Avoiding love is hard. Catching a killer can be fatal…

When Rob's sister passed away, she left him her dog and her house. He can handle the dog part, but he doesn't need another home. Especially a fixer-upper the neighbor swears is haunted. Then he meets Bridget, who's working on getting her life back together after a car accident left her scarred in more ways than one. She can't pass up Rob's offer of free lodging, regardless of the shape it's in. Or the roommate that's part of the package. She's never believed in ghosts, but now she's living with one who wants Bridget's help in catching a killer. There's only one problem: the killer has unfinished business…

Other books by Stacy McKitrick

Bitten by Love Series:
My Sunny Vampire
Bite Me, I'm Yours
Blind Temptation
A Vampire Wedding

Ghostly Encounter Series:
Ghostly Liaison
Ghostly Interlude

Short Stories in the Following Anthologies:
Home for the Holidays
Love's a Beach

Ghostly Liaison
(Ghostly Encounters #1)

Stacy McKitrick

Dayton, Ohio

Mythicalpress.com

Published in the United States of America
Second Electronic Edition: September 27, 2017
Second Print Edition: September 27, 2017
ISBN for print version: 978-0-9967976-4-1

To my parents

Prologue

Charlene Gentry hadn't known what to expect upon her death. She was basically a good person, so would Heaven welcome her? Or would those commandments she'd broken condemn her to Hell? Not that she had a choice, but she'd assumed those were the only two destinations.

Certainly not 5542 Sycamore Lane.

She must be dead. How else could she explain the view of her bedroom from above her bed? She didn't own a mirror on the ceiling, though she'd dreamed of putting one there, and the eyes of the body—her body—lying on the bed below were closed. Then there was that damn needle…

Oh God no. What had that bastard done?

She needed to get back into her body. Maybe then she'd be okay. She moved her arms as if performing the breaststroke, but remained hovering over her bed.

The front door slammed. "Charlie, it's me."

Robbie. Oh thank God. He'd help her. Her big brother fixed everything.

"I'm in the bedroom!" She flapped her arms like a bird, but still didn't move anywhere. How the hell could she get down?

Barnaby barked from outside. The sliding door scraped opened. "Hey, fella. Charlie? You out here?"

"What, are you deaf? I said I was in the bedroom!" No response. What if he couldn't hear her? What if he left before he found her body? If only she could get off the damn ceiling.

Tick, tick, tick. Barnaby's claws skittered across the kitchen floor.

"Whatcha hurry?" Robbie asked. Soon the chocolate Lab burst through the bedroom door, Robbie close behind.

"Charlie?" His eyes widened at the sight. He rushed to her body and placed two fingers against her neck.

Thank God he'd found her. But did he get a pulse? Was she alive?

"Shit." He pulled out his cell, punched 9-1-1, and tossed it on the bed. Ringing sounded through the speaker. After yanking out the needle, he proceeded to perform CPR on her body.

"That's it. Resuscitate me. Bring me back, Robbie!"

"9-1-1, what's your emergency?"

"I need an ambulance at fifty-five forty-two Sycamore Lane. Hurry! It's my sister. I think she OD'd."

"No, I didn't," Charlie said. "I swear."

"Is she breathing?" the operator asked.

"I don't think so. Just hurry! Come on, Charlie. Wake up!"

"You don't know?"

"She has no pulse. I'm performing CPR."

"Why do you suspect she OD'd?"

"Because… Oh shit."

"Sir?"

"She has a history of abuse, okay? And I found her with a needle up her arm. Just get the fuck over here!"

Barnaby sat in the corner and whined at Robbie.

"Someone is already on their way," the operator said.

Robbie pumped her chest frantically. "Dammit, Charlie. Come back! Don't leave me."

Charlie pictured standing beside her brother and the next instant she was there. Thank God. "I haven't left you," she said. "Don't you dare give up!"

Her appearance made no difference in Robbie's actions, so she was invisible, too. Figured.

Where were the damn paramedics? They should have been here by now. She only lived a couple of blocks away from the fire station.

Robbie checked her neck again and swiped at his eyes. "Why, Charlie? Why?"

Was he crying? Giving up? "No! Keep pumping on me!" She reached out to shake him and her hands went through his body. "Holy shit."

He continued with the CPR. "I trusted you! How could I be so stupid?"

"You're not stupid, Robbie. It was Carl. He did this!"

Paramedics rushed into the house. About damn time. They shocked her body, but the machine didn't beep with a heartbeat. They zapped her several more times. All with the same result.

They pronounced her dead.

Robbie fell to his knees and hugged Barnaby. His sobs wrenched her heart. But if she were really and truly dead, why did her chest hurt so much?

Oh crap. Maybe she *was* in hell.

Chapter 1

Bridget Quigley slipped out onto the narrow porch and pulled the door shut with nary a click just as thunder exploded through the neighborhood. She jumped and her heart attempted an exit through her throat. Hell's bells. Rain she could deal with—lightning, not so much. The ominous clouds obliterated any indication of a rising sun, making it appear more like sunset than daybreak. Good thing her bicycle had a light.

The driveway was wet, and there were puddles in the road, but no more rain fell from the sky. The storm must have passed. She should be okay.

Her phone rang from inside her backpack. Shit. If her mother heard… She quickly opened the pack and fished for her phone. She frowned at the display and hit ignore. When would the guy get the message? She tossed the phone back into her pack.

She zipped up her slicker to the sound of the door opening. Her mother stood in the safety of the house, wearing her pink, fluffy bathrobe over her equally pink nightgown.

So much for slipping out unnoticed.

"You were leaving without saying good-bye?" Leave it to Mom, making it sound as if Bridget were moving across country instead of going off to work.

"You were sleeping. I didn't want to disturb you."

Piercing blue eyes stared back. If not for the wrinkles and some gray in her blonde hair, Bridget could be looking in a mirror. "You can't ride your bike in that. I'll drive."

That bossy tone only meant one thing if Bridget let it: total control. No more. Time to break free.

"It's not raining anymore. And I have a change of clothes in case I get wet." Bridget slipped on the backpack, then flipped up the hood of her slicker and cinched it around her chin.

"Why are you doing this to me?" her mother asked.

They would have the same argument as last night if Bridget gave in. For too long she'd relied on others. It had to stop now, regardless of the weather.

"Mom, I'm just riding my bike to work. Lots of people do that. I'll be fine. Please stop worrying."

"But what if you run into a rapist? I heard they target bicyclists."

"What? Now you're just trying to scare me."

"Is it working?"

The overly hopeful expression on her mother's face caused Bridget to chuckle. "No."

Her mother frowned. "Then take my car. I don't need it."

"And have Auntie Eileen ream me a new one? Oh no. You're not using me as an excuse again. You're going to Cincinnati."

Apparently this job would be as beneficial to her mother as it was to Bridget.

"Fine. Where's your helmet?"

Shit. How the hell could she have forgotten that? Maybe because her brain wasn't working the way it used to. "I don't have one yet. I'll buy one tonight, okay?"

Her mother pointed her index finger upward. "Hold on. Don't go." A few moments later she returned with a pink helmet. "Here, take mine."

Bridget took the offered item. "When did you get this?"

"Your father and I started riding before..."

Before. Her mother said it that way all the time. As in before the accident. An accident that wouldn't have happened if Bridget had only said no. How many lives had she screwed up? More than ever she needed to get away and stop relying on everyone.

Bridget secured the helmet over the hood of her slicker. "Thanks. I'll call you when I get to work."

"Don't overdo it. If you get one of your headaches, pull over and—"

"Good-bye, Mom." Bridget climbed on her bike and coasted away before her mother could launch into another lecture about her headaches.

Bad enough she'd been caught wincing. If her mother knew about the constant nagging pain, she'd haul Bridget to the nearest doctor. Wouldn't matter that the doctor had never found anything wrong with her head.

But what was a little pain? It wasn't anything she didn't deserve.

Her parents lived in a new neighborhood, the oldest house only five years old. Small trees decorated most yards, providing little to no shade and certainly nothing large enough for climbing. Not that the owners would want trees hiding their homes. Most were two-story estates with three-car garages and manicured lawns. Even in her old profession, Bridget never would have fit in with this crowd, not that she wanted to, but after spending nearly a year in the hospital and with medical bills up the wazoo, where else could she go? Until she earned enough money, she was stuck living with her parents. But someday she would move. Somewhere where she fit in, somewhere closer to work. It was next on her list.

It had been years since she rode a bike, but she'd gone through enough physical therapy she was sure this would be easy. However, she wasn't prepared for the small seat digging into her butt. After buying her own helmet, she would find a larger seat.

She stopped at the end of the road. So far, so good. Her head didn't hurt any worse than it had every other day and her leg was doing fine. No sharp twinges or stiff joints. She checked for traffic. Left would take her to another new housing development, a couple of small contractor-type businesses, and the river. Right would take her to the main road and into town. With the way clear, she turned right.

Lined with trees and not much else, the road was hilly and narrow. On a dry day, she could ride on the shoulder if a car got too close. Today, the shoulder was a raging creek. Which only proved her assumption: the storm had passed. It would be her lucky day.

Almost as if saying Bridget was foolish to think such things, a fat drop landed on her nose, followed by another. She lived in Ohio, where the weather could change without notice. Well, the hell with the weather. It wouldn't stop her from being independent again.

As she approached the first hill, she stood on the pedals to get some speed. After several pumps, her thighs stung. Damn, she was going to be sore. A car passed and hit a pothole. Water splashed her way.

"Nice going," she yelled as she wiped her face. "I think you missed a spot." Her chest burned, but she wouldn't stop. If she stopped, she would have to walk the rest of the way uphill as she wouldn't have enough oomph in her to start again.

Cresting the top, she breathed deep and relaxed. She coasted for a bit. Her thighs ached, but not enough to ditch her plan. And to think, there were only two more hills to conquer. Give her a week of riding and she'd be in shape for anything.

A sharp pain stabbed behind her eyes. She braked and pulled over, avoiding the creek called a ditch. She massaged her temples. Damn! What brought that on and why did it hurt more than usual? Was she overdoing it? Her jubilation wavered.

She closed her eyes and focused on the patter of rain as it hit her slicker. Then she took deep breaths. In. Out. Nothing was working. Her head still throbbed. What the heck was wrong? Well, standing out in the rain wasn't helping any. If she couldn't get past this little roadblock, how did she hope to survive an entire day at work?

She wiped her face and opened her eyes. A man stood in the middle of the street looking in her direction. He wore jeans and a light blue T-shirt. No jacket. No umbrella.

The sound of an engine from behind alerted her. A car. She screamed and frantically waved at the man to get out of the road. When he saw her, his eyes lit up, but he didn't move.

She turned and waved at the driver. With a cell phone to his ear, he didn't see her and passed her by. The car never slowed. Nor did it hit anything. What the— Where did the walker go?

Thunder boomed overhead.

"Shit." She couldn't worry about a missing man, not at the threat of electrocution. At least the throbbing pain subsided. Her face and hands froze from the beating rain, but she pedaled hard, anxious to get to the main road. As she reached the top of the next hill, her stabbing headache returned and the same man stood at the bottom, blocking her path. She skidded to a stop. How did he get there so fast?

A car crested the hill in front and the man turned into mist.

What? Not again! Panic weaseled its way into her chest. Her first hallucination had appeared after waking from the accident. But they had stopped months ago, once she'd left that damn hospital. So much for thinking she'd gotten better. She continued pushing onward, using the decline to its full advantage.

A car passed close by. In her frenzied state, she jerked hard to the right and slipped in the gravel. Her tire hit something hard and she fell onto her side, splashing into the mini-creek. The bike tangled with her legs. She kicked it away, twisting her left knee. Knife-cutting pain radiated up her leg. She cried out. Big mistake. As soon as she opened her mouth, dirty water and chunks of gravel filled it. Spitting and coughing, she sat up.

Water continued splashing into and around her. She'd take deep breaths to calm her racing heart if drowning wasn't a good possibility.

Hell's bells! All this because she wanted to be on her own? Maybe she should be put away—for stupidity.

* * * *

Rob Gentry sat at the breakfast table and sighed at his neighbor's rambling voice from the other end of the phone. He had given old Mr. Murdock his number in case of an emergency. With his late sister's house unoccupied, Rob requested he be notified of any suspicious activity. And while Murdock was being a good neighbor, this was the third time in a matter of days.

"I tell you, I think you have a squatter," his neighbor went on. "Lights just don't come on and off for no apparent reason, not if someone isn't living there."

They would if I had a timer. Unfortunately, Rob didn't. "I appreciate your concern, but I was just there yesterday. No one's living there. The place is locked up tight. Maybe you saw a reflection."

"So you checked for an open window?"

"They are all closed and locked. And the flue is secured. I don't know what's going on, but it couldn't have come from the house."

"I know what I saw and where I saw it. You sure it's not a ghost? I mean your parents died, then your sister…"

Not the ghost thing again. Rob pinched the bridge of his nose. "It's probably some kids playing a practical joke. Don't worry about it. I'll come by later and take you through the house myself. Okay?"

"You're probably right. I'm sorry to be a bother…"

"You're not a bother. I appreciate your concern. We'll talk later, okay? I need to get to work."

"Do you think you'll be renting the house again? That might solve some of these problems."

Yeah, like renting it the first time had worked out so well. "The place needs some work first, but that's the plan." Rob said good-bye and hung up.

He should have sold the house. Instead he held onto it like some melancholy fool.

Thunder cracked in the vicinity. Rob looked out the French doors. The rain had stopped, but would most likely return. It was going to be a long week. Rain only delayed projects.

Barnaby scampered into the room, the hardwood floor causing his feet to slide. Rob grabbed hold of the dog before he could slide into the wall and scratched him behind the ears, where the fur was super soft.

"So, you gonna stay in the house where it's safe, or go with me to work?"

As if answering, Barnaby barked and headed for the door to the garage, his tail wagging wildly. Rob liked to think the dog was smart like that, when in reality, it was a routine for the animal.

Hell, maybe bringing Barnaby to Murdock's later would get the old man to forget about anything to do with ghosts.

* * * *

Bridget stood hunched over with her hands on her thighs. She took a deep breath and assessed the damage. Her headache was back to normal—annoying—but other areas of her body demanded attention. She straightened her knee. While it moved without effort now, it would most likely swell later. Mud covered the right side of her body and had even managed to make its way inside her coat. Showing up on the first day of a new job all wet was one thing. Needing a shower quite another. After flinging off what mud she could, she straightened and hobbled over to her bike.

The front rim bent at an unusual angle.

"Dammit!" She rubbed her temples. Her first job since the accident and now she'd be late. Five miles was a long walk, even on a clear day. She looked back the way she'd come. Home was closer, but not necessarily quicker. One look at Bridget and her mother would insist on taking her to the hospital.

And since there was no way she would go back to that hellhole, she scratched off home as an option. She needed to get herself together. Standing in the rain like an idiot wasn't getting her anywhere. As soon as she found cover, she'd call Kate and let her know she'd be a little late. Bridget readjusted her helmet, tightened the hood around her face, and bent over to pick up the bike.

A big, red truck—the four-door variety—came up the hill and pulled over. A Good Samaritan or…a rapist?

"Damn it, Mom. Why'd you have to put that into my head?" Of course, with all this mud on her who'd want to rape her? Even a rapist had taste, didn't he? Still, it was a mile to the main road and she was in a vulnerable state. Home was starting to look good about now.

A tall man climbed out of the truck. He wore a rain slicker, but the large hood obscured his face. "You hurt?"

"I'm fine, thank you. I don't need any help." She pushed the bike forward, but with the bent tire, straight wasn't an option.

The man reached for the bike and his hands brushed against hers. Large. Calloused. Warm. He was definitely real. "I don't think your bike is cooperating. Let me help. Where are you headed?"

Deep and melodic, his voice wrapped around her like a warm blanket. Maybe he was a rapist. They've been known to be charming. And he could certainly take her without much effort, being a good six inches taller than her. Her heart pounded against her ribs and she would have swallowed if someone hadn't sucked all the moisture from her mouth. She pulled the bike away from his grasp. "I'll be okay, really. I…I don't need to bother you. Besides, I'm headed the other direction." *So take a hint and leave me alone.*

He straightened. "I'm sorry, I guess I should have introduced myself first. I'm Robert Gentry, but you can call me Rob. I own Gentry Construction."

He pointed to his truck and sure enough, a big white sign was displayed on the door with GENTRY CONSTRUCTION written in blue. How did she miss that?

"And I have a chaperone by the name of Barnaby inside the truck. He'll make sure I'm a perfect gentleman. Now, let's go. I don't know about you, but it's kind of wet out here."

He hoisted her bike onto his shoulder and headed for his truck. She numbly followed. What just happened? Was she going to let him take over like this? She'd just gotten free from her mother.

So much for the helmet protecting her head. She certainly wasn't thinking straight.

While removing the headgear, she walked around the front while he went to the back. His license plate read GENTRY2. She'd seen the truck in town before. Okay, maybe he wasn't a rapist. A rapist would most likely drive around in something less conspicuous.

So who was Barnaby? Could she trust two men she didn't know?

After depositing her bike in the bed of the truck, Rob came around and opened the passenger door. "He won't bite. I promise."

Bite? Who's biting? The whimper made her look inside. A chocolate-brown Labrador stared at her with soulful eyes, wagging his tail. Her heart warmed at the sight. Barnaby, she presumed.

"Well, aren't you a sweetie," she said.

He barked, as if he agreed with her.

"Barnaby. Behave." Rob held a hand out. "Do you need help up?"

Anyone who owned such a magnificent animal couldn't be all bad. Most dogs had good taste and this one seemed well cared for.

"I'm all wet and muddy."

"It's a truck. It expects mud."

Well, if he was okay with it, who was she to argue? She slipped her backpack off, tossed it on the floor with her helmet, and grabbed onto the oh-shit handle. Barnaby backed up on the bench seat, giving her room as she heaved herself inside. Rob closed the door. Heat blew into her face and she pushed her hood back, feeling the full effect. Ah, much better. Another fifteen minutes of this and she might thaw. Why did sixty-degree weather always feel so much colder when it rained?

Trying not to spread too much mud around, she carefully pulled the seat belt over, clicked herself in, and tugged. All secure. Barnaby rested his head on her lap, sharing his warmth. Using the least muddy of her hands, she stroked his head.

Rob climbed in behind the wheel and slid the hood back from his face. Wait a minute. She knew him. But from where? Maybe she *had* hit her head. How could she ever forget a face like that? Square jaw with a small dimple in his chin. Dark hair and eyes that could rival Barnaby's. She'd read how some people resembled their pets.

"You look familiar. Did we meet? Or do you advertise on TV or in the newspaper?" Or maybe posed for the cover of a romance novel?

He smiled, revealing straight, white teeth. "I think I would have remembered meeting you. And no, I don't advertise like that. So, where to?"

Her heart skipped a few beats. She definitely remembered that smile. So where the heck had she met him? Her faulty memory was going to drive her nuts.

He raised his eyebrows, apparently waiting for her answer.

She lowered her head. "Can you take me to Woodland Heights Animal Clinic? Do you know where that is?"

"I can and I do." He put the truck into gear, checked the road, and turned the truck around. "So, you work for Kate?"

He knew Kate? Of course he knew Kate or else he would have said Dr. Kelly. Was that how she knew him? "Yes. She's my cousin, actually."

"No kidding. Her husband is my best friend. Were you at the wedding?"

Holy shit. That was it—the wedding pictures. How many times had she secretly drooled over them, wondering what his arms might feel like around her body, or what his lips might feel like against her own? And here she was sitting in his truck, not that she could do anything about it now. Too many scars. Too many flaws. And then there was that whole going insane thing. Her fantasy of hot, unbridled sex exploded into millions of tiny pieces. Could this day get any worse?

Chapter 2

Rob glanced the woman's way. Had he said something wrong? Her eyes nearly bugged out of her head when he'd mentioned the wedding. He was pretty sure she hadn't attended. Not that he could be one hundred percent certain with all the mud and gunk on her face, but he wouldn't have forgotten her beautiful blue eyes.

"I wasn't able to go," she said as she stroked the dog. "But I saw the pictures. That's where I recognize you from."

Ah, the pictures. Sitting through those hadn't been all bad, but being forced to wear a monkey suit for more hours than he could recall had been pure torture. What a person wouldn't do for a friend.

"That's too bad. It was a fun wedding." Listen to him. Acting as if he'd been to lots of weddings when in fact he'd only attended the one.

Barnaby had taken a shine to her. He hadn't moved from her lap since she got inside the truck. Having his ears scratched wasn't hurting any, either. He probably missed having a woman's touch. Charlie had doted on him. Actually, she had spoiled him rotten. But now she was gone, leaving Rob to take care of the animal. Not that he minded. Barnaby was good company and a reminder of the sister he'd lost.

"So what happened back there?" he asked.

She kept her head down. "A car got too close and I overcompensated."

"Is there a reason you were riding a bike in the rain?"

"Well… I don't have a car and I thought it would take too long to walk."

Okay, so it wasn't his business. She didn't know him so why should she open up? He wouldn't mind getting to know her, though. Some strange urge to protect her had come over him after they'd touched.

The ride was going to be too short. Normally, he'd catch at least three red lights. Today, they were all green. Was someone playing games with him? He even drove five miles under the speed limit and yet he still arrived at the vet's in record time. He drove around the back and parked. Barnaby looked up and whined.

"It's okay, boy," he said. "We're not here for you."

"Someone doesn't like the vet, huh?" She patted him on the back. "Can't say I blame you. I don't care for doctors, either." She gazed at Rob and smiled. "Thanks for the ride." She opened the door and hopped out of the truck.

"Wait," he said to the closed door. Why hadn't he asked for her name? Calling her "hey you" didn't seem right. Regardless, she'd already entered the building. Damn, she was fast.

Barnaby looked at him beseechingly, as if saying, "You idiot, you're letting her go?"

No, he wasn't letting her go. Not that fast, anyway. He opened the window a crack, letting in some of the rain. The seat would most likely be wet by the time he returned, but so what?

"Stay," he said as he climbed out of the truck. The dog had no problem following that command and sat back on his haunches.

Rob pulled her bicycle out of the back and jogged over to the building. After leaning the bike against the wall and making sure it wouldn't fall over, he helped himself inside.

He'd never come in this way, he'd always used the front entrance. A round table with chairs inhabited the middle of the room and a refrigerator stood at the end of a counter containing a coffeepot and microwave. The coffee aroma nearly masked the antiseptic smell the place always held.

His breath caught in his throat. She stood by the coat rack, her long-sleeve T-shirt clinging to her breasts like a second skin. Rain had always been a nuisance, costing his business time and money, but if he could see her like this every day, rain would be welcomed.

Kate appeared from the hallway wearing a white lab coat over casual attire. "Bridget, what the hell happened to you? And what are you doing here, Rob?"

This was Bridget? He'd heard about her accident. She wasn't anything like he'd expected. He'd assumed she was disfigured, or something worse. Not a vibrant, beautiful, woman.

"I fell off my bike and Rob was kind enough to stop."

Oh yes, her bike. "Yeah, about that. I put it out by the door. Is that okay? Or I could take it to get repaired." Then he'd have a real excuse to visit her again.

Bridget grimaced in embarrassment. "Oh my gosh. I'm so sorry. The door's fine. I can take care of it. You've done enough. Thank you."

Damn. He'd have to figure out another way.

"You fell off your bike?" Kate grasped Bridget's shoulders and turned her around in an examination. "Did you hurt yourself?"

Bridget shrugged free. "I'm fine. The bike is in worse shape." She picked up her backpack. "If you'll excuse me, I'm going to go in the back and clean up. Thanks again for the ride, Rob."

"No problem. Glad I could help."

She turned and walked away, showing a fine ass, too. But she favored her left leg. Maybe she'd gotten hurt more than she would admit.

"Rob?"

He tore his gaze from Bridget. Kate stared at him with hands on her hips.

Shit. Caught red-handed. He played it innocent and smiled. "Yes, Kate?"

She curled a finger her way. "Follow me."

She led him to her office, a small room with a desk and not much else. A computer monitor took most of the desk space. She closed the door behind Rob and remained standing, probably because she couldn't offer him a chair.

He figured she would chastise him for staring at Bridget's ass. Or worse, her breasts. But damn, he couldn't keep his eyes off the woman.

"Is Charlie's house still empty?" Kate asked.

He certainly hadn't expected her to talk about the house. "Considering I haven't fixed it up yet, yeah."

"You need a house sitter while you fix it up?"

"Are you and Brian having problems? I mean, I know the guy can be an ass sometimes…"

She snorted. "He may be an ass, but he's my ass and I love him very much. No, I was thinking about Bridget. She's living with her parents and I know she's looking to move out. Problem is, she doesn't have a lot of money right now. I thought since the house is nearby, maybe you could use her to house sit. That way she's out from under her mother's watchful eye and she won't have a long commute to work. What do you say?"

"I don't know. Like I said, the house is a mess. There's a hole in the bathroom wall."

"How the hell did that happen?"

He shrugged. "Who knows? I think they were high on something." How else could he explain finding a chair embedded in the wall? Apparently, good credit did not make a good tenant. And they'd had the nerve to ask for their deposit back.

"I tell you, she won't care," Kate said. "If she agrees, can you do this?"

Could he? Hell, if Bridget did house sit, he'd see her more often. Hmm, not a bad idea. Not a bad idea at all.

Kate smacked him in the shoulder. "Stop it. She's off-limits."

His heart sank at her words. "She has a boyfriend?"

"No. But she's in a vulnerable state. Let her get her life together first, okay?"

Rob smiled. All right. No boyfriend.

She smacked him again. "Did you hear what I said? Off-limits."

He rubbed his arm and sighed. "Fine, I'll be a perfect gentleman. That satisfy you?"

"Thank you. You're going to make her day. I just know you will."

He didn't know about Bridget's day, but his was certainly looking brighter.

* * * *

Bridget ran a comb through her hair, working out the knots. Each pull exacerbated the ache in her head. A headache that had disappeared in Rob's presence. Wonder why that was? Guess hormones trumped craziness. Whatever, the headache returned. Not even the blessedly warm—although brief—shower had relieved it any.

She walked to the grooming station and borrowed a blow-dryer. Soon her hair was dry and she pulled it into a ponytail. Returning to the break room ready to face the day, she found Kate and Rob sitting at the table drinking coffee. Bridget had been sure Rob would have left by now, but something inside of her was glad he stayed.

With his coat off, he was quite a vision. Even though he wore a flannel shirt, his biceps filled the sleeves quite nicely. And his shoulders were wider than wide. Well, he owned a construction company, so what did she expect? Then again, he could be management. If he was, he must be the hands-on kind. An office worker didn't normally sport calluses like he had. And he'd lifted her bike as if it weighed nothing.

Hell's bells. The last thing she needed was to fall for a hunk like Rob. Maybe he was full of himself. Maybe he looked at himself in the mirror every chance he got. Yeah, that was the ticket. Staying away from someone like that would be easy.

Rob turned his head and spotted her. A slow smile spread across his face and her heart melted at the sight.

Dammit, dammit, no! Conceited. He was conceited. She must stick with the plan.

Kate waved her over. "Come sit down."

Bridget grabbed a cup and poured herself some of the dark brew—with her requirement of cream and sugar—before sitting. She picked a chair closer to Kate and as far away from Rob as possible. "What's up?"

"Rob needs some help, and I think you're the perfect person to do it. His sister passed away about six months ago and left him her house. He needs to fix the place up before he can rent it. How'd you like to be his house sitter? If after he's finished, you wish to remain living there, he'll be glad to rent the place to you. What do you say?"

Bridget had been staring at Kate as she rambled on. When Kate had mentioned Rob's sister passing, Bridget glanced at Rob. There was great sadness in his eyes. Shit, shit, and double shit. Conceited persons didn't care for others, and he had clearly cared for his sister.

"Why me?"

"Because I know how badly you want to move out of your parents' home. Oh, and the house is around the corner."

Around the corner? As in walking distance? And free? Let's not forget that! So what if she had the hots for Rob. That was her problem, not his.

"I should warn you," Rob said. "The house is a mess. The plumbing works, but there are holes—"

"I'll do it," Bridget blurted. "When can I move in? Oh wait, I don't have any furniture."

Kate laughed. "I believe it's furnished. Right, Rob?"

"Most of the furniture's intact, yes."

Bridget smiled. Her life was turning for the better. Finally. And she'd only had to fall off her bike for it to tumble into place.

Rob stood and grabbed his slicker from the rack. "How about I pick you up after work and take you to the place? Let you see it before you make any decisions. Okay?"

She must have nodded. He smiled at her and left.

Kate placed an arm around Bridget's shoulders. "You ready to start work now?"

Bridget's heart was near bursting. She hugged her cousin. "Thank you, Kate. You don't know how much this means to me."

"Hey, it's the least I can do for my favorite cousin. Now, let me show you where everything is kept before the patients start showing up."

Oh yes, patients. The furry kind. Bridget could handle that.

Chapter 3

When Kate had said the house was right around the corner, she wasn't kidding.

True to his word, Rob, accompanied by Barnaby, picked up Bridget and her poor, deformed bike. It took him longer to make the two left turns than it did to drive down the street. Third house on the left, he pulled into the short driveway.

The rain had finally abated, so she didn't need an umbrella upon exiting the truck, though Barnaby dashed to the front door as if a tornado was on his heels.

The neighborhood reminded her of the one she'd grown up in. Small houses, built forty to fifty years ago, all contained the same basic floor plan and consisted of brick and siding. Big, climbable trees dotted the landscape—every lot had at least one.

The windows on Rob's home sported fake shutters, painted to match the dark brick and contrast against the cream-colored siding. The yard was small, but well cared for, the grass a lush green. From the outside, the house seemed perfect.

Rob stepped up to the small, covered porch. "Remember, I warned you." He unlocked the door and pushed it open. "Ladies first."

The dog ignored his statement and barged into the house. Rob laughed, but made no effort to give her room to pass, forcing her to brush up against him as she entered the home. Man, he smelled good, like cut wood. Hell, he probably worked with it all day. Sitting in the truck with Barnaby between them had been bearable.

Now with no barrier, her heart leaped. Would she be able to have a business relationship with someone who sparked such desire?

She stepped into the living room and took a deep breath. Much better. She would just keep her distance. It was the only logical solution. Even if the house sported a hole in the roof, she would probably live here, which would make him her sort-of landlord. Better to think of him in a business manner than a romantic one. Better for her heart, anyway.

Because who would be interested in someone who hallucinated?

What little light shone through the clouds came through the big picture window. No walking naked in this room. Not until she got some curtains.

A beautiful stone fireplace adorned the end of the room, but the brass-trimmed doors hung askew, as if someone had tried pulling them free. Who in their right mind would do such a thing?

The wood paneling covering the wall across from the window and surrounding the fireplace would look impressive if big chunks weren't missing. Whoever lived here last had some serious issues. Hopefully not with Rob. "Are you a bad landlord?"

He chuckled. "I didn't think so. But then, I've never been one before. Surprisingly, the couch and love seat are fine and I believe the TV still works. All I have is the digital converter, so if you want more than that, you'll have to get cable or satellite."

Television was the least of her worries. She hadn't watched much since coming home from the hospital.

Rob shut the door. "The kitchen is all electric. I have the pots and dishes in some boxes at home. I can bring them if you need them."

For someone who didn't do a whole lot of cooking, the small galley kitchen was just the right size. Better yet, it included a microwave. Perfect. The window over the sink and the sliding glass door in the dining nook both looked out into the backyard. More uncovered portals to the open world. "Did the place ever have curtains?" she asked.

"Yes. You don't want to know what shape I found those in. I guess I should get those replaced."

"No, don't bother. I can get some. It's the least I can do, since you're letting me live here rent-free." She gazed out the back door. The yard was fenced in—*yay!*—and a cement patio extended from the house. A tall circular deck utilized most of the room in the backyard. Dare she hope?

Barnaby pressed his nose against the glass and whined, as if reading her mind.

"Can I?" she asked, while holding the door handle.

"Sure, go ahead. The gate's closed."

She unlatched the lock and slid the door. The dog squeezed through before she had a chance to open it all the way. "Must be a squirrel or something out there." She stepped outside and examined the deck further, confirming her suspicions. "You have a pool!"

The redwood deck surrounding the covered aboveground pool made it appear built-in. Stairs on the side led to the top. She was dreaming. Who in their right mind would have someone live here rent-free? She could almost kiss those stupid tenants.

"Yes, but it needs to be cleaned." Rob's cell phone played Huey Lewis and the News's "Working for a Living" and he pulled it out of his jeans pocket. "Excuse me. I have to take this call."

He stayed inside the house so she explored the yard. The neighborhood was quiet, a surprise living close to the main road. The surrounding homes featured at least one tall tree and bushes lined Rob's privacy fence. She could picture lying out here in the summer, with no one to see her. The pool was a bonus. It was perfect.

Barnaby whined behind the pool.

"Hey, boy. Is that squirrel giving you a hard time?"

Pain exploded behind her eyes and she doubled over, massaging her temples. Great. She wasn't but a stone's throw from Rob and already the headache returned. She closed her eyes. *Breathe in. Breathe out.* It wasn't working. Maybe she should go back inside and sit. She straightened and opened her eyes.

A woman about her age was standing by the pool wearing blue jeans and a dark red flannel shirt with the sleeves rolled up. Straight brown hair reached her waist. Familiar brown eyes stared back. Barnaby walked in circles around her, still whining.

"Hello," Bridget said. "Should you be here?"

The woman's eyes lit up. "Holy shit! You can see me?"

What a stupid question. She wasn't exactly hiding anywhere. The sliding door opened. Bridget turned around and found Rob coming her way.

"So, was it a squirrel?" he asked.

"You have a vis…" The words died on her lips. The woman was gone. There wasn't any way she could have left without being noticed. Bridget rubbed her temples. Oh great. Now she wasn't only seeing people who weren't really there, she was hearing them, too.

* * * *

Charlie waved her hand in front of the blonde's face. "Hello! I'm right here. You just saw me a second ago."

No reaction. Almost as if the woman couldn't see her. But that wasn't right. Was she playing some kind of game? Why wasn't she flinching or saying anything?

"I have a what?" Robbie asked.

The blonde looked around. Fear etched across her face. "I…uh…nothing. I thought I saw…"

"Me!" Charlie said. "You saw me. You talked to me. What happened?"

"Bridget?" He placed a hand on her shoulder. "Are you okay?"

Bridget backed away. She'd been rubbing her temples, but now she held her stomach. "Can I look at the rest of the house?"

"She saw me, Robbie! She saw a ghost!" Charlie laughed. Oh man, she cracked herself up.

"Sure." He took Bridget's elbow and guided her back to the house.

Charlie crouched to Barnaby's level. "She did see me, right? Well, you can still see me, can't you, fella? I just wish I could pet you. I sure miss you, baby."

The dog wagged his tail and licked, but there wasn't anything to lick. He would find no solid body to match her image and whined as he ambled through her.

"Barnaby, come." Robbie whistled and patted his leg. The dog took off.

"That's right. Go to the living. I'm just a stupid ghost." Charlie willed herself to the living room and appeared, like a magician's trick. All she lacked was the cape and hat. Too bad no one could see her. Except maybe this Bridget woman.

Charlie arrived as Bridget and Robbie were walking down the hall. At least Barnaby stayed by her side. "So, Robbie, who's the cutie? I haven't seen her around before."

No reaction. He'd never heard her before, but Charlie kind of hoped maybe Bridget would give something away. But no, the chick was closed tighter than a clam shell. Charlie popped into the bedroom.

Since dying, she'd taken a few days to get the hang of moving around and a couple of months before she managed to venture outside of the house. She never wandered far, though. If someone or something came for her, she wanted to be close to the site of her death. How else would they find her? Problem was—she'd been waiting and waiting and…nothing. Maybe no one moved on.

But if that were the case, wouldn't she see her parents or other dead people roaming around? Or Nick for that matter?

Man, if she could see Nick, she wouldn't mind being a ghost.

Barnaby rushed into the room ahead of Robbie, who grabbed onto the jamb. "One of these days he's going to knock me over."

"He does seem rather hyper." Bridget stopped and stared at the destroyed wall. "What happened here?"

Charlie bent over and peered through the hole into the bathroom. She was still shocked over how she'd managed that. Those last tenants had pissed her off with their destruction and the next thing she knew, a chair had flown through the room and embedded in the wall. Certainly scared those guys away. Hell, it had scared her, too.

"I have no idea, but I plan on fixing it first," he said. "Unless you think having a peephole would be a good rental feature."

Bridget laughed with him. "I guess it depends on who you rent the house to, but if it's me, then no."

Charlie's chest ached. Robbie hadn't laughed in this house since before her death. It sounded good. Was he interested in Bridget? Were they dating? They did look cute together. God, she hated not knowing anything anymore.

But if they were dating, why the tour? Maybe she was some kind of real estate *mongrel,* as her father had been known to call them. Damn it. Charlie would have kicked something if she could. More strangers in her house. What gives?

"Why didn't you just sell it?" she asked. "Is that why I'm still stuck here? Because you can't let go?"

She followed them back to the living room.

"When can I move in?" Bridget asked.

Charlie's chest lightened. Wait a minute. Bridget was the renter?

Robbie smiled and stepped in close to Bridget. "Tonight if you want." He pulled a key out of his pocket and handed it to her. "Do you need any help moving?"

Bridget took the key and stepped back. "Thanks, but no. I'll have my parents drive me over later with my stuff. My mother will insist on seeing the place. But she won't talk me out of this. Consider me your house sitter."

House sitter, huh? Bridget would certainly be an improvement over the other renters Robbie had found. Not that he was totally to blame. Those idiots had been there for one purpose. But Bridget was different. Charlie pumped her fist in the air. Finally. Someone to help put Carl away.

Life, death, *undeath*, whatever—it was starting to look brighter.

* * * *

Rob drowned in the depths of Bridget's eyes. The more he stared at her, the more beautiful she became. And now he'd be seeing her on a regular basis and his heart soared.

But was he scaring her away? Every time he got close, she backed off. Was that why Kate told him to stay away? Guess he would just have to bide his time. He didn't need to fix the house that quickly. It was paid for and money wasn't an issue. No, this summer project would be more than fixing an old house. If he came by all the time, she'd eventually become comfortable in his presence, then maybe they could get to know each other better.

"Want to grab a bite before I take you home?"

She smiled. "As tempting as that sounds, I better not anger my mother any more than necessary. I'm sure she has dinner ready."

A twinge of disappointment settled over him. Oh well, it'd been worth a shot. There were other nights.

"Maybe another time." He held the door open for her and Barnaby and then locked up once they were all outside.

"Hey, Rob! You here to give me the tour?"

Crap. The tour had slipped his mind and Bridget had filled the gap and then some. Rob smiled and waved at Murdock as the old man ambled his way across the yard, walking in a slow determined pace. His wiry gray hair bristled in the breeze.

"I'm sorry," Rob whispered to Bridget. "I'll try and make it brief."

"Don't worry about it," she said. "Guess it won't hurt to meet the neighbors."

When Murdock reached the porch, Barnaby gave him a royal sniffing of a greeting. "Hey there, boy. Haven't seen you around in a while."

"Mr. Murdock, this is Bridget Quigley. She'll be staying here while I fix up the place."

Murdock held out his hand. "Well how do you do? Aren't you a pretty little thing?"

Bridget took the offered hand and smiled. "Nice to meet you, Mr. Murdock."

"Call me Henry, please. I'm tired of feeling like an old man."

She laughed. "Okay, Henry."

Henry? Murdock had never suggested Rob call him Henry. And what was with the lingering hand holding? She was young enough to be his granddaughter. Jealousy pricked at Rob.

"Were you a friend of Charlie's?"

She glanced at Rob. "Who's Charlie?"

Of course she wouldn't know who Charlie was. Kate had never mentioned his sister's name. But before he could explain, Murdock saved him the breath.

"Charlene Gentry, Rob's sister."

"Oh. No, I never had the pleasure."

The old man continued holding Bridget's hand, even brought the other to join it. Rob gritted his teeth. Why did he get this urge to pull the old man off her? Murdock was only being Murdock.

"She was something. I think you would have liked her. Rob, did you know she used to stop by every day just to check up on me?"

Staring at their linked hands, Rob forced himself to look up once Murdock included him in the conversation. "She did?"

"Well, she wouldn't admit to checking up on me. She always had some flimsy reason. 'Mr. Murdock, did you know your hose is out?' or 'Mr. Murdock, did you know your garage was open?'" he said with a feminine twang. "I saw through her, though." He released Bridget and lowered his head. "I should have known something was wrong that day. She never came by. I sure do miss her."

Damn. Guilt came crashing down on Rob. Murdock wasn't acting crazy to get attention. He just missed Charlie and their friendship.

* * * *

Bridget stared at Henry and her heart went out to him. He was lonely. Maybe she could make a habit of visiting him. It certainly couldn't do her any harm, and she might get a new friend out of the deal.

"So what kind of tour was Rob going to give you?" she asked.

Henry dismissed her with a hand gesture. "It doesn't matter, I suppose, seeing as how you'll be living here now. But if you ever need anything, don't hesitate to stop by." He held his hand out to Rob. "I'll let you kids go on. Good night."

Rob took the offered hand. "Good night, Mr. Murdock. Thanks for all your help."

Henry waved and left. Intent on the old gentleman, Bridget hadn't realized how close she stood beside Rob. His mere presence not only made her head pain-free, but it made her heart rattle. He made no effort to back away. Was he hoping to get in her pants? She probably wouldn't have hesitated before… Ah, hell. Now she sounded like her mother. Still, she might look fine covered up, but no way would he want the real her. She would hate herself for blowing this great opportunity, but she couldn't lead him on.

She walked to the truck and opened the door before he had a chance. Barnaby hopped inside. Rob circled the front of the vehicle and climbed in behind the steering wheel.

"So, where am I taking you? I assume your parents live someplace close to where I found you this morning?" Rob turned the ignition and the truck roared to life.

She buckled the seat belt, tugged the latch, and took a deep breath. Here went nothing. "Before we go, can I ask you a question?"

"Sure, shoot." He flashed that perfect smile her way. Damn, if she didn't watch herself, she'd give him anything and that wouldn't turn out well.

"What are you expecting to get out of this relationship?" *Relationship? Shit!* That hadn't come out right.

"Relationship?" His brow furrowed in confusion.

Shit, shit, and double shit. She was wrong, wrong, wrong. Her fragile ego deflated. He wasn't interested in her. Why had she thought otherwise? "I mean, you have Mr. Murdock watching your place. Why do you need a house sitter?"

"Oh. Well… If you must know, I hadn't even thought of one until today."

"It was Kate's idea, wasn't it?"

"Yes, but—"

"I'm not a charity case. If you don't really need a house sitter—"

"But I do. She did me a favor in suggesting it. Mr. Murdock has been driving me crazy. I don't think his eyesight is what it used to be, and he's been calling me every day. With you living here, maybe he won't be looking for things to be wrong. If you don't move in, I might be forced to get an actual house sitter, because I'm not quite ready to sell the place." His voice cracked at the end and he turned his head away.

"You were close to her, weren't you?"

"Not close enough, apparently." He rubbed Barnaby's head.

She wasn't going to pry. Everyone had their own demons to slay. "Well, as long as you really need a house sitter…"

"I do."

Feeling confident that he'd probably get one anyway if she didn't agree, Bridget gave him her address. So what if the attraction went only one-way. It was what she wanted, wasn't it?

Chapter 4

"Are you sure you're going to be okay here by yourself?" Bridget's mother peeked into the bathroom, avoiding the walls, as if her white blouse and peach slacks would become contaminated. Her eyes widened.

"Now, Mona. Bridget's a big girl." Bridget's dad placed an arm around Bridget's shoulders and gave her a reassuring shake. "It's not like she's in another state."

Standing tall and straight in his green shirt and beige Dockers, he appeared to have stepped off the golf course. He had the body of a younger man—thanks to his daily morning run—and if not for the shock of white hair, no one would guess he had ten years on her mother. Bridget loved her father dearly and not because he usually took her side. If she misbehaved, he would be the first one on her case. But Mom loved to worry for worry's sake and he did his best to balance the scales.

"Owen, there's a hole in the bathroom wall."

"Rob said he would fix that first," Bridget said.

"What does it matter anyway?" he said. "She's living here by herself. Who's going to see?"

Mom trudged into the living room, shoulders down in defeat. Damn her, but she was good. Her actions always managed to cause Bridget's chest to constrict with guilt. And who was to blame? Bridget, of course. One of these days she would grow a backbone.

"Who is this Rob Gentry?" Mom asked. "Do we know him?"

"What do you mean do you know him? He was Brian's best man."

Her mother looked at the floor. "Oh. Well, see…"

"What your mother is trying to say is that we didn't go to the wedding," her father interjected.

"Then why did you tell me you went?" Bridget asked.

Mom set to wringing her hands the way she always did whenever the topic of conversation made her uncomfortable. "Because it made you happy. But there was no way I could go to a wedding when my baby girl was lying in a coma."

Bridget closed her eyes and took a deep breath. Now it was her fault her mother hadn't gone to Kate's wedding? "Mom, I don't think I would have noticed you being gone."

"That's what I told her, but you know your mother." Dad kissed Bridget on the cheek. "We'll leave you to unpack. I'll take your bike and get the tire fixed for you. Call us if you need anything." He picked up her mom's purse from the couch and held it out to her.

Mom eyed her purse for several seconds before taking it and placing it on her shoulder. "You call me tomorrow and we can go out shopping for curtains and things."

Bridget's pocketbook wasn't quite ready for a shopping spree. "The weekend would work better for me."

Her mother pointed to the window. "But there are no curtains!"

"I'll throw a sheet over it. Really, Mom, it'll be okay."

Dad nudged Mom toward Bridget. "Give your daughter a hug good-bye. We're going."

Sometimes Bridget wished for siblings. Maybe then she wouldn't be stuck being the center of her mother's universe. She would have been able to spread the wealth.

Mom hugged her tight. "I love you, sweetie."

"I love you too, Mom."

Bridget walked out with her parents and stood on the porch until they drove out of sight. Pink and orange clouds dotted the western horizon and a cool breeze ruffled her hair. She inhaled deeply, taking in the rain-cleaned air. Finally, on her own. She owed Kate big-time.

After the colors faded away, she went back inside to unpack. Not that she owned much, but no sense in letting her clothes wrinkle. Then her mother might find the need to buy her an iron. Or worse, come over and iron. She shuddered at the thought.

She closed the door and flipped the light switch. Pain flashed in her temples. She winced and rubbed the offending areas. So much for tranquility.

"I was wondering if you were ever going to come back inside."

"Hell's bells!" Bridget jumped and grabbed her chest. The woman from the backyard was standing in her living room, near the fireplace.

"I knew it!" The woman stomped her foot. "You *can* see me. Why did you ignore me earlier?"

"I didn't… Who are you? What are you doing in here?" Bridget glanced at the sliding glass door. Had Rob left it unlocked?

"I'm Charlie and I live…er…reside here."

"Rob didn't mention anyone living here."

The woman smiled friendly-like, not threatening at all. And her name sounded vaguely familiar. Bridget massaged her temples and the pain lessened, but her heart still pounded from being startled.

"That's because he doesn't know. So why did you ignore me?"

"What are you talking about? Is that why you ran off earlier?" Which made more sense than assuming she had spoken with a hallucination. The woman was clearly a squatter, so of course she'd run off earlier. "I'm calling Rob." Bridget hurried to her backpack, which sat on the kitchen counter.

"Umm, you might not want to do that. He'll only think you're crazy."

Bridget froze. The word *crazy* tended to do that to her.

Charlie materialized in the kitchen. "But you're not crazy."

Shit! How had she done that? Wasn't she just by the fireplace? A moan escaped Bridget's mouth. Good Lord, she was hallucinating again. What else could it be?

She needed to lie down. It had been a long and stressful day and she was tired. That's all it was. She was sure of it…almost.

Without making eye contact, Bridget turned and scurried to the bedroom. She quickly closed the door and leaned against it. Eyes closed, she concentrated on calming her racing heart. Thank God her father had stashed her suitcases in the room. No way would she go back out there tonight.

"You can't get rid of me that fast."

Bridget jerked backward—rattling the door—and opened her eyes. Her hallucination stood mere inches away. Dread came crashing around her and she slunk to the floor. It wouldn't be long before the men in the white coats carted her away. And to think her life had been getting better.

* * * *

Way to go, Charlie. Appearing out of thin air had only made things worse. She needed Bridget calm, not on the verge of a heart attack. But how else could she get through to the woman? Knock on the door? Yeah, right.

Charlie backed up a few inches and crouched. She could have lowered herself to be at eye level—walls and floors no longer a barrier—but why risk it? "Please don't freak out. I need you to be calm. Do you hear me?"

"Are you my punishment?" Bridget asked as she covered her face.

Punishment? Shit, she'd never been anyone's punishment before. Well, except maybe Robbie's, but that's what little sisters were for. "Hey—this has nothing to do with you and everything to do with me. You're the first person who's been able to see me."

"Which just goes to prove I'm crazy." Bridget flew her arms out and flung her head back against the door. "Of course I'm crazy. I'm talking to a hallucination."

"Hey! I'm not a hallucination. I'm a ghost."

"What's the difference?"

"A hallucination isn't real." Charlie straightened and tapped her chest. "I'm real."

Bridget gestured toward Charlie. "So says the hallucination."

Well, this wasn't going anywhere. "Listen. I can prove I'm real. It's just going to take some work on your part."

"And I can prove you're a hallucination and it won't take much work at all." Bridget stood, took a deep breath, and stepped toward Charlie.

What did Bridget hope to accomplish? Neither a hallucination nor a ghost was corporeal. Charlie closed her eyes. A person walking through her body was a bit disconcerting and not one of her favorite activities. Not that she could see inside them. That would be gross. But damn if she would get out of the way.

The collision was unexpected.

Charlie opened her eyes. Bridget's widened.

"Holy shit!" Charlie grabbed Bridget's upper arms and her feet hit the ground. She grinned. "I can touch you!"

"You're real?" Bridget's voice barely squeaked out.

Joy wrapped around Charlie and she hugged Bridget close. How could this be? Sure, she'd moved some furniture around, even got the lights to go on and off a couple of times, but never touched the object. "Oh my God! You feel warm!"

Bridget shoved, dislodging Charlie. "And you're cold. What are you?"

"I told you. I'm a ghost. My name is Charlie Gentry and I died. Here. In that bed. But I think the real question is: what are you?"

* * * *

What was she? Was she crazy? Sick? She must be to talk to ghosts. Bridget covered her face with her hands. None of this was happening. How could it? Ghosts didn't exist.

"Will you quit looking so defeated?" Charlie said, pulling Bridget's hands down. Her eyes glistened. "This is a great day! No one has ever seen me before. I just wondered why you're different."

"Oh, God. I *am* crazy," Bridget muttered. Crazy people saw things all the time. But did those things feel real to them? Charlie was as solid as the floor. Well, when they touched. She currently hovered an inch above it.

"You're not crazy. I used to be alive. Go ask my brother. He'll tell you."

Her brother? Bridget blinked. Hell's bells! "You're Rob's sister? The one who died?"

Charlie stepped back. "Yes. Finally!"

"You expect me to tell Rob about you?"

"Hell, no! He'll think you're crazy."

Bridget's head swam. Her eyes filled with tears and her vision blurred. She didn't want to be crazy. She just wanted her life back. Not that she deserved it. Maybe this was her punishment for killing Suzie. If she had refused to drive, if she had only said no, she wouldn't have stalled the vehicle and Suzie would be alive and she'd be sane.

She walked around Charlie and plopped on the bed. "Why is this happening? Can you go away? Is that all it takes, for me to wish it?"

"Probably not, but you might be able to help me go away. I figure I'm still around because I was murdered."

Murdered? Damn. Rob and Mr. Murdock had never mentioned that. Was that why Rob couldn't sell the house? "So, what? You're waiting until they catch the guy?"

"Uhhh, actually, everyone thinks I committed suicide. But I didn't. I was killed."

"What do you want from me? I'm not a cop. I'm not even a private investigator. I'm just a nurse who isn't a nurse anymore."

"But you don't have to investigate. Don't you understand? I already know who killed me. I just need you to find the proof."

Okay, sounded easy enough. Find the evidence and the ghost moves on. It was the least she could do, right? Help another murder victim? She certainly hadn't helped Suzie. Besides, Charlie was Rob's sister, or so she claimed. "Where is this proof located?"

"Well…see… I don't have any." Charlie's face lit up. "But Nick might. If you can see me, maybe you can see him, too."

Bridget rubbed her temples, trying to alleviate the throbbing pain. Of course there wasn't any proof. Why would anything be easy? She was a murderer. Murderers didn't get breaks. "Who's Nick?"

"He was my boyfriend. I'm sure he's still around. That's if murdered people don't move on right away, like me."

"You're asking me to go find another ghost when I'm trying to get rid of you?" The throbbing in her head advanced to a hammering blow. The loony bin was looking mighty tempting. Mainly because of all the drugs they gave out. She could use a few right now.

"Well…yeah. I'm sure Nick knows everything. So, will you do it? Will you go find him?"

"Listen. I'm having enough problems believing in you. Will you let me decide if you're real first before I agree to anything?"

"You won't take long, will you? I mean, you're the first person who can—"

"See you, right. I get it. But right now I want to ignore you. Because I'm sure you're just a figment of my imagination." Or a tumor. That was a strong possibility.

Charlie put her arms akimbo. "I told you, I'm real."

No angering the ghost, especially a ghost who could touch her. "Fine. If you are who you say you are, then Rob will have a picture, right? And since I've never seen you before…"

"Yes, he'll have a picture. He has one in his wallet." Charlie jumped or acted as if she was jumping. Instead of bouncing as expected, she hovered over the floor. "Thank you, Bridget. Thank you for giving me hope. I'll leave you alone tonight, I promise."

"And the morning? You'll leave me alone then, too?"

Charlie frowned. "Sure. I'll stay away. I'll check in tomorrow night. But could you do me a favor?"

"What kind of favor?"

"Could you turn the TV on for me? It gets awfully boring."

Bridget flopped back on the bed. Heaven forbid her ghost got bored!

Chapter 5

Rob closed the lid to his laptop and leaned back in his seat. The start of a headache had formed behind his eyes. He was no college graduate, but even he knew a business should have money in the bank, not be nearly broke. Barnaby sat up and stared at him as if anticipating his departure. He reached down and scratched behind the dog's ears. "What am I gonna do, huh fella?"

As if answering in his own unique and totally speechless way, Barnaby placed his head in Rob's lap.

"That's what I thought." And to think, it had only taken a year for him to screw things up.

This wasn't the life he'd envisioned for himself. For one, Dad would still be alive and running the business. All Rob wanted to do was work with his hands. Build things. Building a bigger business had been David Gentry's dream, not his. And now that dream was crumbling.

The front door to the office squeaked open and slammed shut. Rob had meant to fix the door, but every time he'd started the project, something or someone pulled him away. Carl Anders poked his head into Rob's office. "Oh good, you're still here."

The fifty-three-year-old had been with the company since day one, nearly thirty years. Not only the first salesman/foreman, he'd become a good friend of the family. Rob would have been lost without him this past year.

Barnaby growled.

"Stop it!" Rob said.

The dog just hadn't been the same since Charlie's death. Barnaby slunk to the floor and placed his head on his paws.

"Sorry about that. I don't know what's gotten into him. So what's up?"

Carl grinned and took a chair. "We won the office-park project."

Rob sat up. "I thought we weren't going to bid on that. It's too big for us."

Carl waved his hand in dismissal. "Nonsense. Nothing's too big. It's what your father always said. Besides, with this recession, we shouldn't have any problems hiring people. Heck, we might even get them cheaper. This is great news. Why aren't you smiling?"

"How are we going to pay for more people?"

"Rob... Have you been looking at the bank statement again? How many times have I told you to quit worrying? The bank doesn't reflect what we have due us. This is a big contract. It will pay for the new hires and you'll still come out ahead. Trust me. Have I steered you wrong yet?"

Rob couldn't answer that. Not truthfully, anyway. While he had nothing against hiring new people, he'd rather work with the men he trusted and right now they were stretched thin. "When does the job start?"

"Next month."

Panic sparked through Rob's chest and he bolted out of his chair. "That's not enough time!"

Carl rose, his arms outstretched. "Ease up there, son. I have it all taken care of. That's my job."

Rob dragged in a ragged breath and collapsed onto his chair. "I'm not cut out for this. I should have sold the business after Dad died."

"Why would you say such a thing? Business is great. You're doing a great job. Your father would be proud."

Proud or rolling in his grave?

Rob stood and paced the small office. "Maybe I should stop working in the field and spend more time in the office. Take some night classes and get a business degree. Then maybe I'll feel more comfortable once I understand it better."

College. The thought made his stomach churn. He'd barely passed high school.

"If that's what you want, then go for it. But I know how much you love to work out there. Better yet, why don't you take a few days off? Go fishing or camping or something. While you're away, I can get a crew into Charlie's house and fix it up for you. Then maybe you can sell the place."

"You don't have to do that." Rob waved a dismissive hand and returned to his seat. "I'm taking care of the house. I got a sitter and I plan on fixing it up myself."

"A sitter?"

An image of Bridget and her fine ass made him smile. "Yeah, a sitter. She needed a place to stay and I needed someone there during the night."

Carl leaned back and raised his eyebrows. "She? Is this *she* pretty?"

She was pretty and sexy and...oh yeah, off-limits. At least until she gave him the green light, and he would certainly do everything he could to get it. "It's not like that. She's Kate's cousin."

"Which one? The pretty one you hung out with at the wedding?"

"No. The one in the accident."

"Really? Is she disabled? Unable to work?"

"No, nothing like that. She's just getting back on her feet and Kate asked if I could help. You know, now that I think of it, I *will* take the afternoon off. I promised her I'd fix the hole in the bathroom first. No reason why I couldn't start now." And then maybe later he could talk her into dinner.

* * * *

Bridget's bike riding stint had come back to bite her twofold. Not only did every muscle protest the abuse, her knee had swollen causing her to walk with a slight limp. But she was smiling. And why? Any day living on her own was a good day in her book.

Bridget approached her house—though not technically hers, it seemed like it all the same—and found the garage door open with Rob's truck backed in the driveway. Just thinking about seeing him again made her heart skip a few beats.

Any thought of Rob got her motor running, which would only lead to heartache later on. The man would probably stop by frequently to fix the place. She needed to get herself together. Better to think of him as being a slob or an ungrateful pig, not the hunky and sweet specimen he projected.

The door was unlocked, of course, and she let herself in. Slopping and scraping noises came from the bathroom. Bridget stepped around the small workbench and peeked into the bathroom.

A chalky, dusty smell mixed in with the scent of her shampoo and soap. Rob crouched in the small room holding a trowel in one hand and wearing a blue chambray shirt with the sleeves rolled to his elbows. He hummed a tune she didn't recognize, but his jeans caught her attention. Or at least the ass that filled those jeans. *Oh crap!* She shouldn't be looking at his ass. He and his ass were off-limits. But damn. His ass looked finer than fine. Her heart palpitated and her body clenched in need for something she hadn't experienced in a very long time. She tore her gaze away and paid attention to what he was doing. He'd applied spackle around the new section of drywall. The hole was gone.

"Wow! You work fast!" she said.

He jerked and looked her way, pulling the earbuds free. His shocked expression morphed into a growing smile. "You don't mind, do you?"

"Well, now that you ask, I was growing attached to the passageway. I didn't have to walk around to toss my towel back in the bathroom."

He scanned the area. "I don't recall seeing a towel lying around."

"Oh. Well, I had to go back in and pick it up." She laughed. "Can't stand a messy room."

He laughed with her. "Me either."

So much for him being a slob. Sexy and clean. She was doomed. Oh wait, he could still be an ungrateful pig. There was hope yet.

"I'm finished for today," he said. "Care to join me for dinner?"

She would have declined except for Charlie. Or would that be the hallucination who called herself Charlie? Better to have dinner with Rob, find out his sister had red hair and green eyes, and then enjoy her last good meal, because her next one would be at the loony bin when her hallucination reappeared.

"Sure, as long as I pay my way. What did you have in mind?"

The grin lasted a moment, but the sparkle in his eyes remained. Rob picked up the bucket of spackle and his tools and carried them into the hallway. "Well, I'm not exactly dressed for anything fancy.

How about a fast-food joint?" He placed his items on the workbench. "By the way, did you know you left the television on?"

Bridget still couldn't believe she had done that, and for what? A ghost? She really was losing her mind. "I heard if you leave a TV on, you're less likely to get robbed."

He tilted his head as if contemplating what she said. "So you're saying I should just leave the TV on and forget about having a house sitter?"

What the hell had she done? Talked her way out of a free place to stay? "No! I'm not saying—"

Rob covered his mouth, but his eyes crinkled in mirth and a chuckle escaped. "Sorry. Couldn't resist. You have valuables. I understand."

She shook her head. "No valuables. Just clothes. Which are valuable. To me." God, could she babble any more? Maybe dinner was a bad idea. She'd most likely make a fool of herself. Of course, if she said no now, he'd probably think horrible things about her, and she couldn't have that. Or could she? Oh great. Now she was babbling in her mind. She had to face it: Rob Gentry was trouble.

* * * *

Rob smiled. Bridget sure was cute.

First, the panicked look on her face when he'd hinted at reneging on their agreement. As if he'd do that. What other way could he see her every day without actually dating her? Second, her string of little sentences, each said as an afterthought. He nearly laughed aloud, but squelched it, thinking she might take it the wrong way.

She also exuded sex appeal, and it had nothing to do with her wardrobe.

The weather had turned warmer, yet Bridget wore a long-sleeve T-shirt underneath hospital scrubs. Covered from neck to toes. Maybe no one else would find her irresistible, but all he could think about was uncovering her layers.

The lower half of his body awoke with a jolt. Why had he told Kate he'd stay away?

"Let me clean up here and we can go." He turned toward the workbench and affixed the lid on the bucket, taking his time for the bulge in his jeans to disappear.

Bridget walked to the sliding glass door and gazed outside. "Where's Barnaby?"

"I took him home. He was driving me nuts. First he wanted out. Then he wanted in. Then he wanted out again. I'd have left him outside, but he wouldn't stop barking. Maybe I should take him to Kate's. He's never acted this bizarre before."

"I'm sure he'll be fine. Maybe he needs to get used to my scent."

Rob doubted that. If anything, Barnaby liked Bridget. No, something was wrong with the dog, hopefully nothing serious.

He walked to the door to the garage and she held it open while he carried his gear to the truck. Pieces of drywall littered the ground and a white film of dust covered the table saw and truck bed. He shoved the saw toward the cab and picked up the debris, tossing it nonchalantly as he went. Turning back toward the house, he nearly collided with her carrying his workbench.

"You didn't have to get this," he said as he took it from her.

"I don't mind helping. Besides, I'm hungry."

He'd thought for sure he'd have to bribe her one way or another; instead, he thanked his lucky stars she'd accepted so quickly. How many other ways would she surprise him? He couldn't wait to find out.

He placed the bench beside the saw and closed the gate. "Do you need to change? I can wait."

She shook her head. "If you're good enough, then so am I."

Wow. Had he ever gone out with a woman who hadn't felt the need to dress up and wear makeup? And if Bridget wore makeup, it was minimal, not that she needed it. Even with her hair in a simple ponytail, she aroused him.

They washed up, locked the house, and climbed into the truck. Since she voiced no preference where they ate, he drove to the closest joint and parked. While walking to the entrance, she favored her left leg.

"You hurt yourself yesterday, didn't you?" he asked as he opened the restaurant door for her.

The scent of burgers caused his stomach to rumble, but the sounds of screaming teenage girls invaded his ears. So much for a quiet dinner. The high school softball team took over more than half the dining room.

Bridget either ignored his question or didn't hear and stepped up to the order line.

He stood behind her. "If it's too noisy, we can go someplace else."

"This is fine." She glanced behind him and frowned.

"Are you sure? You don't look fine."

She assured him she was, breathed deep, and turned her attention to the front of the line. Something had upset her, but what? He searched the dining area.

The screams and giggles had turned to whispers.

Teenage girls. He hadn't understood them as a teenage boy; he certainly didn't understand them now. Could they be the reason Bridget had become upset?

She ordered a plain grilled chicken sandwich, a salad with low-fat ranch dressing, and a cup of water. He went with a double cheeseburger, large fries, and a Coke. After acquiring napkins and straws for both of them, she sat at a table as far away from the girls as she could get, yet she faced them. He grabbed several ketchup packets before sitting across from her.

He opened his burger and, near starving, tore into the ketchup packet. Red stuff squirted everywhere, including all over his shirt. *Way to impress the lady, Rob!*

Laughter bubbled out of her and set his heart alight. He needed to make sure she laughed more often, but not at the expense of his shirts.

"Guess you can't take me anywhere, huh?" He grabbed a napkin and proceeded to wipe up the mess, leaving orange spots in his wake.

She cleared her throat. "Sorry. I shouldn't have laughed." She opened her sandwich and cut the meat into tiny pieces. Then a snicker escaped. "But your expression was priceless."

He spread his arms wide. "I aim to entertain."

After popping off the lid to her salad, she dumped the chicken on top, leaving the bun alone.

"Why didn't you just order a grilled chicken salad?"

She tore open a packet—managing to keep the dressing off her clothes—and drizzled the mixture on her salad. "I didn't want all that other crap on it. Lettuce and tomatoes are enough. I don't need cheese, nuts, and fruit, too."

He took a bite of his burger, the more stuff on it the better. He probably should watch what he ate, he wasn't getting any younger, but as long as he worked it off, he should be fine.

She eyed his french fries. Maybe she wasn't actually a health-food nut. Using his finger, he turned the opening her way. "You're allowed."

"I shouldn't," she said as she reached for one. "But it has been a while. I guess one won't kill me. Thanks."

"You didn't answer me earlier. Did you hurt yourself yesterday?"

"I overdid it on the bike, yes. I think every muscle I own has screamed at me at least once today. So much for thinking I was in shape."

Her shape looked fine to him. In fact, he wouldn't mind seeing more of it, which he shouldn't even be thinking since his boner already strained for release. Better to eat and not think.

"Hey, Rob!"

The high-pitched voice triggered an involuntary groan from Rob's mouth. And the hard-on he had sported? Gone. Unfortunately, he hadn't escaped seeing Tori Masters again.

* * * *

Bridget stared at the one cousin she could never be friends with. How did Tori know Rob? Was he why Tori had pulled that U-turn outside?

Rob stood and smiled. "Hi. What brings you here?"

Bridget could have sworn he groaned earlier, but he seemed pleased to see her. Was he only being nice, or was there something between the two of them?

"Sit, sit." Tori ran her hand across the back of Rob's shoulders as he sat before sliding into the seat beside him. "I saw your truck out there, so I had to come in and say hi."

Where Bridget favored her mother's side of the family, Tori favored the Quigley side. The daughter of Dad's younger sister, she'd inherited the trademark auburn hair and green eyes. And she possessed a killer body to go with them—big boobs, small waist. Her skintight dress only accentuated her assets. Bridget was sure men didn't run screaming after undressing Tori. But was Rob one of them?

A twinge of envy tugged at Bridget's heart.

"Hello, Tori," she said. "You meeting someone for a hot date? I don't recall you wearing that to work today."

Tori flipped her hair and flashed one of her fake smiles—all lips, no eyes. "Well, hello, Bridget. I didn't even see you sitting there. But no, I don't have a date. I just take pride in my appearance. How come you're not at home taking care of that knee like you promised Kate?" She shook her head and frowned. "Won't she be disappointed."

First a dig, which Bridget may have earned, then a statement from a private conversation. What did Tori hope to accomplish?

Rob sat straighter and put his burger down. Lines of concern crossed his face. "You *did* hurt yourself."

"I'm fine," Bridget said. "Really. I was waiting to eat before I took some ibuprofen." And why was she explaining herself to him?

"Yes, Bridget is made of some tough stuff, aren't you?" Tori placed a hand on his shoulder, getting his attention. "How's that beautiful dog of yours doing?"

"He's doing fine. Although, I'm sure he's due for his shots." Rob's cell phone played "Working for a Living" and he pulled it from his jeans. "Dammit," he muttered. "Sorry, ladies. I need to take this. I'll be right back."

Bridget stabbed her salad while Rob stepped outside. God, she hoped he didn't have to leave early. She still hadn't had a chance to ask about his sister.

"Just so you know, I saw him first," Tori said. "In fact, we got rather close at the wedding. I would have pursued him sooner, but I've been letting him grieve."

"Ahh, so you met at the wedding."

Tori usually zeroed in on the best-looking available man at any occasion she attended. Problem was, she usually had no problems snagging them. It almost hurt thinking Rob had fallen under her spell.

"Actually, I met him at the clinic. We just got closer at the wedding. It was very magical. Too bad you couldn't be there."

Right, because she'd had a choice in the matter.

"How do you suppose he'll react if he ever got a real good look at you anyway?" Tori whispered.

"Good look at me?" Bridget took a bite of her salad. The lettuce tasted bitter.

"Oh, don't play dumb with me. I saw you in the hospital. I saw your body."

And Tori wouldn't have any problem spreading the news, either. Didn't family mean anything to her? Or was that what four older sisters did to a person?

Bridget played it cool, unwilling to let Tori know how much her words hurt. "Then I guess you don't have anything to worry about. Besides, the only thing between us is business."

"Business? You mean charity, don't you? I heard Kate beg him to take you in."

"Well, if that's what you heard, then you've got nothing to worry about, do you?" The back of Bridget's eyes stung. Suddenly, the salad was unappealing and her appetite went out the door. She wouldn't put it past Tori to make up such a thing, but it also sounded like Kate. Bridget would find out the truth in the morning.

"I'll let you go back to your business dinner, then." Tori rose and brushed the back of her dress as if she'd sat in filth. With a pivot, she hoisted her purse onto her shoulder and marched out of the restaurant.

This whole dinner thing was a huge mistake. Sure, it started out fun. Watching those teenage girls drool over Rob made Bridget feel special, because she got to sit across from him. The poor guy hadn't a clue, which was kind of nice. But then Tori had driven past and pulled a U-turn. She should have known something was up.

Maybe she could find out what Charlie looked like without going through Rob. Henry Murdock, for instance. Or she could quit being a wimp and just ask Rob straight-out. Why would he object?

Rob was leaning against the glass, talking on his phone and Tori stood a polite distance away. She glanced Bridget's way several times. The hairs on the back of Bridget's neck prickled. What was Tori planning?

He pocketed his phone. Tori glanced once more, her devilish grin telling Bridget the show was on. Standing in a position giving Bridget a full view, Tori took his hand and swayed her hips back and forth. She batted her eyes, rested a hand on his shoulder, leaned in, and planted her lips on his cheek.

Why stop at his cheek? Go for his lips and twist the dagger a little more.

Bridget pursed her lips and clenched her fists. Tori's conduct had never bothered Bridget before, so why did her chest hurt? Maybe if it were anyone else but Tori. Still, who was she to tell him who he could and couldn't see? She had no intention of dating him.

Tori caressed his cheek with her thumb, probably rubbing off her lipstick as an excuse to touch him some more. If Tori thought Bridget was a threat, she would have left it on as a brazen reminder of what she owned.

Rob returned, sat, and smiled. No sign of lipstick on his cheek. "Sorry about that. It was one of the guys at work."

Bridget pushed her salad around with her fork. "I guess when you own a business, the place never closes, huh?"

"Something like that." He took a bite of his burger. "Something wrong with your salad?"

She shook her head and took a bite, but her stomach wasn't in it.

"Tori's your cousin, right?"

"Yeah. Kate hired her straight out of college." A smarmy comment was on the tip of her tongue, but she refrained.

"You have a lot of cousins?"

"My dad was one of five and they all had kids. You do the math."

"Wow. I can't even imagine. How about you? Any brothers or sisters?"

She shook her head, but took the opening. "Did you only have the one sister? Or do you have other siblings?"

"Just Charlie."

"Did she go to Woodland High?"

"Yeah. Why? Did you know her?"

"I don't know. The name's not familiar, but that doesn't mean anything. Do you have a picture of her?"

"Sure." He put the burger down and wiped his hands on a napkin before pulling his wallet from the back of his jeans. "It was taken a few years ago, but if you knew her in high school, then it's probably okay."

He removed the photo and handed it over. She hesitated for a moment. What if the woman wasn't her hallucination? Then again, what if she was? Fear wouldn't solve her problems, only the truth would. Bridget took the photo.

Rob had a goofy grin and an arm wrapped around a woman—his sister. Bridget smiled at the sight, at his happiness. Again, she pictured herself in his arms, like she had done with those stupid wedding photos. As if that would happen now. He belonged to Tori, which was for the better.

Bridget blinked back to reality and paid more attention to the woman in the photo. A woman with long dark hair and dark eyes. A woman who was every bit the hallucination she'd conjured. Or should she say ghost guest? Did that make her any less crazy though?

"Well?" he asked.

She returned the photo. "She looks familiar, but that's all. How did she die?"

"I'd like to think she died of a broken heart, and maybe she did, but the reality is, she committed suicide." He returned the photo to his wallet.

"No foul play?"

He frowned and shook his head. "She left a note."

Wow. She not only had a ghost for a roommate, but a lying one at that.

Chapter 6

Rob dumped the remnants of their dinner into the trash bin and placed the empty tray on top. Ever since Tori had left, Bridget had been quiet, reserved. Gone was the sweet laughter that lifted his heart. Gone was the smile that brightened her face. Did she think he was dating Tori? Or had he depressed the heck out of her with their talk of Charlie?

Bridget emerged from the ladies' room, limping. In fact, she'd had a hard time standing, claiming her muscles went on strike from her bike ride the other day. But if that were the case, shouldn't it have affected both legs?

Only her left leg seemed to give her difficulties. She'd either hurt it falling off her bike, or it was the result of her accident last year. Would she ever tell him about that? Probably not until she knew him better, and the only way for that to happen meant ignoring Kate's request—or demand—to stay away.

Bridget didn't appear to be some fragile waif. She was strong and willful. Riding her bike in the rain proved that. Kate might hate him for making the moves on Bridget, but he wasn't looking to date Kate.

"All set?" he asked.

She nodded and he held the door open for her. When she'd placed one leg inside the truck, he resisted the urge to lend her a hand. She grabbed the inside handle and slowly pulled herself up, wincing with each movement.

Once she was settled, he closed the cab door and sprinted to the driver's side. On the ride back to the house, she kept her gaze focused on her lap. Something she had also done on the trip to the restaurant. Even on the day of her bicycle mishap, she had kept her gaze on Barnaby.

"Does my driving make you nervous?"

She smiled. "I wouldn't say that, exactly."

"Then what would you say? Exactly."

"I've discovered I'm…less of a distraction if I don't see what's out there."

She distracted him all right and it had nothing to do with her gazing out the window. "Then I'll make sure to bring Barnaby next time. He'll give you something to do."

She gripped the armrest. "Next time?"

He pulled into the driveway and turned off the ignition. "Sure. The next time we go out."

She shook her head. "I don't think there should be a next time."

"I'm not dating her." That only made her furrow her brows in confusion, so he clarified. "Tori, your cousin."

Her face softened. "Oh."

"But I'd like to date you." He scooted across the bench.

The movement was a mistake. Her eyes widened in alarm. "I don't think that's a good idea."

"Are you saying you're not interested?"

"That's not it." She grasped the door handle. "It's just a bad idea."

She slipped out, but he wasn't letting her get away so fast. Not that she was fast. He climbed out of the driver's side and easily blocked her way. "Why is it a bad idea?"

"I hardly know you." She stepped to the right.

He mirrored her movement. "So we should date."

"I don't think so." She stepped to the left.

Again, he followed. "Am I repulsive to you?"

She huffed and folded her arms across her chest. "No, of course not."

"Do I stink?" He brought his shirt up and sniffed.

A chuckle escaped as her lips curled at the edges. Her face softened.

"There it is," he said.

"What?"

"Your smile. I thought it had left." He ached to kiss her, to taste everything she had to offer. But it was too soon. Wasn't it?

* * * *

Bridget nearly swooned with excitement. Part of her leaped for joy from his interest, thrilled he wasn't dating Tori. But that was the old part. The part that existed before… The part that wasn't scarred.

"What are you afraid of?" Rob took a step toward her, staring intently.

"I'm not afraid." She stepped back right into the garage door. Oh yeah, that was showing him.

"Then why do you run?"

You're dangerous to my heart. "You're my landlord. Sort of."

"You think I'm going to kick you out into the street if it doesn't work out? Is that it?"

Sure, let him think that. It was better than the truth. "Maybe."

"I wouldn't do that."

I know. "Like I said, I hardly know you."

He stepped back and ran a hand through his thick, dark hair. Oh, how she'd love to do the same. Was it soft or coarse? Would it tickle her or feel luxurious?

And his lips. She'd dreamed of kissing those lips since the day she saw his photo. Now he was standing in front of her, wanting to date her, and she couldn't say yes. It was better to dream than live in reality.

His face lit up. "If I can make it where you feel safe from eviction, would that help?"

He affected her brain. Or maybe her hearing. "What?"

He stepped in and placed his hands on the garage door, trapping her. Being this close caused her heart all sorts of commotion. And her brain? Gone. So was her headache. Her head was blissfully peaceful.

"How about I write up a contract leasing you the house for six months? I can't evict you no matter what. Would you date me then?"

"Why? You hoping I'll date you out of some kind of obligation, then?"

"I don't want you to feel obliged. I just want a chance." He leaned in closer. "I've never felt like this with anyone else before.

I've never wanted to be with anyone like I want to be with you. Are you telling me you don't feel anything?"

Oh, why couldn't she have met him before? But if she gave in, it would only end badly. She blinked back the sting of tears.

"Bridget." He lifted her chin. "What are you afraid of?"

Of falling in love and having her heart stomped on. Of seeing the repulsion in his eyes once he saw the real her. She ran her tongue over parched lips and stared at him.

He stroked her cheek and she closed her eyes, enjoying the stimulating sensations coursing through her body. Without the pain in her head, she should be able to think. But she couldn't. Even breathing became a chore. The man sure knew how to mess with the elements.

His breath tickled her mouth. "May I kiss you?"

If she'd had any common sense, she would have said no and pushed him away. Instead, she must have nodded because his mouth covered hers. Soft and hesitant and oh so good.

* * * *

Her lips were softer than he'd imagined and he wanted to devour her, but he had to practice restraint. She was a flight risk. Still, his body ached with need and his cock sprang to life. He slid his hand behind her back, intending to pull her close.

"Bridget?" A woman's voice came from behind.

He froze. Damn, he hadn't heard anyone drive up, no less a car door close.

Bridget pulled away and muttered a curse. "Mom, what are you doing here?"

Mom? He straightened and turned to face an older version of the woman he'd been kissing.

"I came to take you curtain shopping." She fixed her gaze on him and narrowed her eyes. "Who's your…friend?"

Oh great, just what he needed. An angry mother would not give him any points to win Bridget's favor. Time to put on the charm.

Bridget stood beside him. "This is Rob Gentry. Rob, this is my mother, Mona Quigley."

He held out his hand. "How do you do Mrs.—"

"Is that any way for a landlord to treat their tenant?" Her glare rivaled that of a *Star Trek* phaser that wasn't set to stun.

Holy shit! Mama Bear was out and ready to defend and he was her target.

"Mom! Stop it. You're being rude."

"Rude? He was molesting you."

Now there was a strong word. He'd barely touched her.

Bridget clenched her fists. "I hardly think a kiss is molesting." She held out a key to her mother. "Will you wait for me inside, please?"

Mona glanced between the two of them before taking the key and heading for the front door. Bridget waited until her mother was inside before she spoke.

"I'm sorry about her, but I can't do this." Her hand waved between them.

He placed his hands on her shoulders. "So she caught us kissing. We're adults. Next time I'll make sure we're inside."

Her eyes widened. "There can't be a next time."

His heart sank for a moment, but he wouldn't give in to despair. She was scared, that's all. Instinctively, he caressed her cheek to soothe her. She closed her eyes and he leaned in close. "You feel something, too. I know it. Why are you fighting it?"

She jerked away. "It's complicated. Please don't ask."

"Bridget, I'm not giving up on you."

Her eyes glistened. "I wish you would." She lowered her head. "Do you have any more work to do in the house tonight?"

He could make up something to stick around, but he couldn't very well convince her to change her mind with her mother in the house. There would be other days. "No. I'll be back tomorrow and finish the bathroom."

"Good night, then." She limped her way inside.

Well, he certainly had work to do. Maybe the road to Bridget was through her mother, which meant he needed to mend fences with her. Flowers had always worked with his mother. They certainly couldn't hurt with Mona.

He left in higher spirits, with the memory of Bridget's lips against his. An act he planned on repeating in the near future and often.

* * * *

Bridget leaned against the door as she closed it. Her heart raced with excitement. She still couldn't believe Rob wanted to date her, not Tori. No one had ever picked her over her cousin.

She could still feel his lips against hers. How wonderful would it have been to feel his arms around her, too? She so badly wanted to give in, and almost had, but once he got a look at the real her and knew the truth… It would hurt less to end it now. Before she got in too deep.

"Are you okay?" Mom pulled the measuring tape across the bottom of the window sill.

That little action caused Bridget to burn with anger, a welcome change from the sexual frustration. "I'm fine." She limped to the kitchen and placed her backpack on the counter. Her knee had swollen tight. "I told you I couldn't go shopping until the weekend."

Her mother reeled in the tape with a snap and wrote on a small notebook. "I assumed that meant you didn't have any money until then. But since I planned on giving them to you as a house-warming gift, I didn't think you'd mind. I didn't realize you were dating the landlord."

"I'm not dating him."

"So, you're only having sex?"

"What? No! Oh God. We're so not having this conversation."

"Then tell me what I should assume when I catch you kissing in the driveway?"

Her mother still had the power to transport her back to high school after she'd been caught kissing the boy next door. "Assume whatever you want. It's none of your business."

"Bridget! Is that any way to talk to your mother?"

"And how should I talk to you? I'll be thirty this year and you treat me like a child."

"I'm sorry. It's just that since the accident…"

"You were hoping I'd need you more? You want me to stay being your little girl?"

Mom put the notebook on the sill and placed the tape on top. "I suppose there might be a little truth in that. I almost lost you, Bridget. It was the worst time of my life. And now you've moved out."

"I wasn't living with you before the accident." Bridget couldn't stand on her leg any longer and sat on one of the dinette's chairs. A warm bath called for her, but would have to wait.

"Yeah, well, I wasn't happy then, either." Mom sat in the chair beside Bridget. "What's the matter? You're hurting."

Oh great. A lecture from Kate was bad enough. Now she would have to get one from her mother. "Muscles have tightened up a bit. I'm fine."

"I told you not to ride that bike."

"I know, but you don't have to worry any more. I can walk to work now." She looked at the worry lines across her mother's forehead. Was this normal for all mothers or had she just been lucky? "Mom, you need to get you some friends. Better yet, why don't you and Dad go on a cruise or something? I can't be your life. It isn't healthy for either of us."

"You know your father won't go on a cruise. He has a hard time taking any vacation."

"He might surprise you. Have you even tried?"

Mom looked down at her lap. "You're really trying to get rid of me, huh?"

The pounding intensified and Bridget reached for her temples but stopped herself. Why worry her mother more? "I'm not trying to get rid of you. I have my life, you have yours. Isn't that the way it's supposed to work?"

"And you don't want me in your life?"

"Of course I do, but I think you need a friend you could talk to."

"I talk to you."

"No, Mom, you don't." Bridget took a deep breath. She hadn't planned on disappointing her mother tonight, but apparently that was the agenda.

"But what if I did? Will you be my friend?"

She loved her mother, but being her friend? Maybe it could work. "On the condition I'm not your only friend and you don't talk about Dad."

"I can't talk about your father?"

"Not in the personal, bedroom-way, no. You have to find other friends for that."

Mom nodded. "Can we talk about your boyfriends?"

Boyfriends? As in more than one? Rob wasn't even one. Bridget briefly closed her eyes. This friend thing was going to take some work. "Only if I bring it up, okay? I need my space."

"And curtains."

Did her mom just crack a joke? Bridget laughed and gave her a hug. "Yes, and curtains."

Chapter 7

Bridget and Mona hung the curtains and chatted. Charlie was almost jealous. Their closeness brought back fond memories of similar times with her mother, who'd died much too young. The pain of losing her had never quite gone away, even in death.

Existence as a ghost was the pits. She could talk, but why bother when all the conversations were one-sided—hers. And having only two of her five senses was frustrating to say the least. Sight was great and she could hear, but not being able to touch, smell, or taste the things around her tortured her. She couldn't even enjoy the heat of the sun. She would remain the same temperature—cold.

Not the shivering-in-the-winter type of cold, but the emptiness-of-never-feeling-warmth type.

That was one area where she did affect others. If anyone walked through her, they shivered. Rob hadn't reacted the first time she had touched him—probably in shock from finding her dead—but he had rubbed his arms and checked the AC the other times. After that, she made it a point to keep her distance. Why give him an excuse to stay away?

Mr. Murdock sufficed at times. At least he liked watching TV. But he seemed more susceptible to her coldness, no matter how far away she stood.

Then there was Bridget. A godsend. Too bad she only had the sight when they were alone. Boy, what fun Charlie could have then, making it look as if Bridget were talking to thin air. Nothing better than a good prank. Of course, that might cause Bridget to move out, so maybe it was for the best. Still, that didn't mean Charlie couldn't have fun in other ways.

She popped into the doorway of the bedroom, where mother and daughter were currently hanging curtains and getting along a little better than earlier—actually laughing at times.

Mona sat on the bed and slid a panel onto one of the rods. "Rob's kind of cute, isn't he?"

"Mom, we're not going to talk about him again, are we?"

"Oh, yes," Charlie said. "Please talk about Robbie. I want to know what you think."

"All I said was he's kind of cute. Can't you talk about him as a friend?"

Bridget smirked. "I can, but can you?"

"If at any time you feel I've reverted back to being a mother, let me know. But I need the practice."

Bridget laughed as she took the covered rod from her mother. "Fine. Yes, I think he's very good-looking. There. Satisfied?"

Charlie smiled. She liked Bridget and she loved her brother. The two of them would easily make a terrific couple. Maybe then Rob wouldn't look so sad all the time.

Mona picked up another curtain rod. "Are you interested in him?"

"Am I interested? Yes. Will I act on it? No."

"What?" Charlie said. "Why not? What's wrong with my brother?"

"So what I saw on the driveway—"

"Wasn't started by me. I know better than to get involved." Bridget stood on the stool and snapped the curtain rod in place.

"What did you see? What did you see?" Charlie asked Mona, as if the woman could hear her. She'd been over at Mr. Murdock's watching the Reds game when Robbie and Bridget returned from dinner and hadn't thought her brother would make any kind of move. Not yet, anyway. "Dammit. I miss all the good stuff."

"But, honey, if you like him…"

"It doesn't matter."

Like hell it didn't matter. Charlie floated back and forth. Bridget didn't know a good thing when she saw it. There was no one better than Robbie.

"Sweetie. Are you going to push away every young man that shows interest?"

"You tell her, Mom." Someone needed to talk some sense into Bridget.

"Weren't you just telling me not to get involved with my landlord?"

Bridget stepped down and Mona stood, placing a hand on Bridget's shoulder. "That was your mother talking. Your friend is trying to understand you."

Bridget fluffed out the hung curtain. "Can we talk about something else?"

Mona scooped the trash into a bag. "Okay. I'll butt out for now. It's getting late anyway. I should probably go home."

Charlie had meandered to the hallway when both women walked through her.

Mona rubbed her arms. "Did you feel that?"

"Feel what?"

"That blast of cold air? Do you have the AC on?"

"No. I don't think so." Bridget went to the thermostat in the hallway. "It's all turned off."

"Maybe you have a leak somewhere. You might want to have Rob check it out."

"Did you really feel the cold air, or are you giving me an excuse to get him back here?"

"Why would you need an excuse? Isn't he coming back to fix up the place anyway?"

"Good point. I'll have him check into it."

Charlie floated into the living room. How was it Mona felt her, but not Bridget? Bridget had also walked through her. What was up with that?

Mona grabbed her purse and kissed Bridget good night. As soon as her mother left the house, Bridget grabbed her temples and doubled over.

Charlie popped over to her. "Are you okay?"

Bridget jumped and bumped into the door. "Shit!" She looked up. "Oh great. You're back."

"I was never gone. You just can't see me when someone else is around. What's the matter with your head?"

"I think you are." Bridget stumbled into the kitchen, opened a cupboard, and pulled out a small bottle. "I get these bursts of pain whenever you appear." She took two pills and washed them down with water.

"My little calling card, huh?" When that didn't elicit a laugh, Charlie forged ahead. "Do you believe I'm real?"

"I believe you're the ghost of Charlene Gentry."

"Hot damn!" Charlie rushed to Bridget and hugged her. Ahh, warmth. She could get used to this.

Bridget squirmed free and went into the living room. "I want you to leave me alone. The last thing I need is the depressed ghost of someone who committed suicide."

Coldness enveloped her once again. "I am not depressed. And I did *not* kill myself. Carl did."

"Yeah, really? Then why did you leave a note?"

"What are you talking about? I can't leave any notes. I'm a ghost, remember?"

"I'm not talking about now. I'm talking about your *suicide.*"

"I didn't commit suicide, and I didn't leave a note. I swear to you, I didn't."

Bridget paced the living room with a limp and her arms akimbo. "Then explain how Rob received an e-mail from you saying you couldn't live without Nick."

"Robbie got an e-mail? From me? No wonder he thinks I offed myself. I swear, it wasn't me. It had to be Carl."

"And how would Carl do that?"

"From my laptop." Crap. How many times had Nick told her to password protect that thing? "Maybe Robbie could get my computer dusted for prints? Wouldn't that prove Carl used it?"

Bridget stopped her pacing. "Had Carl ever used your computer before?"

"Sure. All the time. Whenever I needed help, he'd be the one...." She stopped when Bridget had raised one eyebrow. "Okay, so I'm not thinking straight."

"You're right. You aren't. Neither am I. I was crazy to think I could help."

"What? No! You have to help. How else will my death be avenged? How else will I be able to leave?"

"What good will I be when they put me in the loony bin?" Bridget made a circling motion around her ear. "Because that's what will happen if I tell people you were murdered because you told me."

"So you don't tell anyone how you know."

"Then what proof do I have to even suspect a murder?" Bridget collapsed onto the couch. "Listen, I want to help you. I can't imagine what your life is like. But I need something concrete. And preferably easy. Do you understand?"

Charlie understood all too well. There must be something. She gazed at the fireplace and then the damaged walls.

"I think Nick might have hidden something here," she said. "Would that help?"

"What makes you say that?"

"Why else would Carl tear this place apart? Can't you find Nick and ask him? If you can see me, you have to be able to see him, too."

"Carl made this mess? Rob said they were tenants."

"Technically, they were. But they worked for Carl."

"You have proof? Did he come over?"

"No. They talked on the phone. I know it was Carl."

Bridget nodded, but more like a sarcastic, yeah-sure kind of nod. "So why the hole in the bathroom? That doesn't make any sense."

"Oh…well…that was me. Pretty impressive, huh? Scared the shit out of them!"

Bridget's eyes rounded. "You did that? You can actually move things?"

"Yeah, but don't ask me how, 'cause I still don't know. I've tried to do it again, but only got small stuff to move. I guess I have to be superangry or something. It sure freaked me out, but at least I got rid of them."

Bridget leaned over. "You have nothing."

"Don't give up. Please. You're the first bit of hope I've had since I died. I'm certain once you bring Carl to justice I'll be on my way. You just have to find Nick. He's got to be the key to this whole thing."

"Then why don't you go looking for him? What's stopping you?"

How could she tell Bridget she'd been no farther than Mr. Murdock's without sounding pathetic? Even if she did venture farther out, it wouldn't have mattered. "I don't know where he died."

* * * *

Bridget stared at her houseguest and shook her head. This was probably the most bizarre conversation she'd ever had. "What do you mean you don't know where he died?"

"I was kind of out of it at the time and Robbie refused to give me the address. But it was at one of his constructions sites. I just don't know which one exactly."

"So, you don't know where Nick died and you expect me to find him? If his spirit is still around, how come he hasn't contacted you?"

Charlie stared at the floor. "I don't know. I don't have all the answers. But maybe Nick does. Just ask Robbie for the address."

Bridget closed her eyes. No, not Rob again. Would every conversation she had end with him? She wouldn't be surprised if he starred in her dreams tonight. Actually, that wouldn't be such a bad idea.

"Why don't you want to go out with him?" Charlie asked. "Do you think you're too good for him?"

"Oh my God. How much have you heard tonight?"

"I've heard everything. What else is there to do?"

"Will I have no privacy?"

"Of course you'll have privacy. I'm not a perv."

The ibuprofen was useless. Bridget's headache remained and her muscles still objected to any kind of exertion. Walking around at the store shopping for curtains had only aggravated her knee. She stood and faced Charlie. "I'm going to take a bath, and then I'm going to bed. I'd prefer to do both without you hanging around. Will that be possible?"

"I left you alone last night and this morning, didn't I? But I gotta know. Are you going to ask about Nick?"

"I'll see if I can find out where he died without bringing Rob into this. Then you can go find him."

"Okay, okay. I can do that. Thank you."

Bridget took a step toward the bedroom.

"Before you go," Charlie pleaded. "Will you turn on the TV?"

Chapter 8

Rob parked in front of the office and hopped out of the truck, Barnaby right on his heels. Two more items on his to-do list and then he could head over to Charlie's. Except, now it would be Bridget's. At least temporarily.

When he opened the door, the dog dashed inside, knocking him off balance. He gripped the frame, preventing him from landing on his ass. One of these days Barnaby would break his leg.

He tossed his paperwork into the in-box. Item one scratched off. On to item two. He went to the receptionist area, but instead of Linda greeting him with her sunny disposition, the part-time bookkeeper, Margo, scowled. She couldn't be more than five years older than Rob, but with that frown, she looked ancient. Why couldn't she smile at him like she did at Carl?

Barnaby trotted around the desk and jumped into her lap. With a yelp, she pushed the dog away and stood, brushing her white skirt, which now contained dusty paw prints that just wouldn't go away. "Now look what he's done."

Dammit. Okay, so maybe she directed the frown toward the dog. Linda never minded Barnaby's affection. In fact, she always egged him on. Margo, on the other hand, seemed to hate everything and everyone. Well, everyone except Carl.

Rob came around the desk and grabbed the dog's collar. Margo's designer suit looked great on her curvaceous body, but totally inappropriate for the job.

"I'm sorry. I'll take care of the cleaning bill. Like I told you before, you don't have to dress up. You should consider wearing jeans." As if he hadn't told her at least a dozen times. He dragged Barnaby back around the front of the desk and snatched a leash, which hung on a hook by the door. "Where's Linda?"

Giving up on her skirt, Margo sat back in the chair with a grunt and straightened some papers. "She had some kind of an emergency. Car—Mr. Anders called and asked if I would sit in for the day. But if I had known you were bringing that monster in here, I would have declined."

She'd almost slipped up there. He wouldn't be surprised if Carl was sleeping with the woman. She was just his type—big breasted, well dressed, and young.

He secured the leash on Barnaby's collar and hooked the end around his wrist. The dog may be over anxious, but hardly a monster. At least this visit would be short. "I need the envelope a courier dropped off for me."

"I gave that to Mr. Anders."

If he'd held a pencil in his hand, he'd have surely snapped it in two. After counting to three, he placed both hands on the desk and leaned forward. "Was it addressed to Mr. Anders?"

Margo flinched and scooted back into her chair. "No, but it was from the lawyer's office. I thought Mr. Anders took care of all the legal paperwork."

"He does, but if I recall, business documents are addressed to him." He straightened and headed for the hall. Damn. So much for leaving early.

Carl's office was situated on the other end of the small building. Years of pictures, many including Rob's father, cluttered the walls. A credenza lined the left wall and included several pictures of Carl's family.

Barnaby stopped in the doorway and growled. Rob tugged on the leash, silencing the dog. How did he manage to mix the two people up? Shouldn't he growl at Margo and be happy to see Carl?

"Is Linda okay?" Rob asked.

Carl was leaning back in his chair reading what appeared to be Rob's documents. He looked over his glasses. "Her sister went into labor."

Rob let out an easy breath. Thank God. That meant he wouldn't have to see Margo tomorrow.

Carl sat up and placed his glasses on the desk. "By the way, Rialto is back on. They paid their bill."

And it was a huge bill. But he doubted it was completely good news for Carl since his son had died there. "How will this impact the new office project? Will we have enough workers?"

"Taken care of."

"Do you need me to take over Rialto?"

Carl stared at him for several seconds. "Thanks, but I'm good, actually. It'll be a relief to get it finished." He waved the papers in the air. "What is this?"

And that was his cue to leave.

"None of your business." Rob snatched the papers and turned toward the exit.

"Wait. I think we need to talk."

Rob respected Carl, but didn't need him interfering with his life. "Talk about what? That you opened my personal mail? This has nothing to do with work."

"I didn't realize it was personal until I started reading it. Sit. Please."

If he didn't stay and hear Carl out, he'd probably never hear the end of it. He grabbed a seat. Barnaby lay on the floor beside his feet.

Carl pointed to the papers. "Does this have anything to do with your house sitter?"

House sitter or future girlfriend? Rob was betting on the latter. "She seems to think I'm going to kick her out into the street if we don't get along. I thought a contract would ease her worries."

"But the contract stipulates she gets the property if you should die before the six months are up."

"Yeah, so? Who else am I going to give the house to? Some cousin I don't even know?"

"No, but you have a business. Have you had your will drawn up yet?"

Rob sat straighter. For once he was ahead of the game. So what if the lawyer had practically bribed him. It was worth it. "Already done. And just so you know, I'm leaving you the business."

"Rob, you don't have to do that."

"You deserve it. Besides, I don't have anyone else to leave it to. Not that I plan on dying any time soon."

"Well, at least you can change it if you get married or have kids."

If Carl had mentioned that last week, Rob would have laughed in his face. But after meeting Bridget, it didn't seem so funny. True, he hardly knew her, but it didn't stop him from wanting to spend every free minute with her. She was all he thought about. Marriage was looking less scary, but first he had to convince Bridget to start dating.

* * * *

Sitting in Kate's office using the computer, Bridget typed Nick Anders's name in the search box and waited. Damn slow computer.

"Does Kate know you're in here?"

Bridget flinched at the squeaky voice and inadvertently clicked the page closed. "Gee, Tori. Way to sneak up on a person."

"Well, if you didn't have your nose buried in the screen, you would have seen me approach. What's so interesting?"

"It's personal. And yes, Kate knows I'm in here."

"Listen, while I got you, I need you to do me a favor." Tori closed the door and leaned against it. "Don't ask Rob over to fix the house on Friday. I want to ask him out, and I don't want him feeling obligated to work on the house."

"For your information, he comes over when he feels like it, not by my request. If he wants to go out with you, I'm sure the house won't stop him." Well, it wouldn't stop anyone else. Rob might use the excuse to be nice.

"You think so?" Tori looked downright hopeful.

"Any man who'd want to date you wouldn't let a little work get in the way." Unfortunately for Tori, that man wasn't Rob. But hey, she could learn the hard way.

Tori smiled and nodded. "You're right. Thanks, Bridget."

"Any time." Maybe she was a horrible person leading her cousin on, but she didn't care. Tori had it coming.

Once her cousin left, Bridget stared at the ocean scene on the monitor. Sun, sand, and palm trees. Now there was a place she'd probably never visit, at least not in the summer wearing something skimpy. Not like she used to, anyway. Oh well, she was getting too old for that crap anyway. Right?

She clicked on the Internet icon. Why was she bothering searching for Nick? Besides wasting her time here when Rob would be the easiest route, did she really think she'd be able to see another ghost? If ghosts were floating all over the place, how come she hadn't seen them?

Or maybe she had. Could that be what she'd seen in the hospital? And how about that guy on the road? Shit. So what made her crazier: seeing hallucinations or seeing ghosts?

She turned off the machine and stood. Forget about Charlie. Forget about Nick. They weren't her concern right now, her job was.

By the time five o'clock rolled around, her concern had shifted from performing her job to making it home before she collapsed. Being on her feet most of the day—cleaning cages, feeding animals—only made her headache worse. Her muscles could stand a break, too. How could riding a bike one time create such misery? Another bath was in store for the evening, and more ibuprofen. Not that the pills helped with the headache much. She pulled her backpack out of the locker and slipped it on.

Kate pulled a bottle of water from the refrigerator. "You got any plans for tonight?"

Bridget grabbed her coat from the rack and hooked it on her arm. The weather had been chilly in the morning, but warmed nicely by lunch, so she wouldn't need to wear it home. "Rob's supposed to come over and work on the bathroom. Other than that, nope."

"How's it working with Rob? Is he behaving?"

Was kissing her behaving? "So far it's good. I'm thankful you suggested me for a house sitter. But you didn't coerce him, did you?"

"Coerce him? Why would you think…. Oh, Tori. I keep forgetting she's got the hots for Rob and is within earshot whenever he visits. She must feel threatened." Kate lifted an eyebrow. "Should she?"

"I'm not doing anything to threaten her." Except maybe existing.

"Then she must be her regular paranoid self. Well, I didn't coerce him or beg. I knew he was having difficulty with his neighbor and I merely suggested you as a solution. And since I could vouch for you, he jumped all over it. Does that make you feel better?"

"A little, thanks. I feel like all I've been doing lately is asking for help."

"Hey, if family can't help out, what good are they, huh? Do you need a ride home?"

Cramps had threatened Bridget's leg all day and while a ride home would be nice, she couldn't accept. Maybe family was meant to help, but there was needing help and there was being needy. She would not be needy. She shook her head. "I'm good, but thanks."

"Let me walk out with you, then. I think I need some air after the Mitchell's dog. I've never seen a dog fart so much."

Together they laughed and stepped outside. The sky was a dazzling blue without a fluff of cloud and the scent of pine filled the air. Bridget took it all in.

"Is that why you don't need a ride?" Kate nodded to the front of the lot.

There stood a big red truck, with Rob leaning against it. He smiled and waved. Bridget's heart fluttered at the sight.

"I didn't know he was coming here." Why did he keep pursuing her? How many times did she have to tell him no? Maybe when her noes stopped sounding like yeses. Because deep down inside, she was glad he was there. Something inside her came alive in his presence and wiped out the nagging headache.

* * * *

When Bridget stepped out of the building, Rob's heart had lifted. All day he'd thought of her and now here she was in the flesh. Damn, he had it bad.

As he sauntered their way, Kate practically scowled at him and a smile flitted across Bridget's face. Maybe he was making headway after all.

"Hey, ladies!"

"What are you doing here?" Kate placed her hands on her hips.

He couldn't blame her for being wary. He had promised to behave. Could it be she knew he'd kissed Bridget? No, that couldn't be it. If Kate knew, she'd be flat-out fuming.

"I finished patching the wall in the bathroom and thought Bridget would like to pick out the paint color."

"You have to paint the bathroom?" Bridget asked.

"Well, yeah. You see, there's this big patch on the wall." He stretched his hands about a foot apart.

Bridget chuckled. "That's not what I meant. Why can't you just paint that one spot?"

"I could, but I'll never be able to match the color."

"You can't match white?"

"Uhhh, the walls aren't white. They're kind of peachy."

"They are?" She looked at Kate, who only shrugged.

"So, what do you say?" he asked.

Bridget shifted her weight. "Do you really need me to pick it out?"

This conversation wasn't going anywhere near how he'd hoped it would. He'd never met a woman who didn't enjoy picking out paint samples, and while Bridget didn't come right out and say no, his heart ached with her lack of enthusiasm for the project.

"No. I only thought you would like to pick a color, but if you don't want to, I can get white."

"I guess I can pick out a color. I've never done it before. It won't take long, will it?"

"Only as long as you make it."

"I thought you were going to relax tonight," Kate said. "Wasn't your leg—"

"He just said it won't take long."

Oh crap. If she was hurting, he didn't want to make it worse. "Is your leg still—"

"I'm fine," she interrupted. "Let's go. I'll see you tomorrow, Kate."

Bridget headed for the truck, and Rob had to jog to beat her to the door. If her leg gave her problems, she hid it well.

"Hey, Barnaby," she said as she climbed inside. "How's my favorite puppy doing?"

Barnaby thumped his tail against the back cushion and licked her face. Lucky dog. Rob closed the door and headed around the truck.

Kate grabbed his elbow. "You said you would behave. What kind of game are you playing?"

"I'm not playing any game." He was dead serious about Bridget. How else could he get her attention if he didn't make himself indispensable? He just never dreamed he'd have to work so hard. "She'll pick out the color, and then I'll take her home." And then maybe have dinner with her or stay awhile and talk. Or better yet, finish that kiss he'd started.

"Why don't I believe you?"

He kissed her on the cheek. "Chill, Kate. She's in good hands. I promise."

Rob entered the truck and Barnaby's tail smacked him in the arm. He pushed the dog's furry butt out of the way and buckled up.

On the drive to the paint store, Bridget kept her attention on the dog and didn't glance out the window once. Not that Barnaby minded. Rob drove as smooth as the road allowed.

After he parked the truck, he left the windows open a crack. As Bridget slid out, the poor dog whined and followed.

Rob grabbed the beast's collar before the he could escape. "We won't be long, fella. You'll see more of her, I promise."

Barnaby stared at him as if saying, "I'd better."

* * * *

Bridget stood in front of the paint store. What the hell was she doing? She should have told Rob no and walked home. But once her headache disappeared, she couldn't walk away. A painless head was a blessed gift. And then Kate had turned all "Mom" on her and every sensible thought escaped her brain. No one would tell her what to do. Even if it was the right thing.

But it was wrong to get his hopes up. Wrong to lead him on. If her guilt and scars weren't bad enough, once he found out she saw dead people he would pretty much run screaming. And who could blame him?

He locked the truck and joined her, his arm brushing against hers. "So, what's your favorite color?"

Her heart pumped erratically, making her head woozy. She stepped away, but the light-headed feeling stayed. "It sort of depends on the item. But for a bathroom, I guess I'd want something light and soothing. Maybe a green or blue."

"Not white?" he said with a hint of a grin and a glint in his eye.

"So sue me for being unobservant."

"I can't. If it weren't for the spackle, I would have said they were white, too."

A snort escaped and she covered her mouth in embarrassment. She hadn't done that in ages, but it felt good. He laughed with her as he held the door open.

The owner stole Rob away, but not before Rob indicated where the samples were located.

Bridget had never painted or even bought paint. When she'd lived with her parents, her mother handled the decorating, and when she'd had her own apartment, she never touched the walls. Hadn't cared to. Maybe she was missing the decorator gene.

She perused the selection. How many stinkin' blues and greens were there anyway? And what would they look like in the bathroom? White was beginning to look like a good possibility, but even that color came in shades. Sheesh! She could be here forever.

Her leg tightened and, stretching her foot, she bent her knee back and forth. Not again. She should have gone straight home and soaked it, but no. A pain-free head beat out her tired leg. So did Rob's company for that matter. Well, she'd come to pick a paint color, so she'd pick a paint color. What could she live with? She started pulling several samples.

"Well, well. Fancy meeting you here," a man said from behind.

The all-too-familiar voice caused her heart to catch in her throat. She spun around and confirmed her suspicions. Hell's bells! Her body suddenly forgot how to breathe.

"Why won't you take my calls, Bridget?"

* * * *

Mac, the owner of McGruder's Paint, was closer to David Gentry's generation than Rob's, but Rob probably dealt with the man more often than his father ever had. When Mac had pulled Rob aside, wearing a frown, Rob showed Bridget where to find the paint samples so he could talk to his friend.

"Hey, Mac. What's up?"

"I don't know how to ask this except to come right out. Have we done something to displease you?" Mac rubbed at his salt-and-pepper beard, a sign of his agitation.

"What do you mean?"

"I'm talking about the big order you canceled. Did you lose the job, or did we do something wrong?"

"You still lost me, Mac. What order did we cancel?"

"Wait here. I'll go get the paperwork."

While Rob waited, he stared at Bridget. He might have had to work at getting her here, but she seemed to be enjoying herself. That snort she'd made outside confirmed it. He'd love to make her laugh more often. And with the way she was examining those paint samples as if she was being tested, maybe he could tease her a bit, too. She was certainly teasing him a lot right now. Even in her scrubs, he could make out the shape of her ass—round and firm—especially when she bent over just a bit. He hoped to God that one day soon he could walk up behind her and show her what she did to him. The erection he sported strained against his zipper, and he shifted his legs hoping the adjustment would help. It didn't.

Mac returned and held out some papers. "This order. We got the cancellation today."

Rob snatched the forms a little rougher than he intended, but it helped ease the tightness in his jeans. "Can I take a look at these tomorrow and get back to you?"

"Sure, sure. But you'd tell me if there were problems, wouldn't you? We've been supplying your paint for years. If it's a matter of price—"

"Mac, relax. I'll check it out. As far as I'm concerned, we're still good. Besides, would I be here if we weren't?"

Mac chuckled and rubbed his beard. "I guess you have a point there. I'll let you get back to your lady friend there. If you need any help, let me know."

His lady. He liked the sound of that. But as he turned to join her, some man was standing beside her and the samples she'd held fluttered to the floor.

Chapter 9

Bridget had seen her share of angry men and had dealt with many while working as a nurse at the hospital, but never anything resembling the man who stood in front of her. Devin's eyes were cold…flat. Dead. He had probably died the same night she'd killed his wife, Suzie.

"Is everything okay, Bridget?" Rob bent over and picked up the dropped samples.

Her heart gave up beating regularly a moment ago, but thank goodness her long-sleeve shirt hid the goose bumps on her arms, because she refused to let either man know how terrified she felt. She held her head high. "Everything's fine. Devin was just leaving. Weren't you, Devin?" Too bad her voice cracked.

Devin scowled at her. "I guess you can speak after all. So, have you forgotten her? Have you moved on?"

Never and never. "Now's not the time."

"When is the time, huh, Bridget? You don't take my calls." He got into her face, slurring his words and reeking of booze.

The man Suzie had loved no longer existed. He'd become Bridget's third casualty.

"Excuse me," Rob interjected. "She's right. Maybe if we went outside—"

"No!" she said. "I can't talk to you now, Devin. Please go."

His face turned red and his eyes glistened. He grabbed her arm. "You took everything away from me. Why couldn't it have been you? It should have been you!"

His grip hurt, but she welcomed the assault. He didn't say anything she hadn't thought herself. A tear trailed down her cheek and she whimpered. Nothing she said would ease his pain. Nothing he did would make her feel better.

Rob pried Devin's fingers loose. "I think you better go, or I'll be forced to call the police."

Devin yanked his hand away. "I'm going."

After Devin stormed away, Bridget wiped her eyes and turned back to the paint samples. Why had she lived and Suzie had died? Suzie'd had a husband who loved her and a baby on the way. Bridget had no one.

"Are you okay?" Rob asked.

She would never be okay. "I'm fine. But I'm not in the mood to pick colors right now. Do you mind taking me home?"

"No, of course not. Let me make sure he's left, though. I'll be right back."

While Rob went outside, she pulled nearly every paint sample from the display. She'd let Charlie help pick out the color. Better than dwelling on her friend's death.

* * * *

Rob pulled into the driveway and turned off the engine. This was not the way he had envisioned the day. He'd pictured having dinner with her. Laughing with her. Kissing her. Instead, he needed to tamp down his anger and find out who this Devin guy was. If he punched someone, he should at least know why.

"Thanks for the ride," Bridget said. "Do you mind if I get back to you tomorrow regarding the color? I think I took every sample they had."

He brought his knee up on the bench and faced her. "Is Devin an old boyfriend?"

She ran a finger over Barnaby's collar as if she were doodling. "No. He was married to my best friend. She died."

"I'm sorry. He blames you?"

With her head down low and her gaze on Barnaby, she shrugged. He got the impression Devin not only held her responsible, but she shouldered the guilt. Why else wouldn't she talk to the man? While that was something she would have to work out for herself, right now he was more concerned with her safety.

"Do you think he's violent enough to come after you?"

"He's never been violent before, but he's grieving. Still...." She shook her head. "I don't think so. He would have done it by now. It's not like I'm hiding. Besides, he's got that whole Hippocratic oath thing going."

"He's a doctor?"

She nodded. With one hand on the door handle, she scratched Barnaby with the other. "I'll see you later, then."

"Bridget, wait." This wasn't how he'd planned it, but she gave him no other option. He pulled the contract from his back pocket and held it out. "Here."

"What's that?"

"The lease which lets you live here free for six months. So you won't feel threatened with eviction."

She stared at his hand, but didn't take the offered item. "Why are you being so nice to me?"

"Why shouldn't I be nice?"

"You don't know me."

"Are we going to go through this again? Bridget, I want to know you."

"Then you should talk to Kate. Maybe then you'll change your mind." She grabbed her backpack, opened the door, and slid out of the truck without taking the papers.

Damn, she was stubborn. Well, he could be, too. He bolted out of the truck and blocked her way. "This is a done deal, already signed and is being filed. This is your copy. The place is yours for six months whether or not you live here. I'd prefer you lived here, though. I still need a house sitter."

Bridget stared at his hand. He placed his bet with her living in the house, because he was pretty sure she didn't want to live with her parents.

Slowly, she raised her hand and took the offered document. "Thank you. This doesn't mean we're dating, though."

"I know. But will you do me a favor? Will you call me if Devin becomes a problem?"

"He won't be." She walked around him and he allowed her.

Rob waited while she let herself in. Maybe she didn't think Devin was a problem, but the man had serious anger issues and directed them toward her. She had told him to talk to Kate, but maybe Brian would be better. With Kate, he was liable to get a lecture and little to no information.

Barnaby whined. If Rob stayed, he'd only be making himself a pest. He'd rather be on her good side. He was heading back toward his truck when she cried out. Curtains covered the window, blocking any view of inside. He knocked. Moans filtered through the door. Something was wrong and he couldn't ignore it.

"Bridget?" He knocked again. No response. Ah, the hell with it. He opened the door and found her curled on the floor, grabbing her left calf. "Bridget!" He rushed to her side.

Tears filled her eyes. She panted through clenched teeth while kneading her leg. Her shoeless foot pointed unnaturally.

"Here, let me." He massaged her rock-hard calf. This was his fault. He'd kept her on her feet too long.

She grabbed her head and leaned back. "Oh God. It hurts so bad."

Her agony twisted his gut. He'd gladly take the pain himself if it were possible. "I know, honey. You need to relax. Try and relax."

Bridget took several deep breaths, but her leg was still stiff. He couldn't get the knot loosened. Seemed her muscles were just as stubborn as her.

* * * *

Bridget couldn't flex her foot to save her life. Had someone cut her calf open and squeezed her muscles? She refused to cry in front of him. She would not be weak.

All she had wanted was a bath. But as soon as she closed the front door, her headache had returned, along with Charlie, scaring the crap out of her and distracting her enough to be careless as she slipped off her shoe. One twist the wrong way and the pain had sent her kissing the carpet.

Rob's large hands offered some relief, but not near enough. Tears formed and blurred her vision. Breathing deep kept her cheeks dry.

"Why don't you try standing?" he asked.

Walking had always helped in the past, but she usually caught it before it got this bad. She wasn't sure she had the strength to do it. The cramp was draining her dry. She moved to her side, looking for a way to stand without it hurting more.

Rob lifted her by her armpits and she cried out a little, but he got her upright. "Try and put your weight on it."

He put an arm around her waist and she did the same to him, his hard muscles against her body. She did as he suggested and her leg relaxed. Finally. Her breathing returned to normal as he walked with her around the small living room. Well, she limped while he walked. She sat a couple of times, but each time the cramp resurfaced. Tired and weary, she wanted to sleep, like, forever.

After the fourth attempt at sitting, her leg quieted down. She breathed a sigh of relief. Her achy muscles relaxed.

Rob went to the kitchen and brought her back a glass of water. "You feeling better?"

Nodding, she took the water and downed it. She couldn't look him in the face. Embarrassment heated her cheeks. That he'd witnessed one of her cramping episodes was humiliating to say the least. But, oh, how he had helped her. Offering gentle suggestions instead of barking orders, like her physical therapist always had, did the trick for her. Maybe he should take some lessons from Rob.

A sound of wood hitting wood caught her attention. He had gone back into the kitchen, searching through her cabinets.

"Don't you have any food in the house?" he asked.

"I have some frozen dinners." One, but then maybe he wouldn't…look. Crap.

He opened the freezer, reached in and pulled out the box of Lean Cuisine Chicken and Broccoli Alfredo. "This is all you have?"

"I planned on doing some shopping this weekend." As if it was any of his business.

"But it's Wednesday. There's not enough here to last the week." He tossed the box back into the freezer and shut the door. "Do you need me to get you something?"

"Nooo. I'm perfectly capable of getting my own groceries, thank you." Tentatively she stood, being careful with the weight on her left leg. Having a cramp was like pulling a muscle, and she had pulled a major one.

"Sit down."

Okay, now he was beginning to sound bossy.

"I don't want to sit down." She took two steps, limping. Damn, she wanted to sit. "Thank you for your help, but you can go now. I can manage by myself."

He appeared in her face faster than she anticipated and she teetered backward. Quickly, he grabbed her waist. "I'm sure you can, but I'll feel better knowing you ate a semidecent meal. I'm gonna get a pizza. What kind do you like?"

His scent engulfed her. Damn. Her physical therapist never smelled this good.

"Pizza is a decent meal?" Her question came out breathless. What had he done to her?

"I said semidecent." He smiled and her resolve melted.

One pizza wouldn't kill her and she hadn't eaten any in over a year. Of course, she was in a coma during most of that time. And would it really be that bad spending time with him? He was going to be working there anyway. Might as well get used to him. "Fine. Surprise me."

His smile turned into a grin. "Can I leave Barnaby with you? I don't trust him with food in the truck."

She chuckled. "Sure, why not?"

He was so close—she was so weak—he could kiss her now and she wouldn't stop him. Instead, he placed his hands on her shoulders and pushed her onto the couch.

Rob fetched Barnaby, who bounced in toward her. He placed his head on her lap.

"Anything else you'd like me to get?" Rob asked.

"How about some beers?" Beer and pizza. Couldn't get any better than that.

He placed his hand on the doorjamb. "Surprise you?"

She nodded, petting the top of Barnaby's head. His fur was soft and comforting against her fingers. How the hell had Rob finagled his way to having dinner with her? And why was she thrilled at the idea?

He wasn't gone a minute when pain slashed through her temples.

* * * *

"Hey, fur face!" Charlie clapped her hands and the dog whipped his head around.

Bridget, on the other hand, held her head in her hands. "You're back."

"I never left. I guess it's not an exaggeration if you say I'm a pain in the head, huh? Is that better or worse than being a pain in the ass?"

"Ha-ha," Bridget deadpanned. Slowly, she raised her head. Her eyes widened. "Barnaby can see and hear you."

The dog ran through Charlie. "I thought you knew that from the other day."

75

"It didn't register. Remember, I thought I was going crazy."

"Does that mean you didn't ask about Nick?"

"Then again, I could have a brain tumor and I'm just seeing things. Why else would I have these headaches?"

Charlie went to Bridget and knelt. "I'm sorry I give you the headaches, but you're not crazy." She placed her hand on Bridget's knee. "You feel me, don't you? How can you say I'm not real?"

"A damaged mind can trick you into all sorts of things."

"Damn, you're stubborn, you know that? What do I have to do to get you to admit I'm not a hallucination?" Barnaby bumped into her. Instinctively, she pet the mutt with her free hand. His fur was soft through her fingers. "Holy shit! I can touch him."

Barnaby licked Charlie's face. More like slobbered. Charlie hugged the dog with both arms and Barnaby fell through her, landing at Bridget's feet.

"What did you do?" Bridget asked. "He touched you, didn't he?"

"Give me your hand."

Once they connected, Charlie reached out. The couch became solid. The dog became solid. Keeping her hold on Bridget, she sat on the couch and sunk into the cushions. What a rush. She stared at her dog and slapped her thigh. "Come here, boy."

Barnaby lobbed over and jumped up, his front paws landing in Charlie's lap.

"Sweet Jesus!" She bent down and nuzzled the top of the beast's head. His fur tickled her face and he smelled just like she remembered. "Oh baby, how I missed you."

Barnaby slobbered some more and wagged his tail.

She turned to Bridget. "You're a miracle. I knew it the minute you saw me. But this is just…wonderful. Thank you." Her vision blurred and she blinked back tears. Damn, she could cry?

"Don't thank me, yet. I haven't done anything." Bridget rubbed her temple.

"So you didn't find anything about Nick?"

Bridget shook her head. "I didn't have enough time during lunch. I'd ask Rob, but how do I bring up Nick without sounding crazy?"

"Yeah, that would be a problem, unless…." Charlie stood, breaking the connection. "Follow me." She led the way to the desk in the spare bedroom. "Open the top drawer."

The desk, one of those old wooden monstrosities, had belonged to her father back at his office. After he died, Rob hadn't wanted it, but Charlie had no problem keeping it.

Bridget tugged and freed the drawer. "It's empty."

"Not quite. Look inside."

Bridget turned on the lamp. Her eyes widened.

"Can you use that?"

"I don't know. Maybe." Bridget rubbed her temples.

"Then I'll give you a break." Charlie willed herself to the backyard.

It wasn't fair. Spending months being invisible and soundless had been sheer agony. Now when someone broke those barriers, and more than that, made her world solid once again, her mere existence was painful to that person.

What was a ghost to do? Maybe Bridget just needed to be eased into her ability—small doses of Charlie. Yeah, that was it. No reason to bombard Bridget.

Charlie clenched her teeth. But, damn, that would be hard. Like rehab all over again. Who knew her addiction would evolve into a ghost-seeing woman?

Chapter 10

Rob closed the box on the half-eaten pizza. "You like leftover pizza?"

Bridget drained her beer. "Nothing better than cold pizza for breakfast."

Lots of things were better. Such as kissing her, or loving her, or waking up beside her. Hell, anything to do with her. Right now he was thankful to have had dinner with her.

He slid the box into her empty refrigerator. As tempted as he was to buy her more groceries, it wasn't his place. Instead, he'd use it to give him some leverage in asking her out again. She had to eat and she clearly wasn't doing that at home.

"Who's Nick?"

Rob sat back at the table. "Nick who?"

"The Nick of Charlie and Nick. I noticed the engraving inside the desk drawer."

Ahh, Dad's desk. "That would be Nick Anders, Charlie's boyfriend."

"Do you still see him?"

"No. He died before…." Damn, were they going to talk about dead people all the time? Of course, it didn't help that most of his friends and family had passed.

Bridget placed her hand over his, warming his heart. "Was she there? Did she witness it?"

"No. She was spared that." He needed to change the subject to something cheery if there was any possibility of finishing the kiss he had started yesterday.

"How did he die?"

"Could we not—"

She withdrew her hand. "I'm sorry. If you want to go home, I'll understand."

In an instant he missed touching her. But home? How did that happen? "I don't have to go anywhere."

"Is talking about Charlie painful? Should I drop it?"

"Why are you so fascinated?"

She shrugged. "Curiosity? I guess because I'm living in her house I feel some kind of connection."

If staying meant talking about death, he'd do it. Maybe if he shared, she'd feel obligated to do the same.

* * * *

"Why don't we move this conversation to the couch?" Rob stood and offered his hand.

If guilt were food, she'd be stored up for several winters, but how else could she get the information she needed without sounding like a raving lunatic?

Bridget took his hand, warm and comforting. If she weren't careful, she could easily lose her heart to him. She was already hankering for him more than she liked. To keep her distance, she sat on the far end of the couch, turned, and placed her knee on the middle cushion, using the back as an armrest.

He frowned as he took the other end. "So, what would you like to know?"

Ah, straight to the subject. Well, at least she didn't have to hem and haw. "How did Nick die?"

"He fell at the Rialto job site. Although I have no idea why he was there."

"He wasn't an employee?"

"He was, but not on that job. Carl thinks he went out there looking for equipment. Or maybe he went out there looking for Carl. I guess we'll never know."

"Who's Carl?"

"He's my head salesman slash foreman. Nick's father."

"You know him long?"

"All my life. He's like an uncle to me. He was there when my parents died and when Charlie passed, even though he still grieved for Nick. I don't know what I'd do without him."

Oh crap. How could she attack Carl without Rob shutting down? She needed information, not him defensive. Maybe if she had studied how to interrogate without being insulting, she'd have better luck. "It's nice you have someone you can confide in. Did Charlie feel the same way toward him? After Nick died?"

Rob sighed. "Carl and Charlie had an up and down relationship. She made the mistake of hanging around the wrong crowd and using drugs, and Carl voiced his opinion on that subject. When she became involved with Nick, she and Carl became more at odds. Then Nick helped Charlie get clean and Carl began to relax around her. I think Nick was the glue that kept her and Carl amicable. I just wish I'd known…."

"Known what?"

He pulled a loose thread on the couch. "That Nick's death would trigger her addiction. Carl had warned me."

Carl had warned him? Well, wasn't that convenient. "How did he know?"

"He told me she'd gone off the deep end when she learned there wouldn't be another investigation."

"But there *was* an investigation."

"Yeah, but there was no proof of foul play. Nick had no enemies. I think Charlie wanted to blame someone and couldn't handle that there wasn't anyone to blame."

He scooted closer and placed his hand on her knee. "The whole incident was in the papers. Could we please talk about something less depressing?"

Her heart sped up from his touch. "Like…like what?"

"I don't know. Movies, TV, the weather." He removed his hand from her knee and stroked her fingers. His warmth zinged through her extremities.

Her heart went from double-time to whoa-baby-come-to-mama. She had to stop his advances and sitting with her legs wide open was probably inviting him in. She lowered her knee and straightened. Wrong move. That only gave him more room and he scooted closer.

He smelled good—of soap and wood—and grasped her hand before she could pull it away. "What are you afraid of, Bridget? Did some guy break your heart?"

"Sure, what girl hasn't had her heart broken." She stared at his lips. Would it be so bad if they kissed? Kisses were just kisses, not a commitment. "How is it you're still free? You a playboy?"

His smile made his eye gleam. "Not a playboy. Never found the right woman. Until…maybe…now."

He held the back of her head. With the sound of blood rushing in her ears, she closed her eyes. He brushed his lips across hers and she leaned into them. What started out soft gradually became hard, almost as if he was staking a claim. She opened to him and he thrust his tongue in, exploring. He tasted better than she imagined, a mix of beer and pizza and something uniquely him.

He rubbed his thumb against her nipple and she moaned into his mouth. It had been too long since someone had last touched her. She craved everything he had to offer.

Slowly, he trailed his hand down her body, ending at her core. Frozen in place, she gradually thawed as he stroked her. She grew wet for him. Tentatively, she placed her hand on his chest, wishing the shirt would disappear. The buttons were at her fingertips. Could she slip her hand in?

He was nuzzling her neck when her mind cleared. Shit! Charlie was probably in the room.

Watching.

"I see dead people." Hell's bells. That had come out all wrong.

* * * *

Rob backed up and blinked several times as if someone had poured cold water over him. His heart was racing overtime, but his erection was slacking. "What? Isn't that a line from a movie?"

"Is it?" Bridget pulled away and stood, averting her eyes.

"And I'm not dead."

"I know."

"What kind of game are you playing?"

"It's not a game. I wish it were. God, do I wish it were. But it's real. At least as real as Charlie tells me."

"Charlie? Charlie who? Shit! You mean my sister?"

Bridget nodded. "She's a ghost and is probably in this room. Watching us."

He looked around like an idiot. What did he expect to find? "What do you mean, probably? Do you, or don't you see ghosts?"

"I see Charlie whenever I'm alone."

"That seems convenient."

"It's true. And Barnaby can see her, too. Show him, Charlie."

The dog lifted his head at the mention of his name; otherwise, he remained lying by the fireplace.

"Bridget, are you all right?" A crushing pain enveloped his chest.

She wrung her hands. "Come on, Charlie. Show Rob. Why are you doing this to me?"

He placed his hands on her shoulders. Tears formed in her eyes. "Easy, now. Why don't you sit down?"

"I'm not crazy. She said I wasn't crazy." Her eyes widened, loosening one lone tear. "Oh, God!" She buried her head in her hands. "Maybe you should leave."

He couldn't leave her in this state. He hugged her close and took in her scent of flowers and a little bit of pizza. She was scared from the kissing, right? She didn't actually believe in ghosts, did she?

"Was your sister always unreliable?"

He laughed. "Boy, was she." Oh great, did he actually believe her? "Listen, I don't know what you think you saw, but ghosts don't exist. They're just stories people make up to scare one another."

"Yeah, stories," she muttered.

"Why don't we sit down?"

She pulled away and looked at the floor. "It's late. Would you leave, please? I want to go to bed."

Maybe sleep was all she needed. She'd been through a lot today, what with Devin and her leg cramp.

He lifted her chin. "Are you going to be okay?"

She nodded, but averted her eyes. "I'll have a color picked out by Saturday, so you don't have to bother coming back until then."

She might as well have sliced him with a knife, the pain felt the same. Being away from her that long would be damn difficult, but if she required space, then he'd give her some. "I'll see you Saturday, then. Come on, Barnaby. Let's go."

The beast followed Rob to the door. He'd give her the rest of the week and take the time to do some investigating. There was more to her than she was sharing. He would find out what.

* * * *

A car door slammed and Charlie glanced out the window. Robbie was leaving? Already? She was sure he and Bridget were getting it on.

"Thanks for the TV, Mr. Murdock. We'll have to do this again some other time."

No response from the man in the chair. He couldn't hear her, and not because he'd fallen asleep.

She willed herself back to her living room. Empty. "Yo, roomie! Where are you?"

"Go away."

Ahh, the bathroom. She appeared at the door. "Why did Robbie leave so early? The way he was looking at you, I thought for sure you two would still be at it."

The door swung open. Bridget wore her pj's—a long-sleeve tee and flannel pants. Her eyes were red and swollen, as if she'd been crying. "You weren't here?"

"No. Once I saw you two hit the couch, I hightailed it over to Mr. Murdock's. I may be many things, but I'm not a voyeur. Especially where my brother is concerned."

"Oh, great. Now you tell me."

"Did he hurt you?"

Bridget stormed into the bedroom and slammed the door. As if that would keep out a ghost.

Charlie popped into the closed room and hovered as far away as she could, hoping distance would help with the headache. Bridget lay face down on the bed, hugging her pillow. "You're scaring me. I love my brother, but if he hurt you, I'm gonna…well, I don't know what, but I'll figure something out."

Bridget flipped onto her back and held her head. "He didn't hurt me. He just thinks I'm crazy. Hell, so do I."

"You asked too many questions about Nick, didn't you? I was afraid he might get suspicious."

"I told him I saw dead people."

"You did wha— Hey, isn't that the line from *The Sixth Sense*?"

"What, did you watch it with your brother?" Bridget crawled under the covers and turned out the light. "You might have warned me that he didn't believe in ghosts."

"I would have if I knew you were going to drop the G-bomb." Damn Robbie and his closed mind. "You're not giving up, though, are you?"

Bridget sat up and sighed. "Don't worry. I'll get what you need. But I need a computer. Rob said the whole incident was in the papers. I just have to find the articles. Kate's computer is too slow, and I don't have that kind of time during lunch."

"What about your folks?"

"Mom would want to know why I needed it. I don't need her snooping around. One person thinking I'm nuts is already one too many. I'll go to the library on Saturday."

"I got a better idea. Ask Mr. Murdock. He's got a computer. And he's all alone. He'll probably welcome the company."

"I don't know."

"I'll even leave you alone, so your head won't hurt."

"My head doesn't hurt any less when you're not around. I only get the stabs when you first appear."

Charlie smiled. She wouldn't have to leave as often. Hot damn!

Bridget pulled the covers up. "However, when I'm with Rob, I have no pain whatsoever. Almost seems unfair."

Charlie understood unfair. "If Robbie helps, why not take advantage? Apologize and tell him you were only joking. I can tell he likes you. He'd probably believe it."

"No. I won't lie to him. And I certainly won't use him like that. Besides, nothing is going to happen between us. Got it? And if thinking I'm nuts will stop his advances, then I'm not going to change his mind."

"What do you have against my brother?"

"Nothing. Now, do you mind? I'd like to go to sleep."

"Wait, Bridget. Before you do, could you...."

The covers flew off the bed and Bridget stomped over to the door. "What channel?"

"Seven." Charlie wrapped her arms around her new friend. "Thank you. You're the bestest roomie a ghost could ever have."

Chapter 11

Rob entered the sports bar and scanned the area. No Brian at the pool tables or dartboards, or even the bar. Figured. Giving Brian a specific time to meet was as useful as giving one to Barnaby. Hoping his wait would be short, Rob took a seat at the bar.

"Hey, Rob. What's your pleasure?" John Pennington, bartender and owner of Wings, placed a napkin on the dark wood surface. Rob had become friends with him while working on a home-improvement project.

"I'll have a Bud Light." Yeah, he'd start out light. Then maybe hit the hard stuff after Brian left.

The day had been torture, and he was such a sap. Mooning over someone who clearly suffered from post-traumatic something or other shouldn't drive him to drink. As if booze would solve any problems. It usually only added to the list. Still, getting lost for a little while seemed like a damned good idea.

John placed the pilsner glass on the napkin. "Everything okay?"

"Not really." Rob took a swig of the beer. "Can I ask you a stupid question? If you don't want to answer it, I'll understand."

"My mother always said the only stupid question is the one not asked. Shoot."

"Smart mother." Rob rubbed his face and took a calming breath. He should have downed the beer first, and then he wouldn't care what John's reaction would be. Oh, hell. Another sip wouldn't hurt any. After another swig, he asked, "Do you believe in ghosts? I mean, really believe."

John raised his eyebrows, clearly surprised by the question. Then a smile formed on his face. "There was a time I didn't believe in anything but my work. Then life took a strange turn and opened my eyes to a whole 'nother world."

"But you haven't seen a ghost, have you?"

"I couldn't tell you if I have or haven't. I can say no one has ever introduced themselves to me as a ghost. Doesn't mean I haven't seen one. And not seeing one doesn't mean they don't exist. There are a lot of stars in the sky. More than you can see. Does that mean they don't exist?"

"How do I know if she sees ghosts or is just delusional?"

John leaned against the bar. "Ahh, so there's a *she*, huh? Someone you like?"

Rob ran his finger over the lip of the glass. "Probably too much."

"Talk to her about other things. If she's delusional, it will come out. Just pay attention."

Now why hadn't he thought of that? Bridget was smart and before that episode, had seemed totally sane. "You're probably right."

"I hope it works out for you."

So did Rob, because no matter how hard he had tried, he couldn't get her out of his head. He took another swig. "So, how are those UV windows working for you?"

John's face lit up like a little boy at Christmas. "They're great. Having sunshine in the house once again is a miracle. It was the best present I could give my fiancé."

"I didn't know you were getting married. Congratulations." Rob extended his hand and John shook it.

Brian slapped Rob on the shoulder. "Better watch out. You might be next." He laughed and turned to John. "Congratulations, man."

John placed a napkin on the bar. "Thanks. The usual?"

Brian answered in the affirmative. "I see you started before me. Is that any way for a friend to act?"

"I'm sure you won't have any problems catching up." And then when Brian left for his wife and home, Rob could really get hammered. Maybe. "I'm glad you called. Because I wanted to talk to you about Bridget."

"Yeah, about her." Brian picked up his beer. "Let's get a booth."

Well, that couldn't be good. Rob took his drink, followed his friend to an empty booth, and sat across from him. "Is something wrong with Bridget?"

"Not that I know of. Man, I hate this, but you know how Kate can be. I haven't seen her this agitated since before we got married."

Rob should have known Kate had instigated this meeting. No way would his friend call for an impromptu meeting in the middle of the week. Leave it to Kate to give him more grief than Bridget's mother. "Does she think you'll change anything?"

"I don't know. I just know I'll have peace if I'm able to truthfully tell her we talked." His friend leaned across the table. "So how bad do you have it for Bridget?"

So bad he was willing to ignore the fact she might be crazy? "Why don't you tell Kate you told me to stay away? It's what she wants, isn't it?"

"Oh, man, you do have it bad." Brian took a drink of his beer. "Are you aware of what happened to Bridget?"

Finally, getting to the information he craved. "I heard about the car accident, but she doesn't look like she was hurt all that bad. I figured she broke her leg or something. How bad was it?"

"Try the or something. She technically died. And after they brought her back, she was in a coma for almost nine months. No one thought she would come out of it until one day she woke up."

Died? That one word lingered in his head, and he couldn't shake it free.

Died. That one word caused him all sorts of pain in his chest.

Death was more than a broken leg. Death was final. Well, usually. Thank God this time it hadn't been or he'd never have met her.

Wait. Could that be why she saw ghosts? Had her near-death experience opened some kind of spiritual doorway or had she always had the ability? Shit! He did have it bad when he not only started to believe her, but didn't care if she did or didn't see ghosts.

Rob sucked down some brew. "She seems okay now, though. So what's Kate so worried about?"

"She thinks Bridget is still grieving. She lost her best friend in that accident. A friend who was eight months pregnant."

"Ah, man." How much guilt was she carrying around? Worse yet, was anyone blaming her? "Was this friend's husband by any chance named Devin?"

"Yeah. Some doctor hotshot."

"Does he blame Bridget?"

Brian shrugged. "I don't know. He shouldn't. Bridget was driving, but she wasn't at fault. In fact, she pulled over after stalling out the car. It had started snowing and the roads were untreated. Some drunk lost control at a stop sign and plowed right into them, sending them into the river. By the time the emergency crews arrived, Suzie had drowned and Bridget nearly bled out."

Wiping the gruesome scene from his mind, Rob concentrated on her pretty face instead. She was alive. He held onto that.

"Kate's reaction still doesn't make sense. So what if Bridget is grieving. Does that mean she's not allowed to date?"

"Hey, I never said I understood my wife. All I can say is that before the accident, they were close. Like sisters. Now, Kate only sees Bridget at work."

"You can't blame her for that, now can you? I mean, you two are still newlyweds. Maybe Bridget thinks three's a crowd. You don't see me as often."

"Which reminds me, we're having a Memorial Day barbecue on Monday and you're invited. Should I tell Kate you'll be over?"

Rob smiled. Guess Kate wasn't too mad at him if she could reprimand and invite all in one visit. "Will the invitation still stand if I continue seeing Bridget?"

"So you are seeing her? You're dating?"

Hell, yeah, if he had any say in the matter. "It's still a work in process. Can I ask you a question, though? Do you think Bridget has changed? Is there something I'm not seeing because I hadn't met her before?"

Brian drained his beer. "I only met her a few times before the accident. She's probably a little more subdued now. Quieter. She used to crack some pretty raunchy jokes, ones she heard at the hospital, back when she was a nurse. I haven't heard her laugh since the accident."

Rob had *made* her laugh. That had to mean something.

"If she's a nurse, how come she's working for Kate?"

"No idea. You'll have to ask Bridget."

"You don't think she's crazy?" Oh shit. Why the hell had he asked that? He downed the rest of his beer.

"Crazy? Why? Did she do something?"

"No, no, no. I just wondered because of the way Kate is acting." Yeah, that was why.

Brian shook his head. "I've never seen Bridget act anything but serious since the accident. Listen, Kate goes a little overboard where family is concerned. Can you imagine what she'll be like as a mother?" They both laughed and then his face became stone-cold sober. "Shit. Guess I'll have my work cut out for me, huh?"

Rob laughed. "You said it. I didn't."

Chapter 12

Summer arrived early on the Saturday before Memorial Day. The clock hadn't even struck noon and the temperature already hovered around eighty-five. Bridget pulled the long-sleeve T-shirt away from her chest as she stared out into the backyard. The covered pool stood out there, but with the temperature barely reaching the seventies for the past week, the water was probably too cold, if not dirty.

Well, what better way to spend the day than finding out? If it was dirty, then she'd just clean it. It would not only pass the time, but keep her mind busy. She turned and headed for the bedroom to change. With a fenced-in yard to hide her, she might as well get comfortable and wear something that wouldn't give her heatstroke.

"Why don't you walk?" Charlie asked. "Your feet work, don't they? Of course they do. I can see you walking right now."

Bridget shook her head. Ever since she'd gotten the address where Nick's accident occurred, Charlie had done nothing but hound her. "Oh my God! Is this what being a ghost has done to you? You're sounding like a spoiled teenager. I told you. I get my bike back today. You can wait a few more hours."

"I don't see why you won't tell me where it is. You're the one who said you wanted nothing more to do with this. Man, if I knew you were going to hide it, I would have been watching the monitor."

At first, Bridget had wanted it over, but in the short time they had lived together, she was considering Charlie a friend—albeit a strange one—and friends looked out for one another. If Nick didn't appear, it would break Charlie's heart. "I didn't tell you to watch the Reds game."

"If you had cable, I wouldn't have been jonesing for a baseball fix." Charlie crossed her arms across her chest. "This life sucks."

"I'm sorry. But I am not walking fourteen miles. Not for anyone." Even riding her bike that far would test her knee.

"You said it was seven miles away."

"Yeah, and seven miles back. Duh!"

"Hey! I never said I majored in math."

Bridget opened her dresser and rummaged through the shirts. Long sleeves. Long sleeves. Long sleeves. She must have a short-sleeve one somewhere. Didn't she?

"There is another way you could go," Charlie said.

"I'm not cutting the sleeves."

"What? No, not your shirts. Although, I do have to say, you got a lot of long-sleeve shirts there. Was there a sale?"

Bridget slammed the drawer shut. "What are you talking about?"

"Finding Nick. Why don't you ask Rob for a ride?"

"And tell him what? That his sister's ghost told me to go find Nick? He already thinks I'm nuts because I blabbed about seeing you."

"Okay, so Rob's out. How about Mr. Murdock? He likes you. You probably won't even have to beg."

"Stop it, Charlie. I'll go when I get my bike. But keep it up and I'll make you wait another day."

That threat widened Charlie's eyes and her mouth clamped shut. Wow. Bridget nearly flexed her muscles. Sometimes words were stronger.

"So, what are you looking for?" Charlie asked quietly.

"A short-sleeve shirt so I can go clean the pool and not get heatstroke doing it."

"How about a bathing suit? You got one of those?"

"I do. But it's at my parents."

"You sure? What about the box your mom brought?"

"What box?"

"That one." Charlie pointed to the closet. "She brought it in when you were putting away all those groceries she bought."

Bridget swiveled. First, her mother had brought bags of food over, as if she couldn't shop for herself, which she couldn't, not without help, but still, she planned on calling this weekend for just that. Now her mother was boxing her stuff and bringing it over?

She knelt before the box and opened it. No wonder her mother hadn't said anything. Packed neatly inside were the skimpy summer clothes she'd tended to wear before the accident, along with her old swimsuit.

"I guess you have something to wear after all, huh?" Charlie said.

Maybe. Bridget rummaged through the box. Not one short-sleeve shirt. All tanks and shorts. And her swimsuit? The turquoise suit with the low-cut neck looked smaller than she remembered. No way. She'd have to be the only person left on the face of the earth before she went outside wearing that.

"Why do you suppose she didn't tell you she brought that? Wouldn't she think you'd want them?"

"She probably hoped I'd want them." Bridget closed the box, leaving all the clothes inside.

A gentle hand landed on her shoulder. She turned her head as Charlie solidified.

"It's not that bad, you know."

Horrified at what Charlie was insinuating, Bridget breathed slowly through her nose. "What do you mean?"

"Now, don't get mad at me. I found out by accident. You were coming out of the bathroom from a shower, I presume, just as I returned from Mr. Murdock's."

Bridget stood, breaking the connection. "You spied on me?"

Charlie shook her head. "No, I swear. I thought the coast was clear. Honest."

"Why didn't you make yourself known, then? Huh?"

"I don't know. I guess I just—"

"Became disgusted with what you saw?" Bridget finished.

"Hardly. So you have a few scars. Big whoop. At least you're alive."

Yeah, she was alive. But Suzie and her baby were dead because of her. How fair was that?

"What does it matter I know? Who can I tell? Huh?"

Charlie had a point. And the yard was fenced in. Having a ghost for a friend wasn't all bad, in fact it was rather nice. Bridget opened the box once again and pulled out a blue tank and white shorts.

* * * *

Rob leaned back in his chair. He'd come to the office hoping for a distraction, but the quiet solitude on a Saturday morning wasn't any different here than it was at home. All he had done was change the scenery.

At least he had gotten some work accomplished. Work he could have done Friday if he didn't have his head up his ass. When had a woman ever consumed every thought in his head? He had just about resigned himself to the fact he might be a bachelor forever. And then Bridget came along.

What did it mean when he was willing to get involved with someone whose emotional scars ran deep enough a relationship was nearly impossible? So she had guilt issues and believed she saw ghosts. Everything else about her was perfect, or at least pretty damn close. He didn't want to walk away, he wanted to help her.

So why was he sitting here mooning over her when he could be at her place visiting? She had told him to come over for that paint sample. Then once he bought the paint, he could start painting this afternoon. And it would be just like her to pitch in, too. What better way to spend some time with her—in a cramped bathroom at that. Oh yeah, the day could turn out wonderful.

Before he left, he needed to send Linda an e-mail. After having checked the canceled paint order Mac had questioned, Rob was more confused than ever. The project still required paint, but Carl had placed the order with some unknown vendor, with the same price as before. He probably had some rational explanation—he usually did—but this didn't seem right.

Then there was the Rialto job. Carl should have scheduled the men to start work on Tuesday, but nothing had been done. Clearly, he wasn't okay with working there again. Rob should have taken over the project.

He sent the e-mail to discuss the situations. He'd broach the subject with Carl only if needed. The man was getting defensive in his old age and Rob wasn't in the mood to fight.

He shut down the laptop and snapped the lid closed. Barnaby lifted his head at the sound.

"Let's go find out what color the bathroom will be, shall we?"

* * * *

Charlie hovered over the backyard. Being a ghost had many disadvantages, but flying wasn't one of them. Too bad she couldn't feel the breeze in her face or smell the air. She could if she touched Bridget, but then she'd be Earth-bound.

Bridget was busy pulling weeds behind the pool. As if anyone could see them. At least she'd dressed more appropriately for the weather, even if the outfit hung a little baggy on her. Wearing it wasn't the obstacle, though. Going outside with it on was. It had taken Bridget a good fifteen minutes to finally venture off the porch and another five before she made it to the pool. She seemed oblivious now, though. The high fence probably made the difference.

Charlie could almost understand Bridget's reluctance. Her left side was riddled with scars. White and puckery, a long jagged line ran from the top of her shoulder to just below her elbow, accompanied by smaller lines as if her skin had burst open. Her left leg looked worse, though. Something had stabbed her in the thigh and pulled away, taking a chunk of her with it. And a more surgical-like scar radiated around her knee. If she wore longer shorts, no one would notice the thigh abnormality and the rest could be attributed to a sports injury.

Thing was, Bridget never seemed to care what people thought of her or else she'd dress differently. Who went around wearing long-sleeve shirts in eighty-degree weather? Who wore hospital scrubs to dinner with a guy? So maybe the scars weren't the concern. Maybe it was the questions the scars brought about.

Well, if her roomie was willing to locate Nick for her, maybe she could return the favor and make Bridget forget about the scars. And what better way than through harassment?

Besides, harassing was just plain fun. She used to do it to Robbie all the time.

"Why aren't you cleaning the pool?" Charlie asked.

No answer. Either she was being ignored, or someone could see her. And why wouldn't the whole neighborhood be outside. The sun shone brightly and big fluffy clouds dotted the sky. Sounds of lawn mowers filled the air. Charlie descended until she was out of sight, hovering above Bridget.

"Can you hear me—"

Bridget screeched and fell on her butt. "Hell's bells! What are you doing?"

Charlie laughed. "You cuss like my grandmother."

"What do you want?"

"Why aren't you cleaning the pool?"

"I am. I'm starting on the outside."

"You can't swim on the outside, though. You should clean the water. Or maybe you don't like getting near bugs." Many of which were floating amongst the fallen leaves.

"I'll clean the water when I'm good and ready."

"But you said you were going to swim today." Not that Bridget could. It would take a day at least to clean, but she wouldn't know that until she read the instructions, which she hadn't done yet. But why spoil a good hassle.

"I never said that. Besides, the water's too cold."

"How do you know? Were you in it?"

Bridget's eyes bugged out of her head and she grew a little pink in the cheeks. Aha! Just the response Charlie had hoped for. Nothing like getting someone all bent out of shape for no good reason. Well, no good reason to Bridget, anyway.

A car door slammed out front. Bridget's widened eyes got even buggier. She looked down at her outfit.

So much for getting her mind off her wardrobe. "Hold on. I'll go check it out." Charlie willed herself to the driveway and was greeted by Barnaby.

So... Robbie returned, huh? Should she be a good friend and warn Bridget? Or should she be a good friend and prove to the woman her scars didn't matter?

"Decisions, decisions."

* * * *

Bridget stood and looked over the pool. Exposed. Nothing blocked her way to the back door. Whatever made her think she could get away with being comfortable? The sun and air might have felt refreshing against her skin, but at what cost? Right now her blood pressure would max out a sphygmomanometer.

What was taking Charlie so long? Either someone had come or hadn't. How long did it take to figure it out? Her nerves twisted her stomach inside and out. Staying out in the open was a bad idea. If she ran fast enough, she could make it to the house and change, provided she didn't pass out first.

Charlie arrived in a blink of an eye. "It's Robbie. I'm sorry, I don't know how to get rid of him. I can distract Barnaby, though."

Something scratched at the side gate. Charlie disappeared. The dog whined.

Bridget muttered a curse under her breath. "I have to get inside. I have to—"

"Barnaby, cut it out," Rob said. The gate squeaked open. "Bridget? Are you back here?"

Shit, shit, shit! She hunkered behind the pool. Of all the blasted luck. She waited for Barnaby to give her away, but surprisingly he didn't appear. Charlie's intervention must have worked. Bridget risked a peek.

"Where is she, boy?" Rob, looking downright scrumptious in a light blue T-shirt, walked over to the sliding glass door, and knocked. "Bridget?" He opened the door. "Hello! It's Rob!"

How long could she stay in the weeds? The bugs were already sampling her for lunch. The grass in front of her rustled. Or did she imagine that? No, it happened again. Something in the grass was moving. Something long and…

"Snake!" She squealed and scrambled with such speed she tripped over the vines and fell smack-dab into a wall called Rob.

* * * *

Bridget's scream came from behind. As Rob rushed toward her voice, she slammed into him. "What's wrong? Are you okay?" He grabbed her upper arms. "Didn't you hear me calling you?"

"Snake! There's a snake in the yard!"

"What?" Did she say snake?

She hopped from one foot to the next and bounced out of his grasp, becoming nothing more than a blur of arms and legs. The sliding door slammed shut.

Crap! Did she expect him to kill the stupid thing? If there was one thing he avoided, it was those slithery monsters. Ah, but he could save the day if he slayed the little biter. Of course, that meant actually slaying the little biter. Shit.

Barnaby ran off to the corner, doing his strange routine once again—jumping up on the fence, licking the air. The dog was seriously going crazy.

Rob searched the yard. By the side of the house his ax proudly stood embedded in the pile of wood. After wrenching the potential weapon free, he tiptoed over to the pool, making sure he wouldn't inadvertently step on the creature.

His arms trembled as he gripped the wooden handle and held the blade above his shoulder. Thank goodness she wasn't witnessing what a wuss he'd become. That would certainly deduct some points in his favor. "Okay, buddy. Show yourself and be prepared to meet your death."

The weeds reached above his ankles. He hadn't been back in this part of the yard since Charlie's death. With the amount of rain that had fallen this spring, he'd never gotten around to clearing the area like he should. Then again, his last tenants should have taken care of the yard as part of the lease agreement.

A pile of branches and weeds lay off to the side and the dirt had been turned over beside the pool. Is that what she'd been doing back here, clearing the weeds? Then why hadn't she answered him? Or had she been hiding? He straightened and lowered the ax. There wasn't any snake. She'd said that to avoid him. But why? Was she still upset about the other night? Dammit. He should have called sooner.

Something landed on his shoes. A dark ropelike item with a yellow stripe down its back lay across his foot.

He yelled and kicked out. The creature went flying and bounced off the fence. With his heart ready to pound out of his chest, he charged the snake, roaring like a mad man on a mission.

"Don't kill it!"

He stopped at Bridget's command. "What? Why not? I can see it."

She wore her standard outfit—long-sleeve T-shirt and jeans— holding a green trash bag. Had he imagined seeing skin before or had she changed?

"Put him in here," she said.

Like hell. That required touching. But what kind of wimp would he look like if he didn't? Shit. He turned toward the creature and held out the ax to scoop up the varmint.

"What are you doing? You can't pick him up like that."

"If you're such an expert, be my guest."

She pulled on her gloves and shoved him out of the way. "Where is he?"

He pointed with the ax.

She bent over and examined the creature, then picked up the snake near the head and held it out. "He's harmless."

He scuttled away from the hanging creature. Ew, ew, ew. The only harmless snakes were dead ones. "Then why did you scream?"

The thing coiled and uncoiled, tangling up in the bag as she placed the bugger inside. "I overreacted. I wasn't expecting a snake in the yard. Why did you? You knew it was there."

"Well, maybe I didn't believe you."

"Why would I lie about a snake?"

"Why would you hide from me?"

"I wasn't… I didn't…" She clamped her mouth shut and hung her head. "I don't know. I guess I wasn't ready to face you after the other night."

"Well, I shouldn't have left the way I did. I'm sorry."

"Yeah, I don't know what I was saying."

She might have continued talking, but the open bag creeped him out. "Would you close that?" The damn biter was liable to jump or slither out.

She tied the bag closed. "Do you get many snakes?"

"God, I hope not."

"You're not a fan, I take it?"

Shit! Had he said that out loud? "Let's just say I'll leave them alone if they do the same to me."

"I'll agree with that statement." She walked over, swinging the stupid bag. "So, what brings you here? You working on a new project?"

"No. Still the same one. I came to paint." With the way his hands still shook, he doubted he'd do a good job. Whereas, she seemed cool as could be, holding the bag as if it only contained trash, not some slithering monster.

"Oh, I have the paint sample inside." She placed the bag beside the stack of wood. The plastic moved.

"You're just going to leave that there?"

"Why? Does it bother you?"

Hell, yes. "No, of course not. I don't want Barnaby to get into it."

She glanced at the dog, now walking in circles. "I think it'll be okay for the next couple of minutes." She opened the door and stopped. "You coming or staying?"

Staying? No way. But he needed to put the ax back and couldn't stop staring at the bag. She took the tool out of his hand and hurled it into the wood. *Thunk.* Tempted to feel her biceps, he rushed inside instead. She closed the door behind them. Damn reptile. Nearly gave him a heart attack.

She waved a hand in front of his face. "Are you okay? Do you need to lie down or something?"

"No. Why would you say that?"

"Because you haven't heard a word I said. Come on." She grabbed his arm and led him to the living room. "Sit and I'll get you something cold to drink. Do you like iced tea?"

"Yeah, that would be great." He sat on the couch and placed his head in his hands. His body trembled all over. What a wimp.

The couch moved. And like a wuss, he jumped. He knew it was only Bridget, but some kind of wire inside his brain had fried. She placed a glass on the table.

"How old were you when a snake first scared you?"

So much for looking heroic. He laughed. "Fourteen."

"Camping?"

"Yeah, with the folks. I complained about wanting my own tent that year. I didn't want to share one with Charlie, so they bought a tent big enough for three and I used one of the old ones. Sometime during the day, the little biter must have crawled inside my sleeping bag. I didn't notice it right away. Not until it crawled up my pajama leg. My parents probably thought I was being attacked by a bear or something significant."

Memories about the people he had loved—the family he would never see again—crushed his chest. God, he missed them. They'd been taken away much too early. He picked up the glass and chugged the iced tea, the cold trailing down to his stomach—his empty stomach. He needed to change the subject.

"Do you want to get some lunch?" he asked.

"If you're hungry, I can make you a sandwich."

"You have food?"

"Yes, I have *food.*" She smiled. "Do you like bologna?"

"And cheese?"

"Sure."

He followed her into the kitchen and sat at the dinette table. When was the last time someone had fixed him a meal? It had to be his mother. No woman had ever offered to cook him dinner.

Their interests had consisted of being seen with him, not that he'd minded at the time.

After finishing the preparations, she brought over two plates containing sandwiches—cut in half, even—and potato chips. She refilled his glass and brought over one for herself.

"This is nice. Thank you."

"You're quite welcome."

They sat in silence as they ate. The food tasted great. Sometimes the simplest sandwich could be the best. He didn't mind the company, either.

And it felt natural being with her.

She finished her sandwich and washed it down with some tea. "I want to explain about the other night."

Oh, man. He had thought he could believe, but now he wasn't sure. "About what?"

"My crack about seeing dead people. You were moving so fast, I wasn't sure what to say to get you to stop."

"How about 'stop'?"

The ends of her mouth curled into a weak smile. "I guess I should have tried that first."

"So… You don't see ghosts?"

She furrowed her forehead. "You want any more chips? I've got plenty."

"I'm good. Answer my question. Please."

She stood. "How about some more tea?"

He wouldn't let her get off that easy. He grabbed her arm. "Bridget—"

The doorbell rang and her face brightened. He released her. This discussion was far from over, though.

* * * *

The young man handed Bridget a brochure regarding the upcoming spiritual retreat being held at the church around the corner. She'd had her fill of spirits, one in particular, but smiled and thanked the man.

"Who was it?" Rob asked.

"No one important." She desperately needed to avoid the subject of ghosts because she would not lie to Rob. So why not just admit it? It would probably send him away for good. That's what she wanted, wasn't it?

She tossed the brochure on the counter. The paint sample floated toward the floor and she caught it, giving her the excuse to change the subject. "Before I forget, here's the color I picked out."

Rob took the card and looked at it. "It's neither blue nor green."

"It's not?" She leaned over to look, but he placed it against his chest.

"Don't you know what color you picked out?"

Actually, she didn't. Her mind had been elsewhere when Charlie picked it out. "Maybe I gave you the wrong card."

He looked at her as if she'd sprouted wings, then turned the card around.

The color on the card bore a strong resemblance to the color in the bathroom. Couldn't Charlie pick something different? Bridget had no one to blame but herself. "Oh yes. That's right."

"It looks like the same color that's in there now."

"Then maybe you don't have to paint the whole room. Just that one wall."

He finished the last of his chips. "Do you want to go with me to get the paint?"

"Thanks, but I'm expecting my parents and I told them I'd be home."

"Okay. Then I guess I'll go get the paint. I shouldn't be long." He went to the back and called for Barnaby.

"You can leave him here if you want. I don't mind."

Barnaby rushed inside and jumped up on Bridget. He panted with his tongue lolling about. Charlie must have given him a good workout.

"Thanks. I don't think he likes me leaving him in the truck anyway." He patted the dog's head. "Thanks for lunch. It really hit the spot."

He stood close and stared at her like he wanted…something. A kiss, maybe? And while that would be nice, she could never stop at just a kiss. She'd proven it the other night. If it weren't for Charlie, who knew how far she would have gone. She couldn't let it happen again. Could she?

She backed away, giving him space to the front door. Keeping a safe distance, she followed him and saw him off. That had been close. She hadn't been forced to lie about seeing ghosts and she hadn't ripped off his clothes and taken him on the floor.

As she turned toward the house, her father pulled into the driveway.

Chapter 13

Bridget stood in the garage and examined the map from the Internet. According to the news article she'd found, Nick's accident had occurred seven point three miles away. It would be quite a bike ride, but she was determined to try if it helped Charlie on her way. And it had nothing to do with the fact that the ghost could bug fleas off a dog.

She would miss Charlie, but it was for the best. Rob didn't need to know his sister was toddling around the old home instead of floating somewhere in heaven, and Bridget should have never said anything. The sooner she sent Charlie on her way, the better, because she wouldn't lie to Rob and he most likely wouldn't let the ghost issue drop.

"I can't believe I'll see him soon."

"Charlie, about that. Maybe you shouldn't come." Bridget still doubted she'd see Nick's ghost and Charlie's hopes rode too high.

"I want to come. Why can't I come? You can't stop me." Charlie crossed her arms.

Bridget folded the directions and slipped it in her back pocket. "You're acting like a spoiled teenager again. How the heck am I supposed to get you there? As soon as someone sees us, you'll disappear."

"Just because you can't see me doesn't mean I'm not there. I'll be floating by your side the whole way."

"Exactly. Your brother already thinks I'm nuts. I don't need the whole neighborhood suspecting it, too. Besides, who's going to stay with Barnaby, huh?" Bridget hoped her appeal worked and zipped up her backpack. Two bottles of water should be enough. If not, she'd stop and buy more. She pushed a button on the wall. As the garage door loudly rumbled upward, light entered the area. She rubbed the top of the dog's head before shutting him inside the house.

"Barnaby's been on his own numerous times. I wouldn't worry about him. And why would the neighborhood think you're crazy if they can't see me?"

Bridget checked the tire on her bike. Nice and straight. "Because I'm sure I'd end up talking to you whether I see you or not." She looked up and Charlie was gone. "Which I'm already doing."

"Who are you talking to?"

Bridget jumped and spun around. "Mr. Murdock! I didn't hear you enter. How are you doing?"

"It's Henry. How many times do I have to tell you?"

"I'm sorry, Henry. Blame my mother."

He laughed. "No. I think your mother did a wonderful job raising you. Except, do you normally talk to yourself?"

"Sometimes it helps clear my head to say things out loud." Ouch. Could she come up with anything lamer?

"I hear you. Must be a habit of living alone, huh? So, you going out bike riding? Aren't you going to be hot in that outfit?"

Yes, she would be. Long sleeves and jeans in eighty-degree weather with the added exertion of bike riding and she'd be lucky she didn't fall over with heatstroke. Maybe two bottles wouldn't be enough. "I don't want to get sunburned. I'll be fine."

"You might want to be careful. Newscaster predicted rain."

"Rain? When?" The sky was a brilliant blue with a few fluffy clouds.

"I don't know. One of those pop-up situations. I'm sure you'll be fine. Just keep your eye out. You won't be gone long, will you?"

God, she hoped not. "Nah. I'm not going far."

"Do you need me to give you a lift? I don't mind."

"Thanks a lot, Henry, but I'll be fine. I think I need the ride to help clear my head. Plus I could use the exercise. You understand, don't you?"

Her heart twisted at the sad look on his face, but having him drive her to a construction site, if it still was one, would only bring on more questions. Questions she wasn't willing or even able to answer. He gave her his phone number in case she needed a lift. If she met with another unfortunate incident, or got caught in the rain, she'd have no problem calling Henry over her mother or even Rob, because those two would definitely give her a lecture.

She pulled up the backpack, but inadvertently stuck her right arm in the left strap, tangling them. Of all the stupid things… She lowered her arms forcefully and the pack landed with a *thud*.

"Where are my manners? Here, let me help you."

She picked up the pack and handed it to him. "Thanks."

With the backpack on correctly, Bridget wheeled her bike out of the garage and closed the door. "See ya later, Henry."

No sign of Charlie, but then Henry stood in view waving good-bye. She waved back and headed on her way.

* * * *

Charlie willed herself to Bridget's bike and floated along. Once hidden from public view, she'd materialize for Bridget and then probably get reamed out, but nothing would stop her from seeing Nick.

With the road busy with traffic, Bridget waited several minutes before pulling out into the main highway. She quickly crossed the street and headed south.

The traffic kept Charlie's presence hidden, which suited her just fine. Why get chewed out if she could avoid it?

The light ahead turned red, but Bridget was too far away to slow. Charlie kept pace with the bike, not exerting herself one bit. She couldn't say the same for Bridget. Man, the girl was out of—

"What the—" Charlie stared at the ceiling as she floated above her old bed. How'd she get here? What had Bridget done?

She willed herself to the main street. Bridget had pedaled beyond the light. Willing herself to the bike, she remained stationary. Okay, she'd float over. As long as she kept Bridget in sight, all would be good.

She'd only moved a few inches when she arrived back in her room.

What the hell? Why did she keep ending up here? Had Bridget put some kind of hex on her?

This was so unfair. Charlie sat up and swung her fist at the wall, but of course, it sailed through it unscathed. When Bridget returned, they were so going to have one serious powwow.

105

* * * *

Rob backed the truck into the driveway, still musing over Bridget's color choice. He'd been sure she would have picked out something in the blue or green range, and even she seemed surprised, which made no sense at all.

He knocked on the door. Barnaby barked, but other than that—nothing. He rattled the knob. Locked.

"She's not home, Rob." Murdock meandered his way across the yard.

"Did her parents come by?"

"I don't know, but she didn't leave with them. She took off on her bike. Wouldn't accept a ride from me, either. I guess she just wanted to go riding."

Bike riding? Maybe she was on a disposal mission. "Did she have a green trash bag with her?"

"No, but she had her backpack. Actually, I thought someone was with her, with the way she was talking, but it was just her. Or maybe she was on her phone and I didn't notice? You know, one of those ear thingies." He removed his glasses and wiped the lenses with the tail of his shirt. "Getting old is the pits. Don't let it happen to you."

Rob punched in the passcode for the garage. It must be the snake. What other reason would make her take off? She knew he would return. He shivered thinking about that thing being in her backpack. The woman had more guts than he did.

* * * *

Nick sat on the roof and stared out over the buildings. A breeze had kicked up, not that he could feel it. The trees in the distance were doing their little wind dance and the plastic window coverings were flapping in annoyance. Soon the rain would appear, not that the scent warned him. Dark clouds grew on the western horizon and he could hear a rumble in the distance. Sight and sound were all he had left.

Even without smell or touch, he liked the rain. It was quite the thing experiencing a storm without getting wet. Or feeling threatened by lightning.

The door downstairs slammed shut. His roommate must have returned. Pretty bad when the high point of his day was watching someone get piss-assed drunk. Man, what he wouldn't give for a drink right about now. Or a doughnut. He missed those, too.

He floated down into the building. Wires hung from unfinished ceilings and metal studs stood naked awaiting drywall. Windows above the first floor lacked coverings. There the birds could come and go—the shit on the pressed-wood floors evidence of their existence.

Once he reached the first level, he headed for the elevator shaft. The cables had been secured high enough so no person would climb or accidently hang themselves. Contained in the alcove below sat a ratty old pillow, a stained blanket, and some discarded empties, but no roommate.

Damn, that meant *he'd* arrived. Again. Nick never should have said anything. Then maybe he'd be alive today, spending his life with Charlie.

God, he missed her. Of all the people in his life, she'd meant more to him than anyone and he hurt being apart from her the most. Had she moved on? Was she happy? He never got to tell her good-bye. But then, how could he? Forget the drink. Forget the doughnut. He'd give anything to see his girl one last time. But what were the odds she'd ever show up here?

Footsteps echoed on the stairwell and Nick headed in that direction. Something must have happened in the past few days to bring the traitor back to this building. But he'd have the last laugh because his father was searching for something he would never find. There was some entertainment in watching his old man go over the edge. After every visit he became more agitated.

Nick might have been able to forgive dear old Dad if he had only shown remorse for what he'd done instead of covering it up and making it look like an accident. Only a sick father could leave his son's dead body to the birds and rodents until discovered in the morning. If Nick could, he'd haunt his father's house. But for some reason, every time he ventured beyond a certain point, he'd return to the spot he'd perished.

So, no haunting his father and no visiting his girl. Just a small diameter of space, a space devoid of homes. Days weren't horrible, but the nights were long. Long and quiet.

Dad stood on the second of five levels. Eventually he would run out of floors and rooms to inspect. Then what would he do? Start over?

Nick smiled. Maybe Karma was on his side.

****

Charlie couldn't believe her peepers once Rob opened the garage. On the floor lay Bridget's folded map. It must have popped out of her pocket after she struggled with that backpack. Charlie smiled. Maybe her problem had to do with her mode of transportation. If she hitched a ride with Rob, could she make it to Nick? Or did she just need to know the address?

Of course, she couldn't get the address unless Rob picked up the paper and opened it. And he wouldn't pick it up unless she drew his attention to it. She stood behind the paper and swooshed her arms out.

The map might as well have been glued to the floor for all the movement it made. Seemed to be her lucky day—not!

Barnaby whined at the door. Hmm. Barnaby could help.

"What are you painting?" Mr. Murdock asked.

"The bathroom."

She stood beside Rob. Man, what she wouldn't give to wrap her arms around her brother one last time. She missed those big bear hugs he used to give her. The wrestling, not so much. Even if she was the one who'd always started it.

The old man stared at the paint can. "Peach Sundae? Sounds more like a food than a color."

Rob laughed. He opened the back of his truck and pulled out paint supplies. "Bridget picked it out, not me."

"No, I picked it out, you doofus." Charlie popped back into the house. "Come on Barnaby, bark. Scratch on the door. Like this." She demonstrated, hoping that would help. "Let Robbie know you want out."

She popped back into the garage and the dog barked. That was her boy.

Rob sighed and opened the door. "What is your problem?"

Barnaby dashed through the door, nearly knocking Rob over. Charlie laughed at his surprised expression.

He grabbed at the door, steadying himself. "I think the dog's gone bonkers."

"He does seem rather anxious. Is he licking the air?"

Barnaby licked a face that wasn't there and she'd kiss him back if she could, but first she needed him to do his thing. "Follow me, baby. Follow me."

She led her faithful friend to the paper and made scratching motions. Barnaby got the gist and copied her.

"Need any help?" Mr. Murdock asked.

"Sure." Rob opened a box and pulled out some plastic sheeting and placed it in a roller pan, along with a roller. He told Mr. Murdock where to go and followed him into the house carrying the ladder. Both men ignored the dog.

Charlie grumbled. "What are you? Blind? Geez, what's a girl gotta do to get some attention?"

"What do you have there?" Rob asked.

He picked up the paper. Her heart soared. Finally, something had gone right.

"What is it?" Mr. Murdock asked.

Rob unfolded the map. Charlie hovered over her brother and got what she desperately needed. Hot dog! Yeah, that's right. Time to go. Time to hit the street. Nick was waiting. He just didn't know it yet. She willed herself to the address.

Nothing. She remained in the garage.

Mr. Murdock pointed at the paper. "Oh, that's the directions she printed out the other day. Maybe that's where she went."

"She printed this? When?"

"Thursday night. She came over to borrow my computer. Do you recognize the address?"

Of course Robbie did—Nick had died there. But why couldn't she pop on over? She had the address now. That should have been enough, but nooo. Robbie better damn well be curious because she had a date and her brother was her last hope.

He folded the paper and slipped it in his back pocket. "Nah. If you don't mind, I'm going to get to work. Thanks for your help. I'll talk to you later."

"Work? No, not work. You need to go to Bridget." Charlie swatted at her brother for all the good it did her.

"Yeah, I guess the room is a little cramped for two people to paint. See ya later, Rob."

Rob watched Mr. Murdock shuffle back to his house. Once he meandered out of sight, Rob pulled the paper out of his back pocket.

Holy shit! Had he been only trying to get rid of the old man? Would he make her dreams come true?

He knelt beside the dog. "I wish you could talk. I'm sure you know what she's up to. I guess my curiosity has gotten the better of me. Wanna go for a car ride?"

"Yes, finally." She popped inside the truck and waited.

The passenger door opened and the beast jumped inside. By the time Rob climbed in, Barnaby hung over the back of the front seat, reaching for Charlie. He shot his tongue out several times.

"You keep that up and I'm taking you home," Rob said.

No, not home! "Barnaby! Sit!" The dog settled and planted his butt on the seat.

"That's more like it," Rob said. "Now, let's go see what Bridget is up to."

He started the truck and pulled into the street. It took some maneuvering on Charlie's part, but she managed to somehow link herself with the vehicle and even though she basically floated, she stayed within the confines of the cab.

Barnaby stared at her.

Rob stopped at the stop sign and glanced back. "Whatcha looking at?"

"He's looking at the best owner he's ever had, that's who."

The dog squirmed in his seat, his body twitching as if he wanted to stand or jump over the seat rest. Rob kept looking between Barnaby and the back seat.

"Charlie?"

She patted her chest. "What? Can you hear me? Can you see me?"

He shook his head and turned around. He wasn't answering her questions. Most likely he wondered about his sanity. Still, to even suspect. Could it be Bridget might have cracked that wall he called a brain?

He turned left onto the street, going in the same direction Bridget had earlier. Charlie was ready. Would she be able to touch Nick? Maybe kiss him, even? Could they have a life together as ghosts? She dreamed of all the possibilities.

A red signal loomed ahead. No, no, no. Green lights. Green lights all the way. The sooner she got there—

"Son of a...."

She was back in her old room.

Chapter 14

Bridget braked at the construction site. The ride had been better than anticipated—the flat terrain a big help—but she still had a long way to go before being considered fit. Breathing hard, she pulled the backpack around and retrieved her water. If she had prepared better, she would have brought her aspirin. As she sucked down the semiwarm refreshment, her heart rate slowed to a fast gallop.

The wind picked up and cooled her heated face, but the rest of her smoldered. Her long-sleeve shirt stuck to her back and her jeans chafed. She swiped her arm across her drippy brow and then put the bottle back into the pack. Clouds formed on the western horizon. Rain or plain ol' clouds? She prayed for the latter.

The unfinished building—a five-story stand-alone—stood among other finished ones in a business area. It didn't appear anyone was currently working on it, either. Brickwork stopped halfway up the front, leaving the Tyvek-covered boards exposed on top and the sides. The upper windows were open to the elements, but plastic covered the lower ones, which currently flapped in the breeze, making the place a bit creepy. Had the project shut down due to the accident or just the economy?

She slipped her backpack on and rode around to the back. If Rob's construction crew was still working, there would be some sign—a trailer or trucks or something. It looked deserted. She climbed off her bike and leaned it against the building. She looped her helmet over the handlebars. The stench of urine burned her nose, even in the breeze.

Someone must be watching from one of the many windows overlooking the parking lot, even on this three-day weekend, else, she'd see Charlie. Unless… Shit. Would she go inside without her? Of course she would. That girl waited for no one.

Bridget walked to the door and found it unlocked. Not that locking it would keep people out. It wouldn't take a tall person to crawl through one of the windows. Was it still considered breaking and entering if the place lacked a no trespassing sign? She stepped through and the door slammed behind her, causing her to jump. Little tremors formed in her chest and radiated to her hands. She shouldn't have come. What if Nick hurt her?

Stop it! Charlie wouldn't have gotten involved with someone like that. And Rob never indicated Nick had been a bad person. She was letting her imagination go wild.

Even with sunset hours away, darkness greeted her. So did the heat. A stuffy mustiness hung in the air. All the rain earlier in the week, and the fact minimal light and air made it through the windows, probably created some mold growth. She pulled out her trusty flashlight.

"Charlie? Where are you?" No sign of her ghost-friend. No splitting headache announcing her arrival. Was it possible she hadn't followed her? Maybe something happened causing her to stay behind. Seemed unrealistic, but stranger things have happened. Like seeing Charlie for one thing.

The hairs on the back of her neck tickled. Scuffling sounds came from her left.

"Charlie? Nick?" Could there be rats? With her heart rate picking up speed, she turned, pointing the flashlight. The beam didn't go far, but illuminated the plastic window covering flapping inside the building.

Idiot. She took a deep breath. She needed to calm down. Too bad Charlie wasn't here. She could use the encouragement and the company.

Cupping a hand around her mouth, she leaned upward and yelled. "Nick! Are you here? Charlie sent me. Please show yourself. I'll be able to see you."

Her voice echoed through the building and still no Nick. Damn. Exactly what she'd feared—Charlie was wrong. She wandered around the interior and came to an elevator shaft. Shining the flashlight upward only illuminated the hanging cables. She shone the light below.

Hell's bells. Someone lived here. She spun around, the beam slicing through the room. Was that person hiding from her?

A scratching sound came from the shadows. She swung her flashlight. The shaky beam barely made a dent. Was he in the shadows? Something hit the wall from behind. She spun. Nothing. Didn't stop her heart from beating triple-time, though. Okay. Time to go home. Coming here alone was a bad idea. She turned off the flashlight and headed for the exit.

Pain exploded in the back of her head, and darkness engulfed her before she hit the floor.

* * * *

"What the hell?" Nick stared at his father as the young blonde lay on the floor.

He and his father had just arrived on the first floor when she'd entered the building, so Dad had nowhere to go. He'd become pale at the mention of Charlie's name and then picked up the loose board. Nick had called out a warning, since the woman said she could see him, but never got a response.

Dad lifted the backpack and pulled out her wallet. Upon inspecting her driver's license, he cursed.

So, he knew Bridget Quigley. But why would he hurt her? What did Bridget have to do with his criminal activity?

His father dashed into the elevator shaft and returned with some plastic grocery bags. He tied Bridget's hands behind her back and secured her feet. When she moaned, he stuffed a bag in her mouth and secured it with another plastic bag. Blood oozed from her head wound.

His father was a madman, clear and simple. And Nick couldn't do a damn thing about it.

Dad pulled on her arm and dragged her to the elevator shaft, grunting in the process. He pushed her and she dropped onto the moldy mattress. The backpack followed. For the finishing touch, he took one of the ratty blankets and covered her like a mummy.

He fled the scene, leaving her to die, and rode away on Bridget's bike. Must be his modus operandi, since he'd pulled the same stunt with Nick. The man lacked a conscience.

Nick floated back to Bridget. He nearly reached out for her—old habits and all that. She couldn't feel any comfort he could offer, but he spoke to her like someone would to a coma patient. It certainly couldn't hurt and it made him feel a little useful.

* * * *

Rob drove toward the construction site with Barnaby lying quietly by his side. Quite a turn of events from the way the dog had acted at the house. For a moment he'd suspected Charlie rode with them. But that was crazy, right? Or could there be some truth to Bridget's claim?

Is that why she'd gone to the scene of Nick's death? He truly didn't believe she was crazy, but could he actually believe Charlie communicated with her? It would explain why she'd be at the site, her color choice, and Barnaby's odd behavior.

His cell phone played "Who Are You" by The Who, indicating an unknown caller. Most likely some potential client needing information and while the intrusion was annoying, he still had a business to run. "This is Rob Gentry. How may I help you?"

"Wow! I finally got you. Does this mean you've been ignoring me?"

The familiar whiny voice grated on his skin. "Hello, Tori. Sorry, I've been busy."

"Too busy to return my calls? Doesn't matter. I got you now. What are you doing?"

The signal turned red and Rob rolled to a stop. "I'm driving, so I can't talk now. Can I call you back?"

"No, this won't take long. Are you doing anything tonight?"

"Yes."

"Well, I guess it is last minute. How about Monday? Are you going to Kate's barbecue?"

He wanted to take Bridget, if she wasn't already going. "Yes, I'll be there, but—"

"Great. I'll see you then."

"Wait, Tori. I should tell you…." Crap. What should he tell her?

"Tell me what?"

The truth? Well, part of it anyway. Why not? "There's someone else."

Dead silence. Had they been cut off? The signal turned green and Rob gunned it a little too hard.

Finally, her breathing came over the line. "I hope she, or he, makes you happy then."

Or he? Great. Now she thought he was gay? "She does. Thank you."

"Are you bringing her to the barbecue?"

"I don't know what her plans are, yet. I might."

Tori muttered something unintelligible and said her good-byes. He hadn't meant to hurt her, but she'd left him no choice. Hopefully now the phone calls would stop.

Rob pocketed his phone and continued on his way, anxious to find Bridget. If he had been smart, he would have programmed her number in his cell. Then he could have just called her and found out…what? That she was ghost hunting for Nick? Yeah, like she'd tell him.

No, confronting her in person was the best way. He'd get the truth out of her eventually.

A siren whooped-whooped behind him and lights flashed in the rearview mirror. What now? The speed limit was thirty-five and he was barely doing forty. Shit. He pulled over and fished out his driver's license.

Ten minutes and one ticket later, Rob merged back into traffic. He'd run a stupid stop sign. That's what he got for driving with his mind off the road.

The shell of the Rialto project loomed ahead on the right. He pulled around to the back and killed the engine. Barnaby lifted his head.

Bridget's bike was nowhere to be seen. Could he have missed her? The cop hadn't been all that long, and no one on a bike had passed. He opened the door and hopped out, the dog close behind. "Bridget!"

Wind kicked up the dirt and thunder rumbled in the distance. He headed around the building to search when Barnaby jumped up on the door. Could he sense her? Rob rushed over. The door to the building was unlocked. It should have been locked. As soon as he pulled the door, Barnaby brushed against his legs and squirmed his way inside.

"Bridget? Are you here?"

No answer. He headed for the stairwell and the dog ran to the elevator shaft, whining.

His heart rate picked up speed and he urged his feet forward. He stepped on something cylindrical. Pinwheeling his arms, he regained his balance and then picked up the item—a flashlight.

Barnaby's whining and scratching intensified.

"Bridget?" Dread crushed his chest. He rushed to the elevator shaft and shone the light. The stench of urine assaulted his nose. Not Bridget. It was those damn squatters. Carl should have taken care of this problem long before now. With his panic under control, Rob jumped down and toed the offender. "Come on, fella. Wake up. You can't stay here."

The lump moaned and squirmed. A muffled scream came from the blanket. The squatter had twisted in the fabric in some kind of attempt to get free. Rob reached down and pulled the blanket away from the head. His heart momentarily stopped. Bridget stared at him with terror in her eyes.

She screamed and moved to scoot away from him.

He stuffed the flashlight in his back pocket. "Shh, Bridget. It's okay. It's me, Rob."

"Raw?" The binding caused her words to be muffled, but she seemed to recognize him and relaxed a little, until she gagged.

"Breathe through your nose."

She did as he requested, putting an end to her gags. He pulled her head against his chest and worked at the knot, but the slick surface made it hard to grab. His shaky hands weren't helping any, either. Blood covered the back of her head. Who the hell would do this to her and why? He pulled out his pocketknife and, carefully avoiding her skin, cut the plastic.

She jerked free and coughed up the bag before he had a chance to remove it.

"Oh God! Oh God! Oh God! What the hell was that?" She spat several times as if she couldn't get the taste out of her mouth.

"They look like plastic shopping bags." He sawed the binding at her wrists. "What happened? Who did this to you?"

"I don't know. I was leaving when someone hit me from behind." The tie came free and she rubbed her wrists while he cut the plastic around her ankles.

"I need to call 9-1-1."

"No! I'm fine. I just want to go home."

"You're not fine. You're bleeding. And I need to report this." He pulled out his phone.

She placed his hand over his. "Can I get out of this stinky mess first, then? I think I'll be sick if I sit here much longer."

He couldn't argue with her there. Standing, he lifted her under her arms and sat her on the floor. He tossed up her backpack. She swung her legs around, giving him room to join her. Barnaby waited until they were clear before licking her face.

"Leave her be, boy."

"Oh, he's fine." She nuzzled his neck. "He smells better than this place does."

Rob called 9-1-1 and informed them of the situation. Time to get some answers from her now.

* * * *

Bridget couldn't stay inside the stinky building any longer. Her stomach twisted and whatever remained in it threatened to be set free.

Worry-like wrinkles marred Rob's beautiful face. "Come on, let's go outside. Can you stand?"

Outside sounded great. "I think so." She got to her feet, but her legs gave out. Before she met the floor, he caught her with his strong arms and held her up. "Thanks. How much blood did I lose?"

"I think it might have something to do with a concussion."

That explained why her head throbbed. Normally Rob shooed her headache away. She leaned onto him and took in his scent, as well as his hard body. He was all muscle and she relied on every bit of it to help her to the exit. Barnaby kept pace and didn't rush to beat them out.

A few raindrops hit her in the face and she took a deep breath. Fresh air had never tasted so good. Her stomach calmed.

Rob opened the passenger door to the truck. After she was settled, he pulled a roll of paper towels from the back and ripped off a few sheets. Gently, he placed them on the back of her head. Even that small amount of pressure stung. What'd the guy hit her with? A baseball bat?

He tossed the roll on the seat. "Hold this."

"Afraid I'll get blood in your truck?" It was meant as a joke, but he only frowned. She held the paper towel in place. "Can you put my bike in the back? I don't think I'll be riding it home." Her attempts at making light of the situation bombed big time. Rob wasn't having any of that. His face remained serious.

117

"Where'd you put it?"

She pointed to the building, but there was nothing to point at. "Ah, man. The creep stole my bike?"

"Maybe the cops will be able to find it." He shut the door and circled around the front of the truck.

Why the hell would someone beat her up for her bike? It didn't make any sense. The driver's door opened and Barnaby hopped inside aiming straight for her. She hugged him tight with her free arm. Waking up in the dark—disoriented—and hearing her name called over and over, did a number on her mind. Not being able to breathe hadn't helped her focus, either. And who had been talking to her? Not Rob. Then again, she had gotten hit hard enough to rattle her brain.

But no way would she go to the hospital. Not unless Rob planned on knocking her unconscious.

He slid behind the wheel and scratched Barnaby behind the ears. "How are you feeling? Really."

Her head pounded and her stomach churned. "I'll admit, I've felt better. But I'm fine."

Rob pulled the towel from her head.

The pain seared and she cried out. "Owww. What'd you do that for?"

He held out the blood-soaked paper. Okay, so maybe she was bleeding a bit excessively, but he could have been a little less rough.

"You're evil."

"And you need stitches." He handed her a clean sheet. "Now tell me again. How are you really feeling?"

She gently placed the towel over her wound. "My head hurts, but I know it's Saturday and your name is Rob Gentry. I'm okay. *Really*."

He relaxed a little, but the lines between his eyes remained. "What were you doing here?"

Sirens and flashing lights announced the paramedics' arrival.

Panic nearly made her bolt from the truck. And what would that accomplish if she landed on her face? She needed to keep her head if she had any hope of getting her way. "I'm not going to the hospital. You can take me to Kate's. She knows how to stitch."

"Bridget... You're hurt."

The concern in his voice nearly made her give in. Nearly. "I'm not going. You can't make me." She pointed at the rescue vehicle. "They can't make me."

He gritted his teeth, but nodded his head in surrender. "Fine. But they're still checking you out."

As a paramedic confirmed Rob's assessment of her head wound and handed her some padded gauze and an ice pack, the police arrived. There wasn't much she could tell them since she never got a look at her attacker, but, of course, they wanted to know why she was there. Rob raised an eyebrow, waiting for her answer. Not one for thinking fast on her feet, she used her head injury and avoided the question altogether by claiming she couldn't remember.

The cops bought it. Rob, not so much.

She signed the paperwork declining the medical help and once Rob explained their doctor friend would help, they didn't argue. Of course, he didn't tell them what kind of doctor.

As soon as they'd been cleared to leave, Rob called Kate and explained the situation. He started the truck and drove off.

What should she say to him? Maybe if he believed in ghosts, she'd have an easier time explaining her presence without sounding like a lunatic. And if he believed, she couldn't tell him everything. It was safer for him not knowing all the details. At least until she had some concrete proof. She let the quiet settle between them while she petted the dog's head.

After a few minutes, he broke the silence. "Can I ask you a question? I'm not trying to antagonize you. I'm just trying to understand."

"I'll answer anything except why I was there."

He chuckled. "Anything?"

Hell's bells. What had she agreed to?

He tapped his fingers on the steering wheel. "Have you always seen ghosts?"

Oh crap. "What are you talking about?"

"Come on. First you mention Charlie and then I find you where Nick died. You don't have to hide it anymore."

"How *did* you find me?"

"You left your map behind." He held up the folded paper.

"So…you believe me now?"

"I want to. I need…I don't know, more information I guess."

Well, he didn't tell her she was nuts. That was a positive. And he actually said the G-word. Maybe he was starting to believe? That thought warmed her chest and made her smile.

"To answer your question, no, I've not always seen ghosts. As a matter of fact, Charlie's the...." Wait. What about the hallucination Monday? Or the hallucinations in the hospital? Was it possible they were ghosts, too?

"Charlie's the what?"

"I was going to say Charlie was the first, but I'm beginning to think she wasn't."

"Is it a recent thing? This ghost-seeing?"

"I'd say. If you had asked me a month ago, I'd have told you ghosts don't exist."

"What changed?"

"Lots of things." The accident. Her death. The coma. Could one of them have initiated her ability? Or was it a combination of two or three? She certainly wouldn't get into all that with him. "I'm still trying to wrap my head around it all."

"I want to believe. I do. It's just...." He took a deep breath. "Does she hate me?"

She hadn't expected that question. "Why would she hate you?"

"Because I didn't come when she called. She was clearly depressed about Nick's death. If I had gotten there sooner, maybe she wouldn't have killed herself."

He felt guilty over something he had no control over. Now that was something she could fix. "Rob, she didn't kill herself. She was murdered."

Chapter 15

Rob pulled into the driveway of the animal hospital and parked in the space beside Kate's car. Wind rustled the trees and bushes while the sky spit rain, a tease from the storm headed their way.

A storm brewed in his head, too. Someone had killed his sister? Who? Why? Ever since Bridget laid that bomb on him, he couldn't think straight.

He killed the engine and Bridget opened her door and promptly fell. Barnaby jumped after her.

Damn, but that woman was stubborn. Couldn't she wait until he came around the truck?

Kate scrambled out of her car. "Bridget!"

"I'm fine."

Like hell she was. She kept saying it, but not acting like it. Rob ran around the back of the truck and found her reaching for the floorboards. Blood dribbled down her shirt as if she had reinjured her head on the trip to the ground. He picked up the gauze and handed it to her, then scooped her up before she had a chance to hurt herself again.

"I can walk. I just lost my balance."

"Humor me, then, okay?"

She held the blood-soaked gauze to the back of her head, but her eyes glistened with unshed tears. Kate picked up the ice pack and then led the way. Even Barnaby entered without hesitation.

"Where do you want her?" he asked.

"You can put me down," Bridget said. "I'll sit here at the table."

God! How could she be so cavalier when all he wanted to do was punch something? He should have insisted she go to the hospital. Clearly, something was wrong if she couldn't even stand without falling over.

"Take her to the first room on the right." Kate looked at Bridget. "And no arguing. That's where my supplies are."

Bridget mumbled something unintelligible.

Rob found the exam room and placed Bridget on the cool stainless-steel table. Barnaby settled himself on the floor, keeping watch on her. As soon as Rob let go, she scooted toward the edge.

He grabbed onto her shoulders, stopping her. "You stay here."

"This is a table for animals. I'm not an animal. I can sit in the chair."

"And make Kate bend over to stitch you up?"

"But it's cold."

He folded his arms across his chest. "Then maybe you should have gone to the hospital. I'm sure it would have been more comfortable there."

"Why are you mad at me? What did I do?"

"You nearly got yourself killed, that's what. Why were you out there?"

Before she had a chance to answer, or come up with a way to avoid it, Barnaby leaped up and wagged his tail. He whined and licked the air.

Rob nearly blew a circuit. "What the hell is wrong with you, boy?"

Bridget grabbed his arm. "There's nothing wrong with him. Charlie's here."

Charlie? He spun around the room. "What? You can see her?"

"No. But he can. He always sees her."

Barnaby definitely saw something or someone. A someone Rob ached to see, too. Oddly, as he approached Barnaby a strange coolness enveloped him. All those times he'd suspected the AC malfunctioned back at the house, had it been her instead?

The chill disappeared as Kate entered and sidestepped the dog. "Excuse me, fella." She examined Bridget's wound. "I need to wash this first. Your hair is all matted and I can't see. Can you make it to the sinks?"

"Sure." Bridget stared at Rob as she scooted to the edge. "You gonna let me walk?"

"I will if you can stand," he said.

The look of determination on Bridget's face said it all. Too bad mind over matter did not apply to damaged bodies. She slowly lowered herself to the floor and once her legs remained steady, she stuck her tongue out at him.

That one innocent maneuver lit his soul. Bridget was the only woman for him and damn, if he hadn't almost lost her.

She shuffled to the door Kate went through, holding onto the table. Turning her head toward him, she smiled and held out her hand. "You coming?"

He offered his arm and she grabbed onto it. Though she claimed to be okay, she strode slowly and used him as a crutch. Once they'd reached the sinks, he left her holding onto the counter as he fetched a chair for her to kneel upon. Kate went to work, using the spray to wash away the blood. He'd planned on staying out of the way until Bridget held her hand out.

His hand nearly swallowed hers whole. She gave him a gentle squeeze as if to reassure him. Problem was, she was the injured party. Not him.

She kept her head to the side and smiled at him. But as soon as Kate applied the shampoo, she winced and squeezed his hand. Her eyes glistened, but his girl never cried.

Kate finished and pressed a clean towel to the site. "Hold this, okay? Let's go back."

Bridget released his hand and held onto the towel. As she straightened, the blood drained from her face. "Can you all leave? I think I'm going to be sick."

No. He wanted to help. But Kate turned him around and pushed him out the door.

Once the door shut, she faced him and poked him in the chest. "Tell me what really happened and not that flimsy story you gave me about her bumping her head."

Information he sorely sought, too, but for some reason Bridget wouldn't share. "I can't tell you everything, that's for her to say, but she was attacked at a construction site." Kate's mouth dropped open, but he continued, "The police are pretty sure the vagrant who was squatting there did it and they left someone to watch the place."

"Good God. Why didn't they take her to the hospital?"

"Are you kidding me? Don't you think I tried? She refused treatment. I stopped arguing once she agreed to see you."

Kate proceeded to pace in the hallway. "Her mother's gonna flip. And she'll probably blame me."

Or him. He was still trying to smooth things over from getting caught kissing Bridget. He could only imagine how her mother would react to this news. "Do you think Bridget will tell her?"

"No, but someone has to stay with her tonight and I can't."

"I can." He extended his palm, halting an argument he was sure would come. "I'll be a perfect gentleman. If Bridget doesn't want to call her folks, she doesn't have to. I can be there for her."

"You really do care for her, don't you?"

No more lying for him. "Yes, and I know you're not happy about it."

She smiled and patted his cheek. "Listen, I was wrong before. I should never have interfered. Bridget likes you."

That notion made him all warm inside. "You think so?"

"Uh, yeah. Who comforted who in there?"

He was pretty amazed at that. Seemed as if every time his mind wandered to how he'd found her, she would squeeze his hand or smile. Kind of spooky, actually. "She could have died, Kate. I barely know her and I already know I don't want to lose her."

"Just make sure you don't cage her or you will. She needs you right now, but she also needs breathing room. Something she hasn't had in quite a while. Are you going to be okay with that?"

Whatever it took to keep her, he'd do it. But did Bridget need him? It didn't matter. He liked having her in his life. He only hoped she felt the same about him.

* * * *

Nausea surged, causing her mouth to water. Bridget closed her eyes and breathed slowly. But as soon as Kate and Rob left the room, pain flared in her temples, announcing Charlie's appearance. That was all it took to bring up lunch, or whatever remained in her stomach.

"Ewww. Maybe I should be happy I can't smell. What the hell happened to you? Did you fall off your bike? You should wear a motorcycle helmet if you're so klutzy."

If it were only that simple. Bridget kept her voice low. "What are you doing here?"

"After that spell or whatever you put on me kept me from following you, I waited on the corner. I saw Rob drive by and followed you here."

Bridget turned on the tap and rinsed her mouth. "Spell? What are you talking about?"

"I'm talking about whatever you did to keep me from following. I kept going back to my room. Well, your room, now."

She pulled off a paper towel and wiped her face. "I didn't do anything. I wouldn't know how. So, you weren't there?"

"No. Did you find Nick? How's he look? Is he doing okay? I mean, besides being extremely bored. I can only imagine—"

"He wasn't there." Bridget hated being blunt, but Charlie gave her no choice.

"What do you mean? He has to be there."

"If he was, he never showed. I called for him. Told him that you sent me."

"That doesn't make sense. Why would Carl kill me if he hadn't killed Nick, too? Maybe he didn't actually die there. Maybe Carl killed him someplace else?"

"Ever think he didn't become a ghost? That maybe he had the good sense to move on?"

"Hey! I would have moved on if I saw there was someplace to go."

"Would you? Really? You seem more like the kind of person who demands retribution."

"Nick was that way, too. He must have died someplace else."

"Fine. Let's say he did. You have any idea where that someplace else would be?"

"No." Charlie floated back and forth in her pacing mode. "You never said. Did you fall off your bike on your way home?"

"No. I think there was a squatter at the building and I scared him into attacking me."

Charlie's eyes widened. "So there was someone else there."

"I just said so, didn't...I? Oh, crap."

"You didn't see Nick because—"

"I wasn't alone. Damn."

"You have to go back."

"Oh no I don't. Not until that guy is caught. And I'm certainly not going alone."

Charlie pleaded, causing Bridget's headache to flare. Only one way to shut her up and they stood on the other side of the door.

Looking over her shoulder, she called out, "I'm ready to go now. You can come back in."

"Oh, that is so not—" Charlie misted away just as Rob and Kate entered the room.

It might not be fair to Charlie, but once Rob entered the room, the pain in the front of Bridget's head disappeared. Now if she could only get the one in the back to leave.

Rob placed a hand on the small of her back. "Feel better?"

"Yeah, I do." She looked over to her cousin. "Ready to stitch me up now?"

"I'll be able to use a local, but if I remember correctly…."

"They don't last very long on me." Even when the dentist had shot her full of Novocain, his pain-free window of opportunity had been small. Good thing she had only needed the one cavity filled. And she'd been asleep during the removal of her wisdom teeth. "You can't knock me out?"

"No. But they can do that at the hospital."

"You should go anyway," Rob said. "You could have a cracked skull."

"I'm not going. End of discussion." Bridget placed her right foot on the floor. Dizziness took away her equilibrium and she grabbed the counter. Maybe she *had* lost too much blood.

The hospital was not going to happen, though. Not unless she passed out. That meant no passing out.

Rob grabbed her elbow. "What do you need?"

A lift would be good. She kind of enjoyed being carried in his arms. How old-fashioned was that? "Can I lean on you?"

He placed her hand onto his arm. "Any time."

Kate headed for the exam room and they followed, albeit slowly. The room spun around as if she'd gotten off a twirly ride. Thank God she had Rob for support, since it didn't appear the spinning would stop until she rested. Her bed seemed to be calling her.

Getting onto the exam table proved difficult—her arms acted more like gummy worms than actual arms. Rob waited all of one attempt before he lifted her onto the surface. Some things weren't worth arguing.

Kate pinned up some of Bridget's hair. "I'm going to shave around the site, but it shouldn't be too noticeable. The rest of your hair will cover it. Now, this is going to sting a little."

Sting a little? Try a lot! As soon as the needle pricked her skin, she nearly jumped off the table.

"Rob, hold her head, would you?"

His warm and comforting hands encompassed the sides of her head, his thumbs near her eyes. It was oddly reassuring knowing he held her firmly, but gently.

"You still with me?" he asked

She gazed into his eyes. Eyes showing concern. Eyes she could enjoy seeing every day. If only. "Yep, still here."

Could fire be cold? A burning, stinging sensation which also felt ice-like invaded her skull. She grabbed onto Rob's shoulders.

He looked over at Kate. "Can I place her head against my shoulder?" She must have nodded because he rested her forehead in the crook of his shoulder. "Dig in all you want. I'm not moving."

The electric razor buzzed loudly, but at least she couldn't feel it. How long the numbness would last was anyone's guess. In less time than she had to think, the buzzing stopped.

There was some tugging going on at the back of her head, but thankfully no pain. Rob smelled incredible, though, and she got lost in his scent. He was a drug she could become addicted to so easily. The fact his mere presence eradicated her headaches already earned him high praise.

But when had any man been there for her like Rob? Not ever, that's when. He didn't have to stick around, yet he did.

Pain sliced through her head as the needle pierced her skin. She twitched and gripped his massive shoulders. So much for being numb.

She steadied herself and gritted her teeth. She would not cry out. She would not cry out. But she would certainly squeeze the life out of Rob. God, she hoped he didn't bruise easily. He seemed pretty solid, though.

"You're doing great," he whispered against her ear.

No, she wasn't. She wanted to scream. Or cry. Or cry out a scream.

"Bridget?" Kate asked. "Do you need me to numb it again?"

She took a couple of breaths. "Are you almost done?"

"A few more stitches."

A few? She could tough it out. "Finish, then." The pain couldn't get any—

Holy Mother of God!

"Rob, you need to hold her still."

He gripped her tighter. It might have hurt if all the pain wasn't being directed to that one spot Kate fiddled with. Bridget panted, similar to a woman in the throes of labor. She'd never had a baby, but Good Lord, if it hurt this bad, she may never be a mother.

His shirt became wet. Damn, was she crying? Stupid eyes. How dare they betray her?

"All done," Kate announced.

Bridget let her muscles finally relax and melted into Rob as she wrapped her arms around his neck. "I'm sorry. I think I got your shirt wet. You know, from drooling."

His low chuckle vibrated against her as he embraced her with a hug. "It'll dry."

Kate placed something against her wound and then wrapped gauze around her head. "Try and keep this dry, okay?" She placed a fresh ice pack against her tender wound. "Keep ice on it for a few hours. I'm giving you more packs and some fresh bandages. Change the dressing before you go to bed tonight."

"Too bad it's not Halloween. I could go out looking like a mummy." No laughter. Damn, that was good stuff, too.

"You have any ibuprofen?"

"I do."

"Then you know the drill."

Oh shit. And after all the work Kate had done, Bridget couldn't ask her cousin to stay with her. That meant calling her mother. A groan slipped out.

"What's the matter?" Rob asked. "Are you in pain?"

"I have to call my mother."

"You don't have to call her if you don't want to. I'll be staying with you tonight."

He wanted to take care of her? All night? "I can't ask you to do that."

"You didn't. End of discussion."

She nearly cried. This man who took her headaches away, gave up his Saturday night and for what? To wake her every hour? God, she was such a user.

* * * *

Rob thoroughly enjoyed holding Bridget in his arms. Maybe next time it would be more romantic.

Kate smirked at him. Was he looking dreamy or something?

"Bridget, you will rest tonight and tomorrow. And I'm trusting Rob to make sure you do. Because if I hear you haven't, then I'm taking you to the hospital myself. You hear?"

"Yes," Bridget muttered against his chest. The word mother might have followed.

"I'll see you two at the barbecue on Monday, then."

Bless Kate for making his job easier. He'd kiss her, but then he'd have to release Bridget and he wasn't willing to go that far yet.

Bridget lifted her head. "You said I should rest."

"You should be fine by Monday. If you're not, or if you don't show, I'll personally drive you to the doctor. Got it?"

"Man, you're awfully bossy."

"Yes. And you're pigheaded." Kate smiled and held out a medium-sized white bag.

Bridget took it and returned the smile. "Thanks, Kate. I owe you one."

"Rob, carry her to the truck. I don't want her walking."

Now, those were orders he would leap to fill. He'd reached for Bridget when she put her hand out and opened her mouth.

Kate lifted a finger, stopping Bridget. "Don't even. If I had a wheelchair, you'd be in it. Since I don't, you're getting carried. You don't like it? I can take you to the hospital. Or call your mother."

Bridget's eyes widened momentarily at that last remark, then turned all innocent-like. "All I was going to say was wouldn't it have been more polite to ask Rob if he wanted to carry me?"

He nearly burst out laughing. She was so full of it.

Kate raised an eyebrow. "Rob, do you mind?"

"Not in the least." He scooped the woman of his dreams into his arms. Next, he'd find a way into her heart.

Chapter 16

Bridget couldn't move—her arms and legs bound, enclosed. She couldn't see—dark, so dark. Something blocked her airway—suffocating her. Panic set in. She screamed.

"Easy, easy. You're just dreaming." Rob's soothing voice oriented her. He grasped her shoulder.

Dreaming? No. Nightmare? Possibly. Once her head cleared, she became aware of her surroundings. She couldn't move because the covers had twisted around her body. The sun had set hours ago, putting the bedroom in darkness. No suffocating, either. Blame that on the pillow she had burrowed her face into.

He turned on the bedside light and sat beside her. Gentle fingers brushed the hair from her face. "That's the second time you've screamed yourself awake. Want to talk about it?"

Nightmares were not meant to be shared. She pulled away and rolled onto her back. Big mistake. Pain flared. She sat up. Her head didn't throb nearly as much as it had after Kate stitched it, but it wasn't ready for any pressure, either.

"No. What time is it?" She didn't bother pulling the sheet up. Her jammies covered all the important parts. No cleavage. No scars. Heck, not much skin showed. She certainly wouldn't entice him with her nightwear.

"Eleven-thirty."

"That's all? What have you been doing?"

"I finished painting the bathroom. I hoped it would be dry before you needed to use it again, so if you go in there, be careful."

That might explain some of the light specks in his hair. She nearly reached out to inspect it, but stopped herself in time. As if she had any right touching his hair.

"No, I'm good. I'm hungry, though. Have you eaten?" She'd pretty much collapsed when they returned to the house, but even her exhaustion hadn't been enough to keep the nightmares at bay.

"I made a sandwich. Want me to make you one?"

She shook her head and pulled the covers off her legs.

"What are you doing? Kate said you should rest."

"I'm tired of resting. Besides, I'm not an invalid. And I'm hungry. I want some pancakes."

He stood and offered his hand. "I can make those for you."

"You?"

"Hey, I'm not totally useless in the kitchen. I don't eat out every night."

She took his hand and rose with care. "But I don't have an electric griddle."

"I don't need one. Trust me. If you have the ingredients, I can make you pancakes."

He led the way and as she passed the mirror, she got a good look at herself. Holy moly, look what the dead brought in. Her hair stuck out every which way and the bags under her eyes were nearly purple. She got hit in the back of the head, not the front.

"I think maybe I do need to use the bathroom. I promise I won't touch the walls."

"I'll see you in the kitchen, then."

She closed the door and waited. If the paint fumes didn't give her a headache, Charlie would for sure, but Charlie never showed. Thanking her good fortune, Bridget unwound the bandage and brushed the knots out of her hair. Maybe she should have left it alone. One way to discourage a man was to look like a slob. She looked all that and more. Still, she was vain enough not to want to resemble a complete zombie.

The wall color didn't look any different—her fault for not choosing the color—but the patch work was excellent. If she hadn't seen the hole for herself, she'd never guess there had been one.

Someone knocked at the front door. It was nearly midnight. Who would visit this late? Rob said he would get it. She put the brush down and shuffled to the living room. Her legs were stiff from the bike ride, but not near as bad as the first time. Maybe she was getting in better shape after all.

"Who are you? Where's my daughter?" Her father usually kept his cool, but he sounded frantic with worry.

"Dad? What's the matter?"

He rushed to her and hugged her tight. "Are you okay?"

Bridget glared at Rob. "You called my dad?"

Her father glanced at Rob. "He didn't call me. Who are you again?"

"Dad, this is Rob. He owns this house."

The two sides of his shirt did not line up, since buttons were inserted into the wrong holes, and the tails flapped free. He had always tucked his shirt in before. If he looked that bad, what might her mother… "Where's Mom?"

"She's at home, sleeping. I got a call from my friend, Pete. Said he saw your name on a report and asked how you were doing. Imagine my surprise. Figured I should find out more before I told your mother anything. I know I should have called, but I had to see you."

She pulled away and slowly spun around. "Well, as you can see I'm okay. Kate stitched me—"

"Stitched? You have stitches?"

"Dad. I'm fine. Let's sit down, okay?" Once she got her father settled on the couch, she told him about getting hit, but not about being tied up. There were some things a father didn't need to know. Rob must have felt the same way, because he never offered any more information.

"What were you doing there anyway?"

Rob sat on the edge of the windowsill and raised one eyebrow. Guess avoiding the question twice would be her limit.

"I was riding and when I passed the building, noticed it was one of Rob's projects. I just went in for a peek." Which wasn't a total lie. If she told her father the truth, he'd pack her up quicker than a weekend carnival.

"You were riding your bike? Down there? By yourself? Why?"

Why, why, why. She was sick and tired of having to explain herself. Not that she'd done much of it, but still, avoiding the question had become just as tiring. "I'm not a child. I can go out if I want. It's not like I went to a bad neighborhood. And it was daylight." Her irritation must have gotten the better of her and she might have raised her voice louder than necessary. Her father placed his hands on her shoulders. Even Rob's eyes widened in alarm.

"You're right, you're right. I'm sorry. How am I going to tell your mother this?"

"Don't?" she asked.

"Oh no. I will not do that to her. I protect you when it's necessary, but this is your mess and you can deal with her. I should have you tell her, but then you probably didn't even plan on us knowing at all, did you?"

"I didn't want to worry you. I'm fi—" Rob raised his eyebrows in disbelief and she rephrased her statement. "I'll be fine. Rob and Kate are taking care of me. And you know how Kate is."

"Well, if Kate is looking out for you, that might smooth things a bit with your mother. But I'm telling her tomorrow, so be prepared."

"I understand." Life would be hell for a while. That friendship thing her mother wanted would probably be put on hold.

Her father looked over at Rob. "Why are you here so late?"

"Kate wants her woken every couple of hours. I was going to sleep on the couch."

"Well, that's not necessary. I'm here. I can do that."

She didn't need anyone babysitting her, but if her father stayed… "Dad, won't Mom worry if she wakes up and finds you're gone? The waking part is Kate being overly cautious. I'm not dizzy, I don't have nausea, and I know where I am and what day it is. You don't need to worry about me."

"I'm your father. I'll always worry." He kissed her on the forehead. "But you're right. I'll go and let you get some rest."

Her father stood and approached Rob. "I don't know you, young man, but if Kate trusts you with her, then I guess I do, too." He took his wallet from his back pocket and pulled out a card. "Call me if she gets worse."

Rob took the card and opened the door. "Will do, Mr. Quigley."

"I'll see you in the morning, then. Good night, sweetie."

Once her father drove off, Rob sat on the couch beside her. "I keep meeting your parents under unfavorable circumstances. Think they'll ever like me?"

Her mother already did, the flowers he'd sent pretty much sealed the deal, but he didn't need to know. He might take it as encouragement. "Is that important to you?"

"It is. I have a reputation to maintain."

"And what kind of reputation is that?"

He stared at her intently, as if looking past her eyes into something deep inside her. "I'm the good guy."

He was definitely that and more. And she liked him, but it didn't matter. He could do so much better than her. "I'm sure they'll come around. They value Kate's opinion."

"But not yours?"

"Right now?" She shook her head. "No. Not so much."

* * * *

Rob placed the plate of pancakes in front of Bridget and sat across from her. He'd eaten many pancake meals in this dining room when he was a kid, back before his parents had moved into the house he now called home. His parents were gone now, and he might have felt a twinge of sorrow if he wasn't staring at his future. He wanted her in the worst way, but he needed her to want him, too. Somehow he'd get her to come around.

She still looked awfully pale, the bags under her eyes were darkened, and her father's visit hadn't helped with her mood any. After she cut the stack into little pie shapes, she poured syrup over them then stabbed a portion and shoved it into her mouth.

"I think pancakes made by someone else are always the best," she said with a mouthful and maybe a hint of a smile. "These are really good."

He placed an elbow on the table and rested his head in his hand. "Didn't your mother ever tell you not to talk with your mouth full?"

His bout with teasing backfired. That little curl at the end of her lips bent downward. "Don't you start now. Next you'll be telling me I shouldn't have gone off on my own."

He placed his hand over hers. "I'm not blaming you for getting attacked."

She pulled away, her rejection stinging a bit. "I swear, as soon as I saw someone was living there, I headed for the door. Which reminds me, I need to go back."

"What? Getting hit once wasn't enough?"

She stabbed another pile of pancake and stuffed it into her mouth and then proceeded to talk. "I don't plan on going alone. Will you take me back? I don't know who else to ask."

His temples throbbed, a sure sign his blood pressure was on the rise. He willed himself to calm down. While she couldn't be thinking straight, at least she'd asked for company. "I'm not taking you anywhere until you tell me why you were there in the first place."

"Oh…well…you see." She took a drink of her milk. The longest sip he'd ever seen. All the while, she averted her gaze.

He was normally a patient man, but he'd given her enough chances to come clean. When she speared more pancakes, he held her hand, stopping her from taking another bite. Maybe he could prod her along. "Were you hoping to find Nick's ghost?"

She sighed and nodded. "I thought he wasn't there, but then I talked to Charlie—"

"What? When did you talk with her? When you were in the bathroom?" He still couldn't wrap his mind around the fact Charlie could be sitting in this room with them, listening to their conversation. Did Bridget feel the same way? Was that why she kept pushing him away?

She put her fork down. "No. At the vet's. She reminded me if someone was there to attack me, then there was no way I could have seen Nick."

"Because you can't see ghosts if someone is watching?"

"Exactly. At least, that seems to be the way it works." She forked the pancakes into her mouth.

Which meant she couldn't tell if Charlie was here now or not, except… He glanced at Barnaby, who slept against the wall. Well, he was no help. "Why are you looking for Nick anyway?"

This time she finished swallowing before speaking, probably thinking about what she should say. "Charlie thinks he might have some information about her murder."

Again with Charlie's murder. And all this time he'd been blaming himself for a suicide that never was. "Does she know who killed her?"

"She says she does." Bridget stabbed another portion of pancakes and stuffed them in her mouth. Slowly, she chewed, as if she were savoring every bite instead of stalling, which he assumed was her plan. What wasn't she telling him?

"Who killed her?"

She stabbed another stack and lifted it. Oh no, he wasn't having any of that. For the second time, he reached across and held her arm, the forkful of pancakes hovering over her plate, dripping syrup.

"Bridget...."

"What?" She kept her attention on her food.

"Look at me, please."

After what seemed like forever, she finally lifted her head. Concern filled her eyes. "Please don't make me say."

"You don't think I should know?"

"It's not that. I need to talk to Nick first. That's if he's even there. You'll take me, won't you?"

He released her arm. "You don't believe he'll be there?"

"I don't know what to believe anymore." She put the fork down, having only eaten half of her cakes. "I'm seeing the world differently and I'm not so sure I like it."

He was seeing the world differently, too. One with her by his side. And he liked it a lot.

* * * *

Bridget lost her appetite and not because the pancakes weren't any good. She couldn't remember the last time she'd enjoyed a batch more. But if Rob wouldn't take her back, who could she ask?

"Okay, I'll take you."

She smiled and her appetite returned. "Thank you. Do you think we could go tomorrow, or rather, later today?"

He glanced at his watch. "I don't know. Kate said you should rest."

"What part of talking is exertion? I'm not going to wrestle the guy."

"Can I answer you after you've had some rest, then? When you don't look like you've been hit by a bus?"

Ouch. It was one thing thinking she looked bad, another coming from his mouth. She went back to eating her pancakes. "Look that bad, do I?"

"You just look tired."

Well, she wouldn't go back to bed. Two nightmares were enough for one night. "I'll feel better once I get Charlie off my back." Oh, crap. She was talking about his sister. "That's not to say I don't like her. I do. It's just..."

136

"She won't leave you alone unless she gets her way?"

"Oh. And I thought it might have to do with her being dead and all."

He shook his head.

"I can't really blame her, though. She's lonely and technically only has me to talk to. But if I can help her move on, then I want to." Same with Nick—provided he hadn't already—but if she told Rob that, he might figure out who killed his sister. She would protect him as long as she could. "I mean, why else would I have this ability if I wasn't expected to use it."

"You think what you have is an ability?"

"Well, I certainly don't know what else to call it. It's not like I always saw ghosts." She polished off the rest of the pancakes and pushed the plate away. "Those were really good. When did you learn to cook?"

"I wouldn't call making pancakes cooking, but I was a Boy Scout and I earned that cooking badge." He took the plate and carried it to the sink. "You think your accident had something to do with this newfound ability?"

She froze as panic inched its way up her throat. "You know about…"

He sat back in his seat. "You told me to talk to Kate." He took her freezing hand in his warm one. "But I talked to Brian instead. He told me what happened. You're lucky to be alive."

Yeah, luck. "I'd have been luckier if it never happened."

"But then you wouldn't be able to see my sister. Right?"

She shrugged, but continued holding his hand, taking some comfort from his touch. But how could she admit earning her ghost-seeing ability was worth the death of her friend and unborn baby?

"You ready to go back to bed?"

"No. I'm not sleepy," she said in the midst of a yawn. Damn traitorous body.

"Sure you're not. Want to watch TV instead?"

She stood. Her leg objected to the movement, having stiffened from sitting so long. "You don't have to stay."

"Will you stop? I'm glad to do it. Besides, there's nothing for me at home except a bed, and I can use the couch here." He placed his hands on her shoulders and pointed her toward the living room.

"Now go see if there's anything good on that TV, while I clean up in here."

Of the five stations she could pick up over the air, her choices included *Law & Order*, *Entertainment Tonight*, a blooper show, an infomercial, or an old horror flick. At least she assumed it was a horror movie. Some big, slimy creature was oozing through the theater and kids were running away screaming. She picked the movie as it seemed the most promising.

After Rob finished in the kitchen, he sat on the couch beside her—much too close. "Oh, wow. I haven't seen this movie in ages."

She scooted to the arm rest. "You know it?"

"Yeah, It's *The Blob*. Haven't you ever seen it before?"

"No. Is it good?"

"I liked it."

Good enough for her. She sat back, but couldn't get comfortable. The back cushion irritated her wound, forcing her to lean against the armrest away from Rob. She was more tired than she imagined and nearly dozed herself off the couch. He grabbed her by the arms and pulled her close beside him.

Her heart raced from the intimate embrace. She pushed away and sat up straight. It wouldn't take much to get comfortable around him and then she'd lose whatever willpower she had left.

"Is it me, or is it Charlie?"

Crap, she hadn't even thought about Charlie. Was she in the room watching? "I think it's best I keep my distance."

"Why? Am I not good enough? Is that it? Is it because I didn't go to college?"

Like college had done her any good. "There's nothing wrong with you. Any woman would be lucky to have you."

"Then why do you keep pulling away?"

"Why do you keep getting close?"

"If you haven't realized by now, I'm attracted to you. In a big way. I'm not looking for a one-night stand."

Her heart pounded in her throat, making it hard to speak. "You could do so much better," she whispered, staring at her lap.

"No, I couldn't. But if you can honestly say you're not interested, and I mean say it to my face, look me in the eye and not lie, then I'll drop it. It won't be easy, but I know better than to make an ass out of myself."

Could she say that and not make it sound like a lie? Because it would be. The biggest one she ever uttered. She looked into his dark brown eyes and drowned in their depths.

"What are you afraid of, Bridget?"

"That I won't live up to your expectations."

"If you could relax around me, that would surpass my expectations. Right now I just want you to lean on my shoulder so when you fall asleep, you don't land on your head."

"I'm not tired." Again with the frickin' yawn.

"Sure you're not. But don't be surprised if you wake up in my arms."

Wake up in his arms? No way. She'd stay awake if it killed her.

Chapter 17

Rob opened his eyes, taking a moment to get his bearings. The TV displayed a church service of some kind and sunlight filtered through the curtains. He was nestled on a pillow against the armrest with one foot on the floor and Bridget lying on top of him, out to the world.

Toward the end of the movie, she'd finally succumbed to sleep. As she had drifted off, he'd pulled her close, made a few minor adjustments to make her more comfortable, and it worked. For him as well.

He looked at his watch. Eight AM. So much for waking her every few hours. Gently, he shook her by the shoulder.

She mumbled something unintelligible and moved her hand down his body. He gasped as a rush of excitement flowed through his extremities. One in particular as her hand brushed against it.

She opened her eyes.

"Good morning," he said.

She pressed against his straining erection as she stared at him. He held his breath.

"Morning?" She pushed up and looked around, putting her weight on that hand. He'd never lost control over his orgasms, but there was always a first time.

"Are you okay?" she asked. "You look like you're in pain."

Words failed him. He nodded. No wait, that was wrong. He shook his head. Wait. What was the question?

"Did I hurt you? I'm sorry. I didn't mean to…." His dick jerked and her eyes widened. She lifted her hand as if she'd touched fire. And in a way she had. "Oh, God. I'm so sorry."

The breath he'd held exploded outward. "I'm not."

She scrambled to climb off him.

"Bridget, stop." He sat up and she froze, her face mere inches from his. Taking advantage of such an opportunity, he swooped in and kissed her, sending even more blood to his throbbing erection.

Her lips were soft and warm. She held still for just a moment and then moved forward. She wrapped her arms around his neck and ran her fingers through his hair. Without any prodding, she opened to him. He explored her mouth and tangoed with her tongue. Damn, was he dreaming or was this real?

He found a breast. Her nipple pebbled through the cloth. She was curvy in all the right places, and soft everywhere. He kissed his way to her neck, feeling the rapid fire of her pulse. His heartbeat was doing a good job of keeping up with hers.

"I want you, Bridget. Let me make love to you." Wanting to feel her skin, he found the bottom of her shirt and pulled.

She placed her hand on top of his. "No…don't."

He was losing her. Cupping her face, he brought his forehead to hers. If she was going to reject him, he would make sure she said the words. "Don't what?"

She closed her eyes and one lone tear escaped. It wrenched his heart.

"I can't do this. I'm sorry."

"Bridget… The last thing I want to do is hurt you. If you're not ready, I can wait." He might have blue balls, but it was a small price to pay. "Please, don't push me away."

"I don't deserve you."

"Don't say that. You like me, don't you?"

She nodded, ever so slightly. Hope wormed its way into his heart and he relaxed. He brushed the tear from her cheek.

"Then we'll take it slow. I promise."

"But—"

"No buts. I like you, you like me. Don't over think this, Bridget."

"Slow?"

"Yes. Slow."

She opened those beautiful blue eyes and stared at him. "I guess I can try slow."

Ah, victory. A minor one, but he'd take it. He smiled and lightly kissed her lips. She didn't back away and his heart soared.

* * * *

Nick hovered over the roof of his prison. The cops had come and gone and the squatter had been arrested for a crime he hadn't committed. Well, it's possible he had committed crimes, but he certainly wasn't responsible for assaulting Bridget.

The familiar silver truck pulled into the driveway. Guess his father wasn't sneaking in this time around. So what brought him back? Hoping to discover a dead body?

"Sorry to disappoint you, Dad."

Nick materialized on the first floor just as Dad came in through the door. Sure enough, he headed for the elevator shaft.

All the evidence had been removed, leaving a nice, clean, empty space behind. He turned in a circle, probably looking for any clue as to what had happened, but the cops had been thorough. He pulled out his cell phone.

"Who you calling?" Nick put his ear to his father's phone. Eavesdropping was so much easier when you couldn't be seen.

"Hey, Carl," Rob answered. "What are you doing up so early?"

"Couldn't sleep. I'm going to head out to the Rialto site and check things out. Want to tag along?"

"Carl, if you're having problems, I can take over the management."

"I did have problems at first, but I'm past that. I'll go into work later and see who's available to start work on Tuesday. I'm sorry I didn't get to it sooner."

The project was back on, huh? Explained a lot.

"Hey, it's okay," Rob said. "I understand."

"So, you want to tag along?"

"No, I'll pass. But Carl, there's something you should know. I was there yesterday. Some bum had been living in the place. I called the cops and he's been arrested."

"What were you doing he—there?"

"Ooh, good catch, Dad. Do you think Rob noticed the slip?"

"It's a long story and I can't talk about it now. Just thought you should know in case there's any damage. I didn't have a chance to examine the area. Hey, are you going to Kate's tomorrow? I know she asked you."

"She asked me because she thought I'd be lonely. I don't know...."

"Come on. Go. It'll be fun. Besides, I want you to meet Bridget."

"You sound like you two are an item now."

"Yeah, we are. I finally got her to agree to date. I'll see you tomorrow, okay? I gotta go. Bye."

Nick's father disconnected the call and stared at the phone for a moment before pocketing the item.

"Well, now you know she's still alive. So, you staying or going?" Nick asked.

As if to answer a question he couldn't possibly hear, his father headed for the stairs.

"Guess you're staying."

* * * *

Hell's bells.

Bridget stared at her reflection in the bathroom mirror as she grasped the sides of the sink. Had she just agreed to date Rob? Oh God. He was like a drug. One she would never get enough of. His kiss alone rendered her brain useless, letting her body make all the decisions.

Right now her body screamed for release, but her brain had come back online and put the brakes on that. Slow would have to do. Maybe if she went superslow, he'd lose interest. Of course, if he kissed her like that again, slow would take on a whole new meaning—torture.

The headache she hadn't missed slammed into her brain.

"You decent?" Charlie asked from inside the shower.

Bridget slid the curtain aside with a velocity that rattled the hangers. "How long have you been here?" she whispered.

"I left after you groped my brother."

"Oh, God."

"Yeah, that was my thought, too."

Bridget sat on the toilet seat and held her throbbing head. "What do you want?"

"Nick. Someone else to talk to. The ability to leave this frickin' area!"

"I get it. What do you want from me now?"

"Well, I noticed Robbie seems okay with knowing you can see ghosts and all. So why haven't you told him about Carl?"

"I can't."

"Sure you can. You shape your lips and say 'Carl killed your sister.'"

Bridget looked up. "Don't you get it? Nick knew about Carl. You knew a little bit about Carl. What do you think would happen if Rob found out? Are you looking to have him join you two?"

"But you know. You saying your life's not in danger?"

"I've never met the man. And I won't if I can help it. So no, I don't feel threatened."

"But don't you think Rob can help if he knew?"

"No, I think Rob would confront the man. You have to trust me."

"Like I have a choice. Tell me you're going back, though."

"Rob promised he'd take me today." If she'd rested. Well, she'd definitely rested. Probably the best sleep she'd had in months. And not one nightmare. Was that what she could expect being with the man? It was hard enough not to care for him without thinking about all the perks.

A knock on the door made her jump.

"Are you okay?" Rob asked.

Bridget stood and opened the door. Charlie vanished, as well as her headache. "I'm okay. Just talking with your sister."

"Oh, well, I guess I could leave you alone."

"No. It's okay. The headache was getting to me."

"Headache?"

The alarm in his voice made her pause. Damn. When would she learn to keep her big fat mouth shut? "It's nothing. I get them when she's around."

"Is that normal? Shouldn't you see a doctor?"

She walked passed him and headed for the bedroom. "And tell them what? That ghosts give me headaches? I don't think so." No need telling him about her nagging headaches. Then he might actually drag her to the hospital. Couldn't have that.

He grabbed her elbow. "But you don't have the headache now?"

"It went away the moment I opened the door to you." She beamed a smile at him indicating the conversation was over. "If you don't mind, I'm going to take a shower. Then maybe we could head out to the site?"

Car doors slammed outside. Rob entered the bedroom across the hall and looked out the window. "Your parents are here."

"What? So early?" She had hoped to be dressed and looking lively or, better yet, gone by the time Dad had said anything.

"I'll get out of your hair. Call me when you're free and I'll take you."

She grabbed his arm. "What? Wait. You're leaving?"

Rob smiled. "You don't want me to go?"

Oh, she was a selfish bitch. For days she'd been pushing him away and now it hurt to see him leave? "You're right. I'm sorry. I don't know what I was thinking."

"That maybe you like having me around?"

Oh God, she did, but couldn't admit it to him. She wanted to try that whole slow thing first. "I guess I'm a little nervous about how my mother—" The knock on the door cut her off. She so wasn't ready to face her parents yet. What the hell would she tell them?

"Go on and get in the bathroom. I'll stay and fix them coffee and we'll see how things are after you come out." He spun her around and gently pushed her off. "Go on."

"Thank you," she said over her shoulder.

She grabbed her clothes and rushed into the bathroom, adding "thinks fast on feet" to his growing list of perks. She was doomed.

* * * *

Rob held his breath as he opened the door. Hmm, maybe he should have looked in a mirror first. Or maybe brushed his teeth. Too late now.

"Good morn—"

Mrs. Quigley barged on inside. "Where's my daughter?"

"Mona!" Mr. Quigley followed his wife. "I'm sorry, she's a little anxious."

Rob closed the door. "Bridget's taking a shower. Would you like some coffee? I can put a pot on."

Barnaby jumped up on Mrs. Quigley, wagging his tail.

"Oh my!" she said, trying to push the dog off.

"Barnaby, down! I'm sorry about him. He's harmless."

The dog dropped to all fours but continued wagging his tail. He then turned toward the sliding glass door and licked the air.

Charlie!

"What's wrong with him?" Mr. Quigley asked.

"He wants outside." Rob hurried to the dog and walked through a blast of cold air. He bent down and spoke softly, but it wasn't aimed toward Barnaby. "I know you're here. Please behave."

A cold presence touched his cheek, and he covered it with his hand. Had she just kissed him?

"Why don't you go play?" He opened the door and the icy air vanished as the dog rushed out.

Man, the day he and Bridget made love—and they would, he was certain—he'd make sure they were far enough away where his sister couldn't find them. He shivered at the thought. Creepy.

Rob measured the coffee grounds and water and set the pot to brew. Bridget's parents sat at the dinette table looking anxious.

"I'm sure she'll be out soon." The water was still running, though. How long did she stay in the shower?

"If she just got in, she'll be a while," her mother said. "I guess she's okay if she can take a shower. Is she okay? Really?"

Rob sat at the table. "She'll tell you she's fine, but I think she still needs to take it easy. She got quite a bump on the head."

"I still don't understand what happened."

"Well, that's for Bridget to tell you, not me. But I would appreciate it if you could keep her inside today. She's asked me to take her out, and I promised, but I'd feel better if I could postpone the trip. I don't think she's ready for a lot of activity. And we'll be going to Kate's tomorrow. Are you going?"

"She invited us, like she does every year, but we've never gone. It's mostly for the kids. I think she invites us to be nice. I can keep Bridget in, if you think it's best."

"I do, Mrs. Quigley."

"It's Mona."

Well, maybe he was getting somewhere after all if Bridget's mother could actually smile at him.

She looked to her husband. "Well, Owen. Are you going to stay or go home?"

Owen looked at Rob. "You better hope Bridget never finds out what you just did. She may never forgive you."

"What's that supposed to mean?" Mona asked.

"It means I'm staying. Bridget and her mother don't always see eye to eye when it comes to recuperating. Maybe I should spike her coffee." Owen elbowed Rob in the ribs and chuckled.

"Why would you spike Bridget's coffee?" Mona asked.

"Not Bridget's. Yours. If she needs rest like Rob says, you need to calm down a few notches."

Oh crap. What had he done? If Bridget ever found out, it could ruin what little leeway he'd made. Rob glanced outside. Barnaby was still playing, most likely with Charlie. God, he hoped so. The last thing he needed was Charlie blabbing about how he'd postponed them going to the Rialto site. And if she'd overheard and told Bridget, well, he'd deal with it. Her health was too important.

Chapter 18

Bridget sat on the bleachers at the park behind Kate's house. The baseball diamond lay in front of her. Or would that be softball diamond? Whatever, her view was excellent. Rob stood out there ready to play, wearing a Dayton Dragons baseball cap, a T-shirt indicating he belonged with the Cincinnati Reds and shorts that sported the finest legs she'd ever seen.

The plan to visit the construction site on Sunday had flown out the door after her parents walked through hers. Rob had stayed until she finished her shower, then left with Barnaby. And thus began the slowest day of the whole year. Her mother had refused to leave her alone and her father wouldn't leave without her mother.

Rob and Kate got their wish. Bridget was well rested. All thanks to her parents.

"Hey, Bridge!" Tori waved, slowly stepping up on the wooden planks, wearing orange three-inch heels just asking to get caught in the holes. Any flying insect could zero in on the large orange-and-yellow flowers prominently displayed on her sleeveless dress, which she pulled up in order to step over the seats.

Leave it to the woman to overdress for a barbecue.

"How come you're not playing?" Tori pointed behind her, in the general direction of the field.

Most of their cousins stood out there and Bridget wanted to be with them. Even though she walked without a limp and her head felt fine—provided no one touched it—Rob had practically forbidden her to play. Well, maybe forbidden was the wrong word. More like blackmailed, since he'd threatened not to take her back to the site if she even thought about playing. She was at his mercy. "Headache. What brings you here?"

Tori brushed the wooden seat before planting her butt. "The game, what else?"

"Since when did you like softball? You never watched before."

"Brian's friends were never here before."

Brian's friends or Rob? Of course, Tori had a point. Brian did have some pretty hunky friends. Bridget had never met them before, either. Kate didn't have the barbecue last year because of the wedding and Brian wasn't in the picture the year before.

Rob stood by the players' bench, trying on several gloves. Bridget held back a sigh. She still couldn't believe she'd agreed to date, but maybe it was destiny. If she hadn't been in a coma, she would have met him at the wedding. Or if she hadn't fallen off her bike last Monday, she would have definitely met him today because this barbecue would have been a godsend away from her parents. Was she fighting a losing battle?

Still, it didn't seem right. Her best friend had died because of her. How fair could it be for her life to go on happily?

"What have you done with your hair?" Tori asked. "You look like you just got out of bed."

Bridget brushed a stray hair from her face. She wore her ponytail loose because pulling it tight had hurt her stitches. But even if she had worn it tight with every stray hair tucked, she still would have looked frumpy next to Tori and her immaculate do.

"And aren't you hot in that getup? I think it's already in the eighties." Tori fanned her face.

Bridget's long-sleeve white T-shirt was still dry, but her jeans were soaking in sweat. "I feel a summer cold coming on."

"Uh-huh. Sure. You're going to end up with heatstroke instead. Don't you miss wearing summer clothes? I know I would."

Bridget did miss her shorts and tank tops, but it was a small price to pay if it kept the questions and knowing stares at bay.

Tori shaded her eyes with one hand and looked out over the field.

"Which one appeals to you?" Bridget asked, fully expecting Tori to say one name in particular.

"I'm not looking at the guys. I'm looking at the girls. I know them all. I guess he didn't bring her."

"What are you talking about?"

Tori stared at Bridget. "I called Rob and asked him out, like we discussed. But he told me there was someone else and that he might bring her here today. The only women out there are married."

"He didn't tell you who this someone else is?"

"No. But then, I didn't ask, either. I was hoping he'd bring her so I could check her out. You know, see what my competition is."

Bridget had never been anyone's competition before. Rob trotted over with Barnaby on his heels. Would he spill the beans? She waited in anticipation. He smiled at her and held his hand out—her cue to hand him a water bottle.

"Hi, Tori." He opened the bottle and chugged.

Tori straightened and smoothed her dress. "Hello, Rob. I see you didn't bring your date. Couldn't she come?"

He wiped his mouth with the back of his arm and glanced at Bridget for a split second before returning his gaze to Tori. "She came."

"She did? Well, where is she?" Tori stood and looked out.

Rob asked with his eyes and Bridget shrugged back and smiled, giving him permission to say whatever he wanted.

"She's sitting right next to you," he said.

Tori looked to her left. Oops. No one there. She looked to her right and Bridget smiled.

"No, really. Where is she?" Tori asked.

Bridget shook her head. When had her cousin ever seen her as competition? She'd grown up a tomboy and never strayed from that, while Tori had always been and would always be a girlie-girl.

A frown had flitted across Rob's face, but he was grinning mischievously when he leaned over the seats. Bridget waited for him to hand the bottle back and nearly came in her pants as he planted those oh so luscious lips on hers. Using his tongue, he urged her to open and she obediently behaved, as if she could have turned him away. His kisses sent her brain on hiatus.

"Mmm, you taste good."

She lost the ability to speak. Was her heart even beating?

With his whiskers scratching her cheek, he whispered into her right ear, "Don't hate me. Couldn't resist." With a smile and a twinkle in his eye, he handed her the empty bottle and ran back to the field. Barnaby hesitated for a moment before joining his master.

After Bridget jump-started her heart, she caught Tori's shocked expression.

"Brian does have some nice-looking friends out there."

"Oh, shut up," Tori snapped and carefully stepped her way off the bleachers.

Bridget stifled the laugh that threatened to take over. The man who made it all happen swaggered back to the diamond.

Suzie, forgive me, but I think I'm in love.

* * * *

Rob adjusted his ball cap, grinning all the way back to the diamond. Damn, but that kiss got him hard. Bridget didn't even shy away. He liked that even better.

"What'd you say to Tori?" Brian asked. "I've never seen her get so red-faced before."

Maybe what he'd done was mean, but the woman had it coming. If she were a guy, he might have belted her one. She'd downright insulted Bridget.

"I thought actions spoke louder than words. Especially when she didn't listen to mine."

Brian slapped him on the shoulder. "Yeah, right. That's why you kissed Bridget."

Rob shrugged and picked up his glove. "We gonna talk or play ball?"

They took their positions on the field, Brian pitching, Rob playing first base. He would have preferred to sit on the bench beside Bridget, but Brian would have never let him live it down. There were some things just not worth the aggravation. The first batter stepped up to the plate and Rob's pulse raced. It had been years since he'd actually played. Hopefully he wouldn't look like a fool in front of Bridget, or her family.

By the fourth inning, he gained his confidence, having caught the balls thrown to him. A bruiser of a man came up to bat. Rob didn't catch the guy's name, only that he was married to one of Bridget's cousins. Brian pitched and the monster smacked the shit out of it.

The ball flew over the center fielder's head. Mr. Bruiser jogged toward Rob and grinned on his way by. The center fielder reached the ball as the runner jogged through second. He continued his leisurely jaunt as the fielder heaved the ball to the second baseman.

The catcher, a small woman, looked around frantically. Brian was busy watching the play and not backing her up. Rob ran to cover home plate, because he was sure she wouldn't be able to catch the ball, seeing how she hadn't caught anything yet. She gave him a look of gratitude and he motioned for the second baseman to throw it in.

The runner must have determined his home run wasn't a gimme after all and turned on the jets. Rob held out his glove and caught the ball.

Blam!

Mr. Bruiser drove Rob into the ground. When Rob opened his eyes, several players were standing around staring at him. How long had he been lying there? "What happened?"

Brian laughed. "Artie made a pancake out of you. You okay?"

Before Rob could answer, Bridget's frantic voice cut through the air.

"Let me through!" She shoved at the people stupid enough to stand in her way and fell to her knees by his side.

"It's Nurse Bridget to the rescue!" Artie said.

"Dammit, Artie. This isn't football." She lifted Rob's arm. "You're hurt."

"No, I'm—" The ball dropped out of his glove. "Hey! I got him out."

"You're bleeding, Rob. We need to go clean this up."

Blood trailed from a gash on the back of his forearm. Funny, he didn't feel any pain, but she sure was fussing over him.

She helped him sit up. "Are you dizzy? Nauseous? Do you know what day it is?"

"No, no, Monday. I didn't hit my head." He scrambled to stand and everyone backed away. Except Bridget. She held onto his elbow. Had he hovered over her the same way at the Rialto site?

"Game's over!" Brian yelled. "Let's go eat."

People scrambled outward, picking up bases and gathering equipment. Rob tossed his glove to Brian as Bridget escorted him to the bleachers.

"I'm okay." He couldn't get over her concern for him. Maybe he was growing on her after all.

"You weren't knocked out?"

"No." He rubbed the back of his head. No bumps. No pain.

"Why'd you check, then?"

He sat on the first row of the bleachers and pulled her down beside him. "You worried about me?"

"Artie's a big guy. He's been known to play dirty. When I saw you go down...."

Damn, she *was* worried about him. Kind of gave him the warm fuzzies. "You got a tissue in that bag so I don't drip all over the place?"

She rummaged through her bag and handed one to him. While they walked back to Kate's, he wanted to hold her hand, but holding the tissue in place made that impossible. Once they arrived, he stayed outside and sat at one of the picnic tables while Bridget went inside for a first aid kit. Barnaby followed her.

The rest of the gang straggled in behind them.

Bridget backed out of the house, carrying a box under one arm and holding a bowl of water in her hands. The dog stayed inside, probably taking advantage of the AC. The day had gotten rather hot, yet she still wore clothes more appropriate for cooler weather. Maybe with her lack of finances, she hadn't been able to purchase any summer outfits. He'd like to remedy that, just picturing some skin gave him a hard-on, but she might take offense.

She settled the items on the table and then sat beside him. He would have scooted closer, but wasn't about to overplay his hand. Right now, he'd take what he could. Like that kiss back at the park. Oh yeah.

With gentle hands, she cleaned and bandaged him. He could get used to this kind of treatment.

* * * *

Rob's wound wasn't all that bad, but seeing him go down had rattled her. And Artie was such a cheat. If she could get away with hitting him without breaking her hand, she would have done it. What a butthead.

"You were a nurse before, right?" he asked as he admired her handiwork.

She put the items back into the first aid kit. "Yes."

"Then how come you're working for Kate?"

She swiped her sleeve across her drippy brow, for what little good that did. Her shirt was drenched in sweat. "When you think you're going insane, it's best to stay away from doctors. Not to mention patients."

Rob leaned in close. "I felt her. Yesterday. I think she kissed me on the cheek."

She froze in the process of cleaning. He'd spoken about Charlie as if it were normal. Had he gotten the proof he needed, or did he finally believe her? Did it matter? He didn't think she was crazy and it nearly brought tears to her eyes. She closed the lid and gathered the trash. "Why do you think she did that?"

"Because I acknowledged her."

She stared into those beautiful brown eyes of his and loved him a little more. "Yeah, she would have kissed you for that."

He looked at his bandaged arm. "Do you think you'll ever go back to being a nurse?"

Never, never, and never. That life was over. Before she had a chance to answer, an older gentleman slapped him on the back.

"What the hell happened to you?"

"Hey! I'm glad you decided to make it." Rob lifted his injured arm. "I got scratched making a play at home. Bridget fixed me up, though."

"I doubt washing it and slapping on a bandage is fixing you up," she said.

"So you're Bridget, huh?"

"Oh, I'm sorry," Rob said. "Bridget, this is Carl."

Carl? As in killer Carl? Hell's bells. All the moisture in her mouth disappeared. Her heart might have skipped several beats, too.

Carl went to sit on the other side of the table. "Whoops! One of the kids leave this lying around?"

The rubber snake was probably a foot long, but with the way Rob jumped, it could have been the size of a crocodile.

His face paled. "Where the hell did that come from?"

"What, you're afraid of rubber snakes now, too?" Carl asked.

Rob squinted at it. "Rubber? You sure? It sure looks real."

If she wasn't freaking out, she'd probably laugh. "Give it to me. I'll get rid of it." Anything to get away from that killer. She wasn't sure how much longer she could hold it together. Hopefully the guy wasn't staying for lunch.

Rob's cell phone played "Who Are You" and he pulled it from his pocket. While he took the call, she picked up the bowl and headed to the side of the house, her steps a little faster than normal. She tossed the water into the rock garden and placed the snake in the trash.

"Good riddance, buddy." She covered the fake varmint, turned around, and nearly collided into Carl. Her heart pounded to be free and she grabbed her chest. "Sorry. I didn't hear you follow me."

"Didn't mean to scare you. Snakes don't bother you?"

"Not usually. Especially the rubber variety."

He chuckled. "Then I guess Rob's in good hands with you, huh? So how are you feeling? I heard you got hurt at the Rialto site."

"The what site?"

"The construction site where you got attacked. Rob told me."

"Oh. Well, I'm fine. Thanks for asking." She moved to go around the killer, but he stepped into her path.

"What were you doing there?"

Shit. Best to stick with the lie she started out with, else she would get her stories all mixed up. "I was riding my bike when I saw the building was one of Rob's projects. I only stopped to take a peek."

She stepped to walk around him a second time, but he continued to block her path. Her nerves could start a generator, but she had no reason to feel concerned. There were too many people around and he couldn't possibly know about her investigation.

"How did Rob find you if it was a chance stop?"

Hell's bells. Why all the questions? Did he only care because it was his project? Or did he know more than he was letting on? "No idea, but I'm sure glad he did."

"You get lucky a lot, don't you?"

The way he said it implied he knew about her first accident. Was that how people saw her? As lucky? Heck, maybe she should play the lottery then. "I'd have been luckier if I never went in the building."

He laughed at that. "True."

"There you are." Rob's arrival eased her edginess. She'd never been so happy to see him. "Carl, do you mind if I talk to Bridget in private?"

"No, of course not. Smells like the burgers are almost done anyway."

Rob watched Carl walk out of sight before turning his attention back to her.

"What's so important you had to send him away?" Not that she minded. Maybe he was hoping for another kiss. She could use a kiss now anyway. She'd rather her heart raced in pleasure than unfounded fear.

"I didn't think you wanted anyone else to know about the incident."

"You haven't told anyone?"

"No, of course not."

Those words sat in her stomach like a bad piece of fish. If Rob didn't tell Carl…

"Anyway," Rob continued, "that call was from the police. Seems the vagrant living in the Rialto building couldn't have attacked you. Would you believe he has an alibi?"

Her heart rate picked up tempo, not that it had slowed much. "Alibi?"

"Yeah. He was at the homeless shelter waiting on the next mealtime. Lots of people saw him there during the time you were attacked."

Of course it wasn't the vagrant. She couldn't possibly be a threat to him. But to Carl? Oh shit.

Chapter 19

Carl knows. Carl knows. Those two words kept swimming in her head. Her vision wavered and Rob's voice sounded a great distance away, even though he stood right beside her.

"Bridget! What's the matter?" He grabbed her arms. "Damn, you're burning up. Let's get you inside."

Carl had been there, which meant he'd heard her call out for Nick. Did that mean he was coming for her next? Well, duh!

She shivered and it had nothing to do with the blast of air conditioning that hit her as they entered the house. How did she get here?

"Bridget, did you bring a change of clothing?"

Clothing? Why did that matter? "No." She grabbed onto Rob. "We have to leave."

"You're in no shape to go anywhere."

"What's the matter?"

Kate's voice also sounded distant. Why did everyone sound as if they were speaking underwater? And why was it so bright?

"I think the heat's gotten to her," Rob said. "Do you have something cooler she can wear?"

"I don't need to change. We have to go. I have to talk to Nick."

"Nick? Who's Nick?" Kate asked.

"Bridget, honey." Rob turned her head toward him. "You're not making any sense."

"Take her upstairs to the guest room, first door on the right. I'll be right there."

Bridget grabbed his arms. "Rob, please. We have to go. I have to talk to him."

"After we've cooled you down."

"No!" She ran for the front door, but he caught her around the waist. She pushed against his chest to no avail. He scooped her up and carried her up the stairs.

Feeling defeated, she gave up. She still had time. Carl wouldn't come after her here. Not with Rob around. Right?

He carried her into a cheery room. Flowery wallpaper matched a flowery comforter in colors of pink and purple. Too bad it did nothing for the fear that addled her brain and raced down her spine. He sat her on the end of the bed and knelt before her.

Worry lines marred his face and she ran her fingers over them, hoping to smooth the wrinkles away. "Oh God. I'm so sorry."

He took her hand in his. "No, I'm sorry. I should have known the news would be shocking to you. You're still overheated, though. You need to get out of these hot clothes."

"I need to talk to Nick. If he was there, he knows who attacked me."

"Not now. No one is going to hurt you. You're safe here. Okay? Let's get you cooled down and hydrated. I won't have you collapsing from heatstroke."

She didn't have heatstroke. She had Carl-stroke. But how could she tell him that? If he found out, he'd go after Carl for sure. What was she going to do? A chill permeated her bones and she trembled.

Kate walked into the room and handed her a water bottle. "Here, drink this. Slowly." Bridget took the bottle and sipped. "All I could find that might fit you are these scrubs."

Bridget and Kate may be the same height, but Kate weighed more—a size or two larger at best. Bridget took the offered clothes and shook out the shirt. "This is short-sleeved."

"What does that matter?" Rob asked. "You shouldn't have been wearing these hot clothes today."

"I can get you a sweater, but you'll have to stay inside, then."

If Rob wouldn't take her to Nick anytime soon, what did it matter? "Bring it."

"She should be wearing less clothing, not more."

"She'll be fine as long as she stays indoors. Why don't you wait downstairs? I'll help her change."

Rob brushed her cheek with the back of his hand. "I'll be right back, okay?"

She nodded. He left and Kate shut the door.

"You have got to be the most pigheaded, pea-brain I've ever met."

Bridget drank some water. "Why don't you tell me how you really feel?"

"You think this is funny, but it's not. It's close to ninety out there and you're dressed for fall weather. You of all people should know better."

She couldn't very well tell her cousin why she'd nearly fainted. Better to let her think the worst.

"I hardly think a long-sleeve T-shirt is fall-worthy."

Kate sat on the bed. "Do you honestly believe he'll care about your scars?"

"It's not just him." She placed the bottle on the dresser and peeled off her shirt. Her skin pebbled from the cool air, but breathed all the same.

"No one blames you."

"Yeah, right. Tell that to Devin."

"Devin is a grieving widower. He's looking for someone to blame. That doesn't mean you're at fault."

"Why did I come back and not her?"

"I can't answer that, sweetie. But you have to stop dwelling on it and get on with your life. And you can start by ignoring your own scars."

She couldn't ignore what she saw every day. It wasn't possible.

* * * *

Rob found Barnaby curled in the corner. He slid to the floor and ran his fingers through the dog's fur.

He suspected Bridget didn't have heatstroke. Why didn't he think before telling her about the phone call? If the bum hadn't attacked her, then her attacker was still out there, so of course she would be scared. Who wouldn't?

But who would do that? And why? Had someone followed her out to the Rialto site or had they been there already? If Bridget had a stalker, why hadn't he seen one follow her? Should he start looking? Rob's brain hurt just wondering about all the possibilities.

"You look deep in thought," Carl said.

Barnaby growled.

Rob grabbed the dog's snout. "Stop it." He looked at the person who'd always been there for him. "Sorry about him."

"He's probably hot and tired. Don't worry about it." Carl sat on the floor away from the dog. "I've heard whispers you had to carry Bridget upstairs. Is she ill?"

"I think she had too much sun today, but I may have overreacted. She probably thinks I'm some sort of macho hero. I'm such an idiot."

"You're not an idiot. You care for her."

"Is it that obvious? She's all I ever think about. She's the one, Carl. I never believed that crap before, but it's true. She's the one for me."

"Rob, you hardly know each other."

"I feel like I've known her forever. I wish I knew how she felt." At least she wasn't pushing him away anymore. That had to count for something.

"I'd give her time if I were you. Don't rush into anything."

Rob wanted a life with her and now wouldn't be soon enough. How could he not rush?

Carl patted him on the leg. "I think I'll head on out of here. If you need anything, give me a call."

Barnaby softly growled and Rob nudged the animal.

"Thanks, Carl. I will."

Carl left and Rob turned his attention to his furry friend. "Did the sun get to you, too? You're awfully grouchy. Why don't we go upstairs and wait for Bridget?" He stood as Kate descended the stairs. "Is she okay?"

She pulled him back into the corner. "I don't think she has heatstroke or heat exhaustion. She's just sweaty. What happened outside?"

He lowered his head. "I told her the guy we thought attacked her had an alibi."

Kate smacked him on the arm. "You're an idiot."

"Tell me something I don't know."

"Well, she'll be okay once she gets something to eat. Why don't you take some food up to her? I don't think she's in any mood to come back down here."

He kissed her on the cheek. "Thanks, Kate. Maybe you went into the wrong medical profession."

"Are you kidding me? Animals are so much easier. They don't talk back."

Rob went outside and filled two plates to the brim. Hamburgers—one with cheese, one without—potato salad, coleslaw, chips, and some kind of fruit-salad thing. He didn't know what Bridget liked or didn't like so he'd let her pick and choose.

Gathering the food took longer than he expected since practically everyone asked how she was feeling. Seeing as he didn't know himself, he found it hard to answer.

He put some napkins and eating utensils in his front pocket and stuck a bottle of water in each side pocket of his shorts. One of the cousins opened the door for him. Barnaby followed him up the stairs and bounded toward the bedroom door, squeezing through the small opening.

Bridget paced in front of the bed, wearing the scrubs and a hooded sweatshirt jacket zipped up to her neck. The dog rushed her. She stopped and crouched, accepting Barnaby's licks before she hugged him close and buried her face in his fur.

He placed the food and water on the dresser. "Are you okay?"

She stood and nodded. "Will you take me to the site?"

"You need to eat."

"No. I need to talk to Nick."

"Bridget. You said it yourself, he might not even be there."

"I know." She held her arms across her stomach and whispered, "What if he comes after me?"

He wrapped her in a hug, trying to offer comfort. "You don't know anyone is coming after you. For all you know you stumbled upon a drug dealer who got scared. Don't make things worse than they need to be."

She pulled free and swiped at her face. "I still need to talk to Nick."

"Not right now you don't. Right now you need to calm down and eat."

After pacing for several seconds, she leveled those brilliant blue eyes at him. "I'll eat if you promise you'll take me to the site as soon as we're finished."

"Deal."

"Okay then." She smiled and relaxed, almost as if he'd lifted a weight off her shoulders. He'd gladly bear any burden she carried, if she'd only let him. She sat on the floor. "What'd you bring?"

"Hamburgers and stuff. We eating on the floor?"

She nodded. "It'll be like a picnic."

"And instead of the bees and ants, we'll have Barnaby to fend off." He handed her the waters before picking up the two plates.

"Ah, he won't bother us. Will you, boy?"

"I wouldn't be too sure of that. He's been known to steal my sandwiches in the past." After giving her the plates, he settled on the floor.

"And I'm sure he waited until you weren't watching. So whose fault is that?"

"Man, I'm not going to win this one, am I?"

"Nope." She raised the plates away from Barnaby's curious nose. "Which one is mine?"

* * * *

Bridget sat on the passenger side of the truck, petting Barnaby. The scenery most likely flew by, but she kept her head down and stared at the dog, with an occasional glance at Rob's legs. And man, did he have nice legs. She'd always considered herself a butt person, but he could easily convert her. Of course, his butt was pretty extraordinary, too.

Oh man, she had it bad.

He was the perfect boyfriend. Attentive. Caring. And able to get them out of Kate's and on their way to Nick without an issue.

Not to mention a good kisser. No, make that an excellent kisser. Only problem: she was wanting more than kisses.

Her cell rang from the inside of her backpack. She pulled the noisy thing out and quickly killed the call. Four times in four days. Devin just wouldn't give up.

"Wrong number?"

"Not really, but I'm not in the mood to chat. How much farther?"

"Not long."

Man, he didn't even berate her for not checking for herself. Something her mother had done over and over. Instead, he treated her inability as if it were a normal trait. Even she had trouble wrapping her head around that.

"What are you going to do if Nick isn't there?"

Now there was the million-dollar question. She'd been basing everything on Charlie's assumption—an assumption she couldn't get into with him. "No idea. I'm not sure what makes a ghost. I only know Charlie has unresolved issues. Maybe Nick does, too."

"Listen, I love my sister, but she's been known to stretch the truth a time or two to suit her needs. For the life of me I don't know who would want to murder her. Or why. It doesn't make sense. Is it possible, just possible, she's embarrassed and she really did commit suicide?"

Bridget stroked the dog's head. She might have believed that scenario yesterday, before meeting Carl, but Rob didn't need to know. "I don't know. I guess. But why lie to me?"

"Because you can see her. Hear her. You're someone she can talk to. Maybe she thinks you won't stick around if you knew the truth. If you can't find any proof otherwise, it's something to think about."

She could definitely see Charlie doing something like that. If only it were possible.

"I know you're worried about your attacker, but could it be you were in the wrong place at the wrong time? It's something to consider, anyway."

She'd love nothing better than to consider that, but Carl knew she was at the site and Rob hadn't told him. Of course, maybe Carl had found out the way her father had. Crap. She'd feel better once she discovered the truth. Maybe.

Rob slowed and turned right. A peek out the side window confirmed her suspicions—they had arrived.

"Uh-oh," he said. "Someone's here."

A navy blue pickup, sans the driver, was parked by the back door. "Is that Carl's truck?"

"No." He pulled up to the building and stopped. "It's one of my crew."

* * * *

Nick stood in front of Rob's truck. More company, or a promise of things to come? Existing away from constant human interaction had some perks. Like forgetting that people went on with their lives. But once this building became occupied, he'd have to face the truth—people lived while he just existed.

Rob opened the door. "Let me go find out what's going on. I'll leave the air on if you'll stay with Barnaby."

Bridget nodded and held onto Barnaby until the driver's door closed. Rob brought the dog without Charlie the last time. So where was Charlie and why wasn't she with her own dog?

He remembered the day he brought her the puppy. His gift to her for one year of sobriety. He'd never seen her happier and she'd thanked him in the best way possible.

Nick floated into the backseat of the truck. "Hey, Barnaby. How's it going, boy?"

Barnaby whined and wagged his tail. It was kind of cool how the dog could see him, and a good thing, too. Rob might not have found Bridget if Nick hadn't gotten the dog's attention.

Bridget looked out the back. "What do you see?"

For someone who said she could see ghosts, she wasn't seeing him, but Barnaby could. Nick moved and the dog's gaze followed. Could he hear him, too?

Back when blood pumped through his arteries, Nick had played the howling game with Barnaby. Drove Charlie nuts, so of course he did it all the time. Nothing better than to get her riled up and then excite her with his kisses. Damn he missed her.

"Okay boy, here's to old times." He tilted his head back and howled like a wolf. Barnaby howled along with him.

Wow. That was way cool. Wonder if other animals could hear him. He'd have to give it a try.

Bridget patted the dog on the head. "What are you—" She furrowed her brow, looked outside at the men talking, then returned her gaze to the backseat. "Nick, if you're here, make Barnaby howl again."

Well, this was interesting. Nick howled and the dog followed suit.

"Damn," she said. "Okay, listen. I can't hear or see you with other people present. I need you to go behind that dumpster so we're out of sight." She pointed toward a three-walled enclosure at the end of the parking lot. "Barnaby, you stay here." After a quick glance Rob's way, she exited the truck and ran toward their destination.

"Shit." Was she for real? Only way to find out. He popped over to where she indicated and waited.

* * * *

Bridget ran to the Dumpster holding her side. Her breaths came in gasps. Damn. This being out of shape thing was the pits. Then

164

again, the temperature hovered close to ninety degrees and with the high humidity, fish could probably breathe easier.

She dashed behind the dumpster and an explosion of pain slashed through her head. Well, if she'd wanted proof a ghost materialized, she just got it. She rubbed her temples as she stood in front of a man. "Nick? Nick Anders?"

He looked a whole lot better than the tiny picture in the paper. Death certainly wasn't unkind in the looks department. He wore his light brown hair a bit longer than she preferred, having gotten used to the shortened locks Rob sported, and he wasn't as tall as Rob nor as big as his father, but damn… Wonder how many women had been jealous of Charlie?

He smiled. "Oh my God. You really can see me."

"I can hear you, too. I have to say, I'm kind of amazed. You're the second ghost I've talked to. It's nice to know I'm not going bonkers."

"What's the matter with your head? Is it still sore from Saturday?"

As she stood in his presence, the painful throbbing receded into a nagging ache. The same way she reacted to Charlie. "A little. Did you see who hit me? Do you know who it was?"

"Yes. My father. Although I have no idea why he did such a thing."

"Oh, shit." Her veil of anonymity just got blown away. Fear threatened to unhinge her, but she held it in check. Freaking out wouldn't help her case any.

"What'd you do to my dad?"

She leaned against the dumpster wall. "Nothing directly."

"I heard you say Charlie sent you. Why? And is she okay? Better yet, could you bring her here? I'd like to see her even if she can't see me."

Oh crap. He didn't know. "She misses you, too." If she didn't change the subject, she might not get any information out of him. "Charlie suspects Carl murdered you. Is she right?"

"Are you some kind of private investigator? Is that why you're looking for me?"

Wouldn't that be a cool job? Investigate for the dead. But how would ghosts pay? Okay, maybe not so cool, then. She still needed to make a living. "No, I'm just someone who happens to see ghosts. Do you have unfinished business, Nick?"

"I don't know about any unfinished business, but I need to see Charlie. I've tried to go to her, but I can't get any farther than about a quarter of a mile. If I go beyond, I end up back here. Or, actually, back there." He pointed toward the construction site. "I need to see her and make sure she's okay. Please. Can you bring her?"

That sounded like unfinished business. "So Charlie's wrong? You weren't murdered?"

He floated back and forth the same way Charlie did whenever she paced. "Well, technically she's wrong, but she's not wrong. I don't think my father set out to kill me, and he probably wishes it hadn't happened, but all the same, I don't think he's lost any sleep over my death, either. We argued, he pushed me, I fell to my death, and he covered it up. What kind of father would do that?"

"I don't know. What were you arguing about?"

"What didn't we argue about? But it all started with Charlie. Dad never thought she was good enough for me. But that night? I told him I had proof of his embezzling, except I don't, well, didn't. So, why didn't she go to the police with her suspicions? Or did she?"

"No, she didn't. But how did you know your father was embezzling?"

"Just a hunch. He seemed to have extra money all the time. More than usual. Then I noticed materials being ordered weren't up to standard. Different suppliers were used than quoted. I didn't want to tell Rob without more to go on so I asked Dad if Charlie could work in the office. He paled so quickly, I thought he was having a heart attack."

"I don't understand. If Charlie needed a job, why didn't she ask Rob?"

"Charlie didn't need the job, but Dad didn't know that. I wanted to see his reaction, and boy, did I get it. He started yelling and called Charlie names. I wouldn't stand for that and yelled back. Next thing I know, he's pushing and I'm falling. That's what I get for bluffing, huh?"

"Oh, Nick. I'm so sorry."

"Hey, nothing you can do about it. What's done is done. But I gotta see Charlie. I don't think I'll rest until I do."

He pleaded with his eyes and she couldn't avoid it any longer. "Nick, I can't bring Charlie."

"Why not? Is she sick? Is that why you have Barnaby? She in the hospital or something?"

Bridget lowered her head, avoiding Nick's gaze. How could she tell him and not break his heart? But maybe that's what he needed to move on. She straightened and looked him in the eye. "Nick, when I said you were my second ghost, what I didn't tell you was that Charlie was my first."

* * * *

Nick was enjoying his conversation with Bridget. To be able to talk with someone again invigorated him. Then she'd implied something that just couldn't be true. "What are you saying?"

Bridget stared at him. "Charlie's dead. That's why she can't come here."

His sweet, beautiful Charlie was gone? "But how? When?"

"Carl killed her shortly after your accident."

"Killed?" Guilt ripped through him. Charlie had died and it was all his fault. "Oh my God. Why isn't he in jail? Why is he still walking around free?"

"He staged her death to look like a suicide. A drug overdose in her home."

And of course people believed that because people believed what his father did—once a druggie, always a druggie. But Charlie wasn't a druggie. She'd been clean and leading a good life. And for his father to taint that was too much. He lifted his head and screamed, releasing all the pent-up anger he'd accumulated over the months. "He deserves to die!"

"I'm sorry, Nick. I can't imagine what you're feeling right now. I'm trying to get the proof she needs so she can move on."

Moving on. Something they both needed to do if they ever hoped to see each other again. It certainly wasn't happening on Earth. They were too far apart.

He shook his head. "I don't have anything. But Rob should. Ask him to look in the books. It's got to be there somewhere."

"You don't have anything else? Anything hidden?"

"No, that's just something I bluffed with my father. I'm sorry. I wish I could help her more. Tell me, is she okay? I mean, as a ghost."

"She's coping with her situation. I might have made existing a little easier for her. But I know how badly she wants Carl put away. I truly believe once that occurs, she'll be able to move on. Of course, it could all be speculation on my part. It's not like I know what the heck I'm doing."

"My last thought before I died was of Charlie. I kind of flew off the handle at her, through no fault of her own. I wanted to tell her I love her, to see her one last time. Now you're telling me it's not possible."

"But won't it be, if you both move on? I'd like to think you will. I've always believed we meet our loved ones on the other side."

He'd like to think that, too. "Will you help her?"

"I'm trying. Can I help you?"

He stared at this pretty woman who didn't know him from Adam. "Why do you care?"

She shrugged. "I'd like to think there's a reason I see ghosts. Maybe I'm meant to help."

"You wanna help me? Then help her. Her happiness is all I care about. And since I can't tell her in person, tell her I love her, would you?"

"Sure, but I'm sure she already knows that."

Wind swirled around his feet, kicking up dirt. Bridget raised her arm and backed away as loose strands of her hair whipped around her head. A bright light shone above. An opening to some other dimension provided the light and a warmth surrounded him.

"Do you see that?" When she didn't respond, he looked down. Bridget had fallen to the ground, unconscious. He moved to her, but something pulled him toward the light.

And the pull felt good, right and peaceful. If he couldn't see Charlie on Earth, maybe, just maybe, he would elsewhere.

Chapter 20

Rob returned to his truck. Barnaby nosed the window and wagged his tail, but where was Bridget? Couldn't she stay put for five minutes? He opened the door and turned off the ignition. Barnaby squeezed by and jumped out.

"Where'd she go, boy?"

The dog ran toward what looked to be some kind of mini twister behind the Dumpster at the end of the lot. The oppressive air around him couldn't stir a leaf and no storm waited on the horizon. So what caused that?

He followed the dog and as he came around the wall, the wind abruptly stopped. Bridget lay on the ground in a heap as if she'd collapsed. He rushed to her side and pulled her into his arms. She wasn't bleeding and she breathed normally, as if she were asleep. "Bridget, honey. Wake up."

He tapped her face. No reaction from her, but Barnaby whined.

What the hell? He picked her up and carried her back to the truck. Should he take her to the hospital or Kate's? Better yet, he'd call Kate and ask her. He opened the passenger door. After Barnaby hopped inside, he placed Bridget on the seat and reached for the seat belt.

Her eyes fluttered before opening. "Rob?"

Relief poured over him. "Thank God you're awake. What happened?"

"I don't know. The last thing I remember is the dust kicking up."

"Did someone hit you?"

"No." She moved to slide out of the truck, but he grabbed her by the shoulders, stopping her progress.

"Where do you think you're going?"

"I was talking to Nick. He might know what happened."

When Rob had checked on Carl's security guard, they were within sight of the truck. So it made sense she'd go somewhere private. But collapsing couldn't be a good sign.

"You need to see a doctor."

Her eyes widened in shock. "You said you believed I saw ghosts."

"That's not the kind of doctor I meant. You fainted."

"I didn't faint. I don't faint."

"Then what do you call it when I find you on the ground unconscious?"

Ha! He had her there. She couldn't answer him. She could, however, cross her arms and scowl. "I'm not hurt. I just want to talk to Nick."

"Fine. I'll take you back where I found you. But if Nick doesn't know what happened, then I'm taking you to a doctor."

"No, you'll take me to the fire station. You'll see my blood pressure is normal and then you can take me home."

"And if it's not normal?"

"It'll be normal."

Dear God, there had to be something seriously wrong with him. Her stubbornness—not to mention the fiery look in her eyes— filled him with an excitement he'd never experienced before. If he could get away with it, he'd kiss her.

She shoved his shoulder making room for her to slide out of the truck. He grabbed her elbow to assist, but she shrugged away. "I'm not feeble."

Her rejection stung. "I'm not the enemy here. I'm only trying to help."

She lowered her head. "I'm sorry. I know you're not the enemy. And I appreciate all you've done. But I'm fine and there's nothing you can do to help me right now. Just stay here and wait for me. I won't be long."

He knew he couldn't tag along, but he wanted to all the same. "What if you faint again?"

She let out an exasperated breath. "I'm fine. I'm not dizzy, woozy, or nauseous."

"Would you tell me if you were?"

The lines on her face smoothed out. "Yes. I wouldn't lie to you. Okay?"

That might be the case, but some people thought they were fine when they weren't. "At least take Barnaby with you."

She smiled. "Thank you. I'm sorry for snapping at you."

When she jogged, he called out to her. "Walk. I'm not going anywhere."

She raised her thumb and slowed her pace.

He leaned against the truck and waited. He'd give her ten minutes, tops.

* * * *

Bridget regretted her actions toward Rob. Although, if she continued to piss him off, she'd get rid of him. The problems with that? Number one, she wasn't sure she had pissed him off. Number two, she wasn't sure she wanted to get rid of him.

She looked at the dog. "Oh, Barnaby, what am I going to do?"

He lifted his head at the sound of his name, and stared at her with those soulful brown eyes, but of course he didn't answer. And if she expected he would, then maybe she *should* see a doctor.

As soon as Rob disappeared from her line of sight, she called out for Nick.

Except for the occasional car passing on the street, the area was relatively quiet. No headache, either. She called out again and waited. He couldn't have gone far. So where was he?

Could someone be watching? "Nick, if you're here, make Barnaby howl."

The dog sat beside her feet and looked up at the mention of his name. No howling. No whimpering. No indication anyone spoke to him. Nick was gone.

With shoulders sagging, she shuffled back toward the truck. Technically, Nick couldn't help her any more, but it would have been nice knowing how she'd become unconscious. She'd never fainted before and she wasn't feeling light-headed. Something knocked her out, but what?

"What'd you find out?" Rob asked.

If she told him the truth, they would end up at the fire station and she would have to do her best to stay calm. And if she lied, and he found out, it would doom their relationship for good. A nice plan, if she took that route.

"He wasn't there."

"Maybe someone was watching."

She shook her head. "He made Barnaby howl before."

Rob chuckled. "I forgot he did that. Used to drive Charlie nuts. So now what?"

"Now I guess you take me to the fire station. That was the deal."

He cupped her face with his hands. A sizzle of excitement raced through her while he stared into her eyes. God, he was beautiful. And he could be hers. She only had to say the word.

"I have a better idea." He released her and opened the passenger door. "Get inside."

"You're not taking me to a doctor, are you?" Because if he was, she'd rethink that lie part. Barnaby hopped into the truck and she followed suit. Her heart rate increased, which didn't bode well with getting her blood pressure taken.

He stood holding the door, the corner of his mouth slightly raised. "Relax. It's not bad."

Where could he possibly take her that wasn't bad? As long as it wasn't the hospital, she was fine with any place. He just better not start asking questions she wasn't willing to answer. She needed proof before she said anything, because once she mentioned Carl, Rob would probably do something rash and only get himself hurt.

"Did he see who hit you?" Rob asked.

Oh crap. The one question she wanted to avoid. She leaned to the right as the truck turned left. "Where are we going?"

"You're not even looking out the window. How do you know I'm not taking you home?"

"Because you didn't make any right-hand turns coming out here."

"Oh. That's pretty impressive. I didn't think you paid attention."

"Just because I'm not watching where you're driving doesn't mean I'm not paying attention. So where are we going?"

"Some place safe."

"Safe? Are we in danger?"

"I don't know. Are we? Did Nick tell you anything about that?"

Oh great. Was he fixated on Nick? She so did not want to have this conversation. She concentrated on scratching Barnaby's head, feeling the soft fur through her fingers, so when Rob suddenly covered her hand with his own, she nearly jumped off the seat.

"I know he told you something. And maybe you think you're protecting me by not telling me, but you're not." He rubbed his thumb across her knuckles. That little action, which was probably meant to soothe her, did quite the opposite. Her poor heart was liable to jettison into space.

"Anyway," he continued, "I'm not taking you home because I think you need a break from Charlie. Or more likely, a break from ghosts. You were having fun at Kate's before I told you about my phone call. Weren't you?"

The kiss came to mind as well as the shocked look on Tori's face. She inhaled slowly. "Actually, before Artie plowed into you."

"Yeah, but you were getting over that." He patted her hand. "Relax. We're almost there."

Relax. Relax. Relax. No chance in hell unless he drugged her.

After a couple turns to the right and left, the truck jostled and stopped on an incline. She raised her head at the same time as Barnaby. Rob had parked on a driveway in front of a two-story house.

"Who lives here?"

"I do." He opened his door and got out. The dog followed close behind.

When he said he'd take her someplace safe, she assumed a restaurant or park. How was his place safe?

The garage door rolled up and her hand hovered over the seat belt release. Wow. Her moment of truth had arrived.

The door opened. Rob stared at her. "You okay?"

No, she wasn't okay. "Why are we here?"

He reached across and undid her belt. "Because I'm fairly certain there aren't any ghosts here. And if there are, please tell me and I'll take you someplace else, as well as get a Realtor. I don't think I want to live with one." He offered a hand to help her out, but she couldn't move.

Why was she so nervous? He hadn't done anything to warrant it. She was an adult. If things got, well, heated, would that be so bad? She took his hand and slid out of the vehicle. "Thank you."

He led her inside the garage. When he reached a door, he punched the remote on the wall and the garage door trundled down.

"The place may be a little messy. Hope you won't hold that against me."

She stepped through the opening into the family room and breakfast nook. Mail littered the tabletop and various jackets covered two of the four chairs.

"How long have you lived here?"

"Since high school. It was my parents' house."

"Didn't Charlie's house belong to them?"

"It did. I think they had plans of buying older homes and renting them out, but that never happened. Charlie needed a place, but didn't want to live with Mom and Dad. They rented it to her, so she was already living there when they died. Technically, we owned both houses together, but she didn't want to live here, so I moved back. You want some ice cream?"

He walked over to what she assumed was the refrigerator.

"You collect magnets, do you?" One whole side and the front were covered in an array of colors. Pictures of a young Rob and Charlie in various sports activities littered the front, while magnets of locations covered the side.

"No. Mom did. Whenever she and Dad traveled somewhere, she'd buy one as a souvenir. Said they were cheaper than T-shirts and lasted longer."

"How can you deal with seeing this every day?" Bridget wasn't sure she could handle that kind of reminder if her parents had been abruptly taken from her.

"Strangely enough, it's kind of comforting. I just think of them on a cruise or some kind of vacation." He opened the freezer. "I've got chocolate-chip cookie dough or Oreo. What sounds good?"

The conversation switch caught her by surprise. An offer for ice cream was the last thing she'd expected to hear, but it sure sounded great. "Oreo."

She sat in one of the uncluttered chairs. Habit had her separating his mail into two neat piles: bills and junk. Rob pulled out two bowls.

"If you don't mind me asking, how did your parents die?"

"Drunk driver. It happened quick and they were together, which they always said was the way they wanted to go." While he scooped out the icy treat, his eyes glistened.

Whatever got her onto this conversation? If she didn't change the subject, she'd get them both crying. "Is ice cream a weakness of yours?"

He placed a bowl in front of her and moved a chair to sit close. His smile glowed. "Who doesn't love ice cream?"

* * * *

Rob scraped out the last bit of ice cream in his dish, the spoon clicking against the glass. He'd lick the bowl if he were alone. Bridget had only finished half her serving.

"Don't you like it?"

Her eyes did not reflect her smile. "As a matter of fact, I love it. It's been ages since I ate any."

Why'd he thought ice cream would solve all her problems? She was probably still freaked out about being attacked. He reached out and covered her hand with his. "Hey. I brought you here to relax, so no worrying, okay?"

"Yes sir." She saluted and chuckled before digging back into the bowl.

Maybe she'd relax if she opened up. Didn't she realize he could help if she only spilled about Charlie's murder? Holding all that in couldn't be healthy. But getting her to open up, now that would be the trick. He didn't need it backfiring and having her pissed off at him. "Who do you think has a better shot at survival? A person with all the facts or a person going in blind?"

The smile disappeared and the spoon stopped midway to her mouth. "Sometimes knowing all the facts can lead to overconfidence."

"You think I'll do something rash, don't you?"

She put her spoon down. "Yes."

At least she was being truthful. "Can you go to the police?"

She shook her head. "I have no proof yet."

"But there's proof? Is that what Nick told you?"

She swirled the remaining ice cream with her spoon and kept her head down. "He had none, but he thinks there's some to be found."

"Then let me help. Tell me who killed Charlie."

She shook her head. "No."

"You think it's better I speculate and take care of matters on my own? Is it someone at my work? Maybe I should start asking questions."

Her eyes widened in horror. "No. That'll only make it worse."

Crap. It *was* someone at work. "How do you figure?"

"Rob, he's already killed to shut people up. You don't have to know who he is for him to come after you."

"Exactly why I should know who it is, so I can avoid him."

She lowered her head and played with the corner of an envelope from his stack of mail. He'd cracked that surface of hers, but had he made enough headway for her to tell him everything? She must see the logic in his defense.

"Bridget… How am I supposed to find the proof if I can't talk to anyone and don't know what I'm looking for?"

"I can find the proof. It's not safe for you."

"And it's safe for you? He's already attacked you once."

She lifted her head. "I didn't say that."

"Oh come on. I'm not stupid. Who else would have hit you? And what makes you so sure he won't strike again?"

"I'm not, but—"

"And won't he suspect something's up if you suddenly show up at my work?"

"Why would I—"

"Isn't the proof at my work?"

"Oh."

Beating her down like that gave him a nasty taste in his mouth, but she left him no choice. "Charlie's my sister. Don't you think I deserve to know what happened to her?"

She bit her bottom lip and her eyes filled with tears. The spoon clattered in the bowl.

"Bridget. I want to help her, too. Let me help her. Tell me who killed her."

She scooted away from the table and went to the family room, wiping her eyes. "Rob, please. I can't."

He walked up behind her and grabbed her shoulders. "You can. You just won't."

"It's not safe for you."

"And it's not safe for you, either. You leave me no choice, then. I'll talk to Carl. Maybe he knows who held a grudge against Nick. I'll feel like a heel bringing up his death, but—"

She swiveled around. The blood drained from her face and her widened eyes filled with fear. "No! You can't talk to him."

It all made sense. How scared she'd acted after talking to Carl. "Charlie said Carl killed her? That's ridiculous."

She grabbed his shirt. "Promise me you won't talk to him!"

He placed his hands over hers. "Bridget, honey. There's no way Carl could be involved."

"But he is. Nick saw him attack me. And Carl pushed Nick to his death. Nick doesn't think Carl meant to hurt him, but Charlie was planned. Carl went to her to find out what she knew and who she told. But she didn't know anything, Rob. He killed her for nothing except to cover his own ass."

Her words punched him in the gut and all the air left his lungs. Carl had been like a second father to him. To learn he was capable of such heinous things… "Why?"

"Nick suspected Carl was embezzling funds and confronted him."

"He's been stealing? No. I would have noticed something like that." But maybe he had. How many suppliers had changed without explanation? Then there was Margo, and Mac's painting contract.

"Whether or not you noticed, you can't confront him, Rob. It's too dangerous."

Anger burned inside his chest. He kicked the coffee table and his game controllers fell to the floor. "I can't let him get away with this. She was my sister! And he nearly killed you."

He collapsed to the couch, holding his head. Tears ran down his cheeks. They'd trusted that man and he turned on them for what? Money?

She sat beside him and wrapped her arms around his shoulders. "Rob, I'm so sorry. I didn't want you find out this way."

He swiped at his eyes. "Were you ever going to tell me?"

She released him and scooted away. "Yes. Once I had the proof. Now that you know, well, maybe you can find it. Can you have your books audited? Make it look routine?"

He waved a dismissive hand. "We already do that." Of course, it wasn't the same accountant they'd used in past years either. "What else did Nick say? Did he give you anything to go on?"

"No. He only wanted to talk about Charlie. Then the wind kicked up and the lights came on and I woke up in your truck."

"Whoa. Back up. What do you mean the lights came on? You didn't mention lights before."

"I didn't? Huh. But there was a bright light." Her eyes widened. "Do you think he moved on? Could that be it?"

"But if Carl killed him, wouldn't he want to stick around for justice? Like Charlie is?"

"Carl wasn't his unfinished business. Charlie was. And once he realized he'd never see her again, maybe that's all he needed to go. I wish I'd known. I would have said good-bye."

"I'm sure he understands why you didn't." He leaned back into the cushions and closed his eyes. How did life become so complicated?

"I'm sorry for dragging you into all this." She lowered her head and played with the string on her hoodie.

"You didn't drag me into anything. You opened my eyes." And right now he viewed the most beautiful woman he'd ever known. He tugged on her arm. "Come here."

She hesitated at first, but after wrapping her in a hug, he managed to get her head on his shoulder. He'd lost his parents and his sister. He wasn't losing her, no matter how hard she resisted.

Chapter 21

Of all the crazy, stupid things she could have done, telling Rob about Carl had to be the craziest and stupidest. Sure, he acted all cool, except for the kicking the table part, but deep down she was sure his rage boiled and mind worked overtime, thinking of ways to get Carl.

If only he'd found out after she'd gotten the proof. Then he could lash out at Carl all day long, because Carl would be behind bars and unable to hurt Rob.

He ran his fingers up and down her left arm. Thank goodness she'd worn the zip-up hoodie or he'd feel more than she wanted.

"Aren't you hot?"

She was. In more ways than one. "I'm fine. Do you have any ideas of how we can secretly prove Carl was behind the killings?"

"I might, but I don't want to talk about it right now. Why don't you take this off?" He tugged on the sleeve.

"Because I don't want to." Maybe being in his arms wasn't such a bright idea, no matter how much she loved it. She squirmed to sit up, but he held her tighter.

"I'm sorry. I don't mean to upset you. I know you probably have scars. They don't scare me." He took her hand and slipped it under his shirt.

What the heck? Feeling him up was not on her agenda, no matter how much she craved it. Feeling would lead to other things. Things she might not be able to stop. She tugged to get free.

"Relax, will you? I'm not looking for a cheap grope. But I won't stop you if that's your inclination."

She closed her eyes and stopped herself from laughing. Although groping him was kind of appealing.

When he'd guided her hand to his side, she relaxed. His skin was hot and smooth until her fingers trailed over the bumps of a scar, a good four to five inches long.

"Feel that? That's what happens when you're young and stupid. And showing off. Saw got me good. Certainly took enough stitches. Dad thought for sure I'd bought it that day."

"You almost died?"

"But I didn't." He tilted her chin in his direction. "You didn't either."

He cupped her jaw, his touch scorching and leaving a trail as he caressed her neck. She held still, her heart beating overtime. She *had* died that night, but came back and her body was very much alive, screaming for release. If this was so wrong, why did it feel so right, right, right?

He leaned forward and kissed her. All rational thoughts left her head. His lips were soft, imploring and she opened for him, their tongues dueling. He tasted good with just a hint of chocolate. He explored her mouth while his hand trailed down her shoulder and rested on her breast. She wore no bra—it was at Kate's—but her jacket provided some protection. Still, her nipple hardened and her sex throbbed. She could kiss him forever.

The sound of a zipper brought reality back with a crash.

Her hoodie. Oh God, not that. She struggled in his embrace.

He stopped and broke the kiss, but held on to her tight. "Bridget, when are you going to trust me?"

She trusted him, but could she trust herself? If she let him continue he would expect more. Hell, she needed more but wasn't quite ready for that...yet. If ever. "I like you."

He smiled. "That's good to know. I'm pretty crazy about you, in case you hadn't noticed. But do you trust me?"

"Yes, but...."

"But?"

She pulled free and looked him in the eye. "I'm not ready for this yet."

"Then we won't. Not until you're ready. Bridget, I'll do anything for you. You gotta know that."

And that was the problem. If she stayed any longer, she would only hurt him more, when the only person who should feel pain was her. He deserved better. Once she helped Charlie move on, she would be out of his life for good. Until then, she'd keep her distance.

"Can you take me home? Please?"

"Bridget, you don't have to leave. I'm sorry. We'll just watch a movie."

His pleading wrenched her heart. What had she done? "I'm tired. I want to take a bath and then crash."

"I guess you have been through quite a bit today. Forgive me for being selfish. I just want to be with you."

No more than she did with him, but she'd already let it go on too long. She stood and went to her backpack.

"What about Carl?" he asked. "You're not going to do anything foolish are you?"

"Don't worry. I'll keep my distance." She'd faced death once and won. The second time she might not be so lucky.

"Good, because I might hire a private investigator to check into some things. Maybe find the proof we need."

Thank God he wasn't getting involved. Her stress lightened significantly. "That's a good idea. My investigative skills suck." She slung her pack on her shoulder.

He grabbed his keys off the counter and they walked to the truck. Barnaby hopped in first and she took the seat beside him. He nosed her hand. Clearly it wasn't working as it should. She hugged the animal and rubbed his back.

Rob drove a short distance and stopped. No cars had passed so she took a peek and immediately wished she hadn't.

* * * *

Out of all the women Rob had dated in the past, not one had ever made him feel so helpless. Not until Bridget.

When would he learn, being with Bridget meant slow and steady, not fast and reckless? But damn, she drove him wild with desire. He had to go and get greedy, didn't he?

She appeared on the verge of bolting and he couldn't have that. Not after all the progress he'd made. He still had the house to fix. Getting her involved in the next project might be one way to get back on her good side. He needed to do something fast or he'd lose her for good.

"Why did we stop here?" she asked.

He blinked. Hell if he knew. He'd stopped at the sign and then his mind wandered. He glanced at her and her pale face, but she wasn't looking at him. She was staring out the window, across the street, to the river. Horror etched across her pretty face.

Shit. Good going, Rob. Got any other ways to blow this relationship? Of all the places he could stop, he chose the site of her accident. And without even trying.

"Sorry. Mind wandered." He turned left and she lowered her head. "How about I work in the living room next? You don't have a problem with that, do you?"

"It's your house. I'm just house-sitting. Remember?"

Yeah, he'd moved back a few steps. Hopefully not too far back.

He drove up the driveway, and she jumped out before the truck had finished rolling. He scrambled to meet up with her at the door.

"I hope you feel better."

"Thanks." She unlocked the front door and stood in the doorway, her head lowered. "Let me know how the private investigator goes. Hopefully it won't take long."

With that attitude, he wanted it to take a good long time. True, nothing would give him more pleasure than seeing the bastard put away for killing his baby sister, but Rob got the impression Bridget would dump him the minute that occurred. And while it might seem unfair to Charlie, she'd understand. Wouldn't she? He couldn't lose the only woman he'd ever loved. He needed more time so Bridget could see how good he was for her.

He leaned over for a kiss good-bye, but stopped at the last minute. No need scaring her away any more than he already had. "I'll call you about the next project. Okay?"

"Sure. Good night, Rob." And with that, she was gone.

He hit his forehead with the heel of his hand. Stupid. Stupid. Stupid. He'd played with fire and got burned. Royally. He only hoped he hadn't scorched the whole relationship.

* * * *

No sooner had Bridget closed the door when pain slashed through her temples so intense her eyes watered. She turned her back to impending doom and rested her heated head against the cool door.

"Hey, roomie. Did you have fun with my big brother? You were gone long enough."

The headache may have triggered the waterworks, but remembering the hurt look on Rob's face kept them flowing.

"Any idea when you'll go find Nick? Good thing Mr. Murdock was watching the Reds game. I've been going crazy waiting."

Yak, yak, yak. Bridget had had enough. "Can you give me an hour? I'd like to take a bath in peace."

"Why are you crying?" Charlie spun Bridget around. "Was Carl at the party? Did he hurt you?"

Bridget wiped her eyes. "He was there, but he didn't do anything." Except maybe scare the bejesus out of her. "I just don't feel well."

"Oh. I keep forgetting I give you a headache." She floated back a few feet. "I'll go watch the rest of the game. Enjoy your bath." Charlie dematerialized out of the room.

Bridget felt a tinge of regret letting Charlie assume her ghostly presence caused so much grief. She tossed her backpack on the couch and headed for the bedroom. A bath would be nice, but having Suzie around would be nicer. Then she could be with Rob guilt-free.

She unzipped her jacket and slid it off her shoulders. What if Suzie were still around? As a ghost? Damn. Forget the bath. She was going for a walk.

After quickly changing into something a little less revealing—scrubs had their purpose, but weren't meant to be worn without underwear—she grabbed four bottles of water and stuffed them in her backpack. Thank goodness Charlie was next door. She could only follow so far, but Bridget would prefer to avoid the incessant questioning that was sure to come. This trip had nothing to do with Charlie and her problems and everything to do with Bridget's future.

The heat had let up a bit, but still hugged her body. A hot breeze blew from the west, and clouds formed on the horizon. This trip would have been a lot quicker with her bike, but Carl must have taken it after he bopped her on the head and the cops couldn't find it anywhere near the construction site. The walk might do her good. Her headache was down a couple of notches—more like a dull throb—but the possibility existed she'd be sore in other places before the day was through. That way she could share the wealth.

She pulled her iPod out and put in the earbuds. Thirty-seven songs later with her shirt stuck to her back and her thighs chafed, she arrived at the river. The sun hung low on the horizon. She blocked the rays with her hand and looked both ways before crossing the street. A new guardrail lined the road. Maybe if that thing had been there before, Suzie wouldn't have drowned. Then again, she might have been squished to death.

After stepping over the railing, she inched her way down the grassy slope, being careful not to slide to the bottom. Be just her luck to end up in the river and drown, not her purpose at all. Suicide was the coward's way out and Suzie deserved more than that.

If the car had left any sign of rolling, it disappeared long ago. The river breached the banks, still high from last week's rain, and a branch traveled past at a good clip. Unimpeded, it would reach the Ohio River at the Indiana and Kentucky borders by daybreak.

Bridget ventured to the water's edge, in an isolated spot deep in shadow, where no one in their right mind would wander. So what did that say about her mind?

She turned off the iPod, removed the earbuds, and listened. Birds chirped. Water lapped at the shore. An occasional car drove by.

"Suzie?" she whispered.

No answer, but what did she expect? Even the birds didn't flee.

She cupped the sides of her mouth. "Suzie!"

Her voice echoed and she waited. Each second that passed, her hopes sunk deeper. Bridget sat on the ground with a *thud*. What a foolish trip. Suzie's only unfinished business was her unborn baby, who had died right along with her. Of course she would go with little him or her. Wouldn't any mother?

"I'm so sorry, Suzie." She rested her head on her knees and wept.

Her cell phone rang. After wiping her eyes, she slipped her backpack off and fished for the noisy item. Devin. Would he ever give up? She pressed the ignore button. If it weren't for the fact her mother might call, she'd turn off the phone. And while she had no desire to speak to her mother, she certainly didn't want an argument as to why she'd turned off the stupid thing.

No sooner had she deposited the phone back into the pack, when it rang again. Would he ever get the hint? Her thumb hovered over the ignore button. Not Devin. Rob.

She should have never agreed to dating. Now she would only hurt him. She took a deep breath and hit the ignore button. She might as well have stabbed her heart with a stick. The result was the same.

As she placed the phone back in her pack, pain slashed through her temples. Only one thing had been known to do that and her hopes rose. "Suzie?"

Not Suzie, but a woman wearing a black dress with white-polka-dots that came straight from the sixties.

"Who are you?"

Her eyes widened. "You can see me?"

Bridget rubbed her temples. She'd come to find a ghost and got her wish. Too bad it was the wrong ghost. "Yeah. How long have you been here?"

"Not long. You were playing with some strange device when I arrived. My name is Mary Alice Walker. Who are you?"

"Bridget Quigley. But I meant, how long have you been dead?"

Mary grinned. "Hello, Bridget Quigley. I don't know. I lost count."

The woman seemed much too cheerful for a ghost. "When did you die?"

"That would be June thirtieth, nineteen sixty-three. How long ago was that?"

"About five decades."

Mary's mouth opened. "Five? I guess my baby girl isn't a baby any more, huh? How is it you can see and hear me? Are you a ghost, too?"

"No. I just see them." No need to mention touching.

"Who's Suzie? Is she your little girl? Did you lose her? Is that why you're crying?"

"Suzie was my friend. We were in a car accident a little over a year ago and she died here."

The woman floated closer and squinted her eyes before widening them in surprise. "That *was* you! I thought you looked familiar. What a night. I don't think I've seen so many people since."

"You saw the accident?"

"I heard the crash. By the time I got here, your car had rolled into the river and the other car on top. Were you hoping you'd see your friend as a ghost?"

"Something like that. Why are you still hanging around? How did you die?"

"I jumped off that bridge."

The little bridge didn't seem tall enough to cause a death. But then, the river was rather shallow. "Was there a reason you jumped?"

"Seemed like the right thing to do at the time. If I had known what I was getting myself into, I would have stuck around. Can't say this life is any better than the previous one."

"Was life really that bad?"

"Having the baby wasn't anything like I thought it would be. I should have been happy to be a mother, but all the baby did was cry. I couldn't shut her up and no one would help. I was expected to do it all and I couldn't. I just couldn't take it anymore."

Bridget had seen patients with postpartum depression. Thankfully, they'd been treated successfully. Back in the sixties, it probably wasn't even diagnosed. Was that why Mary Alice hadn't moved on? Was suicide a big no-no?

"Suzie tried to wake you, did you know that? But I guess you were too badly injured to hear, huh?"

"I don't remember anything after stalling the car."

"And the guy who hit you? I think he was drunk."

"Yes, I had heard that." Bridget stood and slipped on her backpack. Staying here wasn't doing her any good and she still had quite a walk home.

"You're leaving? You can't leave. You just got here."

"I came to find Suzie and she's not here. I'm sorry I can't help you."

"Please. You don't know what it's like."

Guilt dropped her chin to her chest. From the little time she'd spent with Charlie, Bridget had learned how frustrating being a ghost was. At least neighbors with televisions kept Charlie occupied. What did the river and wildlife offer Mary Alice?

"I'd stay, but I have a two-hour walk ahead of me and I don't want to get caught in the dark. I'll come back." Bridget turned and climbed the slope. Mary Alice materialized in her path and they bumped.

"I can touch you?" She grabbed Bridget's wrist and then stomped on the ground in amazement. "Stay. You have to stay."

There was a madness to Mary Alice's eyes, giving Bridget chills in the stifling heat. Panicking, she pulled free and ran up the hill. *Please let there be people at the top.* She reached it and caught her breath. Traffic. What a wonderful sight. Once the cars had passed, she dashed across the street.

Mary Alice appeared out of nowhere and Bridget stopped. "You can see me now?" She searched the area. "You walked through me a second ago, but now you can see me? Why?"

"I can't see you when others are around. But I have to go now. I'll explain it all when I come back." Like never.

Mary Alice grabbed Bridget's wrist with an inhuman force. "I don't believe you. You have to stay. I need you."

"I promise, I'll come back. Just let me go." Pain flared and if Bridget waited much longer for that magic car to arrive, she might end up with a broken bone. She bent Mary Alice's fingers back, hoping to get free. No such luck.

The ghost stared in surprise. "Wow, that doesn't hurt. Am I hurting you?"

Bridget's wrist screamed in pain and she lost the feeling in her left hand, but admitting it might only make things worse. Might make Mary Alice worse. "This is useless. As soon as someone comes by, I'll get free. So just release me."

"Not if I get you out of sight, you won't." Mary Alice squeezed harder and pulled, as if she meant to drag Bridget back to the river.

Kidnapped by a ghost? Really? The pain nearly sent her to the pavement. She bit back a yelp and punched Ms. Walker in the face. The act apparently shocked the ghost more than hurt her and she released Bridget, but now Bridget's left wrist not only throbbed, her right knuckles stung. Still, she ran.

She must have reached Mary Alice's barrier, because the woman never reappeared. Bridget had wanted to help the woman, but now, not so much. She rubbed her tender wrist. If ghosts could become violent, maybe she shouldn't be alone. Better yet, maybe she should hole up and never venture out. It's what she deserved, anyway. Unfortunately, holing up didn't pay the bills.

Chapter 22

On Thursday morning, Bridget's sleep came to an abrupt halt. Something heavy landed across her back followed by sharp, shooting pain in her head. She scrambled out from under Charlie.

"Sorry."

"Dammit, Charlie! That's the third time this week. What's your excuse this time?"

"Man, what a grouch. I left you alone so you could sleep and this is the thanks I get?"

Bridget rubbed her throbbing temples. Sleep? Tossing and turning all night, as she had the past three nights, did not amount to any kind of rest. Thoughts of Rob certainly didn't help in the dozing department. If anything, it only made it worse. "Maybe I wouldn't be a grouch if you didn't wander out of your zone and pop on top of me in the middle of the night."

"Excuse me, but it's morning, not night. And I said I was sorry. Did you ever think about moving the bed? Then maybe this wouldn't happen."

"I did move the bed." Bridget could understand it happening the first time, but after the second, she had moved the bed against the other wall.

Charlie looked around and then burst out laughing. "Yeah, you moved it all right. I just landed across you instead. This room isn't that big and, unless you move the bed across the hall, I'm going to disturb you."

"Or maybe you stop with your midnight exploring."

"But that doggie was sooo cute. How was I supposed to know I went too far unless I attempted it? Huh?"

Ever since Bridget had told Charlie her theory about Nick moving on, Charlie had ventured further from the house, and more often. The fear of missing her light—the light that had found Nick—was no longer an issue.

Bridget jerked the covers aside and stomped to the bathroom. Charlie materialized.

"Can't I even pee without your hovering?"

Charlie floated out of the room and Bridget shut the door, as if that would stop Charlie from talking.

"What the hell happened on Monday anyway? I think I deserve to know."

"I told you about Nick."

"Not Nick. Robbie. I want my brother back."

"What are you talking about? He's been here. I can tell." The fireplace doors had been repaired and the rest of the paneling removed. Even the hole in her bedroom had been patched. Seeing the evidence of his work—work he'd accomplished without her help or company—stung, even though that's what she'd wanted. Or so she'd thought.

"I don't mean physically. I mean mentally. He yelled at me. He never yells."

"Did it ever occur to you maybe you caused him to yell?" Bridget flushed the toilet and washed her hands.

"I've teased him plenty, even when we were kids. He never yelled. He swore he never would. He didn't want to be like Dad."

"Your dad yelled?"

"All the time. And Mom yelled back. We loved them, and knew they loved us, but it drove us nuts. How do you tell your parents not to yell? Rob found some kind of inner peace through scouts and football."

And it had only taken Bridget a week to make him go crazy. What might he be like if she let it go any further? She opened the bathroom door and headed for the kitchen. Coffee sounded good.

While Bridget went to work on making a pot, Charlie floated in and out of the room, wearing a frown. Bridget sat at the table. "So Rob found inner peace through football. Where did you find it? Through Nick?"

Charlie stopped her pacing. "No. Drugs. Nick came later."

"I'm sorry. I can see why suicide by overdosing would be a sore spot."

"Hey, it's not your fault. What am I saying? It is your fault! Bring Robbie back. I miss him."

Bridget missed him, too. "It's over. Just give him time."

"How can you say it's over? He loves you!"

"What? He can't love me. He doesn't even know me."

"Bridget. He loves you. I've never seen him look at anyone the way he looks at you."

"That's not love." Was it?

"I've seen the way you look at him, too. So why are you doing this?"

Hell's bells. How *had* she looked at him? Had he noticed? "It's complicated, okay? Just drop it."

"You're nuts, you know that? You have a great guy in love with you and you throw it away? Do you know what I would give to have Nick with me right now?"

"Give up your quest to see Carl put away?" Bridget hit a nerve, but was satisfied in diverting the conversation away from Rob.

Charlie's eyes widened and her nose flared. "Ooo, that's not fair! I can't let Carl get away with murder. Plus, there's no guarantee I'll see Nick on the other side."

"There's no guarantee Carl will be put away, either. What are you going to do if I don't find the proof?"

Charlie turned away. "I don't know. I can't think like that, okay?" She spun around and poked Bridget in the chest. "And that's another reason you have to see Rob. Find out what's happening."

The last message Rob had left informed Bridget he'd hired a private investigator and would call back when he got some news. That was two days ago.

Bridget rubbed her chest. Charlie's poking had hurt, like Mary Alice's grip, but admitting it would be a huge error. Not that she didn't trust Charlie, but why give the ghost any ideas? "When are you going to learn to be patient?"

"When are you gonna admit you love my brother?"

Bridget stormed to the bedroom. She was so not having this conversation. And if Charlie followed her, she might have to bop her one. Her knuckles were just about healed.

* * * *

Rob slammed the file drawer closed. He resisted the urge to ram his fist into something—like Carl's face—because he wouldn't stop with one punch. Knowing that man had killed his baby sister ate him raw. He needed the proof now, before he did something that landed him in prison.

What was taking so fucking long? The investigator had assured Rob he'd hear something by the end of the week. It was now Friday afternoon and not a word. That whole idea about dragging out the investigation was bunk. Putting Carl away sooner would be better. Better, so he could pursue Bridget. How could he start a relationship with his sister's murderer walking around free?

"It's starting to sound like your father returned." Carl poked his head into the doorway. "He used to do that all the time. I think he went through several filing cabinets."

"What do you want, Carl?" Rob practically growled at the guy. Keeping his cool around the murdering son of a bitch was harder than he'd anticipated. Maybe he should have taken the week off. But dammit, this was his business. Not Carl's.

"Hey, no need to bite my head off. Having a problem with a project? Maybe I can help."

"There's nothing wrong with any of the projects. Maybe I'm just in a bad mood."

"I've known you a long time. Something's bothering you. You have a tiff with Bridget?" Carl entered the office and Barnaby growled.

"I don't want to talk about her." And give the bastard more reason to hurt her. Bridget might not be taking his calls, but he hadn't given up on her. Instead, he'd given her the time to hopefully see the error of her ways. And if the investigator got off his ass and did his job, then Rob could finally get Carl put behind bars where he belonged. And wouldn't that be a wonderful present for his soul mate and future wife.

Carl raised his hands in surrender. "Whoa, that bad, huh? Well, you really don't know her, now do you?"

"We're not talking about her."

Barnaby growled again and then barked.

"I think you might need to leave the dog at home, Rob. He's starting to get on my nerves."

Rob patted the faithful animal, who knew the truth. "Why do you suppose he doesn't like you, huh? Have you done something to him?" Like maybe, murdered his master?

"I've never touched that animal. Maybe he just senses I'm a cat person. You ever think about leaving him at home?"

"I'm not leaving him alone all day. He doesn't bother anyone but you. Maybe you just need to stay away. I do find it interesting how he's never shown a dislike for you until after Charlie died."

"I don't think he liked me before. She was able to control him. If you can't do the same—"

"Listen, this is my business. If I want to bring Barnaby to work, I will."

"Rob, what's the matter with you? I've never seen you so agitated. Why don't you go back to Charlie's house and work out your frustration."

"Maybe I should. My paneling order came in and I need to pick it up." And then he could see Bridget. Man, he'd missed her.

"While you're there, push them about the Bonner project. Maybe you'll have better luck."

"Sure." He snatched his truck keys from the desk. "Oh, by the way. What do you know about Sylvester Paint?"

Carl stood still and acted calm, but his face paled and he averted his gaze toward the dog as if Barnaby would attack. "Why do you want to know?"

"We always get our paint from McGruder's. Why the sudden change?"

Carl crossed his arms. "To tell you the truth, Mac was getting on my nerves and we got a better deal at Sylvester's. Since when did you care where we got our supplies?"

"Since now. I want to be more involved. You don't have a problem with that, do you?"

"You're the boss. I just assumed you'd rather work in the trenches than deal with paperwork. Do whatever you want." Carl turned and left.

Yeah, he'd do what he wanted. Except what he wanted—watching Carl being hauled off to jail—couldn't be done without proof. Since that wasn't happening soon enough, there was something he could do. Rob sat back behind his desk and called Linda, requesting her to get his lawyer on the phone. Maybe he would never get Carl behind bars, but he'd be damned if Carl got his business.

* * * *

Bridget's coworkers avoided her completely. Even Kate kept her distance. Four days with a nonstop headache would put anyone in a foul mood. Living with Charlie only made it worse.

It had nothing to do with the fact Rob hadn't called since she put him to voice mail on Monday evening. Not at all.

She should be happy. She got her wish. Instead, her heart sat like a lead weight embedded in her chest.

Bridget trudged into the storage room and pulled out a bag of dog food. How had she gone from a successful nurse to being a maid at a veterinary clinic? Feed the animals. Bathe the animals. Clean the cages. Without a tech license, she couldn't help Kate with the patients. Maybe she should go back to being a nurse. She'd make more money at least, and then she could afford her own place.

Of course, that meant going back to the hospital. Not happening.

Then again, she could move back with her parents. She wouldn't have access to Charlie or Rob there. So why hadn't she? Because then she wouldn't have access to Charlie or Rob. Crazy as it seemed, Charlie had become a friend. And even if she couldn't date Rob, it didn't mean she never wanted to see him again.

Yeah, she was into that whole self-torture thing.

She hoisted the bag of dog food as pain flared in her head. The bag landed with a *thud*.

"There you are. Man, I didn't think I'd ever find you."

Bridget rubbed her temples. "Dammit, Charlie. Can't I even get a break at work?"

"I'm sorry about your headache, but you have to call Rob. Now."

"Is this some sort of plan for you to get us together? Because it's not working."

"No. This is about Barnaby. I think he's sick and I can't get Rob's attention." Charlie wrung her hands and floated back and forth across the room.

"Sick how?"

"He's throwing up. Stop talking and call."

"I need to get my phone. It's in my backpack."

193

"Then get it."

Bridget went to her locker and pulled out the phone. She wouldn't put it past Charlie to come up with some concoction to get her and Rob talking, but if the dog was in some real trouble and she did nothing about it, she would feel the guilt forever. She'd had enough of that dish already.

She entered Rob's number and pushed send. The phone rang twice then directed her to voice mail. The pain in her head radiated to her chest. Oh God. How many times had she done the same to him? Had he finally moved on?

* * * *

The quiet phone stared at Rob from the carpet. What a dumb ass.

He'd been installing the paneling when Warrant's "Cherry Pie" played from his cell. Back during his teenage years, he couldn't play the song enough. Being a lover of the dessert hadn't helped, either, and caused him all sorts of teasing from Charlie. "If you love the pie, why don't you marry it?" "If you love the song, why don't you marry it?" If anyone else had tortured him that way, he would have slugged them and then listened to the song again.

So when he'd found it as a ring tone, he couldn't resist and used it for Bridget. She was his cherry pie. But stupid him, the song had played and transported him back to high school. In a nervous fit, he'd pulled the cell from his jeans and fumbled with the device. As it had slipped through his fingers he must have hit the decline button. The song had died the moment the phone landed.

For the past few days he'd stopped himself from calling her. Each time he'd convinced himself that giving her time and space was better. Now she'd think he cut her off. "Well, don't just stand there like an idiot, pick up the stupid phone and call her back."

But how could he explain what happened without sounding like a total moron? His phone rang again—playing "Who Are You." His heart sank. It wasn't Bridget. Had he blown his chance?

He pushed the accept button. "This is Robert Gentry. How may I help you?"

Silence for several seconds, then, "This is where you tell him who you are."

That voice. But it wasn't possible. Was it? "Who is this?"

The caller coughed. "It's Bridget. Please don't hang—"

"Bridget?" His heart soared, but his mind struggled with confusion. "I must be going crazy. I could have sworn I heard Charlie."

They spoke simultaneously. "You could hear her?" "You heard me? Holy shit!"

He'd believed Charlie was still hanging around, but to hear her voice… Tears formed in his eyes. He could talk to his sister. "How is this possible?"

"I…I don't know. She's in the office with me."

"We can chat later," Charlie said. "Robbie, get your ass out to the backyard. Barnaby needs you."

"What are you talking about? He's in the backyard playing with—" Oh shit.

"He was playing with me until he ate something he shouldn't."

He bumped into the couch on his way into the dining room and gazed out the back door. No sign of the dog. He opened the door. "Barnaby!"

Retching noises came from the side of the house and Rob dashed toward the sound. The dog vomited as he swayed on his feet.

"He's throwing up."

"That's probably a good thing," Bridget said, "but you need to bring him in and let Kate look at him."

As he approached, the dog looked up with glassy eyes. "Hey, buddy. What've you been eating?" Rob rubbed Barnaby's neck. The animal stiffened and keeled over. "Oh God!"

"What happened?" a chorus of voices sounded over the phone.

Rob grabbed his chest as the pressure nearly crushed him. This dog had wormed his way into his heart. *Dear God, don't take him away from me. Not yet.*

Barnaby coughed. Relief washed over Rob. Not dead. Not yet. "He collapsed, but he's still breathing."

"Hang up and bring him in now," Bridget said. "Hurry."

She didn't have to tell him twice. He disconnected the call and pocketed the phone. Barnaby lifted his head and struggled to get his legs underneath him. "Easy, boy. We're going to Kate's. She'll make you all better."

Rob slid his arms under Barnaby and he stiffened once again.

"Please don't die. Please don't die."

Rob ran to the gate and unlatched it with his elbow, slipped out, and let it shut on its own. Using his fingers, he lifted the handle to the passenger side of his truck and then placed Barnaby inside. The dog lifted his head and whimpered. Rob shut the door and dashed around the vehicle. In a matter of seconds, he was backing out and heading for Kate's.

Bridget and Kate were standing by the back entrance as Rob pulled in. Kate ran to the passenger side and pulled the door open.

"Wait. I'll get him," he said.

Barnaby had been moving, until Rob lifted him. Again, he stiffened.

"He keeps doing that."

"Get him inside. Bridget, get Tori. I'll need her help."

Rob followed Kate and carried Barnaby to the same room Kate had stitched up Bridget. He placed the dog on the metal table. Bridget arrived with Tori in tow.

"It's a good thing you checked on him when you did," Kate said.

He would have corrected her, but Bridget shook her head. Guess he couldn't say the truth—his sister warned him. "Yeah. I heard him throwing up."

"Did you bring a sample?"

"No. Do you need it?"

"It'll help me determine what he ingested. Bridget, go get a container and bring back a sample. Rob, you need to leave."

Leave? Hell, no. He couldn't abandon him in his need. "I can't."

Kate got in his face. "Yes, you can. Let me do my job."

"Come on." Bridget pulled him by the elbow. "She'll take good care of him. You know that."

Yes, he knew. But it was Barnaby.

Bridget leaned in close and whispered, "*She'll* be with him."

That *she* being Charlie. He nodded and let Bridget lead him back to the employee lounge. She directed him to the couch where he promptly collapsed onto the cushions.

"I'm going to get a container and head on out. Are you going to be okay?"

No, he was not okay. He was numb all over. "Is he going to die?"

* * * *

Bridget sat beside Rob. Seeing Barnaby sick wrenched her heart, seeing Rob despondent even more so. "I don't know."

He covered his face with his hands and hunched over. A sob escaped.

"Oh, Rob." She hugged him and he turned into her, burying his head into her shoulder, holding her tight.

He had no one left. His parents were gone, his sister. And now Barnaby? She couldn't imagine what he must be feeling. She offered comfort as he had with her in the past.

He pulled away, keeping his head low. "I'm sorry. I know he's just a dog."

"Hey, don't say that. You love him. We all do. Kate will do her best, you know that."

"I know." He swiped his eyes with the back of his hand. "Do you need a ride?"

A ride? "Oh… No, thanks. I can walk. You stay here."

He stood and stared at her, his eyes red and dark. "I can't sit here and do nothing. Let me drive you."

"Okay, sure. Let me get the container." Bridget rushed to the supply cabinet and snatched a plastic cup with a lid.

They arrived at the house in silence and Bridget walked to the side gate, where Rob had said he found Barnaby. She found where the dog had thrown up. Instead of being green with grass, which she expected, it was reddish-brown.

"Rob? When did you feed Barnaby meat?"

He'd been looking out over the yard and spun toward her at the question. "Last night. Why?"

She scooped up what she could and then stood. "It looks like he threw up raw meat. Look around the yard and see if you can find any more."

She examined the edge of the fence and walked toward the back. If what she suspected was true, someone had intentionally set out to harm the dog.

"Bridget." Rob stood by the pool, looking down. He swatted the air as if an insect pestered him.

Stepping carefully, she arrived at his side. What he found was small, probably the size of a golf ball, but it brought chills down Bridget's spine—raw hamburger, covered in flies.

"I'm going to get a plastic bag. Kate's going to want to see this."

He grabbed her arm. "What is it?"

"I don't want to guess. Let's get it to Kate."

She found a Ziploc bag and collected the ball of meat. Rob searched the yard for more, but came up empty.

They returned to the clinic in silence. She left Rob in the break area and headed back to Kate. Barnaby lay on the table, his eyes closed and breaths slow. He seemed at peace.

"How is he?"

"I've got him sedated right now. I won't know for a while. You get the sample?"

Bridget nodded and handed them over. "We also found some raw hamburger in the backyard. Do you think it's strychnine?"

"That's what it's looking like."

"Who would do such a thing?" Tori asked.

Kate shook her head. "Someone who doesn't like animals? Who knows? Rob should report it."

"I'll let him know." Bridget turned to go.

"Bridget? Stay with him, okay? I'd call Brian, but he's out of town. Unless you think I should call Carl?"

Hell's bells. He was the last person she wanted with Rob. Probably the last person Rob would want to be with, too.

"Damn, did someone just turn up the air conditioner?" Tori rubbed her arms. "It's like a freezer in here."

Charlie offered her opinion, too.

"Go check it, will you, Tori?" Kate said.

Tori left as requested, what little good that would do. Charlie had been the cause of the little freeze out, not that Bridget could feel it.

"Don't bother Carl. I'll stay with Rob." She departed, hoping her statement cooled—or would that be warmed—Charlie's jets. When she returned to the break room, Rob was sitting on the couch with his head in his hands.

He lowered his hands and then stood. "Well? What does Kate think?"

"It's looking like poison. You should probably report it."

"Shit." He rubbed his head. "How is he?"

"Too soon to tell. Do you want something to drink? I can make some coffee or get you a soda."

He sat back down. "No, thank you. Did you see him?"

"He's asleep. Kate sedated him." He looked so lost, she had to do something. "I still have to feed the animals in the back. You can help if you want. Or not."

He nodded and rose. "Okay. I mean, I'll help."

Rob walked beside her, shuffling his feet and hunching over as if he carried a heavy weight. She just wanted to hold and comfort him, but held back. That would certainly send the wrong message. Well, not so much the wrong message, but a message she didn't want him to receive.

The clinic currently housed three furry guests—two dogs and a cat—which stood when Bridget and Rob entered the room.

"The cocker is Spike, the mutt is Billy—"

"Mutt? Is that politically correct?"

She laughed. "Probably not, but I don't know what he is. Do you?"

He examined the white-and-brown pooch, which stood no taller than the cocker and sported short, curly hair. Billy's tail thumped against the enclosure and he skittered side to side in excitement. Rob stuck his fingers through the cage and got licked for his reward. "No. Guess not. What are they in for?"

Bridget lifted the bag of dog food she'd dropped at Charlie's appearance and placed it on the counter. "Owners are on vacation. You make it sound like they're in jail."

"That's what it looks like. I don't think I could…." Anguish flashed across his face.

Crap. Maybe bringing him here wasn't such a good idea. "If you're more comfortable waiting in the lounge, I'll come back when I'm finished."

"No. I'd rather not. Who's the cat?" He strolled over to the white Persian and stared into the cage.

She scooped out some nuggets and poured them into a bowl. "Mrs. Wiggins. I'd steer clear of her. She scratches."

The cat mewled as if in protest. Rob stuck his fingers in the cage and the little monster rubbed against him. "Seems friendly enough to me."

"Well, you just blew my theory out of the water."

He laughed and it lightened her heart. "What theory would that be?"

"I assumed she didn't like me because I'm a dog person. You're clearly a dog person, but she likes you well enough."

His smile morphed into a frown, and he lowered his hand. Crap. She didn't want to get him depressed again. When would she learn to shut up?

"Dammit," he said.

"I'm sorry. I didn't mean to make you think of Barnaby." She used to be better at this. Her job as a nurse had been to help, not hinder.

He stared at her. "That's not it. You reminded me of something Carl said. And I had to go egg him on. What did I do?" His eyes glistened.

His anguish went straight to her heart, propelling her to his side. She wrapped him in a hug. "This is not your fault."

He buried his face in her neck. "I put it in his head that Barnaby doesn't like him. We both know why the dog doesn't, but damn, if I had only kept my mouth shut."

"Hush. You don't know Carl did this." Although she was pretty sure he had, Rob didn't need to think that way. "It's most likely some deranged person after dogs."

"Did Charlie see anything? Maybe she knows…."

"If she knew anything, she would have told me. Why don't you go back to the lounge and call the police. Maybe that will make you feel better." She loosened her hold to release him, but he gripped her tighter.

"I've missed you, Bridget. You make me feel better."

And the feeling was mutual and not just because her headache had disappeared the second he'd arrived with Barnaby. She reveled in his scent, his strength. If only things were different.

Her mind and body were at odds where Rob was concerned and right now her body craved his closeness. Damn the consequences.

Chapter 23

Bridget made coffee while Rob sat on the couch. They'd fed the animals and walked the dogs all in relative silence, his mind most likely on Barnaby. She didn't know quite what to say about their embrace. She'd only meant to offer him comfort, not start things up again. But that hug was better than all her dreams combined. That hug was home. Didn't matter, though. She would watch what she said or did from now on. If he even got a hint of how much she cared for him, he might change his mind when, clearly, he had moved on—her trip to his voice mail the proof.

"Are you sure you don't want to go home? I'll call you as soon as I hear anything."

He exhaled as if she frustrated him, and maybe she had. "You don't have to stay on my account. I'll be fine."

"That's not what I meant. I only want you to be comfortable."

"Well, I won't be comfortable at home. Not without Barnaby there."

"Oh. I didn't think about it like that." She snatched two mugs from the cupboard and poured the hot beverage. "How do you take it?"

"Black."

Black? Yuck. Coffee wasn't coffee unless it had cream and sugar. At least she didn't have to worry whether or not she got his right. She fixed hers and carried the mugs to him. He took his and she sat on one of the chairs at the table.

"I don't bite, you know."

She chuckled. "I know."

He patted the cushion beside him. "Sit with me. Please?"

She shouldn't, but he was hurting, waiting for word on Barnaby. All the more reason to offer comfort, right? Once he heard the dog would survive, then they would go their separate ways. It was for the best.

She sat on the couch, leaving enough room for a football player to squeeze between. He shook his head, but kept quiet.

For the longest time he stared into his mug looking lost and ran his finger around the rim. What could she say that didn't sound corny?

He ended up breaking the silence. "What kind of poison do you think was in that hamburger?"

She relaxed. While talking about Barnaby wouldn't get his mind off the dog, at least he wasn't mentioning that hug. "Probably strychnine."

Back during her junior high school days, she'd seen firsthand what the poison could do. Some sicko had gone around poisoning dogs with the crap, her neighbor's dog included. They'd gotten treatment quickly for their pet, the only thing that saved him, unlike most of the other animals hit. She prayed Rob had brought Barnaby in on time.

"Shit. That's not good."

"No, but you can't look at it that way. Barnaby threw up and not because of the poison. The meat was spoiling, probably what made him sick. And you were able to get him here quickly. All those are in his favor."

"I want to wring Carl's neck."

Again with the accusation. "What makes you think he's responsible?"

"Ever since Charlie's death, Barnaby has growled at him. I never questioned it, just assumed Barnaby was having a bad day, missing Charlie maybe. But today when he growled, it dawned on me why. He was there that day, which means he knows it was Carl. Then Carl practically ordered me not to bring Barnaby in to work anymore. I kind of lost it and practically accused him of murder."

She scooted closer. "Oh, Rob. No."

"Yeah, I know. Pretty stupid move, huh? And now he's taken it out on a defenseless dog."

Bridget closed her eyes. Carl might be to blame, but Rob wouldn't have lost his temper if she'd kept her mouth shut. Barnaby had to survive. She couldn't handle another death on her conscience. "Would Carl have access to strychnine?"

"Possibly. He had a rodent problem a while back. Said he found the perfect solution, but never elaborated and I never asked. I swear, if he's involved…."

"Have you asked your investigator? Could he have been following Carl?"

Rob's face lit up as if he'd won the lottery. He put his coffee on the side table. "That's it! You're a genius."

He called the investigator and made arrangements to meet. Just as he slipped the phone into his jeans pocket, Kate entered the room.

Bridget held her breath and prayed, *Please be good news.* Any other kind would be devastating.

* * * *

He'll live.

Those were the best words Rob's ears would ever hear. And what manly man thing did he do once Kate uttered those wonderful words? Cried like a baby, what else?

He covered his face, but stopping the flow proved impossible. Barnaby would live. Relief came over him so strong, he couldn't control the dam.

He stood and hugged Kate. "Thank you."

She patted his back. "You're welcome. Now go on home. I'll be staying with him tonight."

He released the best doctor in all the world and found Bridget beside him. He took her hand. With her touch alone she gave him comfort, peace. Without her, he wouldn't have survived the last few hours.

He swiped his arm across his eyes. "Can I see him?"

"He's still sedated and is on an IV. Don't you want to wait until tomorrow?"

He shook his head. "Please. I won't be long. I just need to see him."

Kate nodded. "You know the way."

He held onto Bridget and headed down the hallway.

"Don't you want to be alone with him?" Bridget asked.

Not if he could help it. He was through with being alone. "I want you there."

Barnaby lay sleeping in the middle of a large pillow. Rob rubbed a spot above the dog's eyes and kissed him on bridge of his the nose. The contact didn't affect Barnaby in the slightest. No more spasms. Just an even breathing. What a wonderful sight to behold. Rob choked back a sob.

"You okay?" she asked.

He nodded. "I guess I never realized how much he means to me. Am I being sappy?"

"No, of course not. You love him." She sniffed.

He turned at the sound. Tears filled her eyes, too. He pulled her close. "Thank you for being with me."

"You're welcome." She pulled away and wiped her eyes. "I'm glad he'll be all right. He's a sweet dog."

Rob wouldn't let her get away again. No sirree. He'd been stupid staying away as long as he had and he would make it right. "I didn't ignore your call. When you called the first time."

"What?"

"And I was planning on seeing you tonight. To surprise you with the paneling."

"Really?"

He held her face. "Of course, really. Why would you doubt that? Haven't I made my feelings clear?"

"Yeah, but after I put you to voice mail that night, you stopped calling. I just assumed—"

"I was trying to give you some space." A mistake he would not make again.

"And you've been angry. Charlie said."

God, what else had Charlie told her? She couldn't have told Bridget the truth. That this past week had been the worst of his life and that not being able to hear her laugh, see her lovely smile, or be teased by her, had torn him up inside. And maybe he couldn't say that all to her right now—why give her a reason to run?—but he could show her how he felt.

He held her face in his hands and kissed her. She tensed and might have stopped breathing, but within moments she leaned into him and wrapped her arms around his neck. She molded against him and opened her mouth, inviting him in.

Encouraged, he hugged her closer and kissed her deeper, exploring everything she had to offer, every last sweet and delicious part of her. The way she grabbed him as if he weren't close enough gave him hope. And while he'd love nothing better than to take her right there on the floor, he wanted more than sex from her. He just wanted her.

Footsteps echoed in the hallway, bringing him back to reality. Reluctantly, he ended the kiss and smiled. "Still think I'm angry?"

"No." Bridget's cheeks were inflamed, her lips red and swollen, and she busied herself with smoothing her shirt. But she hadn't hit him and she wasn't frowning. She also hadn't told him to take a hike. Maybe, just maybe, he'd finally made headway.

* * * *

Bridget ran her fingers across her burning lips. That kiss wasn't from someone who had moved on. And she certainly didn't react like she should have. Her body sensed victory over her mind, which hadn't objected in the least.

Rob rubbed Barnaby on the head. "I'll be back tomorrow, fella. Love ya."

His mood had definitely improved and she couldn't blame him. Knowing Barnaby would be okay lifted her spirits, too. Maybe now Rob could go home.

They left the dog and headed for the lounge. He took her hand and squeezed it. "You okay to leave?"

"Yeah."

"Good. Let's go." He pulled her toward the door.

"Go? Go where?"

"To the PI's office. We've got thirty minutes."

She shouldn't go with him. She should just go home. But how could she with him so happy and her headache gone? She couldn't spoil that. Besides, it was only the private investigator, not a date. Plus, being knee-deep in the whole situation, she'd like to see it through to the end. "I need my bag."

He released her long enough for her to fetch her backpack out of her locker.

She climbed into the truck and emptiness settled over her. No Barnaby wagging his tail. No Barnaby resting his head on her lap. Was this what Rob would experience at home?

Rob climbed inside, his presence practically charging the air. Her body tingled. She needed to focus on something else. Anything else.

"Is that what you do all day? Feed the animals? Clean their cages?"

Good, he wasn't talking about their kiss. Work she could discuss. She shrugged. "I take them for walks and bathe them, too. I don't have the credentials to do much more."

"Are you happy? Working there?"

"I don't know. Does it matter? It's a job."

"So was nursing, wasn't it? Why'd you really quit?"

"Well, I had this accident…." She didn't mean to sound snarky; it just came out that way.

"But you seem capable. Is there some reason you can't be a nurse?"

Okay, maybe talking about work was a bad idea. And mentioning the headaches would be bad. He'd already freaked out after her declaration of the ones Charlie brought on.

"Before, you said you quit because you thought you were going crazy. You know better now."

"That was part of it."

"What's the other part?"

"No one wants a cranky-assed nurse, okay? I'm not the same person I was before. I just don't have the patience for it anymore."

He snorted. "Cranky-assed, huh? Okay, so what about veterinary medicine? You think you might go that route?"

"I don't know. What does it matter what I do anyway?"

"Everything you do matters to me."

Oh crap. Did he still think they were dating? Well, she hadn't told him otherwise. Good Lord, what had she gotten herself into? And why was it so hard to tell him no? He held her heart and wasn't letting go, that's why.

The truck jostled onto a driveway and came to a stop. They'd arrived at a one-story house that had been converted over to a business. Most of the homes on the main drag had done the same after the street enlarged to four lanes. The sign on the building indicated the home of Parker Investigations. Bridget slid out and met Rob at the front of the truck. He took her hand and squeezed, as if she'd bolt or something.

He let himself in and pulled her along. She loved holding his hand, but might have let go if not for the fact her body continued to ignore her mind. Not that her mind was putting up much of a fight.

The reception area was deserted. A bell sat on the counter among a pile of file folders and mail. Rob pinged it.

"Be right there!" a man called from down the hall.

Bridget's nerves got the better of her and she squirmed in her skin. She shouldn't fear this guy, because Rob would never give away her secret. At least, she was pretty sure he wouldn't.

A tall, sandy-haired man came through the back door. Wearing jeans and a faded T-shirt, which proclaimed he ran the 5K marathon, he smiled at his two visitors. Bridget couldn't make out the date on the shirt, but if this guy ran the race, it had to be many beers ago. His investigative skills must not require any muscles.

"Mr. Parker? I'm Rob Gentry. This is my friend, Bridget Quigley."

Mr. Parker, who stood a good two inches taller than Rob, held out his hand and Rob took it. "Ahh, yes. Call me Dean. You might not believe this, but I was getting ready to call you when you called. I'm glad you could make it tonight. I didn't want to come in tomorrow." He offered his hand to Bridget and Rob had to release her so she could take it. "Come on in the back. We can talk there."

No sooner had she released Dean's hand, when Rob's took its place. They followed the burly man down the hall into his office, or what used to be a bedroom. The old closet had been converted into a little alcove and contained two file cabinets with more file folders stacked on top. They all settled into chairs, Rob and Bridget in front of an old beat-up desk covered with various papers and files, which Dean slid behind.

The man had a serious filing problem.

"I think your Mr. Anders knows he's being investigated."

Damn. If Carl knew about the investigation, how would they ever catch the guy in the act?

"What makes you say that?" Rob asked.

"Oh, the way he's always looking behind him. The way he drives, as if he's trying to lose a tail."

"You didn't manage to follow him to Sycamore Lane today, did you?"

"I'm afraid not. Like I said, he drives like he's being followed and my man lost him."

Rob fell back into his chair. "Dammit. I was hoping we had him."

"Why? Did something happen today?"

Bridget squeezed Rob's hand. "Rob thinks Carl might have poisoned his dog."

"Oh? Did you call the cops? They might be able to help."

"I did earlier," Rob said. "They're checking it out. Having him spotted in the area would have been a big help."

"I'm sorry. I did look into the businesses you deal with and couldn't find him involved with any of those. Not illegally, anyway. It's possible he's working under the table, but that would require major undercover-type work, and I just don't have that kind of manpower. But if you want to go to that kind of expense, I can recommend someone."

Bridget had hoped for better news. "Are you saying he's not embezzling money from Rob's company?"

"No, just that I couldn't find any sign of it. You've had the books audited, right?"

Rob nodded.

"How about your supplies? Is it possible you're getting substandard parts at premium rates? Could be one way he's skimming you. Some of those businesses you mentioned haven't had a very good record with the Better Business Bureau. You might want to check out some of your projects and make sure you're getting what you paid for."

Rob leaned his head back. "Man. I was hoping you had better news."

"Sorry. The only surefire way to put a stop to it is to let him go. I know you said he's an old friend—"

"Was," Rob interrupted. "Not anymore."

"Then fire him. Problem solved."

Firing him might have solved Rob's business problem, but it didn't give them the proof they needed to accuse Carl of murder. And Rob hadn't seen fit to tell Dean Parker about her ability, of which she was thankful. Who would believe her anyway?

Rob thanked the man and settled his account before they left. He opened the passenger door for her and stood there while she climbed inside. He lowered his head and kicked at the gravel while he swung the door back and forth.

"I'm sorry he didn't have better news."

"He didn't have any news. If I fire Carl, we might as well give up, and I'm not ready to do that yet."

"If you fire Carl, won't he come after you?"

He shrugged. "Probably. But after next week, he won't have any reason to. Not after I tell him he's no longer in my will. So I guess I'm stuck with him until it's all finalized." He shut the door, trotted around the truck, and got in on his side. "Where would you like to eat?"

It never failed to amaze her how his mind worked. She was freaking out and he was hungry. Typical guy. "You can just take me home."

"I've seen the food at your place. Pizza it is, then." He pulled out his phone and actually ordered a pizza with the works while she sat there.

"What are you doing?" she asked.

"Listen, I may not have a degree, but I'm not stupid. Well, sometimes I am, but I learn from my mistakes and I've made several this past week I'm not about to repeat. I'm not letting you out of my sight."

"I never said you were—" His words sank in and irked her. "What do you mean you're not letting me out of your sight?"

"Exactly what I said. Carl is out there. He's not getting another chance."

"And you think I can't take care of myself? He may have attacked me before, but I know better now. I'm not stupid, either."

"I know that. But there's safety in numbers. He won't try anything if we stick together."

"So you think. You can't let him run our lives like this." Not to mention spending more time with Rob. If he planned on sticking around, there was no telling what she might end up doing.

"Better than being dead. We can discuss it over dinner. Buckle up. Gotta make it to your house before the pizza does."

She slammed the buckle into its slot and crossed her arms across her chest. How dare he act all manly macho? She wasn't some weak-assed woman who fainted at the sight of blood.

Amazing how a little anger could clear up her muddied mind.

* * * *

Rob winced at her quietness. Bridget could be a stubborn woman and maybe he'd overreacted a little, but he wasn't letting her get her way. If he could prevent her from getting hurt again, he would. She was too important.

He pulled into the driveway and turned off the engine.

"You might as well get your pizza and go home."

"I'm sorry. I didn't mean to make it sound like you couldn't take care of yourself. It's just that I'm worried. I don't trust Carl."

"Or me." She unbuckled her belt and reached for the door handle.

"Bridget, wait." Surprisingly, she stopped. "I trust you. Can't we talk about this inside?"

"No. Go home."

Home? But Barnaby wasn't there. He sighed. How did he screw this up so royally?

She stared at him and her face softened. "I'm sorry. I forgot. You can stay on the couch if you like, but not because I need protecting."

Well, it wasn't his intention to use the Barnaby card, but he'd take whatever would get him to stay. "Thank you. Does this mean you'll share my pizza?"

"Well, if you insist." She smirked.

He smiled, thankful she couldn't stay mad at him. A big point in his favor, and one he wouldn't overlook.

As he climbed out of the truck, the pizza-delivery guy pulled in behind. Rob paid for the pie and he and Bridget ate a nice dinner, but every time he broached the subject of Carl, she'd either tune him out or talk of something else. If it were anyone else—like say, his sister—he'd be frustrated beyond belief. For some reason he couldn't get mad at her.

The paneling job sat untouched as they watched TV in relative silence. She didn't seem angry any longer, more like cautious, so he made sure not to give her any reason to kick him out. At nine o'clock, she announced she was turning in. It seemed a little early, but maybe she just needed some alone time. She brought him blankets and wished him good night in such a rush, almost as if she were afraid he'd kiss her again or something. Not that it hadn't crossed his mind.

One of these days she would see the error of her ways and realize he was the best thing for her. Until that day, he would patiently wait because life without Bridget was unthinkable.

Chapter 24

After spending the last few hours watching a soccer game at a house down the street, Charlie materialized in the living room and found Rob asleep on the couch. The light from the television illuminated the room and her brother's peaceful face. He must have fallen asleep watching the tube, since he slouched against the armrest on the couch and two blankets and a pillow sat on the love seat. But what was he doing here in the first place?

She popped into her old bedroom. Bridget was curled on her side, tucked inside the covers, definitely asleep. Charlie eyed the backpack on the floor next to the door.

Ever since Rob had heard her over the phone, she'd wondered if she could do it again. She'd been solid when that occurred. That meant she only had to touch Bridget for Rob to hear her. She wanted to talk to Rob. No, she would talk to him.

Waking Bridget would defeat her purpose—this convo needed to stay private—but could she touch Bridget and not wake her? Charlie put her fingers against Bridget's neck. Warmth spread across her hand and her feet landed on the floor. Charlie smiled. She reached for the backpack.

"Dammit," she whispered. The bag was too far from Bridget's head. Ooh, but not her feet. Still touching Bridget's neck, Charlie lifted the sheet and exposed one foot. At least Bridget didn't wear socks. She had enough clothes on, though. Even in the privacy of her own room, she stayed covered. How was she not hot? When

Charlie had lived and breathed, she went to bed in the buff. Now that made for a blissful slumber.

With the way Bridget was curled, even that foot might not be close enough. Only one way to find out. Charlie solidified, causing Bridget to stir. After ensuring her roomie still slept, Charlie reached for the bag.

Still too far. Ugh. Keeping one hand on the foot, she slowly tugged the pant leg until Bridget's leg straightened. Bridget moaned and Charlie froze. Once Bridget quieted, Charlie sat on the floor and nudged her toes around the strap.

Ahh, success.

Staying solid meant she only had one hand to search inside the bag. And without any decent light, she relied on touch alone. After pulling out several wrong items, she finally hit pay dirt.

She turned on the phone and stared at it. Rob had been a name in her cell phone, not a number. She accessed the address book. Not a single number was recorded, not even Rob's. How could Bridget not have her brother's name programmed in her phone?

Going another route, she accessed the call list. A sea of numbers filled the screen. Well, duh. What did she expect? How the hell did this woman ever know who called? How was this normal?

The last outgoing number must be Rob's—Bridget hadn't called anyone since and it did seem a little familiar. She grinned as a marvelous idea popped into her head. After pushing several buttons, she laughed. Now a listing appeared in Bridget's address book and the ringtone wouldn't be boring anymore.

Teach you, Miss Bridget!

Charlie pushed send on the new listing. A few seconds later, "Cherry Pie" sounded from the living room. Now there was a song she never thought she'd hear again. A song which only proved one thing.

"Bridget? What's the matter?" Rob's voice sounded gruff and groggy.

"I was right. You do love her."

Bridget stirred and Charlie froze. Shit, she better keep her voice low or her communication would come to a quick and brutal end.

"Charlie? Where are you?"

"I'm in Bridget's room, where else? Man, I can't believe this is actually working. You can really hear me?"

"Yeah, sis, I can. Damn, I've missed you." His voice cracked and her heart ached at the sound.

If she didn't cheer up the conversation, she'd end up blubbering like an idiot. "Same here. Those one-sided conversations were getting a little old."

"Tell me about it." He chuckled and then fell silent for a moment. "I'm so sorry, sis. I should have known you wouldn't take your life."

The memory of him screaming at her dead body made her chest tighten. "Hey, I get it. You thought I relapsed because of Nick. Once a druggie, always a druggie."

He sighed through the phone. "That's no excuse."

"Don't carry this guilt around, okay? Please? It wasn't your fault."

"We'll get him, Charlie. I promise. I won't let you down again."

"Robbie, you never let me down. You're my big brother. I love you." Man, what she wouldn't give to hug him right now.

"I love you, too. Have you seen Barnaby?"

"Yeah. He's sleeping. I'm so glad he's going to be all right. I was scared."

"Me, too. You didn't see anyone put the hamburger in the yard? Like, maybe, Carl?"

"Oh, please. You think I'd keep that bit of information to myself? I wasn't even around until you and Barnaby showed up. So, what are you doing here? Is your house too lonely?"

"Partly, yes."

Just as her own home felt empty without the dog. "And the other part?"

"Carl. I'm afraid he'll come after Bridget again."

"I was right, though. You love her."

His chuckle held no mirth. "What was your first hint?"

He deserved to be happy and she would do all that she could. "I should kick her butt into gear."

"Leave her alone, okay? She'll come around."

"When? When you're an old man?"

"If that's what it takes."

The man was a fool. Maybe she should kick his butt into gear. "Robbie, there's something you need to know. She's afraid—"

"Stop it. I'm not talking to you about her."

"I was just going to say—"

"No. She'll come around on her own, you hear? Stay out of it."

Well, if she couldn't get through to Rob, then he left her no choice. Maybe if someone had pushed her where Nick was concerned, she wouldn't have wasted so much time.

They talked a bit longer. Reminiscing with her big brother was great. If she could only sit beside him on the couch and see him, touch him, it would have been perfect.

"I wish I knew about this phone thing before Nick went beyond. It would have been nice to talk to him, too."

"And how do you suppose that would have happened? Bridget can't be in two places at once."

"I'd have figured something out."

Bridget rolled over. The phone fell through Charlie's fingers and landed on the floor.

"Shit."

"Charlie? You still there?"

She stood, grabbed Bridget's foot, and picked up the phone. Bridget kicked out. Uh-oh. Better wrap this up.

"I gotta go, Robbie. If you hear Bridget scream, don't worry, she'll be yelling at me. Love you! Hope I can do this again." Charlie hit the End button and dropped the phone into the backpack.

* * * *

Something crawled on her foot. Oh, God! A spider? Bridget kicked out. Her heart thumped wildly as pain sliced through her head. She sat up and grabbed her chest.

"Relax, will ya? It's only me."

Of course. Charlie. Damn woman would eventually give her a heart attack if not an aneurysm. "What are you doing? Isn't landing on me enough for you? Now you have to play footsies?" Although to admit the truth, Charlie was a whole bunch better than a spider.

"Be quiet. You want to wake up Robbie? What's he doing here anyway?"

No, she certainly did not want that. He might come in to investigate and then Charlie would disappear as would her headache. On second thought... Still, Charlie usually didn't wake her without a reason.

Bridget kept her voice low. "I don't think he wanted to be alone." And she didn't have the heart to push him out. She had to face it—she liked having him around. "Is that why you woke me?"

"I just wanted to talk. Didn't think you'd hit the bed so early."

Bridget pointed at the clock. "It's one in the morning. How is that early?"

Charlie waved a dismissive hand. "Just wanted to give you an update on Barnaby so you could maybe call Rob about it. Instead I find a couple of old geezers. Nick and I used to stay up all night."

"Yeah, I'm sure you did. So how is he?"

Charlie shrugged. "Robbie? How would I know?"

"Not Rob. Barnaby." Bridget fingered the pillow and nearly threw it at the ghost. Why bother? She'd only hit the wall.

"Oh. Yes. Well, he's sleeping still. But he sure looks a lot better than before. More peaceful. I heard Kate say it's a miracle he's doing so well. I like to think I had something to do with that."

"You did. You saved his life."

Charlie straightened. "Yeah, I guess I did. Now maybe I can save yours."

"I didn't realize I was dying."

"Not from death, you idiot. From loneliness. You got a man out there, a freaking fantastic one I might add, who loves you and you're throwing him away."

Bridget fell back into the bed and pulled up the covers. She was not having this conversation. "Good night."

"Do you ever wonder why you survived?"

"I wonder every day."

"And?"

Hell's bells. Had she said that out loud? Now she'd never shut Charlie up. "And nothing. There's no reason I lived and Suzie didn't. Period. Now let me sleep."

"No, not period. I thought you were smart. You died and came back. Came back with a wonderful gift. Why can't you see that?"

Bridget sat up on her elbows and stared at her so-called gift. "This wonderful gift is a pain in my head and ass and I wish it would go away."

"You're being awfully selfish. I'm glad you have the gift. I'm glad someone is fighting for me, because I sure as hell can't. Do you realize how many ghosts you can probably help move on? I think maybe that's why you survived and Suzie didn't. You were more useful."

Useful? When had she ever been useful? Charlie was talking out her ass. "Leave me alone. I'm tired and want to sleep."

"And I think you were saved for Rob."

Not Rob again. Was Charlie trying to get him hitched or something? "You don't give up, do you? Have any other fairy tales you want to tell me?"

"He won't wait forever you know. Eventually he'll get tired of your games. Is that what you want? For him to go?"

No. Never. "It would be better."

"I didn't ask what was better. I asked what you want. Do you want a lonely life? Really?"

"With ghosts like you, it's not so lonely."

"Ha-ha. Very funny. How would you feel if Suzie survived and acted the way you do?"

Bridget pulled the covers up and turned her back on Charlie. Her heart ached for her lost friend. But would Suzie have felt guilty if Bridget had been the one who died? If not for Suzie's complaints, Bridget never would have driven.

"Did you know your mother feels guilty because she never taught you to drive a stick?"

Bridget sat up. "What? That's ridiculous. How would you know?"

"You'd be amazed at what people say out loud when they think the only person listening is God. She loves you, Bridget. And she's prayed for forgiveness. She believes if she had taught you to drive a stick, then you wouldn't have stalled the car and gotten hit. Basically, she thinks it's all her fault."

"But it's not her fault." Why couldn't her mother just be happy?

"Oh, then it is Suzie's fault."

Bridget pulled the sheet up over her head. "This conversation is over. Go away."

"It was her car, right? How come she wasn't driving?"

She would not take the bait. "Go away."

"Okay, then if not Suzie's fault, her husband's. I'm sure he feels especially guilty not being the one who drove her home."

Dammit. Is that why Devin kept calling? If he hadn't taken the van that day... No. He was mad. Mad at Bridget for surviving and killing his wife and child. Charlie was only messing with her mind.

"Frankly, I think you're hiding. I think you're using the accident as an excuse to keep people away. If no one is close, no one will see your scars."

"No one wants to see my scars."

"How would you know? You don't let anyone in. You think I was proud of my life when Nick came into it? But once I admitted I loved him, I was willing to do anything for him. Are you telling me you wouldn't do anything for Rob?"

Bridget's eyes stung with tears. Sure, she'd do anything for Rob. Even give him up if that was best. She sat up and faced her tormentor. "Why are you doing this? Isn't it enough I want to help you?"

"If what I'm saying isn't true, why does it bother you so much? You were granted a second chance and you're not honoring your friend by refusing the gift. I wasn't even given that much."

She made it sound so simple. Nothing was that simple.

"Get out."

"No."

Bridget grabbed the sheet and nearly ripped the material. "Get out."

"Make me."

"Getoutgetoutgetoutgetout!"

Her door flung open. Charlie vanished in the midst of laughter. Bridget's headache disappeared.

Rob—coming to her rescue once again. Was that Charlie's plan? Oh God, what was she going to do?

He stood in the doorway. Part of her yearned to run into his arms. The other part itched to hide under the covers. She hugged her legs, unsure which part would win.

* * * *

Rob ran a hand through his hair. Damn Charlie. Why couldn't she just leave Bridget alone? Because whenever Charlie had an agenda, she became obsessed. Death hadn't changed her one bit.

Bridget sat on the bed, hugging her legs and keeping her head down.

He sat beside her and laid a hand on her foot. "What'd she do?"

She shook her head and took in a ragged breath.

The urge to hold and comfort her was strong, but he didn't want to agitate her further. "I'm sorry she's upset you. Why don't I stay so she doesn't bother you again? I can sit on the floor until you fall asleep. I promise I won't sleep until you do."

She remained silent, hugging her legs, creating a barrier between them.

The hell with it. If she pushed him away, she pushed him away. Rob pulled her into his arms. "Don't listen to Charlie, okay? She doesn't know everything."

He held his breath for a moment, waiting for her rejection. None came.

She relaxed in his arms. "Why do you put up with me?"

He leaned back and held her face. "You have it all wrong. I don't think I'm putting up with anything."

"Your life would be so much easier without me in it."

"And not near as fun." He kissed her forehead, stood and held up the sheet. "Go back to sleep. I won't let her bother you anymore tonight." He wagged his finger back and forth for his sister's benefit, just in case she remained in the room.

Bridget took his arm and pulled him back to the bed. "Not the floor."

Not the bed, either. How many times had he screwed that up? "Bridget, honey, I don't have that kind of—"

She put her fingers against his mouth—cutting him off—and stared into his eyes. "What would make you happy?"

That was easy. He took her hand and smiled. "For you to be happy."

"What if that's not possible?"

"Bridget, I won't venture a guess how much your friend's death has affected you. You're still grieving, but I promise, it won't last forever. I'm here for you. Do you understand? I'm not going anywhere."

"Do you believe in fate? Do you believe things happen for a reason?"

"Are you asking me if I think there's a reason you lived and your friend didn't? I can't answer that. But I'm glad you survived, because I can't imagine never knowing you. You've filled in a part of my life I didn't even realize I lacked." He placed her hand over his heart. "With you I'm whole."

Would she notice the rapid beating of his heart? He couldn't make out her expression, since he blocked the light from the hall and the streetlamp outside barely filtered through the window.

She hugged him around the neck and whispered into his ear. "I want to be happy. I just can't remember how."

His heart filled with hope. She wasn't pushing him away.

Chapter 25

Bridget closed her eyes and reveled in Rob's embrace. Her life had been an empty shell even before the accident. Then he popped into her life and filled her up.

Charlie was right. Suzie would have hated anyone dwelling on her death. So full of life, she had lived it to the max and would have been angry at Bridget for acting selfish. And if Suzie had lived, she would have been ecstatic that Bridget found Rob.

They were destined to meet, of that Bridget was certain. Now she couldn't imagine her life without him in it.

And he still wanted her, even after all the crap she'd put him through. Patience had never been a virtue of hers, but if she could learn to be half as patient as he, she'd be a better person.

His stubble scratched her face, but she liked the feeling and rubbed against him. A trace of his cologne or aftershave lingered—some woodsy, musky scent. It suited him perfectly. She kissed his neck, his skin like fire on her lips.

"Bridget, I don't think—"

His voice had cracked and she placed a hand across his lips, pulled away and stared at his face. What little light filtered into the room lit up his eyes. Eyes she could gaze at forever.

She kissed him and he tensed. Not that she could blame him. How many times had he initiated a kiss only for her to slam on the brakes? Well, she wouldn't stop him again. Never again.

He held her shoulders and slowly scooted away. His rejection cleared her head. Oh God, Charlie was right. She'd waited too long.

He cleared his throat. "I'm sorry for pushing you. It's just that… Ah, hell. You don't have to do this for me. I'm not going anywhere. I can wait. I will wait. For however long you need."

Her heart filled with hope. "You still want me?"

He smiled and ran his thumb across her cheek, sending an electrifying warmth through her body. "Bridget, honey, I always want you." He laughed deep. "Don't ever doubt that. But I don't want you doing something you're not into."

Her body ached for him. In a bold move, she shifted so she straddled his lap, his erection pressed against her. Wanting him more than ever, she wrapped her arms around his neck and brushed her lips against his. "I want you, too."

He hesitated. Shit. Had he changed his mind? Then he grasped her head and claimed her mouth. His sheer possessiveness set her heart alight. She welcomed his tongue as he explored her mouth. She'd never needed anyone like she needed Rob. He was air to her.

He lowered her and cupped her breast. Her nipples hardened. Even through the fabric of her shirt, his touch ignited her. She arched into him as he kissed his way along her jaw and down her neck. But when he lifted her shirt, her instincts kicked in and she froze. She'd do anything to take it back.

He pulled away. "It doesn't matter to me, Bridget. If you're not ready…."

Damn, the man was a prince and she loved him even more. "That's not it."

She sat up. Her heart was hammering. She could do this. After a quick breath, she slipped the shirt over her head and tossed it on the floor. Darkness was her friend. She repeated this mantra in her head and relaxed. She reached for his shirt. He obliged and removed it. Now darkness was her enemy, but she had no one but herself to blame there.

She kissed him and smoothed her hands over his chest, feeling a light dusting of hair. His skin was hot, his muscles hard. There was only one muscle she craved at the moment, though.

He nuzzled his way down her body, stopping at her breast. "You're perfect. Just the right size." Using his tongue, he played with the hard nub and she moaned in pleasure. Damn, they were wearing too many clothes.

She found the button to his jeans and slipped it through the hole. As she reached for the zipper, he placed a hand over hers.

"Let me. If you touch me right now I might explode and there's no way I want this to end that quickly."

She didn't want anything to end right now either, so she bit back her disappointment at not touching him and settled for enjoying the ride.

He removed the rest of his clothes and then worked at removing hers. Slowly, he slid her pajama pants off, inch by agonizing inch, taking her panties along with them. He came so close to touching the scars on her thigh and she did her best not to tense, but he must have sensed something and avoided the area completely. Once her garments were discarded, he spread her legs and kissed the inside of one thigh, then the other. He continued in this fashion on his way up to her apex.

"You're so wet and you smell so good." He licked her. "Taste good, too."

She held her breath. With each lick, the anticipation was exhilarating, but torturing, and she grabbed on to the sheets. Using his tongue, he flicked her clit and the breath she held burst from her mouth.

Pressure built inside, like one humongous wave. She rode it as long as she could, avoiding each crest, enjoying the wild and wicked things he did to her with his tongue. He inserted one finger, then two inside her. He sucked on her bundle of nerves. The wave broke, sending her into oblivion.

She screamed.

He covered her mouth with his, and she tasted herself. She jerked as the orgasm waned. He continued kissing her until she stopped shuddering.

The chuckle tickled her cheek. "I didn't know you were a screamer."

She hadn't either. "I'm sorry."

"Don't be. I love it."

"You do?"

He smoothed her hair from her face and ran his thumbs across her temples. "Hell, yeah. I love making you lose control. I love everything about you." He kissed her lightly on the lips. "I love you."

He tensed, probably afraid of her response. And why wouldn't he be? Had she ever given him any encouragement to think otherwise? He was the kind of person who would jump in with both feet, whereas she would start with one toe, then another. And where had that gotten her? Maybe it was time to take a leap. "Oh, Rob."

"Don't say any—"

"I love you, too." She held his face, proving her sincerity, because she meant every word. "I think I've been in love with you since that stupid softball game."

His smile under her palms brought tears to her eyes. She'd actually made him happy.

"And I've loved you since you sat that muddy body of yours inside my truck." He kissed her with such passion, she nearly stopped breathing.

He'd lit a fire in her she wasn't sure could ever be extinguished. When he nudged his erection against her, she nearly burst with need. "I need you inside of me."

"Hold on a sec." He pulled away and bent toward the floor, in the process his penis rubbed against her leg.

She took this opportunity and wrapped her hand around his erection. Good Lord, would he even fit in her? It'd been a while since her last time.

He hissed in a breath. "Oh geez, Bridget. Not yet."

Now who had the control? But she reluctantly released him. He retrieved his jeans, yanked his wallet out, and pulled out a condom.

"You always carry one of those with you?"

He dropped the jeans and placed his wallet on the nightstand. "Only since meeting you. Remember, Boy Scout here." He poked at his chest. "Always prepared."

The packet gave him some fits and she took it from him, opening it with ease. She pulled the slippery thing out and rolled it over his penis, enjoying the sounds of his moans as she touched him. After she'd finished, he lowered himself over her. He ravished her with another kiss while he pressed into her slowly as if she were fragile.

Wrapping her legs around him, she urged him on. He pushed his way, bit by bit, until he filled her completely. She nearly came from his size alone, every nerve ending on fire. As her body adjusted and accepted him, she relaxed and enjoyed the ride. She ran her hands over his nipples, exciting them into little buds and placed her mouth over one.

He jerked. "Damn, that feels good."

She continued her explorations of what he liked and didn't—and so far he liked everything. Each thrust, rubbing against her sensitive clit, became more urgent than the last. She lost control. Her breath came in gasps and she leaned her head back.

"Oh God, Bridget. You're so tight."

The orgasm struck hard and she inhaled for one wicked scream, but Rob was there, covering her mouth with his. She grabbed his shoulders. Dug in her nails. He continued driving into her, prolonging the sweetest orgasm of her entire life. She was still shuddering as he arched his back and cried out. His biceps bulged as he came.

A warm, peaceful feeling settled over her, wrapping her like a soft blanket. Rob was hers. A part of her heart, the other half of her soul. All this time he'd been right there and she'd been so stupid pushing him away. Not anymore. She would never let him go.

Chapter 26

Light shone through the small window and left a path across the bed. Rob spooned Bridget as they lay under the sheet, on their left sides, his erection snuggled between her warm legs. He couldn't remember the last time he'd slept so well or been so contented.

Still, there was this issue regarding her scars.

He hadn't seen anything in the dark, but suspected, when she'd tensed, he'd come close to touching them. Since he'd aimed at getting her relaxed and comfortable, he avoided the area. But now that it was morning, he hoped to God she wouldn't hide them from him. Not that he was obsessed. Far from it. Lord knew he'd acquired enough scars of his own. Somehow he would get her at ease around him, to trust him. To feel safe and know any flaws, scars, or whatever, made no difference. He loved her and nothing would change that.

Bridget stirred and wiggled her butt. "You got a present for me?"

Man, if she kept that up, she'd have a present on her ass. He kissed her temple. "Good morning."

"Yes, it is." She pulled the sheet over her shoulder, then turned, facing him. He missed the warmth of her legs, but her grip on his dick more than made up for that. He gasped in pleasure. "You ready for round two?" she asked.

"I'd love to, but I'm fresh out of condoms." Which was true enough, but not the real reason behind his rejection. Daylight meant Charlie could see them.

"Some Boy Scout you are." A wicked smile spread across her face. "Well, maybe I can improvise."

She scooted down his body, keeping the sheet around her shoulders. And while he wouldn't mind her mouth on his dick, Charlie could be standing right beside them and that thought alone took him to Limp City. Making sure the sheet stayed around her—mustn't have her flee quite so soon—he grabbed her upper arms and pulled her back up. "Gimme a kiss."

The radiant smile on her face warmed his heart. "Gladly."

Her lips were soft and he tried keeping it PG, but who was he kidding? Anytime he kissed her, he grew aroused. Then her breasts pressed into his chest and that was it. Morning wood hell, this went straight to X-rated.

"You sure you don't want me to take care of it?" She ground her belly against him.

Saying no became difficult. "It's not that I don't want you to. It's just now it's daylight and well... I'll feel a little more comfortable at my place, if you know what I mean."

"Charlie assured me she's not a peeper, and I got the impression she'd poof out of here at the first sign of a kiss, but I understand. I'm guessing she's still with Barnaby, though."

"But you don't know for sure."

She laughed. "No. Not unless I was alone. But I don't want to be alone right now."

She laid her head on his chest and played with his right nipple. As if that would do anything to relieve him of his erection.

He took her hand and brought it up toward his lips, but stopped halfway. Yellowish bruises encompassed her wrist. "What happened here?"

"An error in judgment. Not all ghosts are friendly."

"A ghost did this? Ghosts can touch you?"

Her eyes widened as if she had said too much. "Umm...."

"Bridget?"

"Oh crap," she mumbled.

"Did Charlie do this?"

"Oh heavens, no. She's never hurt me. Not intentionally."

"What's that supposed to mean?"

She tried to brush off her remark, said her injury came from some crazy ghost of a woman who'd committed suicide, but he wasn't buying it. Some ghost had hurt her. A ghost. Even saying it a thousand times wouldn't make it any less bizarre. Could one kill her? Damn. Now why'd he have to go and think that?

"It's no big deal, okay? Besides Charlie going past her boundaries and landing on me in the middle of the night, I can prevent this from happening again."

"Bridget, you have to be more careful. You could have been seriously hurt."

"I know. Believe me, I know. So quit worrying, okay?" She gave him a peck on the lips, then pulled the sheet tighter around her and slid off the bed. "Want some leftover pizza for breakfast?"

"Whoa, whoa, whoa, hold on there." He grabbed the sheet and pulled her back. "Do you really need this?"

She scrunched her face and bit her lip.

He sat on the edge of the bed. "Bridget, honey. Don't you trust me?"

"Yes."

"Then lose the sheet." He tugged at the opening. She resisted. "Please?"

She lowered her head, but stood still. At least she wasn't running away anymore.

"Bridget. I love you. Nothing will change that." He stood and kissed her. She melted against him and he slid a hand inside the sheet, caressing her ass. The erection he had sported earlier returned, but this wasn't about him. She had to know he found her beautiful, regardless what was under the sheet.

And if Charlie was in the room, well, so be it.

* * * *

Bridget loved kissing Rob. Loved how her body tingled and clenched and swooned. She could kiss him forever.

He grabbed her butt, his hand warm and calloused, and pulled her closer. His erection pressed against her belly. Heat radiated from every pore of his body. She ached to wrap her arms around him, but that would require losing the sheet. Her heart beat rapidly. She did trust him. Damn, she loved him. Why was it so hard to let it go?

He pulled away and held her face. His brown eyes beseeched her. "Can you drop it? For me?"

"I…I want to," she whispered.

He smoothed his hands down to her neck and massaged it. "You know you'll be more comfortable."

227

"I don't care about my comfort."

"Yeah, but I do. You gonna hide from me forever?"

She pressed her forehead against his chest and moaned. All she had to do was let go. Let go of her fears. Let go of the sheet.

He rubbed her back. "Never mind, honey. It's okay. I'm sorry I pushed."

No, it wasn't okay. God, she was such a wimp. She wrapped her arms around his neck as the sheet puddled around her feet. The hairs on his chest tickled as she practically melded her body against his. Her heart pounded.

"Mmm, you have a nice ass, but you don't have to do this. If you need me to close my eyes, let me know."

He still gave her an out and she nearly took it.

She had acted the same way the first time she'd jumped off the diving board back when she was nine. Standing on the board and staring at the pool below, she'd spent several minutes thinking about all the things that could go wrong. It wasn't until her father had yelled at her to quit thinking, take a deep breath and jump, that she'd done it. Was that how it would always be? Someone yelling at her to get her butt in gear? Maybe she should start yelling at herself. God, she was such a wimp. No more. She could do this. Maybe.

She took a deep breath. Here went nothing.

She closed her eyes and stepped back and, just to be safe, covered her face with her hands.

Warm hands encompassed her wrists and he pulled her arms down. She kept her eyes shut and lowered her head. Watching his repulsion would have been too much.

"You're beautiful."

No, no, no.

"Bridget, look at me."

No, no, no.

"You scars aren't any worse than mine."

"What are you talking about? You only have the one scar."

"No. I showed you the one scar, but I have more. Didn't you see them?"

Was he trying to trick her into opening her eyes? His chest was perfect, nicely sculpted with a dusting of dark hair. He showed the makings of a six-pack and a trail of hair leading straight to heaven. And last night she hadn't felt any scars.

He placed her hand against his skin and the bumpy scar. "You've already felt this one." He lifted her hand to another part of his body. More puckered skin, but longer and thinner than the first. "I did this when I was eleven."

She opened her eyes. The scar ran the underside of his upper arm. "What happened?"

"Had a fight with a fence. The fence won." He pointed to his thigh where several older scars crisscrossed. "Had a run-in with a glass door when I was six. Are you disgusted?"

"No. Of course not."

"How come? They're scars. I even got one on the back of my other leg."

"I don't care about your scars. They aren't what define you."

"Thank you." He leaned over and kissed her and then pulled her left arm out. "These don't define you, either. Do I wish you weren't scarred? Sure. That would mean you were never hurt. I don't like seeing you hurt. But I'm not about to not love you because of them."

Damn him for using logic on her.

"You do have quite an interesting pattern going here," he said as he rubbed her upper arm. "Ever think about getting it tattooed?"

She laughed. "You and Charlie are definitely related. She pretty much asked me the same thing. Do you think it would make it look better?"

"I don't think it looks bad now. But if it'll make it look better to you, then maybe that's what you should do." He pulled her close. "Now, don't you feel better?"

"Yeah, I guess I do."

"Good. Then get dressed. Because if I have to keep staring at your naked body, I might just explode I want you so bad." He playfully swatted her behind.

She stared at him. God, she was an idiot. He still desired her—obvious from his erection—regardless of her scars. Probably no more than she desired him. First thing Monday she would call her doctor and get a prescription for birth-control pills. Then maybe they wouldn't need the stupid condoms.

He pulled on his jeans and zipped up. "Well, don't just stand there. Let's have some pizza. Then we can go check on Barnaby."

Her brain finally came back on line and she rummaged through her dresser, pulling out a long-sleeve T-shirt and jeans. She might be able to bare it all to Rob, but the public? Not so much.

She put on a pot of coffee and pulled the box from the fridge. To think she'd almost sent him home with this pizza. So glad she hadn't. She placed the box on the table and went to take her seat, but he grabbed her around the waist and settled her on his lap.

"I like this. Sleeping with you. Waking up with you. Having breakfast with you. I could get used to this." He pulled her head down for a kiss. His lips seared hers and a telltale lump formed under her butt.

If only they had another condom. Or two or three. Slowly, she broke the kiss and picked up a slice of pizza. "I wouldn't exactly call this having breakfast. More like leftovers."

"You know what I mean." Rob kissed her temple before reaching for a slice.

She never would have pegged him for a touchy-feely kind of man, and never thought she'd want one, but sitting on his lap felt right.

"I was wondering," he said. "You say Charlie can be solid when she touches you. Do you think if she wrote a note saying she knew Carl killed Nick, that maybe it would be enough to get the cops interested?"

"Probably not. Where would you have found this note so long after her death? And why wouldn't she have just told you? I don't think the police would buy that story."

"We gotta do something. I don't think I can go back to work and not hurt him."

The coffeepot beeped and she gave Rob a brief kiss before leaving the warmth of his lap. After she filled two mugs, she returned with a smile on her face. He was still hard for her. She could get used to this, too. Probably a lot faster without Carl hanging over them like a black cloud. If only…

"What if I flush him out?" she asked. "Tell him I know what he did. Then when he comes after me—"

"No way!" He'd only gotten the mug halfway to his mouth when he dropped it as if the item had become too heavy. Coffee splashed. "I'm not putting you in danger like that."

She grabbed a napkin and wiped up the mess. "How about I just get him to confess? We could record—"

"No! I don't want you near the man. You hear me? Dammit, Bridget. I just got you. I don't want to lose you." He squeezed her so tight he nearly cracked a rib.

Okay, no more voicing those opinions aloud. She caressed his face and gave him a little kiss. His lips were tight at first, but softened, and he loosened his hold on her. The worry lines still marred his forehead. She needed another plan. "How about Henry?"

He rolled his eyes. "I'm not putting him in danger, either."

"Not that. I mean, maybe he remembers if Carl visited the day of Charlie's death. Maybe he saw him around the house on Friday. If not him, maybe someone else in the neighborhood saw Carl. Maybe all we need is a witness of Carl's whereabouts."

Rob rubbed his forehead. "Damn, I wish I had thought of that sooner. Then maybe Barnaby would have been spared."

"Probably not. You couldn't have gone to the cops before, but now we have something to report."

Rob smiled and gave her a gentle squeeze. "I knew there was a reason I loved you so much. I sure hope someone is as nosey as Mr. Murdock."

"You have a picture of Carl?"

His smile turned mischievous and he smoothed her hair away from her face. His fiery touch branded her soul. "I do. At my house."

"At your house?" she whispered as she closed her eyes. He continued caressing her cheek and neck, and she could think of nothing but his fingers touching her everywhere. Then it hit her. At his house. The home of his condoms. She snapped her eyes open and stared at his wonderful brown ones. "When do you want to leave?"

* * * *

Rob climbed into the truck near tears. He'd been told Barnaby would be okay. Charlie had told him. Kate had told him. Bridget had told him. But seeing the dog wag his tail after he and Bridget had entered the room had been the proof he needed and it wrenched his heart. If it weren't for Kate in the room, he would have broken down in relief. But one breakdown in front of her was one breakdown too many.

Now in the truck with Bridget, he felt as if he could let his guard down and she would still see him as He-Man. Wouldn't think any less of him. And boy, did his guard come crashing down. His heart pounded and tears threatened to fall. He rested his forehead on the steering wheel.

Damn, if he could react this way to a dog, how could he survive without Bridget? It scared him how important she'd become in his rather empty life. And she wanted to confront Carl? Why not just shoot him through the heart and get it over with?

She rubbed his back. "What's the matter? Kate said you'd be able to take him home tomorrow."

Dammit, Rob, man up already. He straightened and blinked back the moisture in his eyes. "Nothing's the matter," he snapped. "You ready to go?"

"Sure."

The cab became eerily quiet. They were headed to his place to have wild sex. He was sure of it. So why'd he have to go and spoil the mood? "I'm sorry. I didn't realize how much Barnaby affected me. I didn't mean to snap."

Bridget stared at her lap. "Don't be sorry. You love him. I understand. Would you like me to drive?"

"No. I'm good." He started the truck and drove off. "Wait a minute. I thought you were afraid to drive."

"I'm not afraid. I have my license. I just don't have a car."

"But you never look outside the windows."

"I told you before, I'm a distraction."

She had and he hadn't pressed her at the time. "And how are you a distraction?"

She ran her fingers along the door handle, drawing imaginary curlicues. "When I was ten, my mother rear-ended a car. So when I'm a rider, I'm a little jumpy and I grab the dashboard. That kind of thing."

"Did you get hurt?"

"Yeah. Seat belt wasn't secure and I hit the dash."

"That's why you double-check your seat belt."

"Wouldn't you?"

"I guess I would. But grabbing the dash won't bother me. My mother did that."

"Nah-ah. You're just saying that."

"Nope. Scout's honor." He held up three fingers together. "So who said you were a distraction?"

It became quiet in the cab, besides the road noise. He'd almost changed the subject when she spoke. "Suzie. It's why I was driving her car in the first place."

"What? You're telling me Suzie complained about you being a passenger, but had no problem with you driving a car you weren't comfortable in? During a snowstorm? Sounds more like she needed an excuse for you to drive."

"It wasn't snowing when she asked. She didn't want to drive. She was eight months pregnant."

"Come on, Bridget. She talked you into driving by making you feel guilty. Now you feel guilty because she died while you drove her car. Am I right?"

"I could have refused, though. I didn't."

"I'm betting you told her no and she insisted. And you, being you, obliged." He glanced in her direction. She scrunched her brow, but kept her head down. He reached over and grasped her hand. "You will not be a distraction to me. Well, you *are* a distraction, but for a whole 'nother reason."

She chuckled, tilted her head, and looked at him sideways. "You're not lying to me about your mother?"

"Hey, did I not give you Scout's honor? Besides, I wouldn't do that to you."

He pulled into his driveway. They climbed out of the truck and headed for the front door. She took his hand. It was the first time she'd ever initiated anything and that little gesture filled his heart with love.

"How is it you've never been snatched up by someone? You're like the perfect guy."

"I'm far from perfect. Don't put me too high on that pedestal. I don't want to get hurt when I fall."

"But you are. You hardly lose your temper. You're the calmest, most patient person I know. Any woman would be crazy to have you."

And many women had tried, but he hadn't been ready to settle down. Plus, the women never did anything emotional for him. Sure, the sex was good, but when they'd expected more than he could offer, he ended the relationship. He hadn't believed in love or that it could hit him as hard as it had with Bridget. "I seem to recall losing my temper when you were getting stitched up."

"Yeah, but I kind of deserved that."

"As for other women, well, no one compares to you." He smoothed her hair behind her ear. "I think we're perfect for each other."

"Like soul mates."

He smiled. "You believe in that?"

She cupped his face and pulled him down for a kiss. Her lips were soft and ripe for plucking and his dick responded.

She broke the kiss and smiled. "Oh, yes. I definitely believe in soul mates."

That might explain the connection he'd felt from their first meeting. The connection he was feeling right that minute. Suddenly, the bedroom was too far. So was the front door.

She took his hand and tugged. "Come on. You still have to show me around the house."

Around the house? Hell. That could wait.

Chapter 27

Rob opened the door and tossed his keys on the foyer table. "That's the living room. You've seen the kitchen and family room. Come on."

Bridget laughed as he pulled her up the stairs. "What's the hurry?"

He was about to burst through his zipper. "You wanted to see the upstairs, didn't you?"

"Actually, I just want to see your bedroom."

"Okay, now you're talking." Tugging her along, he grinned until a lone sock stared at him from the landing. Oh crap, the bedroom. At the top of the stairs he quickly pocketed the sock and turned toward her. "I…uh…can you give me a minute?"

"And if I say no?" She tilted her head and smiled.

Was this a challenge or a form of torture? Well, two could play that game. He pushed her against the wall and kissed her deeply. She tasted so sweet and it only got him hotter. He tore himself away panting. "Then we'll just do it in the hallway."

She gasped. He liked how he took her breath away. Now to get her to scream.

"You keep the condoms in the hallway?"

Shit. "No." He hung his head. There was no getting out of this. If he went into his bedroom to get one, she'd only follow.

"It can't be that bad."

"I hate to wreck that perfect image you have of me."

"Maybe I want to see the real Rob."

"Thing is, it doesn't look like the real me. I had a pretty rough week. Let me just straighten it." He pleaded with his eyes. She had to reconsider.

"Don't be silly. I'll help. Which room is yours?"

He knew he'd fall from her pedestal, just not so soon. After one look at the mess, she'd run screaming from the house. Well, maybe not screaming, but he'd be lucky if he could talk her into coming back. He lowered his head and sighed. "The one on the right."

She intertwined her fingers in his and peered up at him, smiling. "You're cute when you're nervous."

Nervous? Hell, yes. But cute? He'd take it if it meant she wouldn't run away. Then again, she hadn't seen the room yet.

"Come on." She tugged at him to follow. When she'd peeked inside, she stopped. "Are your drawers full?"

The laundry he'd done earlier in the week wasn't folded inside the dresser nor hung in the closet. No, he'd been too lazy for that. Instead, he'd dumped his clothes on top of his dresser in one big heap and yesterday had tossed the pile on his bed so he could find some socks to wear.

It didn't help the bed was unmade, too.

"I meant to put those away." Eventually. Maybe. When he got around to wearing them.

Bridget stepped up to the bed, picked up a T-shirt and folded it. No running or screaming. Maybe that pedestal wasn't so tall.

She turned toward him, holding another shirt up to her chest in the midst of a fold. "Are you going to let me do this all by myself?"

Oh shit. "No. Stop. You don't have to do any of this." He took the shirt from her hand. "I'll just put them back on the dresser for now."

Bridget picked up another shirt. "I don't think you noticed, but that would drive me nuts. It won't take long if we both do it."

Now that she mentioned it, her house was rather tidy.

Normally, he would just fold shirts in quarters, but wanting to impress, he folded it like she'd demonstrated—sort of. Where her folds looked professionally done, his looked worse than a four-year-old's attempt. If only she would do all the folding while he put everything away. But how would that make him look if he suggested it? Probably get him buried under that pedestal.

She snatched the shirt from his hand, giggling. "Why don't you let me fold and you put away?"

Thank God! He took the clothes she folded and placed them in the drawers and shook out the shirts meant for the walk-in closet. She asked if he ironed them. If he admitted the truth, she might get it in her mind to do it herself. Not that he owned an iron. His mother probably had, but if the sucker still existed, the location was a mystery to him. One of these days he would have to go through the house and donate his parents' clothes. Maybe he could get through it with Bridget's help.

But not today.

After hanging his shirts in the closet, he returned to the bedroom. Bridget had pulled the covers off the bed and sat in the middle of the king-size mattress. Daylight poured in through the windows above the headboard and bathed her in soft light. She looked like an angel.

His angel.

He crawled up her body and kissed her. "Do you need me to darken the room?"

She shook her head and kissed him back. Her velvety tongue mingled with his. He reached for her shirt just as the house phone rang. He ignored it and kissed along her jaw.

"Don't you have to get that?" she asked.

He nuzzled her neck and fondled a breast. "Nah. Machine will get it."

After four rings, the phone silenced. There was a pause, then a beep.

"Rob! It's Rafe. Call me ASAP."

Rob sat up. Rafe wouldn't call unless it was an emergency. But why didn't he use Rob's cell?

"Who's Rafe?" she asked.

Rob pulled his phone out. "He's the foreman at the Taco Bell project."

"You're building a Taco Bell? That's so cool."

"Not so cool if there's a problem." Rob tapped the screen on the phone and got nothing. Damn. No wonder Rafe called the house. "My charger's downstairs. I'll be right back." He kissed her, which was a huge mistake. The more he tasted her the more he wanted her. He went in for more, but she pushed him away, breaking the kiss.

"I'll be here when you return. I promise. Now go."

Rob hightailed it downstairs. The sooner he got this resolved, the sooner he could get back to Bridget. He plugged in his cell and turned it on. Problem with keeping phone numbers on the cell meant Rob didn't know Rafe's number off the top of his head, so no calling him back on the house phone.

He got in touch with Rafe, who informed him that two of the workers had failed to show. With a deadline fast approaching, Rob couldn't afford to be late on the project. He told Rafe he'd be there as soon as he could. Working on a Saturday was usually no big deal. He'd done it enough in the past. But now Bridget was in his life. Dammit. So much for spending the whole day with her.

He trudged up the stairs and found Bridget sitting on the edge of his freshly made bed.

"I hope you don't mind. I had a feeling we weren't staying."

"I'm sorry. I can't afford to be late on this project."

She stood and wrapped her arms around his waist. "It's okay."

He kissed the top of her head and reveled in her floral scent. "I'll drop you off at home."

She pulled away, frowning. "Can't I come with you?"

He liked that she wanted to go, but… "I'll be working. Won't you be bored?"

"I got a book in my pack. Besides, I really don't want to face Charlie any time soon and I'd like to see what you do."

"Well then, let's go." He put out his elbow and she took it. They'd arrived at the top of the stairs when his brain kicked in. "Wait a minute." He rushed inside the bedroom and yanked open the nightstand drawer. He pulled out half the condoms from the box.

"Gee. How many women do you bring here?"

He supposed it did look suspect as he owned the economy-sized box of condoms. Truth was he'd been dry for nearly a year and he certainly wouldn't have brought any women to this house while his parents lived here. "Just you."

"What about Tori?"

"I told you, I didn't date her. I haven't gone out with anyone since my parents died. Believe it or not, I bought these for us."

"What if I hadn't come around?"

He stepped up to her and stroked her cheek. "You keep forgetting. I wasn't giving up. I knew sooner or later you *would* come around. I'm just glad it was sooner rather than later." He held several strands of packets. "Now, where's your backpack?"

She laughed. "Downstairs. Don't forget we want pictures of Carl, too."

The bookcase in the family room held all the photo albums. Rob opened the book that contained the cruise pictures. Blinking back tears, he turned slightly away, hoping Bridget wouldn't notice his weakness. Damn. He hadn't expected to get overemotional seeing his parents stare out at him, but they looked so happy together, and Mom had always said she couldn't live without Dad. Why, Rob had no idea. He loved his father, but the man had been mean at times. Still, he missed them both. Even their fights.

Bridget stared at the photos. "You look like your father."

Same thing his mother always said. He found a picture of Carl and his lady friend and handed it to Bridget. "Here, put this in your backpack."

"I'll ruin it. Don't you have any snapshots?"

He shoved the picture at her. "I don't know. Doesn't matter. Just take it."

Carefully, she inserted the photo into the bag. "Is she Carl's wife?"

"No. She died of cancer when Nick was a kid. I have no idea who the woman in the picture is." Rob had never kept up with Carl's sex life. Too much like thinking about his parents having sex, which he'd rather not do.

"Too bad. Maybe she knows something that will help us."

Short of asking Carl straight out, Rob wasn't sure if anyone could help them. Their only hope—find someone who'd spotted Carl nosing around the neighborhood.

* * * *

Charlie waved bye-bye to Barnaby, but he slept and didn't see her. Knowing he would be okay filled her with happiness.

She floated through the back wall and met a brilliant blue sky. Not a cloud in sight. Taking advantage of seeing and not feeling the wonderful day, she took flight and floated back to her house. Below, Carl climbed over the fence into the yard. The vet took up most of the property behind Charlie's house, so she had no backdoor neighbors, making it easy for him to travel without crossing into anyone's yard.

She lowered to the creep and air-punched him, wishing one of her swings connected. What the hell was he doing now? Looking to poison Barnaby again? Because he'd done it—she knew it in her being. Ooh, if she could get her hands on that bastard, she'd squeeze his neck until he joined her.

Carl picked up a black duffel-type bag and headed for the pool. He opened the bag and pulled out a rubber snake with a cord out the back. If Rob saw this sucker, he'd probably avoid it for good.

Rob hated snakes and had ever since she'd put one in his sleeping bag. Who knew she had such power over her brother? Or how fun it would be? Of course, no one ever found out. Her father would have skinned her alive. It was the best secret she'd ever kept.

The black-hearted bastard placed the snake into the tall grass. He laid the cord, camouflaging it all the way to the outlet behind the pool, where he plugged it in. Once he finished, only the snake's head and upper portion could be seen.

The stupid thing didn't move or light up or anything, so why the plug? Carl picked up the bag, zipped it, and carried it to where he'd landed. Then he hoisted the bag over the fence. With more agility than Charlie would have credited the guy, he grabbed hold of the fence and climbed back over. She followed him to the next street, where he'd parked his truck. After he drove off, she popped back over to the house.

She needed to warn Bridget, but there was no sign of her or Robbie. Where were those two anyway? They'd seemed awfully cozy back at the vet's. Did her little talk do some good? Maybe she had come on hard, but Bridget needed a good swift kick in the butt.

It saddened her to think she might never see her big brother get married or have children. Actually, if she were still around to witness all that, she might become one of those grumpy, mean ghosts, and then Bridget wouldn't have anything to do with her. But she couldn't leave while Carl ran around free. It wasn't right. It wasn't fair.

* * * *

The air warmed up, but not as hot as it had been on Memorial Day. Rob had tossed a lounge chair in the back of the truck and Bridget placed it in a shaded area, away from any danger. The workers fascinated her, one in particular, and the book remained in her backpack untouched.

Now that Rob knew she didn't mind driving, he asked if she'd pick up lunch. A few of the men overheard and asked the same. She hadn't driven since she'd gotten her license back and it felt good being behind the wheel. As soon as she earned the money, she would buy a car. Something big, though. No more compacts.

Around four o'clock, the men stopped working and cleaned up. Rob pulled his T-shirt off and wiped his face, but her gaze stayed glued to his torso. His skin glistened. Watching him all afternoon had given her an appetite and if she wasn't careful, she might start the main course right here.

And to think she'd been pushing him away. She *should* get her head examined.

"You ready to go?" he asked.

"You're all sweaty."

"Yeah." He placed his hands on the armrests of her chair and bent down for a kiss. His lips tasted salty. "Is that good or bad?"

Good if they were alone, bad they weren't. "Can I tell you in private?"

He smiled. "Sure. How 'bout the shower? We could go back to my place."

Ooh, a shower with him would be heaven, but the outdoors sounded better. "How about a swim instead?"

He straightened and wiped his chest and back with the shirt. "Sounds good, but I haven't cleaned the pool."

"I have." Amazing what sexual frustration could do to a person. Cleaning the pool had expended a lot of that energy.

He nodded. "Okay. We'll still have to go back to my place for my trunks."

She stood and ran a finger down his arm. "The yard's fenced in. Who's going to see?"

"Lady, I like the way you think." Desire filled his eyes and in one quick movement, he pulled her in for another kiss. She'd just wrapped her arms around his neck when he broke it off. "Umm, what about Charlie?"

"Trust me. She's not going to be a problem. Would you want to watch your sister?"

"I think you ruined a perfectly good boner."

She laughed at the look of disgust on face. Soon, he joined her.

Life with Rob was more fun than she'd dreamed possible. She wished the weekend would never end.

* * * *

Rob pulled into the driveway and brought the truck to a jerky stop. Man, her idea of love in the pool got him a kind of hard that wasn't going away until he had his way with her.

"Afraid we've got a visitor," Bridget said, staring out her window.

He followed her gaze and sure enough, old Mr. Murdock was ambling his way across the yard. Of all the dirty rotten timing. "Can you get rid of him?"

"Now, Rob. He's an old man and he's lonely. It won't hurt to say hello. Besides, I want to show him Carl's picture. Maybe he saw him lurking around on Friday."

She had a point, but why now? They could do it after their fun in the pool.

Bridget climbed out of the truck. "Hey, Henry. How's it going?"

"Hi, Bridget. It's such a wonderful day, thought I'd go for a walk. I was coming to ask if you wanted to join me, but I can see you're busy. Hi, Rob."

Rob smiled and waved, but kept his mouth shut. The sooner this was over, the better.

"Sorry. Maybe next time," she said. "Since you're here, I have something to show you."

As she opened her backpack, Rob stared at her lush curves. He craved running his hands over her breasts, then taking one in his mouth. Damn. That thought had his dick rubbing his jeans to the point of pain. He moved behind her. No sense in having the old man snicker at his bulge.

She pulled the photo out. "Have you seen this man around the neighborhood yesterday or Thursday?"

Murdock examined the picture. "That's your father's friend, isn't it? Carl Anders?"

Rob nodded. Maybe standing close to her was a bad idea. Her scent enticed him further. He placed his hands on her shoulders, causing her to tense for a moment. Another mistake. His fingers itched to touch her soft skin. Once they were done with Murdock, her shirt would be history. As well as the rest of her clothes.

"He used to come by all the time when your parents lived here. Him and his wife. This isn't his wife, though. I remember a time…."

Murdock rambled on. Getting the guy to shut up wouldn't be easy without being rude, and Bridget was never rude to the man. If Rob didn't do something soon, they could be standing here until sunset. Better to give her a clue to move things along. Using his thumbs, he lightly massaged the back of her neck while he rubbed his groin against her back. Major mistake on his part, but damn it felt good. He bit his lower lip.

Bridget turned her head a bit, her lips curled at the edges, giving him hope. She cut off Murdock. "So, have you seen him recently?"

"No. The last time I saw him was the day Charlie died. He acted real strange, too. Probably about Nick. I know she had it bad for that young man. Shame how he died."

Rob stopped his massage. Damn. Bridget was right. "Are you sure you saw him here the day she died?"

"Yeah. That was the day she didn't stop by. I told you about that."

He might have told, but Rob was sure he hadn't listened. That's what he got for being jealous of the old guy.

"How was Carl acting strange?" Bridget asked.

"Well, for one, he didn't drive, he walked. And he carried a black bag. Like a gym bag. Then he kept looking around kind of nervous-like. Almost like he thought someone followed him. Didn't do a very good job, if you ask me, cause I don't think he ever saw me. Charlie seemed happy enough to see him. Why do you want to know if he was around that day?"

Rob didn't want to get into the whole Barnaby issue, it hurt just thinking about how close he came to losing that dog.

"Someone played a practical joke on us, and we think he's behind it. But he won't say," she said.

He could have kissed her right then for not mentioning the incident.

"Mrs. Johnson might have seen something. She's always peeping through her windows. One of these days I'm going to ask her out for a walk. She stays inside much too much. It's not healthy."

"Why don't you go ask her out now?" Bridget said as she stuffed the photo in her bag.

Henry straightened out his shirt. "You think I should?"

"Sure. How can she resist such an eligible bachelor as yourself?" She patted him on the shoulder. "And while you're walking, you can find out if she saw anyone lurking around my house recently."

Rob stared at Bridget. Man, she was good. He could hug her and kiss her and eat her up right here.

"You're right. I think I will. Thanks, sweetie. I'll let you know what I find out." His steps slightly bounced as he crossed the street toward Mrs. Johnson's.

Rob wrapped his arms around Bridget, his jealousy gone, as well as his erection. For now. So Murdock had the hots for Mrs. Johnson. Who would have thought? "I can't believe he saw Carl here that day. He could be the witness we need."

She leaned back into him. "His testimony would certainly help, but we still got nothing. Maybe I should tell Mr. Parker the truth."

"We don't know if it will help, so don't think about it." He kissed the top of her head. Her flowery scent did its number on him once again. The time for talking had ended. There was a pool in his future. "Right now, there's only one thing on my mind, and that's you and me in the backyard."

Chapter 28

If someone asked Rob what he thought the word torture meant, he'd explain it as being with the woman you love in a room full of people, twenty-four-seven. Eventually, you'd give in to your needs, pray she wouldn't mind, and hope no one watched.

As he opened the front door and ushered Bridget inside, relief at being alone with her washed over him. Until cold air surrounded him. Oh no. His sister could just wait. "Charlie, unless you want to see your brother naked, I suggest you stay inside."

Bridget laughed as she placed her pack on the counter. "Well, that's one way of ensuring she'll stay away."

He'd take whatever worked. And if Charlie saw? Well, as long as he didn't see her seeing, he was strangely okay. He had Bridget and a pool and no suits. Couldn't ask for a more perfect combination.

Bridget opened her backpack. "One or two?"

From behind, he wrapped his arms around her waist. Little Miss Air Conditioner wouldn't let up. Goose bumps formed on his arms. A curse nearly left his lips.

"Is she still bothering you?"

"Can't you feel her?"

"No. Why don't I see what she wants?"

"Oh, no. You got your way with Henry, I'm getting my way in this. She can wait." He nuzzled her neck and rubbed his erection against her backside. Touching her wasn't enough. He needed to be in her. "Bring a strand."

She coughed as if she choked. "Feeling lucky, are you?"

He nearly laughed and wouldn't that have blown his cover. He'd only said it to shock his sister. Of course, if Bridget believed he possessed such great stamina, who was he to burst that bubble? He kissed her temple. "I will not be unprepared again."

She patted his arms and extricated herself. Instead of heading for the sliding glass door—and heaven—she walked over to the coffee table and picked up the remote. After turning on the TV, she surfed through the few stations and stopped at the Reds game. "Oh look. Aren't we lucky?"

Lucky? No, lucky would be watching Bridget strip. "Did I miss something?"

"It's for Charlie. Should keep her occupied for a while."

Even better. "Well, then, let's go." He grabbed her hand and practically dragged her out to the backyard, stopping at the deck.

Her laughter lifted his heart. Seemed she hadn't forgotten how to be happy and he would do his best to keep her that way. Taking her face into his hands, he claimed her mouth. Her lips were warm and soft and opened, inviting his tongue, and she leaned into him, rubbing up against his erection. As much as he loved kissing her, another part of his body demanded attention. Slowly, he broke the kiss. "Let's get you out of these clothes."

"I love the way you kiss," she gasped. "You take my breath away every time."

"I'd rather hear you scream."

He regretted those words after her eyes widened. She looked around the yard. "Umm, Rob? Maybe this wasn't a good idea. I didn't think about people hearing me."

Besides a few birds chirping, the neighborhood lacked the sounds of summer. No lawnmowers, no loud music, no kids playing in the sprinklers, just plain quiet. Damn. Okay, so maybe he wouldn't be able to hear her scream, but he could feel it. "No one will hear you. Trust me." He eyed the pool, and the chilly-looking water. Oh great. Was his fantasy all awash? "That's if I can even get you to scream. How cold—"

"It's heated," she said.

"Since when?"

"Since I cleaned it. Charlie showed me how. I've been swimming every night after work." She ran a finger along his dick—now softening—and grinned. "He has nothing to fear."

The seductive quality of her voice stiffened him right up and her touch made his nuts constrict. He inhaled through his teeth. "Who said I was afraid?" Which might have sounded more convincing if his voice hadn't gone up an octave.

"Not me." She grabbed the bottom of his T-shirt and pulled it up. Once she exposed his chest, she licked his nipples.

Damn, that felt good. He finished removing the garment just as her teeth clamped down. Holy— Was she aiming to have him come in his pants? His legs wobbled for a split second.

Gathering his wits together, he pulled her T-shirt over her head, momentarily halting her ministrations, and tossed it into the yard. Before he could admire the view, she unbuckled his belt, unbuttoned his jeans, and lowered the zipper so slowly, each click of the tine rubbed against his dick, which strained to be released. Good Lord. She returned her warm, wet mouth to his nipple as her hand cupped his balls. He closed his eyes and enjoyed the sensations. Who was supposed to be seducing who out here? And did he care?

Yeah, he cared. If he didn't stop her now, there would be no sex in the pool. There'd be no sex whatsoever. At least until he recuperated. He kissed her while he unhooked her bra, but she brought her arms around his waist and grabbed his butt. His jeans had slid halfway down his legs when she ground against him. He all but bit off a groan.

"You're going to take away my fantasy if you keep this up," he said.

"Oh, can't have that." She stood back with arms spread out, the bra loose as it hung from her shoulders.

The big tease. She only needed to lower her arms and he'd get an eyeful.

Well, if she wouldn't cooperate up there, he'd take care of the rest of her. After hiking up his pants, he quickly undid her jeans and slipped them—along with her panties—down her slender legs. Her scars were more evident out in the light of day and he did his best to ignore them. Someday he'd kiss them and show her how much they didn't matter, but not now. He didn't want her to even think about them.

Instead, he concentrated on the patch of hair covering heaven. He grabbed her butt and pulled her in close. Just as he prepared to sample her, the bra landed on his head. Look up or lick? Decisions, decisions.

"Is this part of your fantasy?" She grabbed his shoulders as she teetered. Her jeans kept her feet together.

"No, but it could be." Like later, when he wasn't so crazed. So many things he pictured doing to her. Forever wouldn't be enough time.

He removed her shoes and the offending jeans, tossing them all, along with her bra, into the yard. Gradually, he stood, taking her in. The curve of her hips. Her luscious breasts. "God, you're beautiful."

As he reached out to caress one, she whirled around, dashed up the steps and dove into the pool. "Come on in. The water's fine."

Damn woman. He shook his head and fought back laughter as he kicked off his shoes and slid off his jeans. The condoms lay on the grass where he had first kissed her. He placed them on the deck and then joined her, the water warm enough not to shock his erection completely away. When he met up with her, she grinned. Now this was the Bridget he longed to see more of—happy and smiling.

He kissed her hard and explored her mouth. She sucked on his tongue. What the water nearly took away, she brought back in full force. Every kiss with her was like that—pure adrenaline.

"You make me feel like a teenager," he said, nudging his hardness between the apex of her legs. "Like I'm going to come if you just touch me."

She backed away. "Then maybe I shouldn't touch you."

"Oh no you don't." He reached for her, but she jumped out of the way with a yip. Water splashed as he continued diving for her and missing. This was getting him nowhere. He submerged and wrapped his arms around her legs, lifting her as he surfaced. She squirmed.

Squeals of laughter filled the air telling him her struggles to be free were a big, fat lie.

Her sex stared him in the face and he kissed her there, running his tongue along her womanly folds. The squirming stopped. He waded over to the edge and placed her on the deck, spreading her legs for better access. She tasted a little of chlorine, but mostly of her. As he flicked his tongue over her clit, she grabbed his hair and moaned.

He loved the reactions he got from her. But once she'd tensed and the moaning increased, he stopped. He'd promised no one would hear her scream and he meant it. "As much as I'd love to continue, I need to be in you."

He hoisted up beside her and grabbed a condom. She snatched the packet from his hands and slipped into the water.

She rested her forearms onto his thighs and smiled. "You're evil. I should torture you like you tortured me."

She hovered her mouth over his dick and he gasped as her breath fluttered over the sensitive tip. "Honey, you torture me every second I can't be in you."

"Well, then I guess you'll be tortured a little longer." She wrapped her hand around his erection and then kissed the top.

Oh, shit! His nuts constricted and his dick flinched. With torture like this, he could die a happy man.

Sliding her tongue up the base, she lazily licked it from side to side. He gripped the edge of the deck. Then warm, wet pressure enveloped him as her mouth covered him. She sucked and swirled that little pink tongue of hers until he nearly shot his load.

After a couple of pumps, she withdrew and rolled on the condom. He was ready to burst.

"Come get me!" She swam to the other side.

Oh man, she was killing him. He slid into the water and caught her easily enough. Not that she was putting up much of a fight. He kissed her, pinning her to the edge. With one hand behind her head he positioned himself, grabbed her butt, and thrust into her. Tight. Wet. Warm. He could only imagine the sensations without the condom. Her moans of pleasure drove him and he pumped in rhythm to his pounding heart. She wrapped her legs around his hips.

"You feel so good, Rob. Don't stop."

As if he could. Catching his breath, he leaned his head back while he continued to pump. She gripped him tighter as her breathing became ragged. He covered her mouth before her moan turned into a scream. Damn. The vibrations of her scream turned him on even more. Her body shuddered against his, but he continued to drive into her, her orgasm squeezing him, bringing his own close to the edge. He needed to be deeper, he needed to fill her.

He needed to love her forever. And he would.

His release exploded. Seemed she wasn't the only screamer.

* * * *

Could life get any better?

Bridget held onto Rob, weak-kneed. She'd never done it in a pool. Heck, she'd never done it anywhere but a bed. Fresh air certainly made a difference, but the man—her man—made it better.

Her heart was still beating overtime when he slid out of her. And just like that, she missed his presence. They'd fit perfectly.

He pulled the condom off, tossing it into the yard. "Don't worry. I'll get it later."

"Good. I'd hate to see Barnaby go after that. Or maybe a bird."

He laughed. "Hey, what bird's nest doesn't need some waterproofing?"

"You're silly. What am I going to do with you?"

"Keep me?" He flashed his eyebrows.

Yes, she could definitely see doing that.

He caressed her cheek and she leaned into his palm. "I love you so much, Bridget." He kissed her, his tongue seeking entrance. She opened and welcomed his heat, his passion. He kissed his way to her jawline and nibbled on her ear. "Marry me."

She froze. "What?"

He pulled back and held her face. "I know we haven't known each other long. But I feel like I've known you forever. I want to care for you. Provide for you. Be with you always. Maybe I should have waited to get a ring and do this right, but my heart is so full of love for you right now. Please say yes."

She couldn't deny she felt the same way. She had since they met. But marriage? "Don't you think we should try living together first?"

Disappointment flashed across his face and he lowered his hands. "Oh… I guess. If that's what you need."

Her heart ached at hurting him. "I'm not saying no. It's just that I have a lot to…" What? Think about? Good Lord, she was screwing this up.

"It's okay. I understand. You're not ready."

How could he understand when she couldn't? Just her luck she'd nabbed probably the only man ready for a commitment. She stroked his cheek. What could she say that didn't sound…fake?

He leaned in and kissed her softly. "Why don't you go inside and get us some drinks. I'll clean up and meet you on the patio."

She could kick herself. Why couldn't she say yes?

* * * *

Bridget climbed out of the pool, quickly donned her shirt, and squirmed into her jeans. Rob remained in the water nursing his wounded heart.

Stupid. Stupid. Stupid. Was he trying to scare her away? Of all the idiotic things he could have said, he had to ask her to marry him?

He should be relieved she hadn't said no. Except…why couldn't she say yes? Caught in the moment, he'd been sure she felt the same. Especially since she believed they were soul mates. Living with her would be nice, but nice wasn't enough. He wanted a life with her. Family. Kids. The whole enchilada. Isn't that what soul mates did?

He hoisted himself out of the pool and put on his jeans. Her underwear still lay on the ground and he picked them up, along with their shoes. He placed the shoes on the cement slab and the underwear on the table. He fingered the lace on her bra. In their hurry to get undressed, he hadn't noticed how pretty it was. Light pink and frilly. Her panties matched, too. They were the most feminine items he'd ever seen her wear. Had she bought them for him? Would he ever see her in them again?

God, he hoped he hadn't screwed things up.

He sat for all of two seconds before he remembered his condom. Finding his shirt first, he picked it up. Something long and black lay underneath it.

Shit! He backpedaled and landed on his butt. His heart pounded wildly. How many dammed snakes lived in this yard?

"Man up, Rob." It was just a snake. Hadn't Bridget said they were harmless? Hell, maybe he could make her proud by disposing of the slithery creature all by himself. He only had to pick it up and toss it over the fence. How hard could it be?

However, he could only be so brave. He tossed his shirt on the table as he passed by, heading toward the woodpile and the gloves lying on top. Unfortunately, he couldn't get his fingers inside. He would use it like a potholder, then.

His heartbeat galloped while he practically crawled toward the area where he had spotted the creature. It hadn't moved. Sun glinted off the yellow stripes. As he shuffled closer, the snake appeared more rubberlike than snakelike. What the hell? He threw the glove onto the thing and it didn't move.

Fake. It was that damned fake snake from the barbecue. What kind of trick was Bridget playing?

* * * *

Bridget slid the door shut with a *bang* and headed for the kitchen. Her heart sat in her chest like a cold, dead weight. Why did he have to propose? Why couldn't she say yes? Why, why, why?

"Hey, it's about time you came back. I got something to tell you."

Pain exploded in Bridget's head and she jumped. "Not now, Charlie."

"But it could be important. I saw—"

"I said, not now." Bridget paced. Oh God. What was she going to do? "How patient is your brother?"

Charlie crossed her arms. "Pretty patient. Why? What'd you do?"

Bridget stared at Charlie. Could she confide in Rob's sister? It wasn't like Charlie could go blabbing to Rob and she needed someone other than her mother or Kate to talk to. Of course, she risked getting Charlie's biased opinion, but maybe that's what she needed. "I suggested we live together."

Charlie's eyebrows shot up. "Oh yeah?"

"After he proposed."

Her eyes narrowed and she placed her hand on her hips. "What? You turned him down?"

"I didn't turn him down. I just didn't say yes."

"And how is that different?"

Oh crap. What had she done? She continued pacing within the small kitchen. "He hardly knows me. Don't you think it's too soon?"

"Apparently Rob doesn't think so. When he wants something, he just goes for it. Whereas you"—using her index finger, she made a zigzag motion toward Bridget—"you think it to death."

Oh, God. It was the diving board incident all over again.

"I thought you loved him."

"I do."

"Then what's your problem?"

Having a normal life, but when offered, she couldn't take it. Deep inside it still came down to Suzie, who would probably shoot her right about now. "I don't deserve"—she waved her hand around—"this."

The excuse sounded weak even to her.

"There you go again. Will you cut the crap? Stop thinking about what you deserve and start thinking about what he deserves. Don't you want him to be happy?"

"Of course I do."

"Then stop being selfish and make him happy."

"You think I'm selfish?"

"You're denying Rob the woman he loves. I call that selfish."

Bridget shook her head. Ah, to be like Charlie, who saw everything in simple terms. Why couldn't she be like that? "I wasn't expecting him to propose."

Charlie laughed. "And I never thought he had it in him."

"What if it turns out all wrong? What if he wakes up one day and sees the mistake he made? What if—"

"You're thinking too much again." Charlie grabbed Bridget's shoulders. "You love him. You want him to be happy. You have the power to do it."

Bridget lowered her head. She did love him. More than anything. "He's probably changed his mind by now."

"I doubt it. You're his cherry pie."

Sometimes the words out of Charlie's mouth made the headaches she caused even worse. "And what is that supposed to mean?"

"He has the song, 'Cherry Pie,' as his ringtone. For you."

Leave it to Rob to assign her a ring tone. Bridget didn't even have her address book set up, not that she needed it. "How long has he had it?"

Charlie shrugged. "I don't know. I heard it the other…night…."

The other night? "How? I haven't called him in days."

"I… Well…that's not important. What is important is that Carl was hanging around here today."

Bridget's head almost exploded and not from the usual source. "What? And you're just now telling me this?"

"Hey, you're the one who told me it could wait and then you distracted me with Robbie's proposal."

If it would make a difference, Bridget would punch the ghost, but she didn't relish having a broken hand. "What did he do?"

"Snuck in the yard, plugged in a rubber snake and left. I thought maybe the thing would slither or something, but it didn't even move or light up or anything."

"Plugged it in? Do you suppose it's a camera or listening device?"

"Oh, I didn't even think of that."

If Carl had installed a listening device, how much had he heard them talking in the backyard? And if it was a camera?

Hell's bells! Was it pointed toward the pool? She rushed outside.

Rob stood by the fence, bare-chested and bent over staring at the grass. Her gardening glove lay on the ground in front of him. She stopped at the pool. He'd found the snake.

He looked up, his eyes narrowed. "Is this some kind of joke?"

His words were laced with anger and it stung how he could accuse her so easily, but maybe she had it coming.

"I didn't put it there. Carl did."

Rage flashed in his eyes as he straightened. "Carl was here?"

Bridget nodded. "Charlie saw him plug that thing in. Do you think it's a camera or listening device?"

"Only one way to find out." He bent over and reached for it. His hand shook and a bead of sweat trickled down his temple. After muttering a curse, he snapped his hand back.

The snake might be fake, but his fear wasn't and she wouldn't force him to do something he couldn't. "I can get it."

"No!" He straightened and ran his arm across his forehead. "It's just a stupid rubber snake. That's probably why he put it out here. He knew I wouldn't get near it." His laughter was strained. "I'll show him."

He leaned over. After a quick breath, he grabbed it. His fist clenched around the snake and he shook. He groaned as he fell hard to the ground.

"Rob!"

The smell of burned rubber and flesh hit her nose.

"No, no, no!" She bolted toward him.

Facedown, he jerked in convulsions. Pain gripped her chest and she reached to turn him over, then stopped. Plugged in. Electricity.

She followed the cord and yanked it from the socket. Rob lay still. Too still.

Without thinking, she yelled, "Fire! Fire!"

The front gate slammed. "Bridget? What's the matter?"

Thank God for Henry. "Call 9-1-1!" She flipped Rob on his back and placed two fingers against his neck. Nothing. Placed her ear against his chest. Nothing. Dammit! She performed chest compressions. "Robert Gentry, don't you dare leave me."

* * * *

Rob grabbed at his chest. The shooting pain stopped as quickly as it had started. Damn, what was in that snake?

"Oh, Robbie."

Charlie stood next to him. He rubbed his eyes. Must be dreaming. He looked again and she was still there. "I can see you? How?"

She lowered her gaze and he followed her line of sight. They weren't standing on the ground. They were hovering in the air. Bridget was performing CPR. On him.

"Bridget!" The height disoriented him and he pinwheeled his arms.

Charlie grabbed him. "You can't fall. But she can't hear you or see you. Mr. Murdock is in the yard."

Sure enough, the old man came through the gate. "They're on their way. I told them to come to the backyard."

Bridget stopped and placed two fingers along his neck. Shaking her head, she continued with the chest compressions. "Come on, Rob. Come back here."

"Am I dead?" He pounded his chest. Solid. Charlie's grip felt pretty real, too.

"I think you were electrocuted. Oh, Robbie." She hugged him.

He'd never dreamed he'd touch his sister again, no less hug her. He returned the embrace. "God, I missed you."

"You have to go back. Who's going to take care of Barnaby? Who's going to take care of Bridget? She loves you, you know. If you die on her, she may never recover."

He pulled away and looked down at the love of his life. "Does she? Really?"

Charlie punched him in the arm. "Of course she does, you lunkhead. She's just scared."

Scared. Yeah, he'd suspected as much. She probably needed to think things out, too. So what had he done? Practically pushed her away. He couldn't leave her like that. "How do I go back?"

Charlie shrugged. "Pray?"

Yeah, pray. He could do that.

Sirens sounded in the distance, getting louder by the second. Charlie took his hand and lowered him beside his body. If it weren't for his sister, he would certainly think he was dreaming. Instead, he understood what he was and what he didn't want to be.

Please let me go back. Please.

The paramedics came in through the gate. Bridget was pulled from his body so they could work. One of the medics pulled out paddles and squirted some liquid on them.

They zapped his body with electricity and pain ripped through his chest. He winced. "Damn. Should that hurt?"

Charlie grabbed his arm. "You felt that?"

"Yeah." Another zap rocked him. Some force pulled him toward his body. Yes, finally.

She smiled. "I love you, Robbie. Guess it's not your time after all."

And he hoped it wouldn't be for a long, long time. A family loomed in his future and it began with Bridget. "I'm naming our first born after you, sis."

Chapter 29

Long eyelashes lay against tan cheeks; his face slackened in sleep. Bridget sat in the chair beside the hospital bed and held Rob's left hand. If not for the bandage on his right hand, no one would suspect he'd even been hurt, no less died. The blips on the machine after the paramedics had shocked him had been the most blessed sound she'd ever heard.

He had scared the crap out of her. And it would have been all her fault if he had died. Charlie had told her the stupid thing was plugged in. Why hadn't she suggested unplugging it first?

She rested her head on his arm. "I'm so sorry."

"You're forgiven. What am I forgiving you for, though?"

She raised her head to the most wonderful brown eyes staring at her. Ever since she'd seen him collapse, she'd kept her composure. Now, when he was fine, the tears fell. She quickly wiped them away. "Hey."

"Hey, back." He looked around the room. "What happened? Where am I?"

"At the hospital."

He raised his brows. "And you're here?"

"Yeah. Go figure, huh? Takes your death to get me in here."

"I died?" He moved to sit up, but she placed a hand on his chest and pushed a button on the remote, raising the top part of the bed.

"Technically, yes, for a few minutes." The longest minutes of her life. "Try not to do it again, okay?"

"Okay." He smiled and stroked her cheek. "You look like shit. Oh, shit. That came out wrong."

Laughter bubbled between open tears and she couldn't contain the flood of emotions. "Thanks. You look wonderful."

"I doubt that. I feel…wiped out. Gimme a hug, would you?"

"Gladly." She rested her head on his chest and did her best not to hurt him.

"So, how'd I die?"

Sitting up, she asked, "What do you remember last?"

He furrowed his forehead for a second and then raised his eyebrows. "Loving you in the pool."

He would remember that. But in order to get him around the proposal and her rejection, she skipped to the important part. "Do you remember the snake?"

"Kind of. It was fake, right? My memory's a little fuzzy."

"Yeah, but it was wired and it got you good."

"Figures. The one time I face my fears and…" He paused for a long moment and then squeezed her hand. "I'm gonna kill him."

The menace in his voice sent chills down her spine. The frequent beeps of the heart-rate monitor spurred her to action. "Rob, don't talk like that. You need to calm down."

He stared at her. "He tried to kill you."

Crap. She had hoped he wouldn't come to that conclusion. One that came to her as soon as he had taken that first breath after the longest time. Carl knew Rob hated snakes. Carl knew Bridget wasn't afraid. Therefore, Carl had planted the electric bomb for her, not Rob. But Rob had been through enough and she needed to downplay it. "It's possible it was an accident."

He stared at her as if she'd grown another head. Not that she could blame him. The words sounded weak to her own ears. "An accident? Oh please. What makes you say that?"

She placed a hand on his chest. "Because it's what the police think. The snake was a recording device, with a short in the wire."

"Yeah, a short he put in there on purpose." He clenched his jaw and the beeps on the monitor went wild.

She believed the same thing, but if she didn't calm him soon, they would get company of the nurse variety. And then they might kick her out.

She rubbed his forearm, his hair soft against her fingers. "Let's worry about this later. Please? When you're better? There's nothing we can do now. We still don't have any proof."

He sighed and the beeps slowed. "You keep it up, and I won't care about anything." He pulled the sheet up and scooted over. "Come here. I want you next to me."

"No, Rob. Your body had a tremendous shock."

"And it wants you lying beside it." He lifted the sheet higher. "Come on. Don't make me beg."

She couldn't say no to those beseeching eyes or his pouty lip. After slipping off her shoes, she climbed in beside him. He enveloped her with his strong arms.

He kissed the top of her head. "I'm okay. Maybe a little tired, but other than that, I feel fine."

She rested her head on his chest. His beating heart comforted her more than anything else, but her mind kept replaying the horrible incident. "I almost lost you."

"Nah. I'm not that easy to get rid of."

Wasn't that the truth? She'd done everything but shoot him and yet he kept coming back for more. Somehow she had to fix things, but where to start? *I'm sorry I rejected your proposal? Ask me again?* Or maybe get some balls of her own and propose to him. Before she could say anything, the door opened and Dr. Crawford entered.

Of all the doctors at this hospital, Bridget had always liked him the best, and not because of his ruggedly handsome face. He seemed to actually care for his patients and the nurses. Everyone adored him.

She leaned to climb out of the bed, but Rob held her tight. For someone who claimed tiredness, he certainly had his strength and continued holding her while the doctor introduced himself and asked Rob how he felt. He gave the doctor the same line he'd given her and she found it hard to believe he'd had no adverse reaction.

"Well, that seems to coincide with the results. The tests don't show any significant damage, but I'd like to monitor you overnight, get you walking around, and run some more tests in the morning. If all turns out well, you can go home tomorrow."

Bridget silently thanked the Lord.

"You sure I can't leave now? I have the best nurse watching over me." Rob gave her a gentle squeeze.

"While I won't discount your statement, I'll feel better if you spent the night. So, Bridget, when *are* you coming back? We all miss you."

She might have gone into autopilot saving Rob, but it hadn't changed anything. Walking through those hospital doors hadn't brought back any fond memories and she doubted it ever would. Her nursing days were through. "I haven't decided yet."

"Well, this place just isn't the same without you. Rob, I'll see you in the morning." Dr. Crawford left, shutting the door behind him.

Rob rubbed her back. "You're not coming back, are you?"

She shook her head.

"Because you see ghosts?"

Hallucinating—well, seeing ghosts—made for a good crutch, but not the real reason and she wouldn't lie to him. "Because I don't belong here. I never have."

"Well, that's the beauty of this country. You don't have to do anything you don't want. If you knew bookkeeping, I'd hire you. Provided you wanted to work for me."

"What about Linda? Or Margo?"

"Linda has enough to keep her busy. Margo…." He shuddered. "She was Carl's pick. Not mine. She's gone once we nail his ass."

She laughed. "You're optimistic."

"Always. But I don't want to talk about Carl right now. Since I'm stuck in this hospital, I want to have some fun." Using his finger, he lifted her head by her chin. "Gimme a kiss."

She could oblige him that. Kissing him was definitely fun. His lips were gentle at first, then turned to a hunger she reciprocated.

"You have too many clothes on," he said.

Maybe so, but the room wasn't exactly private. "That's what happens when you're a visitor at a hospital. They require you to dress."

"Well, take them off. I want you now." And to prove his point, he dragged her hand to his crotch and helped her grip his erection. "Oh yeah, honey. Just like that."

Maybe a quickie hand job would shut him up. She didn't think he could handle much more than that. But the privacy curtain was wide open and anyone could come walking through the door. Even if she would never work with these people again, she still knew them.

She rolled away to close the curtain, but he pulled her back.

"No, no. Don't go."

"I just want—"

Cutting off her words, he consumed her with another kiss. He slipped his hand under her shirt and found a breast. Her nipples were already hard and he kept them that way by running his thumb over the nub. "You're not wearing a bra."

"I never had a chance to change."

"Oh? Then you're not wearing any panties, either? Take off your jeans." He brought his bandaged hand to the button.

The curtain. The curtain. "Can I at least—"

Again, he robbed the words from her mouth with another hungry kiss. At this point she was starting not to care. He certainly knew how to get her attention.

"Now, is that any way to treat a patient?"

Bridget froze at the sound of her former coworker's voice.

Rob chuckled. "Busted."

* * * *

Rob had gotten minor electric shocks in the past, mostly from being young and stupid. But none of those had affected him to any degree. Rub the offending spot, shake the arm or foot. That was about it.

It would take more than a rub or a shake this time.

The nurse who'd discovered them in the midst of playing— thankfully a former friend of Bridget's—had come to take Rob walking. Bridget suggested she take him instead and boy, was he glad she had. Who knew his legs would wobble when he first stood on them? Who knew walking down the hall would feel like climbing a mountain? Who knew it would take him thirty minutes to accomplish that walk? Thirty damn minutes!

Except he didn't walk down the hall and back. He leaned on Bridget and let her drag him. At least that's how it seemed.

The only good thing regarding the whole electric-shock incident? It had happened to him and not her. If Bridget had ended up in the hospital or, God forbid, died, Rob would be behind bars for the murder of Carl Anders. No doubt about it. Just realizing how badly things could have gone had him shaking, and not from weakness. Rage bubbled below his calm exterior.

"We're almost there," she said, with an arm around his waist. Damn, if not for her arms holding him up he'd be crawling on the floor. Or lying there in a heap. He had no energy left.

"You sure you didn't take me up a flight of stairs?" Man, even his voice wheezed. And he was going to make love to her earlier? Glad he was saved that embarrassment.

"This is why you walk. To get stronger. Do this a couple more times, and it'll be a piece of cake."

A couple more times? Hell, he'd be lucky if he survived the first trip.

The bed came into view and called to him. Unfortunately, it took him several minutes before he could plant his butt on the side. Once he did, he fell back in relief, panting.

She laughed. "What happened to the man who begged to go home today?"

"Decided to take advantage of being waited on. Where else can I get breakfast in bed, huh?"

"You want breakfast in bed? I might be able to do that one day. And the meal might even be better than what you'd get here. But I'm not promising anything." She swung his legs up and covered him with the blanket. "Give me your robe."

"No." He pulled the front together. "I might decide to get up and use the bathroom. Don't need to be airing my ass for everyone to see." Provided he could even rise on his own.

"Oh, but it's such a fine ass. They won't mind."

"Is that what you nurses do all day? Look at patients' asses?"

"Only the ones worth looking at."

She pulled the drape around the bed and went to sit on the chair, but he shook his head and raised the covers. "Don't worry, I won't be molesting you. I don't think I have it in me anyways."

She kissed him on the lips. "Tired?"

Exhausted. "A little, maybe."

She slipped off her shoes and snickered before sliding beside him. His legs might be done for, but not his dick. Her nearness alone sprung the sucker to life. Too bad he couldn't do anything with it.

"You deserve a reward, then."

A reward, huh? Warmth surrounded his erection and he gasped. He loved her hand.

"Just lay back and enjoy." Her ministrations got his heart racing. Good thing the nurse had disconnected the monitor for his walk. Hate to have her interrupt this time. Each stroke was pure pleasure. If all Bridget's rewards were this good, he would make sure he earned plenty.

"How many times have you done this in a hospital?" As if he really wanted to know the answer to that question.

She leaned up and kissed him. "You're the first. How about you?"

He liked being a first in her life. "A virgin. Just like you."

She tickled his neck with her tongue. "Want me to stop?"

"Hell no." He got harder and savored every moment. Being inside her would have been much better, but plan B wasn't too shabby. He closed his eyes and focused on her attention. On each wave of pleasure. She lifted his gown and suckled on the right nipple, then the left, before running her tongue down his stomach. Fingers teased his testicles. He yearned to be in her so badly, but enjoyed her touch, too, until her mouth came down on him. Holy Mother of— He opened his eyes and found her head under the covers, bobbing up and down. He lifted the blanket. Seeing him in her mouth and the way she sucked was all it took for him to blow his load.

Damn. That hadn't lasted near as long as he'd hoped.

* * * *

Her Prince Charming slept.

Bridget brushed back a lock of his hair. Rob was her life and she'd do anything to keep him safe. If that meant spilling her secret, then so be it.

She lightly kissed his cheek, savoring his scent for a moment before quietly slipping out of the bed. He stirred, but remained sleeping.

Slowly, she opened the bedside table's drawer and found Rob's cell. Lucky for her, he labeled everyone and she quickly found the name. She took the phone into the bathroom and punched in the number, silently praying the guy would answer.

As luck would have it, Dean Parker could see her in twenty minutes. After returning Rob's phone, she slipped the backpack strap on her shoulder and stared at the man she loved. If he knew her plan, he would stop her—or make an attempt—so no sense in waking him. After leaving a note stating she'd be back in a couple of hours, she left the hospital and headed for Rob's truck. The keys were still in her possession.

By the time she arrived at the private investigator's building, her nerves were on edge and she shook. He couldn't hurt her. Couldn't condemn her. But if this didn't work, she would be forced to meet Carl head-on and that thought alone twisted her stomach into knots. She took several deep breaths and entered the building. The reception area was empty.

"Mr. Parker? It's Bridget Quigley."

"It's Dean and I'm in my office. Come on back."

A muted voice followed. She walked down the short hall and stopped before reaching the door. Was he on the phone, or was someone else with him? She poked her head around the frame. He sat alone behind his desk, staring at a monitor.

"Hello? Is someone with you?"

He stood and grimaced for a moment before smiling. "Hi. No one's here. Just talking to myself. Come on in."

She stepped inside and her headache exploded. Guess whatever good luck Rob had given her had finally faded. She'd been with him so long, she'd gotten used to not having headaches.

Dean looked over her shoulder and frowned.

"You act like you can still see me."

She spun toward the man behind her. Lanky and in his forties, he stood by the wall.

"You said you were alone," she said.

"You can see him?" "You can see me?" Dean and the ghost said at the same time.

Now it made sense. The voices. Her headache. Dean's strange behavior. The fact the man standing behind her floated above the ground. She turned toward the investigator. "You see ghosts, too."

He plopped into his chair. "Holy shit."

"Hallelujah! Someone else can see me besides this fat slob!"

"Hey!"

Her spirits soared. Dean saw ghosts. He'd believe her story and might be able to help. She held her hand out to the spirit. "Hi. My name's Bridget. What's yours?"

He floated over and took her hand, solidifying in the process. "Wow! I'll never get tired of that rush. Mr. Party Pooper here doesn't like me touching him. I'm Peter McDermott. Pleased to make your acquaintance."

He continued holding her hand and while she didn't want to begrudge the guy his temporary solidification, it still kind of creeped her out. His grip was strong and thoughts of Mary Alice from the river came to mind.

"Can I have my hand back?"

"Oh, if you must." Peter released her and returned to floating.

"How long have you been dead?" Bridget sat in the chair as he appeared by the window. The popping to and fro unnerved her whenever Charlie did it. Peter was no different.

"I was killed—"

"You were not killed," Dean interrupted. "How many times do I have to tell you?"

Peter folded his arms across his chest and pouted.

Okaaay. "Why do you think you were killed?"

He grinned as if he'd won a prize. "If someone takes your life, it's murder, isn't it?"

Dean shook his head. "The only person who took your life was you."

"I wasn't ready to go yet. It wasn't my time. He was supposed to come save me."

"Yeah, well, maybe you should have made sure he was home answering his phone before you took those pills."

While Dean spoke, Peter mouthed the words and flapped his fingers in a talking motion. He didn't seem to care about Dean witnessing this little rant, either.

"How long ago did this happen?"

Peter averted his gaze. Dean answered, "Thirty years ago."

Thirty years? Hopefully, Peter wasn't as deranged as Mary Alice. Being alone could do funny things to a person. She looked at Dean. "How long have you seen Peter?"

"Three years. After my...heart attack. When I came back to work, I found him. He'd been here all along, but besides feeling a blast of cold every now and then, I never knew."

Heart attack? Sure, he didn't look in the best of shapes, but he didn't seem that old. Maybe a few years older than Rob. "Did you die?"

"Technically? Yeah. For about three minutes." His eyes widened. "Is that what happened to you?"

She nodded. "Do you think everyone with a near-death experience sees ghosts?" Wouldn't that be something? Maybe they should start a club.

"I don't know. It's not like I'm going to ask, though, you know what I mean?"

"I suppose." One person seeing ghosts could be a nut. But several? It was something to consider anyway.

"I'm sure you didn't come to talk about ghosts. You said you had something important to tell me?"

"Yeah, but it involves a ghost." She told him everything she knew regarding Charlie, Nick, and Carl. Telling Dean turned out to be a whole lot easier without the fear of being ridiculed.

"Wow," Peter said. "You saw Nick move on?"

"Not really. I passed out. I only assume he did because he's not there anymore."

"Is there a police report regarding your attack?" Dean asked.

"Yes. But I couldn't very well tell them Carl did it after I told them I didn't see anyone."

"I know this is frustrating for you, but I have to ask. Are you sure Charlie told you the truth, or could she be telling you something she wants to believe is the truth?"

"Rob thought the same thing, but after everything that's happened, even he believes her now."

"Well, this definitely will give me more to work on. Assuming you still want me on the case."

She nodded. Who else could she go to now?

"I might be able to find a motive for murder, but without any witnesses, or concrete evidence, it will be hard to prove."

He mirrored her feelings exactly. "That's why I think we should trap him. Get him to confess. I even bought a digital voice recorder."

Dean held up his hands. "Whoa. Not a good idea. The man has killed. And he's after you already. What does Rob think of your plan?"

She sagged in her seat as if someone had taken the air out of her. Dean was her only hope of not doing this alone. "I haven't told him."

He came around his desk and squatted in front of her, his knees creaking. "Because you know what he'll say, huh?"

Yeah, she knew. "I can't just sit still anymore. He nearly killed Rob today. What's to stop him?"

"I understand how you feel. But let me put someone on him, first. Follow him twenty-four-seven. If we lose him, we contact you and Rob. If he's as desperate as you make him sound, he'll slip up. In front of a witness. Do you understand? You have to be patient."

Patient, patient, patient. He sounded like Rob. She stood and paced. "You don't understand. Rob wouldn't be in danger if I hadn't told him. If it weren't for me…." She stopped and lowered her head as all her guilt came crashing down. "All I wanted to do was help Charlie and I've mucked it all up."

Dean came to her and placed his hands on her shoulders. "Listen, I know it seems like you might have stirred the hornet's nest, so to speak, but I honestly believe Rob's life was in danger long before you got involved. So in essence, you *are* helping Rob."

"I wish I could go to the police."

"Yeah, I know that feeling. Let's try the following part, shall we? At least through Monday."

Monday seemed so far away. "Are you sure I couldn't just call him and rattle him a little?"

"Please tell me that's a joke."

Not hardly. "Don't worry. I won't approach him."

"Good girl. You can keep yourself busy by taking care of Rob. I'm sure he's going stir-crazy in the hospital. I know I did. I'll call you if anything new develops, okay? Are you going to tell Rob you came to see me?"

"Yeah, but I may leave out the part where I suggested I contact Carl."

She left Dean in the process of calling his man. Peter followed her into the foyer. "Do you think once you help Charlie, she'll move on?"

"Yeah, I think she will."

"Do you think I'll ever get to move on?"

Mary Alice had committed suicide and she appeared stuck, but Bridget didn't have the heart to tell Peter her suspicions. "I honestly don't know."

He nodded, then disappeared.

She trudged back to the parking lot. The sun had set, turning the clouds into a pretty pink-and-orange glow. A cool breeze from the west ruffled her hair and she climbed into the truck.

Just as she closed the door, her phone went off. Thinking it was Rob, she hurriedly fished for her cell only to discover Devin's number. Maybe she couldn't do anything about Carl, but she could face Devin. If he could forgive her, then maybe she could forgive herself. She was certainly ready to try.

She pushed the answer button. "Hello, Devin."

"Bridget? You finally taking my call?" His speech slurred.

Good Lord, had he been drunk all those other times he'd called? She'd never listened to any of his messages, having deleted them as soon as they were received. "I'm sorry it's taken me so long to get back to you."

He wept and it wrenched her heart. "I miss her, Bridget. I try to remember her and it's like she's fading from my memory. I feel like I'm losing her all over again."

Tears welled up in her eyes. "I miss her, too. But drinking isn't helping you any."

"It's the only way I know to make the pain go away. It's all my fault she's dead."

Damn Charlie. Did she have to be right about everything? "Why do you think that?"

"I took her van because I was being petty. And now she's gone because I didn't get my way. Please come over and talk. I only want to talk. I need help remembering her."

"I want to talk, too, but not while you're drunk. When are you at the hospital next?"

"I'm not working. I've been told to take some time."

And he spent his time with a bottle. "How about I come over tomorrow?"

"You promise?"

"If you're sober, I promise."

More weeping. "Thank you, Bridget. I'll be sober. I won't drink any more tonight. What time?"

"I'll call you around ten, okay? We can pick a time then."

He thanked her some more between sobs. She felt as small as an ant. Maybe if she hadn't ignored him all this time, he would have moved on by now.

She'd tossed her cell into the backpack when Madonna's "Like a Virgin" played. The music came from her pack. She opened it and her phone lit the interior. The display read LOVER BOY. What the heck? She pushed the answer button. "Hello?"

"Hey, where are you?" Rob asked.

"Did you mess with my phone?"

"Mess with it how?"

No. He wouldn't do that to her. Charlie on the other hand… "Never mind. I'm on my way to the hospital. Do you need something?"

"I need you, but that's not why I'm calling. The nurse came back and took me for another walk. As unmanly as this sounds, I just want to go to sleep. So… I'm giving you an out. If you want it."

"Are you saying watching you sleep isn't entertaining?"

"I don't know. Never had anyone watch me before. Well, except for my mother. But then I was little and I don't remember. I missed you when I woke up. Where'd you go?"

As badly as she wanted to say, she kept quiet. She would tell him in person. "Just had an errand to run. Sorry it took so long. I'll see you bright and early in the morning. I believe they serve you breakfast around six. I'll join you then."

"Six! But it'll be Sunday. Don't they let you sleep in?"

She laughed. "You'll be lucky they don't wake you up several times during the night. Do you want me to bring you something special?"

"Honey, the only thing special I want is you. Damn. I'm getting hard just thinking about you. I think I'm addicted."

"Do you need me to come over and relieve you?"

"Ah, hell. As wonderful as that sounds, I'm sure I'll be out before you get here. I love you, Bridget. Sleep well. I'll see you in the morning."

"Love you back. Good night." She disconnected the call.

A pain radiated from behind her eyes. The pounding headache had left after losing contact with Peter, but the everyday variety remained. And when she got home, the pounding one would return. There would also be a ghost with some pain of her own, once Bridget was done with her. How dare Charlie mess with her phone?

Chapter 30

Someone knocking at the door woke Bridget out of a dream. Darn it, sucker had been a good one, too—Rob starred in it.

"Hey, wake up. Mr. Murdock is here," Charlie said as she shook Bridget's leg.

Mr. Murdock? Why the heck would he be up so early? She opened her eyes. Sunlight filtered through the bedroom windows. "What time is it?"

"Eight-fifteen."

"Eight-fifteen! Hell's bells! I was supposed to meet Rob at six." Bridget sat up and grabbed her cell. Dead. Shoot. How many times had he called?

"I tried waking you earlier, especially after your alarm went off, but you mumbled something unintelligible and smacked me." Charlie rubbed her arm as if Bridget had just hit her.

The knocking became rapid, insistent. She grabbed her robe and headed for the living room. "I'm coming. Hold on."

Bridget opened the door to a relieved-looking Henry. He placed his hand over his heart. "Thank goodness you're okay. Rob was afraid something had happened to you and he called me to check. And then when you didn't answer, I thought maybe he had a reason to be concerned. You are okay, aren't you?"

"Come on in." She closed the door behind Henry. "I overslept and my phone died." Poor Rob. She'd make it up to him in the best possible way.

"Well, you might want to call him. He was rather frantic."

She lifted her backpack, then lowered it, remembering. Crap. "My charger is at work. Can you call him and tell him I'm fine? I'll be leaving soon." She'd pick up the charger on the way and charge the phone at the hospital.

"Sure thing. I'm glad he's doing well. At least he sounded pretty good, besides sounding worried, that is."

"He should be released today." She escorted Henry back to the door. "Tell him I'm sorry to have worried him. I guess I was more tired than I thought."

He patted her hand. "You wouldn't be the first person to oversleep. Let me get out of your hair so you can get ready." He reached for the door handle. "Oh, before I forget, I want to tell you about my conversation with Becky."

"Becky?"

"Mrs. Johnson." Henry's eyes got a little dreamy when he spoke her name. Could he have a crush on the woman?

"Why don't you go call Rob first and then come back and tell me? By then I'll be dressed and ready to go."

"You're right. I'll be right back."

The door hadn't been closed one minute when Charlie reappeared. "Mr. Murdock and Mrs. Johnson? Who'd have thunk?"

Bridget went into the kitchen and prepared a pot of coffee. "I think it's cute he's found someone. Which reminds me." She turned and faced Charlie. "Lover boy? Really?"

"Hee hee." Charlie laughed. "Serves you right for not putting Rob in your address book. In fact, you don't have anyone in there. That's just not normal."

"I don't need the names to know who's calling. Once I see their number, I remember it."

"Must be nice. I had problems remembering my Social Security number. Guess that's not a problem anymore, huh?"

Bridget rushed to the bedroom and pulled out her clothes while Charlie hovered by the door. "Are you staying to watch?"

Charlie stuck out her tongue and vanished. Once Bridget finished dressing, she found the house empty. Enjoying the rare solitude, she pulled a mug from the cabinet and was pouring coffee when someone knocked at the door.

"Come on in, Henry. It's open."

He popped his head around the corner. "Do you think it's wise you leave the door unlocked? You can never be too careful anymore."

Shit. She hadn't given it much thought, not since a certain ghost always warned her. Unless said ghost was engrossed in TV or just not around. Like now. Dang it. Maybe she should have told Charlie to stick around.

"You're right. I'll make sure to lock it from now on." She held the carafe up and tilted in offering. "Would you like some?"

"No, thanks. I've had my caffeine for the day." He sat at the table.

"What did you find out from Mrs. Johnson?" Bridget carried her mug and took a seat next to Henry.

"Before I forget, Rob says hi and he's glad you're okay. He'd also like you to swing by his place and get him a change of clothes."

"I feel bad I worried him for no reason." Yeah, she was definitely making up for that.

"Anyway, back to Becky. I convinced her to go walking with me on a regular basis. All this time I think she was looking for an invitation. So I also asked her to join me at the senior center and she said she'd go."

Okay, if she didn't reel him in, he could go on forever and she had a man at the hospital waiting for her. "That's nice. But did she see anyone around the house?"

"Yes, she did. But it wasn't Carl."

"How do you know? I didn't give you his picture to show her."

"Because it was a woman."

Well, crap.

"She was young, brunette, and dressed like a lawyer—Becky's term, not mine—but no one who lives around here. And she would know."

The description matched Tori, but Tori loved Barnaby, so it must be someone else. Probably someone Carl knew or paid. The creep.

"I know it's not the news you were hoping for. If you want, I can take his picture and ask around for you. But Becky was probably your best bet. She's got an eagle eye. Plus, she's kind of nosy."

"And you like her."

Henry actually blushed. "I guess I do at that. Which reminds me." He glanced at his watch and then stood. "Whew! Thought maybe I was late."

She stood with him. "Late for what?"

"Breakfast at Becky's."

Seemed as if Charlie's baseball games were numbered because Henry might not be home much anymore. "Have fun. And thanks again for all your help."

"My pleasure. See you later."

As he left, she went back into the kitchen and rinsed her mug. Still no sign of Charlie. Well, she didn't need the headache anyway, except… Wait a minute. She hadn't had a headache this morning. Why was that? Too busy thinking about Rob to care? Whatever. It was a gift and she wouldn't complain.

She'd filled a travel mug for the road and turned off the coffeepot when someone knocked on the front door. She placed the mug beside her backpack. A pair of sunglasses sat on the table. Henry must have left them. After snatching them, she rushed to the door and opened it. "Did you forget these…."

The words died on her lips and the moisture in her mouth was sucked dry.

Carl stood on the porch.

* * * *

Rob checked his watch for the fifth time. A whole five minutes had passed since the first time he looked. Why the hell had he told Henry to have Bridget stop home? He needed to see her, feel her, know she was truly okay.

"Hey. You up for a visitor?" Dean Parker poked his head around the door frame.

Rob had no idea why his former investigator visited, but was grateful for the distraction. "Am I ever. What are you doing here? You got nothing better to do on a Sunday morning?"

"I was in the neighborhood." Dean scanned the room and sat in the chair beside the bed.

"How'd you know I was here?"

"Bridget told me. How are you feeling?"

"A lot better." His trip to the bathroom, while slow, was not near as exhausting. "But when did you talk to Bridget?"

"She didn't tell you about our meeting last night?"

273

That was her errand? How come she didn't say? "No. What did she come see you for?"

"She told me everything, hoping it would make a difference."

"Everything?" What the hell?

Dean patted Rob's leg. "Don't worry. I don't think your girlfriend is crazy." He leaned in closer and whispered, "It just so happens I have the same ability as her."

"What?"

"Yeah. Who'd have figured, huh? So where is she?"

"She overslept." Rob explained what Henry had relayed to him. "Does this mean you're back on the case?"

"I've got a man following Carl. It's the best I can do for now."

"Thank God. I was afraid Bridget might try something on her own."

"You and me both, buddy. I wish you had told me about her earlier. I might have been able to get something on Carl by now."

"I didn't feel like that was my secret to tell and I wasn't going to push her. Hell, I'm still trying to wrap my head around it."

"Oh, don't get me wrong. I know *why* you didn't tell me. No one but you two know I see them. It's not something you want advertised. Bad for business. Have to say, it's a relief to be able to talk about it, though. Makes me feel less like a freak."

Is that how Bridget felt, too? "Have you always seen them?"

"Hell no. Heart attack. I technically died for several minutes."

Dean had died. Bridget had died. And now he had died. Or so he was told. "Do you remember dying?"

"Nope. I remember the pain in my chest and next thing I know, I wake up in a hospital bed. The stuff in between is gone."

Rob couldn't say the same thing. Something had happened, but remembering only made the events fuzzier, like trying to remember a good dream. Hell, maybe that's all it was—a dream. "Do you think I'll see ghosts now?"

"Don't know. Guess you'll find out soon enough, right? At least you'll know you're not going crazy. I honestly thought I was headed for a mental ward." Dean reached into his pocket and pulled out his cell. "Excuse me while I take this." He walked to the other side of the room.

Rob leaned his head back and closed his eyes. Would he be able to see Charlie? Would she look the same? Damn. He needed to hurry up and leave this place so he could go check it out.

"Rob? Would Carl be working on a project this early on a Sunday?"

"It's possible. Where at?"

"Out in Kettering. On Stroop."

"It does seem a little early, but yeah, the project hit some snags and we've been busting our balls to get it completed in time. Is that where your guy followed him to?"

Dean nodded and raised his finger, indicating a moment. "Sam, check out the place and then call me with your findings."

"What's going on?"

"It doesn't appear anyone else is working, but Carl's truck is there."

"That job is his baby. He's likely in there doing the work himself. I sure hope he is, anyway."

"Even if it's with substandard material?"

"Ah, shit." Being so caught up in the whole murder thing, he'd forgotten all about the possible embezzlement. "Guess I have my work cut out for me."

* * * *

Carl smiled as he stood on the porch. If Bridget didn't know any better, she would believe he only came to chat.

"Hi, Bridget. Can I speak to Rob?"

"What makes you think he's here?"

"His truck? Would you just get him please? His phone is dead or something."

Rob's phone was definitely not dead, but it didn't make sense he'd be ignoring Carl's calls, especially if he'd thought something had happened to her. So Carl was lying. Whatever the reason for his visit, maybe she could get him to slip up. If only she had her recorder, but it was in her backpack, on the counter. Still, wasn't he being watched?

She glanced out front. The only car out of place was the company truck he drove. Whoever had followed Carl did a good job of hiding. Hopefully not so good he couldn't hear if she screamed. "I'd like to, but he's at the hospital."

"At the hospital? What happened?" The surprised expression didn't appear to be an act. And why should it? Didn't he expect *her* to be the one in the hospital—if not dead?

She willed herself to be calm, to stay cool, and her heart almost obeyed. But staring at a known murderer didn't make the task easy to accomplish. "He received an electrical shock after picking up a malfunctioning listening device. What I can't understand is why someone would record our conversations." She became bold and put her hand on her hip. "You wouldn't know of anyone out to get Rob, would you? Like some nasty competitor or employee trying to take over his business?"

Carl's jaw clenched. "What have you been feeding Rob lately? Ever since you came into his life, he's been suspicious of me. Maybe you should have picked up that snake instead of him. He'd do well to be rid of you."

Man, if only she'd gotten that on tape. All her worries would be over. "Who said anything about a snake?"

Carl glared at her. Hell's bells. Was she crazy or just nuts? Screaming, Bridget threw the sunglasses at him, then slammed the door and locked it. The investigator had better get his ass over here, quick. She ran to the sliding glass door and made sure it was locked, too. As she pulled the drapes, Carl appeared in the backyard.

"Shit, shit, shit!" Bridget scrambled backward. Her butt hit the counter. She grabbed her backpack and dashed toward the front door.

The sound of broken glass hit her like a shot of adrenaline. She reached for the knob and pulled. Nothing.

Shit. She'd locked it.

Chapter 31

Rob's call went straight to Bridget's voice mail, and he disconnected without leaving a message. Unease niggled on the back of his neck. He'd feel a whole bunch better if he could only hear her voice. "She still hasn't turned her phone on. I wish I knew what was taking so long. She should have been here by now."

"Have you tried calling a neighbor?" Dean asked.

"I already have. His phone just rings." Could it be the two of them just got busy talking? Henry tended to be long-winded and sometimes Bridget was too nice to the guy.

Dean pulled his phone from his pocket. "Let's see what Sam has to say." He put the phone to his ear. "Whatcha got?"

Rob sat up. He needed some good news. Let Carl be in Kettering, far away from Bridget.

"Shit!" Dean's outburst popped Rob's little hope balloon. "Head on over to Bridget's. I'll meet you there." He stood and slid the phone back in his pocket. "No sign of Carl at the site. I'll go check on Bridget—"

"No. We'll check on Bridget." And if he found Carl anywhere near her, he'd kill the man. Rob slid out of bed and the room spun. He grabbed the bedside table.

"Rob, you're in no shape to go."

He would be, dammit. Nothing could keep him from Bridget. "If you don't take me, I'll call a cab. But I'm going." He yanked the bottom drawer open and pulled out the only thing in it—his jeans. "You don't happen to have a spare shirt, do you?"

* * * *

"Stop or I shoot."

Bridget's hand froze over the lock. She was probably dead, regardless. If Carl had been followed by one of Dean's guys, he would have shown up by now. At least there was still hope for Charlie. Slowly, she reached into the side pocket of her backpack and turned on the recorder. She placed the bag on the floor and turned around to find a gun pointed at her. "Aren't you going to shoot me anyway?"

"Now, why would I want to do that? It has to look like an accident."

"Like it did for your son?"

"Whoa, wait a minute. I did not kill my son."

"You didn't try to save him, either."

"There was no one to save. He died upon impact. When I finally reached him, the light had left his eyes." Carl shivered.

"You left him," Bridget said.

"I left a body, not my son." He rubbed the arm holding the gun. "Got the air set rather cold, don't you?"

Charlie must have heard the scream. Her presence felt reassuring, in an odd sort of way. If she could only help, though.

"That would be Charlie. You know, the woman you killed."

"Charlie?" He looked around as if he expected to see the woman. "She died from an overdose."

"That you gave her."

He shivered again. "You're crazy. Now get away from the door."

"Am I crazy? You're feeling her, aren't you? How do you think I know so much? It's because she told me."

"She *told* you? I knew something wasn't right about you." He spun around, swatting the air.

"If you want her to leave you alone, admit you did it. And tell her why."

He swung the gun in her direction. "I'm not telling you again. Get away from the door."

"Or what? You'll shoot me?"

"Yeah, maybe I will. You're kind of getting on my nerves."

He must be bluffing. Gunshots could not be covered up easily and would only bring the police. Her only chance was to make a break for it.

He waved the weapon. "I don't have all day. Move it!"

She was pretty sure he wouldn't shoot her, just not one hundred percent sure. Every time he waved the gun, her heart skipped several beats. But damn, if she didn't make a move now, she'd never have a chance. She said a silent prayer.

Inhaled deeply.

And took two quick steps toward the hallway.

He flinched. She dashed to the door, flipped the lock, and gripped the knob. Pain flared in the back of her head.

Had he shot her? Was she dying?

Her hand slipped off the knob as she crumpled to the floor.

* * * *

Being a ghost sucked! How could an incorporeal being hope to stop a bullet? Giving Carl the chills wouldn't stop the bastard from killing Bridget, yet Charlie continued to move into him, to distract him, so Bridget could escape.

When Bridget had run for the door, Charlie cheered and kept up the freeze. But Carl had either adapted or was clued in to Bridget's plan. He clobbered her on the back of the head before she had a chance to open the door.

Anger and helpless frustration burned inside Charlie as her friend, and future sister-in-law, fell to the ground, bleeding. She screamed over all the wrongs assaulted her. Over all the death and despair this one monster had caused. "No one messes with my family!"

The coffee table skidded across the room and slammed into Carl's leg. How the hell did that happen? Wait a minute. The chair in the wall. She'd been angry then, too.

He bent over, rubbing the offending spot. "What the…"

Directing her enraged energy toward the table, she willed it to crash into Carl once again. The end flipped up and landed on his head.

Oh, yeah! Game on.

He kicked the table aside. Pointing the gun at Bridget, he said, "Is this how you want to play? Keep it up and I shoot her."

If he had planned to shoot her, he would have by now. Charlie didn't take the bluff. She directed the framed photo of Bridget and her parents to his shooting hand. Hot damn! He dropped the gun.

He rubbed his wrist and then reached for the weapon. With a flip of her hand, Charlie shooed it into the dining area. This was getting fun.

He straightened and stared around the room, evil etched into every line of his face. "Fine. I don't need the gun to kill her."

* * * *

"You think you can get away with leaving, wearing just your jeans and a robe?" Dean asked.

Rob zipped up. What choice did he have? He figured he would look less conspicuous wearing a robe rather than no shirt at all. "It's Sunday. How busy can this place be?"

"Yeah, exactly. You'll stand out like a sore thumb."

"So what if they stop me. It's not like I'm breaking out of jail." But the less distractions, the better.

They stepped into the deserted-for-now hallway and walked to the stairwell. The floor was cold beneath Rob's bare feet, but it beat wearing those silly booties the hospital had given him. He let out his breath as soon as the door shut behind him. So far, so good. He followed Dean down the stairs toward freedom.

Maybe he was overreacting, but Bridget wasn't the kind of person to make him worry needlessly. His gut twisted inside and out. She was in trouble and he prayed he'd get there in time.

As soon as they arrived on the first floor, he stopped to catch his breath. Someone should give him a walker. Apparently, that shock had turned him into an old man. Three flights of stairs should not be this exhausting.

"You okay?" Dean asked.

"I'll live. Let's go."

Dean directed them to the side entrance, away from the reception area, and a direct line to the parking lot. Two steps later, a man from behind spoke.

"Excuse me."

Oh God. Now what?

* * * *

Carl knelt before Bridget and grabbed her throat. Panicking, Charlie sent the table flying into Carl's back, knocking him forward and on top of Bridget. He sat up and still held her neck, but Charlie counterattacked with every available knickknack from the room. Frames, coasters, remote controls—they all headed for Carl, hitting him in the head, arms, and back.

He raised his arms in defense as she continued assaulting him with the flying debris. Each item took its toll on her, but she refused to give in to the weakness. He stood and staggered into the dining area. With a flick of her hand, she sent the gun flying and it crashed into his forehead. Blood trickled from the gash it left. Another flick sent the gun back into the living room as he stumbled toward the door to the garage.

A block of knives sat on the counter. Weariness settled over her, but she directed the largest knife into the wall, intentionally missing Carl's head by inches.

He turned around. "She said you were stuck here because of me. Would killing me free you or keep you around? I'm guessing you need me alive."

"You killed me. Why shouldn't I kill you?" At least she didn't expect a response. Still, what he said rang true. Dead people never confessed.

But she couldn't let her need get in the way of stopping this bastard. Bridget's and Rob's life depended on her taking action now. She directed another knife toward Carl's stomach. It flew through the air, stopped midway, and clattered to the floor.

"What the—" Weak and used up, she willed the weapon to move. Nothing. She was empty. "Oh, craaap!"

He stared at the knife as if waiting for it to arise for another attack. When after several seconds nothing happened, a smugness came over his face. "Well, well. Isn't that interesting."

* * * *

Rob froze in his steps. His heart hammered. Damn, he'd been so close to freedom. To Bridget.

Dean turned around. "Yes?"

"Do you have a light? My lighter died."

Rob nearly collapsed in relief. Shit. A smoker.

"Sorry. Don't smoke." Dean took Rob's arm and led him away. "You okay there?"

"No. He almost gave me a heart attack."

They arrived at a blue Honda Accord. Rob opened the door. Papers, papers, everywhere. On the seat. Stuffed beside the center console. Even the footwell. At least he hoped it was only paper.

"Interesting filing system you have here. Is it safe to sit in?"

Dean scooped up a handful of papers and tossed them in the back. "Get in, smartass."

Slowly, Rob lowered onto the seat. "Hey, you never know. Some of the guys I work with are such slobs I swear I've seen shit moving around in their trucks."

"Well you won't find anything that will end up stinking or moving in here. I do have some sense." Dean stuck the key into the ignition and turned. Nothing happened.

"Please tell me you forgot to step on the clutch," Rob said.

"It's an automatic." Dean pulled out his cell phone. "But don't worry. I'll have Sam stop by and pick us up. We should be on his way, anyway."

Rob took deep breaths. Exploding in anger would do no one any good, especially Bridget. "Maybe I should call a cab."

Dean held the cell to his ear. "Sam will be quicker. Just be patient."

Patience had always been Rob's strong suit. But then he'd never been tested quite this badly. He leaned his head back and prayed.

* * * *

Bridget was having one wild dream. Or maybe a nightmare. Yeah, more like a nightmare. The kind where she couldn't see anything, but she could sure feel.

The back of her head hurt. So maybe she was reliving her attack at the construction site. Except she wasn't bound and gagged, the way the nightmare normally played out.

Cracks of light offset the darkness as she blinked her eyes a few times before opening them wide. A wall and door stood at an odd angle and the carpet scratched her cheek. Oh, she got it now. She lifted her head. Pain exploded and spots formed in her vision. She swallowed and her throat burned. Not a nightmare, but a monster.

Where was Carl? Had he just hit her and run? Whatever, it didn't matter. She needed to get help. To keep her pain to a minimum, she sat up slowly, using the wall for support, but even slow was too fast. Her vision focused in and out as the room spun. Feeling queasy, she closed her eyes and concentrated on steady breathing to calm her stomach. Damn head injuries. Would she ever be right again?

Once the nausea dissipated, she opened her eyes. The coffee table lay on its side far from its original position. Broken picture frames, several coasters, and the remote control littered the living room as if a mini-tornado came through. Damn. Maybe Charlie had come to her rescue.

Bracing to stand, Bridget placed her hand on the carpet and touched something hard and cold just as Carl came around the corner. He stopped, staring at her.

Hell's bells. Too late to leave, now. She raised the gun and brought her other hand up for support. Her hands shook and her heart pounded in her ears. She'd never shot at anyone, never even held a gun, but wouldn't hesitate to pull the trigger if he took one step her way. He may be unarmed, but he was far from harmless.

He raised his hands, palms out. "Easy, now. You don't want to do something you'll regret."

"What makes you think I'll regret shooting a murderer?" God, even her voice sounded raspy. Her vision became wonky again and she blinked. Passing out would be a bad thing, but if she were to hunt for a phone, she'd have to stand and take him with her. Better to sit still and rest for a minute. Maybe get him to confess, too. The backpack—along with the recording device—was still beside her. She waved the gun at him, like he had with her. "Sit." He moved toward the couch. "Not there. On the floor, where you're standing."

He slid to the floor and leaned against the wall. "You don't look very well. How long do you think you'll last?"

"Tell you what, if I think I'll pass out, I'll shoot you first, okay?"

Carl shivered. "Damn her."

"Charlie making you cold again? I think I know why you killed her, and it had nothing to do with your embezzling Rob's business, did it?"

"I don't know what you're talking about." Carl stretched his legs out and clasped his hands in his lap.

He was probably waiting for her to pass out. Not an unlikely scenario. But she'd get a confession out of him first.

"I talked to Nick. He told me what your fight was about."

"You really are nuts, you know that?"

"You never thought Charlie was good enough for him, did you? I believe you said, 'Once a druggie, always a druggie,' isn't that right?"

He squirmed. "He deserved better than her, but she managed to weasel her way into his life and blind him to the truth. She would have dragged him into the gutter with her."

"You blame her for his death, don't you?" Bridget asked. Her hands shook slightly as the gun grew heavier, but if she rested them on her knees, she might get too comfortable.

"Because it was her fault. He never would have—"

"Never would have, what? Accused you of embezzling?"

"She corrupted his mind. He never disrespected me before."

"Is that why you lost it when he asked if she could work in the office?"

"He was nuts to ask. She wasn't even qualified."

She rotated her shoulders. "Oh, but that's not why you didn't want her in the office, is it? I think I get it now. Why the audits always came out okay. Margo fudged the numbers for you. Didn't she? Did you get her to poison Barnaby, too?"

A stony, cold silence greeted her from across the room.

Bridget's arms burned from the weight of the gun. Holding it was becoming harder and harder and she needed to end this now, even if she didn't get that confession. What she had should at least give the police enough to go on. "Toss me your phone. Then we can all leave unharmed."

Carl sat up straighter, placing his hands on either side of him. Was he going to pounce? At this point, she might be able to pull the trigger, but her aim would be a problem. Of course, this gun held six bullets, one was liable to hit. Hopefully, she survived with those odds.

"I don't think so," he said. "Why don't you let me go so you can get the help you need? You don't want to kill anyone, do you? Besides, do you know how to turn off the safety?"

Spots marred her vision and she blinked several times. She would not give up. This stupid concussion would not get the best of her. She raised the gun above Carl's head and pulled the trigger. Okay, so now she was down to a one in five chance. The deafening sound reverberated in the room and her arms recoiled upward, but she got her point across. Carl jumped.

The jolt also cleared her head. "Guess the safety's not on after all," she said. "Now toss me your phone."

He reached into his pocket and pulled out his cell. "I don't think so." He threw it against the fireplace, where it exploded into several pieces. He grinned as if he had the upper hand. "Now what?"

Damn him! The clearness she'd obtained a second ago faded. Even if someone had called in the shot, they wouldn't get here fast enough. Her breathing grew ragged and her arm was turning into rubber. If she was going to pass out, she might as well do it outside where someone could see her. Carl might make a break for it, but unless she flat out killed him—and no matter how much he deserved it, she still needed to justify it—she couldn't hold him back much longer. With her last bit of energy, she grabbed the doorknob, braced her body against the wall and stood. The room tilted. Her stomach churned.

"I'm guessing someone called the police from that gunshot. You can stay here while I go outside and wait." Simple and easy. That's all she had to do. With her back to the door, she opened it a crack, but the dizziness took over. Her legs gave out.

He ran toward her. She leveled the gun. He slammed into her, shutting the door, and grabbed her wrist. Pain flared, but she held on.

The blast reverberated as they fell to the floor.

Chapter 32

If Rob could jam his leg through the seat in front of him and floor the accelerator, he would have done it. Instead, he sat trapped in the backseat of Sam's SUV, making fists to keep from ripping anything, unable to will the vehicle faster. While Dean had been correct that Sam would be quicker than a cab, the drive was anything but. They must have caught every fucking red light.

Sam turned right onto Sycamore and Rob straightened. Finally! The car could stall out and he wouldn't care, her place was within sight now. Sam pulled over to the right and stopped several houses short.

"What are you doing?" Rob asked.

Dean turned around in his seat. "If Carl is there, do you really want to—"

"Hell, yes." Rob opened the door and jumped out of the SUV. He ran toward the house and was easily beat by Dean, who grabbed his arm and stopped him.

"Rob, use your head. If he's there, he could react badly. He could hurt her just to spite you."

The door opened and slammed shut. The *crack* of gunfire ripped from the house and tore at Rob's heart.

"No!" He shoved Dean out of the way and with a blast of energy he hadn't thought possible, rushed to the house. She had to be all right. She just had to. He burst inside and froze.

Carl, sprawled on top of Bridget, had a knife in his back. Rob felt his heart fall into his stomach. Before he took a step toward them, Carl slid off her and landed on his side. Blood covered half the front of her shirt.

Fear propelled him to her side. "Dean! Call 9-1-1. She's been shot!"

"What?" She blinked. He pulled up her shirt to investigate the wound, but she covered his hand. "Not shot."

"Oh, thank God!" Tears of relief spilled from his eyes as he pulled her into his arms, but the fear returned as he held her. Blood matted the back of her head.

Dean appeared in the doorway. "I called 9-1-1. Is she okay?"

"No. She's hurt."

"I'm fine," she said.

Again with the "I'm fines." Was it the only phrase she knew with a head wound? Her speech was slurred and she could barely control her movements. "She's not fine," Rob said to Dean and then spoke to Bridget. "You're bleeding."

She looked down at her shirt in a slow, lazy way. "Not mine."

"Not your shirt, your head."

"Okay, you two argue about it. Help is on the way, regardless." Dean crouched beside Carl and placed two fingers along his neck. "He's still alive. How did you stab him in the back?"

"That would be me, you idiots! The baddest ass ghost who ever lived! Whoo hoo!"

Dean turned around. "Well, hello there."

"Charlie?" Being told his sister had become a ghost, and getting proof when he'd heard her voice, had surprised him, to say the least. But seeing her—imitating Rocky Balboa at that—shocked the crap out of him.

Charlie's eyes widened and she froze with her arms above her head. "Holy shit! You all can see me?" When everyone had nodded, she lowered her arms and offered them her guilty smile. "Sorry about that idiot remark. But to answer your question, I have this awesome power and once I recharged a little, bam! I let him have it."

"Good thing. I was a goner." Bridget pointed to her backpack, her arm shaking in the process. "Front pocket. Recorder. Hope it got everything."

"You recorded it?" Charlie asked.

"Of course. How else you moving on?"

"Will it be enough?"

Dean pulled out the recorder and turned it off. "We'll find out soon enough."

Rob couldn't believe Bridget had taken such a risk, but at least she was alive and in his arms. He may never let her go.

* * * *

Bridget smiled while something warm and scratchy caressed her cheek. Only one person could make her feel alive with his touch. She opened her eyes to the man she would spend the rest of her life with. Rob.

"Hey," he said. "You're back."

Lying on her side, she looked around the hospital room. "Wasn't this situation reversed just yesterday?"

He laughed. "Guess it was."

"So, I guess you've been checked out now? What are your plans for the day?" She couldn't imagine he'd want to spend all day in the hospital. Not after being a patient.

"Umm, the day is almost over, Bridget. I haven't gone anywhere."

"Almost over?" She sat up. Pain flared and she stopped.

Rob grabbed her shoulders and lowered her back to the bed. "Take it easy. Doctor says you have a concussion."

"Did the doctor say when I can go home?"

"He told your parents they could take you home tomorrow, provided you became lucid before then. You've been in and out of it all day."

No, no, not her parents. "That's not the home I meant."

"No?" He smiled. "You consider Charlie's house your home?"

She shook her head slowly. "Not really."

He frowned in puzzlement. "Then where?"

She grabbed the front of his shirt and pulled him in close. "Wherever you are. If you still want me."

He freed his shirt and kissed the knuckles on her hand. "I'll always want you, Bridget. I love you."

"Then you'll marry me?"

"I think maybe you're still out of it. Why don't we wait—"

She placed two fingers across his lips. "I was stupid, okay? And maybe a little scared. But I don't want to wait. I nearly lost you and I nearly died. I don't want to waste another second. I love you. You're who I want."

A grin grew across his face. "Bridget, honey, you've certainly turned this day around. Gimme a kiss."

He bent down and she held him back by his shoulders. "Is that a yes?"

"Hell, yeah, that's a yes."

"Okay, then." She released him and his lips covered hers, in a tender, consuming kind of way. She could kiss him forever, and now that was possible.

"Hmm, should I come back later?" Dean leaned against the doorjamb, his arms folded across his chest.

Rob lingered for a moment longer and then smiled. He stood and held out his hand. "If I forgot to thank you, well, thank you."

Dean took his hand. "All in a day's work. You're looking better, Bridget. I'm glad everything turned out okay. Which brings me to my visit."

"Any word about Margo?" Rob asked as he sat back down.

"No. I guess she ran off after news hit about Carl's incarceration. They'll find her though. But I came to talk to Bridget."

"Me?"

"Rob told me how you didn't care for your current job and I thought you might want a change. How'd you like to work for me?"

"What?" Rob shot out of his chair. His yo-yo action made her dizzy. "Dean, she's still recovering. And she has a concussion."

"And you're very protective, I get it."

"Hey! Don't I get a say in this?" She took Rob's hand and pulled him to the edge of the bed. "You're not going to control my life, are you?"

He squeezed her hand and solemnly looked at her. "No, of course not. It's your life. I know that."

"And my life includes you now. I wouldn't make this kind of decision without discussing it with you. But first, I'd like to know what kind of job we'll be discussing."

Dean said, "It's not dangerous work, well, usually. I could use someone to help research and analyze what they find, not to mention talking to ghosts. That's a great ability."

An ability, not a disability. She liked the sound of that. "And here I thought you needed someone to file."

"Well, there is that, too." Dean shoved his hands into his pockets and smiled.

"You want to do it, don't you?" Rob asked.

"I think I do. Kate doesn't need me. She only hired me because I'm family."

"And nursing?"

She shook her head.

"Rob, your case has been the most dangerous I've ever taken on. And Bridget did most of the work. You don't have anything to worry about."

Rob ran his fingers down her cheek. "You wouldn't risk your life, would you?"

"Trust me, I won't be doing anything like that again. Not unless your life is in danger. I plan on being married to you for a good long time."

"Married?" Dean slapped Rob's back. "Well, congratulations you two. And no rush on a decision. I'm not going anywhere. Take it easy, Bridget. I think Rob will rest easier then." He wished them both well and left.

"If you're uncomfortable with me taking this job…"

"I'm concerned about you going back to *any* job too early. I just want you healthy first. And I want to be the one who takes care of you. Then there's the matter of our honeymoon. I think two weeks anywhere sounds good."

She hugged him. "Two weeks and a lifetime."

Chapter 33

Charlie hovered over the house. When her brother's truck turned down the street, she smiled. They hadn't been by in like, forever. Not since the paramedics had carted Bridget off to the hospital. Robbie had come by for her things Monday night, smiling as if he had a secret, and the only thing he shared was that Bridget would be fine and they would stop by later in the week.

Well, now it was later. Four days later. Way later than she'd anticipated. If not for Mr. Murdock and Mrs. Johnson, she'd have lost her mind. But watching those two lovebirds had been sweet and enjoyable. Much better than any television show.

Robbie pulled into the driveway and killed the engine. Both doors opened. Barnaby jumped out through the passenger door, with Bridget following behind. Robbie jogged around to help her, not that she seemed to have any problems standing. Charlie willed herself into the living room and waited.

The front door opened and Barnaby burst through first.

"Hey, baby!" Charlie looked up after Bridget and Robbie entered. "It's about time you guys showed. I've been going nuts."

He grinned like he had when he'd been a little boy and hit a home run. "Charlie, I'd like to introduce you to my wife."

"Wife? You two got married?"

Bridget held up her left hand and flashed the gold band. "I followed your advice and listened to my heart." She gazed at Robbie. "And my heart couldn't wait."

Charlie rushed to her and hugged her. "You truly are my sister now." She then turned to her brother as he wrapped her up. "This is the best news ever." She stood back and something was different. "I don't give you a headache anymore? Did all those head injuries cure you?"

"No. It seems that way, doesn't it?" Bridget rubbed the back of her head. "I sure hope no one else sees fit to hit me. Doctor said another jolt just might scramble my brain."

Robbie winced at that news. Charlie was confident he'd make sure no such thing would happen, though. "So if not your head injury…"

"I noticed after I decided to talk to Devin, your presence didn't affect me. Seems it was some kind of stress-related thing."

"And Devin?"

"We had a good visit. You were right. He blamed himself."

Of course she'd been right. When had she ever been wrong?

"We have other news, too," Robbie said. "But first, I want another hug."

"Me, too," Bridget said.

Charlie could certainly oblige them. Being solid felt wonderful, even for a few moments. They even let her give Barnaby a hug and kiss. How she loved the big fur ball.

Robbie kissed her on the cheek. His eyes glistened. "I love you, Charlie." He turned to Bridget. "We better sit down. If this works, I don't want to pass out on the floor."

"Good point," Bridget said and he led her to the couch.

Charlie crossed her arms. "What's that supposed to mean?"

"It means," he said as they sat, "I'm going to miss you all over again."

Bridget grabbed Robbie's hand and smiled. "I'll miss you, too."

This didn't sound good. "Are you moving?"

"No," he said. "But maybe you are. Your death is now being investigated as a murder. Carl said enough on the tape and Margo has been caught. Didn't take much to get her to admit Carl put her up to poisoning Barnaby. Once he's out of the hospital, he'll be sent to jail awaiting trial."

"For real?"

He smiled. "For real."

"Yes!" Charlie pumped the air with a fist. Finally, justice was served. "But why did you have to sit?" A slip of paper floated by her head and Robbie's and Bridget's hair whipped around as if a storm brewed inside the house.

"I love you, sis."

"Good-bye, Charlie…and thank you for everything. You gave me back my life." A tear ran down Bridget's cheek as she squeezed Robbie's hand.

A bright light shone around her from above, warm and comforting, and something pulled her toward it. She turned to tell her brother, but found them leaning against one another, out cold. Barnaby barked. "Robbie?"

A familiar voice came from above. "Charlie, sweetheart. It's time."

"Nick?"

She let herself be pulled up and arrived in a bright white room. Her old house disappeared and her feet hit solid ground.

He stood on the other side of the room, looking as good as ever. He held his arms out to her. "I've missed you more than you could ever imagine."

"Nick!" She rushed to him. His embrace felt better than a hundred sunny days and she cried with joy.

ACKNOWLEDGMENTS

Special thanks go out to the writers who first critiqued this story: Todd Moody and Dana (aka Bobbi Romans). Your comments and suggestions helped me shape this story into what it is today.

Thank you, Kathleen McRae, for suggesting I insert an "Easter Egg" in this story (and if you, dear reader, spot it, please let me know!). One of these days, I'll be able to return the favor for all the help you have given me. I really am in your debt.

Thank you, Paige Christian. You are the best editor this writer could ask for!

Hugs and kisses to my hubby, for teaching me all about electricity and for putting up with my non-stop talking about this book (and all the others). Your support means the world to me.

And a super-duper thank you to Lynn Johnston (aka Madeleine Drake). Your class, "Edit the Life Back Into Your Story," showed me the way. I will be eternally grateful.

ABOUT THE AUTHOR

Stacy McKitrick always had stories in her head; she just never knew what to do with them. Then one day she decided to give writing a try and discovered the passion she'd been looking for all her life. She waived goodbye to accounting and now spends her time writing romance featuring vampires, ghosts, and aliens. All with happy endings, of course. Born in California, she currently resides in Ohio with her husband. They have two grown children. You can learn more about Stacy at her website www.stacymckitrick.com.

Thank you for purchasing this book

Sign up for my newsletter to receive new release announcements, sneak peeks of future books, and bonus content. I sometimes even give away stuff.

http://eepurl.com/-Auwz

Now keep on reading for an except to the next book in the Ghostly Encounters series: Ghostly Interlude.

Ghostly Interlude
Chapter 1

Something poked Maggie in her shoulder and she swatted it away. Time to have a serious talk with her cousin about boundaries and if that didn't work, she would finally install a lock on her bedroom door.

"Ma'am, wake up. You have to go."

Ma'am? That didn't sound like Erica because, well, Erica wasn't a guy. So what was a guy doing in her bedroom? Maggie bolted upright and blinked as the bright room came into focus. Better question: Where was her bedroom?

Keep calm. Keep calm. You've just been sleep walking. Again.

The mantra did nothing to keep her heart from racing. Probably because every other time it had happened she'd woken up at home. Not at some strange café.

Dirty dishes littered the table before her. God. She was eating in her sleep now? Should she be thankful she wasn't wearing her pajamas? She apparently had the sleep-sense to put on a sweater and jeans.

The person who'd poked her was actually a waiter, and a young one at that. He couldn't be more than twenty. "Here's the check. I have to close up."

"What day is it?"

"It's seven. We're closing."

She grabbed his arm. "Not time. Day. Day!"

His eyes widened and he shrugged free. "Sunday?"

"Sunday?" No. No-no-no. That couldn't be. She'd lost two days. Two freakin' days! Who slept-walked for two days?

"Are you okay?" he asked, taking several steps backward.

She was far from okay, but spooking the waiter wouldn't improve her situation. "Sorry, I got confused." Maggie scooted away from the table and found her purse on the floor. Thank God she had her wallet, and money. She paid the young man and stood on unsteady legs. "Can I use the restroom before I go?"

He nodded while he policed up the table. "Just be quick. I want to go home."

Home. That sounded good. But how far was she? Her eyes scratched with each blink and she practically stumbled to the ladies' room. Why was she so tired? If she'd been sleepwalking, wouldn't she be rested? She splashed cold water on her face but instead of shocking her awake, it only made her shiver. Great.

She pulled out her phone. Maybe it would show where in the world she had ended up. She pushed the on button and was faced with a blank screen. She shook it as if it would do any good. Dead. Figured. Now she'd have to make a bigger ass out of herself and ask that waiter where she was. He probably already thought she was high on something.

At least she didn't look high. Tired, definitely, but not high or drunk. She ran a brush through her hair and headed back to the dining room.

Had she driven over here? If she had, she certainly wasn't in any condition to drive home, even if she lived close. God, she hadn't left town, had she?

"What street is that?" she asked the waiter, praying for a familiar name.

"North Dixie?" he answered, as if she should know.

She sighed in relief. Local. Finally, some good news. "May I use your phone? Mine died."

The request did not sit well with the young man, as he rolled his eyes. But he showed her the phone by the register "Just be—"

"Quick. I know," she finished. "I will." She found her cousin's business card—and it was a good thing she had it; she wasn't sure she'd remember the number in her current state—when she spotted the number to a cab company written on a piece of paper attached to the register. Erica would want some answers. The cabbie, not so much. Maggie called the cab company. The address to the café was listed on the menu and she gave it to the dispatcher.

After hanging up, she found a five in her wallet and handed it to the waiter. "Sorry for being a bother."

"No bother." He shrugged but took the money. "Kind of surprised the guy left you like that anyway."

Guy? Oh great. Not only was she having strange meals in strange cafés, she was having them with a guy now. Asking for a description was tempting. So...so... tempting. But who didn't remember their dining mate? Or what day it was?

Clearly, she was suffering from more than sleepwalking. Could dementia hit early? Grandma had been a little whacky at times, but she'd been old. Not twenty-eight.

Maggie stepped outside and was hit with a blast of frigid, February air. Before she had a chance to wonder if she'd brought a jacket, the waiter tapped her shoulder and held out her coat.

"I think you forgot this."

At least her crazy mind had remembered to dress warmly before leaving the house. "Thanks."

The young man shut the door and locked her out. Guess he wasn't too worried about her well-being after all. Not that she was in a horrible part of town. Wasn't exactly pristine, either.

A couple of motels littered the street. Unknown, unbranded, and certainly nothing she would feel safe in. She leaned up against the brick building and did her best not to slump to the ground.

She pulled out her keys and pressed the panic button on her fob. All was quiet, which meant her car wasn't parked close by. She looked to the sky. "God, please let it be at home." She could only imagine what she would tell the police if by some chance it wasn't.

Twenty minutes later, the cab arrived. So much for speedy pickup. She climbed into the warm vehicle and gave the driver her address. Weariness settled over her, and she leaned her head back.

Her house was a welcome sight. She paid the driver and stumbled to her front door. All she had to do was make it to her bed. If she was lucky, Erica was out on a date and wouldn't notice Maggie's arrival until morning.

As she fumbled with the key in the lock, the door swung open.

"Oh my God!" Erica wrapped Maggie up in a bear hug. "Where the hell have you been? I've been worried sick."

Maggie offered a weak smile. Guess she could have called her cousin and saved the cab fare. Seemed she was answering some questions tonight after all. But not the truth, because the truth was she didn't know where she'd been and if she admitted that, Erica would probably whisk her straight to the hospital. And then all the work she'd gone through would be for nothing.

She couldn't—wouldn't let that happen.